THE KNOT

A DR. EDGE NOVEL

ALSO BY J. A. ALLDREDGE

Our Kiss

The Dr. Edge Series

THE KNOT

J. A. ALLDREDGE

This book is a work of fiction. The characters, incidents, and dialogue drawn from the author's imagination included in this book are not to be construed as real persons, incidents, communications, or actual events. Any resemblance to actual persons, living or dead, is entirely incidental.

THE KNOT may be purchased for educational, business, or sales promotional use. For information please write: Joseph A. Alldredge Publishing, P.O. Box 1555, Santa Rosa Beach, Florida, 32459.

First Edition

ISBN # 978-0-9963274-5-9 (hardback)
ISBN # 978-0-9963274-3-5 (paperback)
ISBN # 978-0-9963274-4-2 (e-book)

Introducing Dr. Edge

IN ORDER TO create a superhero there must always be some great disaster or personal tragedy that brings about their incredible transformation. But what makes a person superhuman is not necessarily the incredible new power that they miraculously acquire. They already possessed some superhuman quality. And that tragic transformative event is only the catalyst needed to reveal their *real* hidden inner power—a genuine unconquerable desire to achieve something greater than human.

Such is the case for Dr. Alexander Edge. Once a depressed and unsatisfied psychiatrist dangling at the end of his emotional rope—he's ready to give up on everything he once believed to be true about life. A pure hearted young idealist, he struggles with the grind of everyday existence, seeing little progress for himself, or improvement for his seemingly incurable hapless patients.

Then an extraordinary event shatters his very existence. Witnessing the terrorist attack on the World Trade Center buildings on 9/11, he rushes to the aid of those desperate victims risking everything to try and save just one precious life. He ended up losing his own life—for a brief moment—just long enough to have the curtains pulled back away from his mortal eyes enabling him to see a hidden reality.

After being miraculously saved from certain death by a mystical apparition, Dr. Edge was forced to reevaluate everything about his life. This near death experience sends him on a quest in search of something more *real*—something greater than this *perceived* existence.

Later, while seeking enlightenment in India, Dr. Edge is once again pulled away from the icy grasp of death just at the last moment. He is saved by the same beautiful female deity, known by the Guru to be an Apsara. This time she shares with him a supernatural gift. She leaves him with a mystical amulet—one that allows him to possess incredible powers of inner sight. Allowing him to actually experience what others are hiding deep within their subconscious minds.

Now, when Dr. Edge uses the amulet to delve into the depths of the human psyche he discovers a reality that is far stranger than anything he could ever have imaged possible.

In this Dr. Edge series, follow along as he uses his supernatural power to try and solve bizarre paranormal mysteries—as revealed within the mind's eye.

A NEW EYE

Varanasi, India
April, 2002

D R. ALEX EDGE rolled out of a death bed. Blurry-eyed, swaying light-headed on his unsteady feet, nothing around him was familiar. The entire night before was all just a dizzying haze.

This was not the state of enlightenment he had come searching for. Instead, Dr. Edge had now crossed half-way over to Nirvana—permanently.

Staggering through an open doorway and down a narrow corridor everything around him was dreamlike. *Just a nightmare*, he wanted to believe. It was a terrible reminder of how he used to make his way home after a night of binge drinking back in his college days—blitzed out of his mind and struggling to find his dorm room—right before completely blacking out. Still sporting a six-foot, sleek, taught body, with sprigs of thick wavy-brown hair dangling over sparkling blue topaz eyes, he could still *almost* pass for a frat boy, on a much better day. Only this time he hadn't passed out drunk in the wrong frat house.

Stumbling out into the courtyard of the Ashram Dr. Edge was greeted by pillars of swirling white smoke rising up like silken snakes from many pots of burning incense. The air was thick with pungent smoke. Right outside, large bonfires had finished burning down to smoldering heaps of embers and ash. Corpses of the recently deceased were being cremated in ritualistic fashion. A small hoard of bearded men busily removed the remaining charred bones.

Belonging to the Aghori, a sect of Hinduism, the nearly naked men carefully pulled the still hot bones out from beneath the smoldering piles of ashes.

They had gathered around the Ashram for their daily worship. And Dr. Edge was not at all prepared for what was to come next.

After smearing grayish-white cremation ash over their skin, they filed inside the courtyard. Wild-eyed, with long unkempt hair, they cackled in loud voices, speaking in an unrecognizable tongue. In a shared trance, they all began chanting while shaking rattles, blowing into strange wooden flutes, and beating on calfskin drums. Some clanked long human arm and leg bones together, while others passed around a human skull—all taking turns sipping the hallucinogenic mushroom tea. Moving rhythmically, swirling through the heavy fog of white smoke, they danced about as enchanted ghostly apparitions. Each of them was adorned with a triangle-shaped diagram drawn on their foreheads. The triangle was drawn using dark human ash. In the center of the triangle, there was made a bright red dot using freshly drawn blood.

Dr. Edge was caught-up in this disorienting apocalyptic scene. The ash covered men buzzed around him. Naked or wearing only groin clothes and sandals with jingling beaded jewelry, the Aghori men swarmed around the room chanting and whaling, flowing in and out of his sight as they moved through the thick veil of smoke. Coughing and barely able to breathe—the heavy smoke was burning in Dr. Edge's throat, and in his eyes, as he strained to see what was happening. It was like being a convict in the middle of a prison riot. All he wanted to do was run, but couldn't. The room spun-round beneath his feet. His pulse was pounding and it was getting harder to breathe. A severe panic attack was setting in. *I'm going to pass out.* All he could do was brace himself against the wall, trying not to faint.

Flashing images flew past his eyes. He was mentally transported back to the day of 9/11. The day he died—buried beneath the ashy rubble.

Suddenly he was surrounded once again by the horrendous disorienting sounds of crashing—of metal beating against metal—with smoky acid burning in his eyes and throat—as hysterical ash covered people scattered around him moving in all directions. It all felt the same way. It was all so devastatingly hopeless, amidst the unfolding carnage, waiting for the icy cold hand of death to take him.

That was the reason for his journey to India in the first place—to try and find peace of mind again, some reason to go on living, after his near-death-experience in the middle of the collapsing buildings in New York City on 9/11. But now, it was like he was right back there once again, fighting to survive all over again.

In the midst of this chaos, a distinctive tinkling sound drew Dr. Edge's attention. It miraculously cut straight through the clambering noise from across the smoke filled Ashram. Wiping his tearing eyes, he lifted his head and tried desperately to gaze through the smoky haze. A jingling sound—soft yet piercing—it was the only thing he was able to focus on. There was a glimmer as he momentarily caught a glimpse of her. Glinting jewels on her sari reflected sparkling light as the young woman shimmered through the veil of smoke. He could only make out her outline as she swept across the room, before slipping out of a doorway. *It's her!*

His weakened body and legs felt revived at the site of her. He knew it was the same mysterious woman who had somehow preserved his lifeless body that was buried in the rubble on 9/11.

Pushing through the morass of chanting worshipers, Dr. Edge forced his way to the front gate of the Ashram. His head began to clear along with the smoke as he stepped outside into fresh air. Looking both ways down the dirt roadway, he caught a glimpse of her disappearing around a bend. Racing up the road he scanned the doorways of every building as he passed. But she was gone, along with the gentle jingling sounds that emanated from her as she moved. *I must have been hallucinating*, he thought while standing in the road alone. His heart slowed and he slowly caught his breath. As he turned to return—the jingling tickled his ear once more. *That's her!*

The alluring sound drifted lightly through an open archway just a few feet away from where he was standing. It lured him inside as a siren song. Moving cautiously through the open archway he found himself within another small walled-in courtyard. There was another doorway in front of him, this one veiled by dangling strands of beads. Slipping a hand between the strands, he peeked inside.

She was there waiting for him. Seated on the floor with crossed legs and gesturing fingers as would the Buddha—with her eyes shut in a state of deep meditation.

"Please come in Alexander," he could clearly hear her say. But, her lips didn't appear to be moving, and she didn't open her eyes to see who was there.

"You know English?" Dr. Edge asked shyly, feeling like a shameful intruder.

"Yes," she answered softly, "please come, sit with me."

As he knelt down, he was awestruck by her stunning beauty. She was easily the most beautiful woman he could ever remember seeing—ever. She had long black hair pulled back by a thin shimmering silver headband. With skin that radiated a translucent light. Her sari was like no other he'd ever seen—woven with gleaming strands of golden silk that glowed with the radiance of a tiny sun.

Her wrists, neck, and ears were arrayed with dazzling gemstones that sparkled green and red.

His eyes moved over her, devouring every part, but some power was pulling them back up again—up to the jewel that was dangling from her headdress. It was a glimmering green gemstone. The gemstone was set in the middle of a brightly shinning silver pyramid that was all enclosed within a large silver eye, similar to the ancient Egyptian Eye of Horus. Inside the gemstone were lines that swirled around as they moved toward the center, creating a vortex. Instantly he was pulled inside the gemstone. His gaze was pulled in—drifting ever deeper into it—until he couldn't look away—as he drifted ever deeper into her third eye.

Dr. Edge could hear her voice speaking to him as her sumptuous red lips never moved at all. A strong voice that spoke directly to his sole, saying to him, "You believe that you are lost?" He instantly understood what she meant by the statement. And he knew that he did not need to respond. She already knew exactly what he was thinking. So, he just closed his eyes too, and listened closely, hearing her words speaking within his mind. "Your parents were both successful doctors in New York City. They expected you to follow them, so you reluctantly complied. You went to medical school. You became a psychiatrist like your mother. But you were unsatisfied. Hating every day, making your rounds, diagnosing illnesses, dispensing pills, trying to help, without any sense of satisfaction, day after day, nothing changes—no one ever gets better."

Her voice, her message, was deeply penetrating and probing. Dr. Edge squirmed as she went in deeper—every inch of him fighting to cry out as her words touched his most sensitive nerves—forcing him to confront every repressed demon inside of him. It took every ounce of his strength to stay there and not jump to his feet and run out of there. As if feeling his pain, she pulled him back, by saying, "but you escaped that life that terrible day, on 9/11. The morning those planes struck those tall buildings in New York City, you were working at the hospital close to where they fell, and you rushed into that chaos to try and help the survivors. Running straight into that burning hot cloud of grey dust you fought to save the lives of those strangers. Covered in a layer of thick ash, they were frantic, wandering helpless, searching for safety. But, you couldn't help them either, because you sacrificed yourself. Struck down by a falling piece of a building, then swallowed up and overcome by the chocking, stinging, burning ash, you fell to the ground, helpless, and dying."

Dr. Edge could see it all over again—feeling the acrid burning in his eyes and throat as he gagged for air—as the white, ash covered people ran passed him, screaming for help as they rushed in all directions around him like they were just ghosts being blown around by a rushing wind. Unable to breath, as the dust and ash filled his lungs, he remembered how he fell down on the pavement, blacking-out. Struggling to open his eyes, it was all dreamlike as he moved in and out of darkness. Without oxygen his brain was shutting down. Then he felt his body lifting up weightless. He was looking down at his lifeless thirty-two year old body. Watching himself dying right in front of his own eyes, he remembered thinking; *what a wasted life I lived*.

Then he remembered seeing her approaching his lifeless body. She drifted through the cloud of ash unharmed, somehow impervious, like a guardian angel. And there was that gentle jingling sound. He recalled watching her as she knelt down next to his lifeless body. Bending over him, she placed her lips to his—breathing life back into his lost soul.

Now, she was back—saving him again in another way—breathing new life into his spiritual self. Then, she said to him, "Alex, you have come to India as a lost soul. Your old self died on that dreadful day in New York City. Now, you are searching for a new life… a new direction. Because of your sacrifice that day, I will grant you what you desire most."

At that moment Dr. Edge could feel her presence depart. He opened his eyes. The beautiful woman was gone. On the ground in front of him was the silver pendant with the emerald gemstone.

This amulet he realized was now *his* third eye. It was a new life—with new eyes to see.

Picking up the amulet, he stared at it, with his eyes going in and out of focus, with his head spinning once again. Fighting to stay conscious his mouth mumbled with a feeble attempt to call for help. Feeling his body going limp, his hand squeezed down tightly, holding the amulet as if his very life depended on it.

Out of the corner of his eyes he caught a glimpse of a young woman wearing familiar light green medical scrubs rushing towards him—just as his body finally gave up—his mind going dark. His severely dehydrated body finally collapsed on the floor—with no life left in him.

Later on, some would call it a miracle that he passed out on the floor of the only medical clinic within a hundred miles of that tiny hamlet. Even more amazing was the coincidence that a visiting medical student intern just happened to be there on call that very day. The intern was able to stabilize him. They just happened to have the necessary medicines needed to treat his dysentery. And once again, the mysterious woman had pulled Dr. Edge away from a certain death, at the very last moment.

Following two weeks of intense treatment, Dr. Edge was able to recover his strength. He understood this was no unexplainable miracle—the jeweled amulet still clenched in his hand told him otherwise.

Upon leaving the medical clinic, he sought out a knowledgeable Guru who could speak some English, and who could provide some answers—for why she chose to save him?

"Yes, I know what you experienced my friend," the old man said while examining the triangle that held the third eye gemstone amulet. Sitting cross-legged on a blanket, his long hair and beard were matted and twisted. His wrinkled, cracked, dark brown skin showed his age, and his dedication to his practice. The cremation ash had been washed away by his ritual bath in the Ganges so that the deep lines in his face were clear to see. Looking up at Dr. Edge, he smiled, showing his rotting, cracked, yet friendly teeth.

"An Apsara—she is who visited you my friend," he explained, "a celestial maiden, a nymph, as you English may call her." Laughing joyfully, the old Guru handed back the amulet, saying, "Between this world and the next is where you met her. She was there to guide you. At that moment you decided to stay with the living. She looked into your heart and found it pure, but troubled. So, she has given you a new eye—a third-eye. This is so that you can see what is real, and what is true, while still in this life."

"What exactly can I see with this?" Dr. Edge asked skeptically, unsatisfied with the old man's cryptic response.

Pointing to his head, the old Guru answered as plainly as he could. "You can now see everything that another has known… whatever they have thought, or whatever they believe to know. You will see whatever is in hidden inside their mind."

"Actually read people's minds?" Dr. Edge asked perplexed.

The old man stared disappointed at him. Then he answered as plainly as he could. "Not like a man reads a book. Remember my friend, that nothing is real. Only what you *believe* to be real is *real*. You will experience what the person believes to be true… imaginations, memories, jealousies, dreams and fantasies… all of these are *real* to that person. All of these combined is what creates a mind, a consciousness. Then, you must decide for yourself, what is real?"

Deuteronomy 18:10

There shall not be found among you *any one* that maketh his son or his daughter to pass through the fire, *or* that useth divination, *or* an observer of times, or an enchanter, or a witch…

Bonfire

The name "bonfire" is derived from the fact that bonfires were originally fires in which bones were burned. Some people took to jumping over the fire in order to ensure youth and fertility. The ash from these fires supposedly had a special power to raise crops, and people also walked the cattle through the ashes to ensure fertility.

1

Central State Psychiatric Hospital
Milledgeville, Georgia
July, 2011

NO ONE NOTICED the grey four-door sedan entering through the large ornamental gateway. Opened in 1842 as the State Lunatic, Idiot, and Epileptic Asylum, this place was once the largest lunatic asylum in the world. With its several enormous patient barracks set behind an array of ornately appointed administrative buildings, it could easily be mistaken for a sprawling university campus. It would be hard to tell the difference if it wasn't for all of the patients, nurses, orderlies, and doctors—all of them wearing pajama looking, green, blue, and white scrubs. The expansive grounds spread out behind the large brick buildings, covering another 1,700 acres or more. So, it was easy for Kaitlin to not be noticed driving through the gate. And that's just what she wanted.

The car drove slowly down the long winding driveway just like any other visitor would do. Veering to the right Kaitlin followed a slight fork in the road leading her away from the administration building. Driving around the hospital, she turned down an even smaller dirt road. Thumping over rocks and potholes, she followed the slowly disappearing ruts until she came upon one of the many graveyards on the hospital grounds. Away from the main road, these graves were intentionally hidden from view.

Only the maintenance staff had used this road over the past ten years. No visitors ever ventured to this area anymore. This was where the hospital buried the unclaimed bodies of deceased patients—almost all of them in unmarked graves. For the ones that were marked, there was only a two-foot metal post stuck in the ground, with a number placed at the top. Only the head ground-skeeper could identify who was buried in each grave. He was the only person with the list, and he kept it securely locked-up in his office—always.

Leaving the car door open, Kaitlin wandered off across the rolling grassy field. Still wearing her pajamas and robe, she meandered through the long rows of cemetery markers—over twenty-five thousand. She felt like a tiny flea that was scurrying through thousands of rusting whiskers. It was easy for her to pick out the older ones, those dating back from the first burials back in the 1840's. Some had small roughly hewn granite stones to mark them. Worn down by the weather, they were all tilted slightly at odd angles, or had fallen all the way over. She turned away from those, pacing quickly over to the newer looking iron markers poked into the ground in long straight rows. Slightly eaten-up with spots of rust, they all held a numbered plaque, for identification.

Moving down a long gently sloping hill, her eyes frantically scanned the ground as she passed by each iron marker. It seemed an impossible task, but somehow, she found the grave she was looking for. Suddenly stopping, she fell down onto her knees in front of one of the spikes—marked grave number 19801. Digging her fingers into the ground, she began tearing madly at the matted grass and clumps of clay covered rocks. Her fingers scooped out balls of thick clay like some burrowing groundhog. Her hands moved fast, frantically digging beneath the midmorning steamy-hot sun.

She had made a good sized hole in the ground before a nurse

taking a leisurely smoke-break just happened to notice her. Staring far across the field, the nurse could barely see Kaitlin's back moving up and down. Tossing her cigarette down the nurse raced back inside the hospital to notify the groundskeeper. One of *those* patients got out again, she surmised.

By the time they got to her, the hole was nearly three-feet deep. Kaitlin was soaked from head to toe with sweat from her feverish digging. Red clay inked her hands up to her elbows. Groaning, her hands clenched down on the last handfuls of dirt she managed to scrape up, just before she was grabbed and pulled up to her feet. Without saying a word, two burly orderlies made short order of restraining the fragile middle-aged woman. Quickly subdued and placed into restraints, she was whisked up to the hospital.

As Kaitlin was hauled through a large metal door and dragged down a long corridor, she looked up—and she smiled. This was a familiar hallway. And so was the room they dragged her into. Back inside a familiar observation room, she was sat down on a hard plastic chair—where she patiently waited for the doctor to finally arrive to begin her evaluation. Much like the many other interrogations she had endured—twenty years earlier.

Upon being deemed incompetent to stand trial Kaitlin had been transferred to a small treatment facility up in Atlanta. A place reserved for the wealthy elite. It was all paid for by a large insurance settlement. After a short stay, her treating psychiatrist wrote a report showing that she was in fact "clinically and legally insane" at the time of the incident. Because of that report she could not be held criminally liable for what she had done. So, she was subsequently released back into the general population back in the fall of 1982. But no one ever believed her story.

The present day Hospital Director, Doctor Conrad, sauntered down the hill, gliding through the grave markers on his way to see what damage Kaitlin had done. The young groundskeeper was already throwing shovel loads of dirt back into the hole.

"Did she write those words there?" Dr. Conrad inquired of the sweaty worker.

Sticking the head of the shovel into the ground, the grounds-keeper leaned over and peered down at the dirt up near the metal marker. "Not sure?" He mumbled. "But it sure as hell wasn't me."

"Had to be her," Dr. Conrad murmured. The sun beat down through a near cloudless sky overhead. It quickly became very uncomfortable in his long-sleeved white frock—the one he should have taken off before he left his office. But he never liked to be without his cloak of authority when conducting official hospital business. Tiny beads of sweat appeared on his balding forehead. "You're the new guy… right?"

The groundskeeper nodded, wiping dripping sweat from his own forehead.

"Find out who's in that grave," Dr. Conrad ordered. "Let me know before you leave today—understand?"

He nodded his dripping head again.

Taking a peek up at the blazing sun, Dr. Conrad grumbled, "It's too damn hot to be outside today. Don't know how you guys can stand it out here all day," before he turned and sauntered back up the hill.

Taking the shovel back in his hands, the groundskeeper scratched through the words that had been etched into the clay—written by someone's finger:

I once was where you now be,
prepare with speed to follow me.

2

Two days later

AN ORDERLY SHOWED Dr. Alexander Edge into Dr. Conrad's office. It had the appearance and furnishings that are typical of a state employee office—no frills, a ramshackle wooden desk, dilapidated book shelves, peeling paint and dirty carpet. The musty smell let you know just how old the room was. The state run hospital hadn't been updated or improved for over a decade, nor would it ever be again, since it was slated for closure within two years. Defunded by the Georgia State Legislature, all of the remaining patients were being systematically reassigned to other, smaller, more efficient facilities around the state. Doctor Edge took a seat in one of the outdated and unsteady side chairs.

"To what do we owe the pleasure Alex?" Dr. Conrad smirked. His tone was as cold and unwelcoming as his brief limp and unemotional handshake. It was his way of saying very clearly... *I don't like you or your methods...* without having to say it out loud.

"I won't waste much of your time Conrad," Dr. Edge responded bluntly, "I'm here to see one of your patients... a Kaitlin Singleton. You are most likely familiar with her maiden name, Whitcomb."

The hospital was being shut down and Dr. Conrad was being reassigned—demoted being the more appropriate description—to another facility in downtown Macon. And there was an iron-clad court order confining Kaitlin at the hospital for 72 hours, for evaluation and diagnosis, to determine if she was a threat to herself or others. If Dr. Conrad wanted, he could easily designate her as a threat, and get the court order extended for months. This could quickly escalate to a showdown of egos if Dr. Conrad decided to try and flex his authoritative muscles and try to keep him away from her. It was obvious by the disdain all over Conrad's face that he so badly wanted to just say, *"Hell no... get out of my hospital!"* But he was not about to burn another bridge that may eventually get him back to a lucrative position in Atlanta—even if it meant helping out Alex Edge.

Dr. Conrad huffed, "Yes, she's still a patient here—being held for observation. I have heard stories about her family. They used to be very prominent, owned a lucrative Cotton Mill and half the county at one time. They lived about twenty miles from here, right?"

Dr. Edge merely nodded to confirm that his information was correct so far.

"So, what the hell do you want to see her about Alex... did she kill someone important or something?"

"Something like that doctor?" Dr. Edge replied reluctantly, before adding, "But I'm not at liberty to say right now."

All the records of Kaitlin's prior stay at the hospital had been destroyed years before Dr. Conrad arrived. He still had no idea who Kaitlin really was, or why she was digging up the unmarked grave. Alex wasn't even sure that he really understood what was happening. All he knew for certain was that Kaitlin had suffered an emotional breakdown after causing the accidental death of her middle-school classmate. That had been well documented. The trauma lingered with her until causing her to succumb to a full psychotic break—forcing her to suffer from schizophrenic paranoid delusions—a chronic condition from which she never fully recovered. Housed in a secure boarding home in midtown Atlanta, under constant medical scrutiny, she was eventually able to reconnect with *normal* society.

"It must have something to do with that dead person she was trying to dig up out there in the graveyard… isn't that what you are into these days Alex?" Dr. Conrad quipped. "So, you must know why she was trying to dig up… who was it again? Let's just see," he mumbled as he began flipping through the list of names that the groundskeeper had brought him. "Oh yea here she is… a Catherine Whitcomb… some distant relative most likely?"

Dr. Edge glazed over, his eyes glaring at Conrad without giving up his hand. He only wanted to let him know so much—just enough to get him to Kaitlin—without pissing him off. His bizarre explanation wouldn't suffice, and it may even get him barred from entering the hospital altogether. Dr. Conrad could never move beyond the boundaries of text-book science—he was too afraid. Anything of a paranormal, unexplainable, or improbable nature was way more than he could tolerate. If he was truthful, Dr. Conrad would have him thrown right out the front door.

Dr. Conrad studied Alex's stoic face. His chiding wasn't getting under his thick skin. It was obvious Dr. Edge wasn't unnerved, and not going to budge. It was time to call his bluff. Dr. Conrad leaned forward and looked him straight in the eyes—reminding him of who was in charge, and sternly said, "Well, you don't work cheap so I know someone with serious money sent you here. But without proper authorization, or a formal release, I can't allow you access to my patient. You're just going to have to tell me who sent you here Doctor, just so I can contact them to get confirmation that you have been hired to treat this patient. You understand, just can't break the rules, right Doctor?" Dr. Conrad leaned back and smiled. He had Dr. Edge back against the ropes.

"Her daughter Fiona hired me to evaluate her," Dr. Edge relented, knowing he would have to come clean. "Catherine was

Kaitlin's grandmother. And Kaitlin believes that she is still alive inside that makeshift grave you have out there."

Dr. Conrad dropped his taunting smile. This was exactly what he was afraid of hearing coming out of Dr. Edge's mouth. "You can't be serious Edge? You're about 42 years old… right? Way too old to be still chasing ghosts, aren't we? I'm in charge of a hospital—not a spook-house."

Dr. Edge interjected, slapping his hands down on Conrad's desk, saying firmly, "She's been suffering from this same delusion for thirty years, and she won't let it go. This is not some ghost story to Kaitlin. She is really sick. Nothing has helped, especially not at your hospital Doctor. And I may be able to find out why?"

Dr. Conrad broke off his fuming glare to look back down at the list. His eyes scanned over the pages holding the thousands of names of those buried in the graveyard. Flipping over page after page, seemingly utterly perplexed, he asked, "I have to know how this Fiona, your client, somehow managed to find out exactly where this Catherine was buried?" Looking back up, with eyes burning, he now was demanding real answers. "Nobody gets a look at this list except for the head groundskeeper, and me. There is no possible way that insane woman in there could find that grave, not without this list, or someone to show her how to find it. So, I need you to explain yourself Doctor. Tell me what it is you're doing here, and exactly who really sent you here. Otherwise, I'll have the orderly show you out."

Dr. Edge softened his voice, asking, "I assume you've checked this out and have determined that you have no patient records for a Catherine Whitcomb. Isn't that correct Dr. Conrad?"

"That's correct."

"Yet her name is right there on the list of persons buried in your graveyard," Dr. Edge pointed out, before asking, "how could that be if she was never even a patient here Doctor?"

"Sloppy paperwork I would presume," Dr. Conrad mumbled, "this is a very big, very old institution if you haven't noticed

Doctor, files, records, lots of stuff gets misplaced… that's not unusual at all."

"Doctor Conrad, what if I were to tell you that both Catherine and Kaitlin were patients of this hospital thirty years ago… at the same time? And what if I told you that my client Fiona Whitcomb was born right here in this hospital, thirty years ago."

"That's preposterous, even for you Edge," Dr. Conrad smirked dismissively. "So you're telling me that someone has destroyed all their records, covering up the fact that they may have been patients here before… that a child was born here… all for some unknown reason?"

"That's exactly what I'm telling you," Dr. Edge insisted, "But for a very good reason."

"What reason is that Edge?"

"I'm sure you've heard about the bizarre experiments engaged in by Dr. Emily Karanza?"

"Those are just old rumors… horror stories the staff likes to perpetuate. That's exactly the kind of thing I have to deal with around a place like this constantly, and frankly I'm sick of it." Dr. Conrad leaned in, staring Dr. Edge straight in the eye, saying, "And it's people like you who keep those horrible stories alive." Sitting back in his chair, he said softly, "I believe I've heard enough and it's past time for you to leave this hospital for good."

Dr. Edge noticed the resignation in Dr. Conrad's eyes. He had to make his last appeal—making it good. "Fiona didn't hire me to chase ghosts Dr. Conrad. She hired me to find her father, and possibly the answer to why her mother went insane." Dr. Conrad glanced up with interest as Dr. Edge explained. "She believes that her father was the nurse who was assisting Dr. Karanza when they were trying to find out who killed her grandfather. Both he and Dr. Karanza disappeared. She believes Dr. Karanza poisoned them with some experimental medication she was working on. They are the only ones still missing. If I can find her father, or Dr. Karanza, we may just find a cure for *your* patient."

Dr. Conrad knew the stories about what happened at the Whitcomb home. He knew about the hospital records concerning the incident—the ones that were kept hidden and locked away from public scrutiny. The ones held in reserve—just in case Dr. Karanza or the nurse ever did reappear—to protect the hospital from unjust accusations and lawsuits. The records he was not even allowed to mention.

"We're not reopening that can of worms Alex," Dr. Conrad fumed. His finger stretched out and pushed down on a red button on the keypad of his phone. A feigned smile appeared on his face.

Dr. Edge knew what that smile meant. And he knew what that button was for. The orderly was already opening the door. "She also hired me to find the money," Dr. Edge said quickly, before the orderly stepped inside.

Dr. Conrad's hand shot up—stopping the orderly at the door, saying, "Just give us another minute." Dr. Edge could feel the eyes of the hulking man in the doorway looking him over like a piece of meat he wanted to devour. Like a well-trained guard dog, the orderly slipped back out into the hallway, slowly pulling the door shut behind him. "Go on... I'm listening," Dr. Conrad prompted, "make it quick."

Leaning up close with his arms resting on the desk, Dr. Edge spoke softly, "My client received an anonymous letter from someone who had intimate knowledge about her, her family, and everything that happened with Dr. Karanza and your new patient, Kaitlin. And according to this letter, there is a sizeable stash of cash at the Whitcomb estate just waiting to be found."

"Why in hell would this anonymous person want Fiona to find this money?" Dr. Conrad murmured.

"That's what I'm here to find out. And lucky for you, Fiona doesn't even want the money. She promised whatever I find as payment for my services. All she really wants is for me to find her father. There is little hope of finding out what caused her mother to go insane... so if I did... that would just be a bonus."

"How much money are we talking about?" Dr. Conrad asked, fidgeting with anticipation. He had driven past the Whitcomb estate a few times—it was a nice escape from the everyday grind at the hospital—now and then—spending a couple of free hours just meandering around in the countryside to clear his head. From what he had seen from his car window, he knew that they were obviously wealthy at one time. So the rumors could have some truth to them, after all. A slender greedy smile emerged on his lips as he almost began to salivate.

Dr. Edge smiled, "Enough to leave this dead-end government job and start a new practice… anyplace you like Doctor." He could see the wheels spinning in Dr. Conrad's head—already counting the money. "We can split whatever I find fifty-fifty. All I need is one hour with Kaitlin."

Glancing around his office, taking in everything he had come to despise about this place—he made up his mind quickly. "You have one hour." His finger pressed the red button again and the orderly promptly reappeared. "Take Dr. Edge to the observation room to examine the patient… he has one hour with her." With that, he handed Dr. Edge Kaitlin's file, along with an unfriendly departing smile.

Dr. Edge took the file with a *wink*. He then followed the orderly to where Kaitlin was waiting in the observation room. He hesitated in the open doorway, caught by a foul stench that filled the room. It was the smell of death—rotting flesh—something he was familiar with, but not accustomed. Doused in a strong sweet floral perfume to try and mask the stench, only made it worse—creating a sickening combination. Forcing himself into the small room, he took a chair across the table from Kaitlin. A two-way mirrored glass lined the back walls. Brightly glaring overhead lights bounced of the stark white walls making the room appear to glow. Her skin was nearly as white as the walls and her hospital issued clothing, having a similar reflective glow.

Dr. Edge was taken aback by how young Kaitlin looked.

Glancing inside the file, he checked her birth-date again. "Says here you should be around, seventy-something... that right Kaitlin?" She didn't respond, with her head hung low over her folded arms as if trying to hide her face. From what he could see of her, she appeared to be in her forties. With smooth skin, healthy looking dark brown curling hair, and a sleek aerobicized physique, she actually looked much like his last date—that ended poorly. Still, other than the dreadful smell, he found her to be very attractive. "Kaitlin, will you please look at me?" He asked softly.

No response. Head bowed down. She kept still.

"Can I see your hands then... to check your pulse?" He asked, trying to get her to open up a little—to develop some trust.

No movement.

"How can I allow you to visit with Catherine if you won't help me find out some things first?"

Kaitlin slowly raised up her head at the seemingly bizarre suggestion. She obviously wanted to believe it could happen. Dark circles surrounded her hazel eyes as she glared at him—skeptically. With no make-up, her complexion was pale, and her skin gaunt. She could have just walked out of a Nazi concentration camp. Trembling a little, she pulled her hands out from underneath her arms and placed them on the table.

Dr. Edge shuttered at the sight of her long bony fingers. Her fingertips had all turned black, with her skin in a state of decomposition. A nauseating odor of rotting flesh wafted to his nose forcing him to lean back in his chair. He could see tiny black lines snaking up through her capillaries, moving up each finger as it spread into her hands. Every instinct of attraction instantly vanished. It took everything he had just to stay in the room. "Let's get started shall we... since we don't have much time," he mumbled while trying not to breath in.

Taking the gemstone amulet from his pocket, Dr. Edge held it up near Kaitlin's forehead. Her eyes instantly fixated on the gleaming green jewel and its spiraling vortex lines drawing her in. "Follow my voice and the lines," he suggested, speaking low and soft, over and over again—drawing her in deeper and deeper into a hypnotic state. His hand ever so slowly moved the amulet closer to her forehead, until her eyelids began to close and twitch—vibrating violently—as her eyes rolled back into her head. With one last quick motion he placed the amulet on her forehead, holding it against her skin with the flat of his palm. Closing his own eyes—he focused his mind.

"Show me," he whispered to her.

Kaitlin's soul opened up to him…

3

In the mind's eye
The same observatory room
Twenty years earlier, January, 1981

IT WAS UNUSUALLY quiet for a Monday morning within the *experimental wing*. Inside this section of the Georgia Central State Hospital (formerly known as the Georgia Lunatic Asylum) all of the patients had been locked down, restrained, and sedated under heavy medication. The long sterile corridor was empty and silent.

Dr. Emily Karanza followed closely behind Dr. Jenkins as he stormed out of the observation room. As the door swung shut and latched Dr. Jenkins spun around to face her. With an ominous scowl, clenched fists, and bloodshot eyes, Jenkins lunged forward, forcing Dr. Karanza to lurch back against the door. She winced as the doorknob jabbed into her spine. Jenkins quickly stepped forward and leaned in close—pinning her. His tall lanky frame loomed over her like a raised cobra—carefully watching for any reason to strike.

Dr. Karanza kept her eyes down, unable to look into his dark callous eyes that peered down at her through his *nerdish* thick glasses. It was bad enough, being so close to his gray-tinged beard. Unkempt, with uneven whiskers that clung to bits of his last meal, making her cringe inside every time she saw him up close. If she could only hold him down long enough to run a razor over them, she would cut them off clean down to the skin—till he bled.

Looking down, she instead focused on his crisply starched white physician's frock and the two-toned silver-plated *Cross* ink pen that was tucked inside of his coat pocket. *Ooh... that pen!* The one that he used expertly to betray her confidence while belittling her work; scribbling notes of disagreement, scratching through her diagnosis or prescribed medications, or, best of all, to leave indiscriminately jotted tidbits of sarcastically laced criticism—just for fun. A clicking sound erupted in Dr. Karanza's head as she stared at it—hearing that obsessive *click-click-click-click* noise he would make with it using his thumb. Clicking it impulsively like a hyperactive child. It now starred in one of her diabolical day-dreams—one in which she would grab the pen from his hand and swiftly plunge the metal spike deep into his eyeball, throat, face, or any other place with exposed soft flesh. Imagining Dr. Jenkins screaming in agony, with his pen piercing him like a giant hypodermic needle—she couldn't help but allow a tiny smile.

Dr. Jenkins glanced down. His probing eyes attracted to her breasts by a glint of light. The silver *Sephirot tree of life* medallion was back on her necklace. Having slipped out from beneath the top button on her blouse that had popped free—he saw it. *Stupid bitch!* His blood boiled over like a kettle on a high flame. *I've told her a hundred times. Do not wear that damn thing at work... making us all, look like cultish idiots. Stupid Kabballah witch!*

Dr. Jenkins looked back up just in time to catch a glimpse of Dr. Karanza's sly smile—before she could erase it. Huffing, he raised his head up high on his long thin neck, and growled in low guttural voice, "Last warning Emily. You've been here less than two years and you've already pushed everyone to their limits. This is absolutely your last chance to get some results before I pull the plug. I'm meeting with the Board next week and they'll want my report about this patient. And trust me nothing would bring me more pleasure

than bouncing your ass right out of here." His eyes glanced back down at the medallion with a moment of reflection, before saying. "My reputation is on the line here too you know. This is not some science fiction alchemy project. I'm the Department Head and I'm not going to let you act like some sort of God-damn witch doctor… not this time!"

The doorknob raked across Dr. Karanza's spine as she shifted in place, squirming back and forth like a wriggling worm trying to create some space between herself and Dr. Jenkins. Unable to move in either direction, she felt as if she was one of her own involuntarily confined patients—trapped inside a tiny space to be constantly scrutinized.

At present, a mere four patients were continuously housed in the designated *experimental wing,* all of whom were suffering from some unique mental illness. Only those patients that suffered with the most severe symptoms were permanently housed here. Each of them suffered from a severe chronic mental illness, one that could not be identified, diagnosed, or controlled.

Making her rounds early each morning Dr. Karanza made sure that she was there before any other staff had a chance to interact with any of her patients. Without turning on any lights, she slinked cautiously along the darkened hallway, stopping at each door to peer inside through the tiny square windows. To her, it was the only time when they could be honestly examined, before they became aware that they were being watched—before they became *the patient.*

With a pencil in one hand and a manila patient file in the other she carefully watches them, until after a few moments something would catch her interest or spark some insight. Then, she would begin frantically scribbling cryptic notes in her self-styled short-hand, out of which, upon review and reflection, only she could later interpret some deeper useful meaning. As always, she concluded each patient's notations with a more personal observation.

Carla: a twenty-one year old emaciated blonde who enjoyed

cutting her skin open and writing passages on the walls with her own blood, frequently to be discovered standing on top of her mattress urinating, while giggling like a petulant child. Red spots of fresh blood are splattered everywhere, covering her clothing and bedding. She is feverishly scratching her broken nails down the concrete walls, pricking at the broken and peeling paint as if to uncover something.

Patient notes: *Removing skin and paint, the coverings that would hide what hid inside.*

Rachel: a stout middle aged woman that was nearly bald from her penchant for pulling out her own hair, typically found sitting upright in the corner of the room staring back at me through the window, with bread crumbs and bits of breakfast clinging to the drool on her chin. Wide awake and waiting expectantly, she could sense my arrival and her imminent release from the restraints, allowing her to stretch her aching numbed limbs, take her medications, and escape once again into a drug induced hibernation. If allowed the slightest of opportunities, she would gleefully take her own life—just as she had her own six children—by repeatedly slamming her head into the gray concrete wall.

Patient notes: *A final escape from her perceived miserable state of existence.*

Donald: an obese man in his late fifties who lived each day seemingly without any sense of a moral conscience, who growled in the manner of a rabid dog, hissing, menacingly displaying his black pitted rotting teeth, rolling his head to the side while opening his eyes wide, reminiscent of a real life wolf man. He would greet me each morning in a different location in his room, but always squatting on his coiled haunches ready to pounce on me, or anyone else, if they made the awful mistake of coming within his reach.

Patient notes: *Envious; complete dehumanization, no need for compassion or concern for the mundane, free from the trivial pursuits of life.*

Finally; there was Catherine, her most interesting, and most promising patient.

Appearing to be in her twenties, locks of wavy red hair

surrounded her pale porcelain skin. A sleeping beauty of sorts, Catherine remains trapped within a deep coma since the day she arrived at the Hospital, over eighty years prior. In the same position, every morning, lightly restrained at the wrist and ankles, she spends every moment, peacefully resting like a lifeless corpse, lying motionless on her rolling hospital bed mattress. Her serene expression seemed to never change, much like her soft porcelain white skin that had a doll-like quality—an appearance that was beautiful and mesmerizing, and yet, so terribly sad.

Only the very tips of her toes and fingers had any indication of imperfection. They had become a deep black, as if droplets of black ink had been dribbled from a broken ink pen across all ten of them. Over the decades since she had arrived at the hospital, tiny tentacles of black had slowly appeared, snaking out of the black tips, and moving up through the length of her fingers and toes, like ink was ever so slowly flowing into her veins. An ever-present pungent smell of rotting flesh accompanied the blackening of her skin. The smell grew stronger, and ever more putrid, as her capillaries darkened. With each passing decade, she slowly decayed, while she slept.

Patient notes: *An eternal death while stuck in this place, how ironic!*

"Well Emily?" Dr. Jenkins huffed, trying to goad a response.

Dr. Karanza turned her head to look in the other direction. Her eyes fell on the heavy metal door at the end of the hallway. Large, thick, and heavy, the door stood constant guard, keeping them locked safely inside. A recurring feeling washed over her like an all-consuming tsunami—a longing for freedom. Every part of her just wanted to get on the other side of that door. *Oh my God Catherine, this has just got to work… for both of us.*

The shadow covering her face darkened as Dr. Jenkins leaned in—even closer. She could smell the stale coffee on his breath as he growled at her in a deep voice that echoed through the corridor like rumbling thunder. "I won't let this Department's reputation become tainted by your unorthodox experimental practices. They don't just call you *Ka-razy Ka-ran-za* around here for no reason. Mark my words Emily, this is it… got it!"

Dr. Jenkins abruptly turned and quickly walked away—stomping down the hallway. Her body slumped down and trembled as she released the tension. Clenching her eyes tightly shut, she tried to block out the reverberating sounds of his footsteps. If only she could blot him out of existence completely. *Stupid, jealous bastard! He never believed in me, or in my methods. He wants me to fail. So afraid I will succeed and show him for what he is… a fool!*

Three members of the Hospital Board along with two hospital administrators anxiously awaited Dr. Karanza's return. They positioned themselves for optimum viewing behind the one-way mirror—keenly watching the male nurse who was busily attending to Catherine. He ignored the low pitch hum of whispers on the other side of the glass wall as he picked up a shining silver needle and placed it nearly flat against Catherine's milky white forearm. Using a gentle touch, his fingers danced lightly over her skin as he probed for a suitable vein. He guided the needle inside the vein with delicate precision. Catherine lay absolutely still as the needle pierced her. Not the slightest flinch of a fingertip, twitch of a nerve, or flutter of an eyelash.

After wrapping a cover of surgical tape around Catherine's arm, the nurse switched off the bright ceiling lights. A dimmed spot-light attached to a retractable swing-arm over the bed lit up the patient. The room around her bed was dark. Catherine's upper torso and face glowed under the soft beam of light. Then, with everything ready, the nurse flipped a plastic toggle, releasing medicine that dribbled down the I.V. tube. Everyone watched intently, as Karanza's experimental medicine flowed inside Catherine's vein.

As Dr. Karanza was about to reenter the observation room, the sound of the metal door slamming shut at the end of the hall stopped her cold. *Kaitlin—about damn time!* She could hear Kaitlin's high heeled shoes clicking on the tiled floor. *She's the only one who would wear those shoes in this place.* Turning to face her, she said in a professionally restrained voice, "Good, you're finally here. We need to get started immediately." Her eyes were looking past Kaitlin, focusing instead on the metal door behind her as she spoke. "And where's Gregory?" She asked bluntly.

Kaitlin was strolling down the corridor wearing the white doctor's smock that she had borrowed from her surgeon husband. Way-too-big looking, like a child wearing her father's overcoat. She had rolled up the sleeves to make it wearable. It did the job nonetheless, covering up her knee length black dress that she felt was more appropriate for this morbid occasion. And besides, there was just no way in hell she was going to be seen in those hideous white nurse's scrubs that Dr. Karanza had asked her to wear.

Kaitlin's hands were covered by a pair of surgical gloves—also borrowed from her husband. Not that she needed them for protection from anything that she knew of, she was just feeling self-conscious about the tiny black spots that had recently appeared on the very tips of her fingers. Only Dr. Karanza was aware of her condition. Kaitlin had sought out her medical advice since it was so eerily similar to Catherine's progressing disease. She was mostly concerned that it may be congenital, and begin to spread—just as it was doing in Catherine.

Dr. Karanza had kindly volunteered to help her find a remedy. It only made sense, since she was already treating Catherine for the same apparent malady. The coma like state and the slowly decaying flesh were most likely related anyway. Finding a cure for one symptom just may lead to finding a cause, and cure, for both.

Kaitlin was late, as usual, and was clearly agitated with everything—as usual. The look on her face reflected a resigned frustration—a look that had been drawn on her face by many years of being habitually disappointed by her husband.

"Isn't Gregory with you?" Dr. Karanza repeated.

Kaitlin didn't answer—ignoring the question. Still making her way down the long hallway, a vacant shark-eyed glare came across her eyes as she thought about her absent husband. Lost in reflection while contemplating the answer to the seemingly simple question, her face turned cold and hard, resembling the austere expression of an ancient marble Greek statute.

Dr. Karanza's neck muscles stiffened, realizing the answer, before lashing out, "You do understand this is our last chance… don't you?" Looking Kaitlin up and down like a stern headmistress, she pointed out with contempt, "At least you put on *something* white like I asked. You finally got something right, for once."

The hallway fell coldly silent as Kaitlin stopped walking. Now face to face with Dr. Karanza, the two women glared into each other's eyes like prize fighters anxiously waiting for the sound of the bell. Both women were emotional volcanoes. Primed by mounting stress, they were each ready to erupt and spew out a burning lava of seething anger.

Before the women's emotions could fully erupt, the nurse ripped open the observation room door—stepping in-between them like the referee. "Oh good… there you are Doctor," he said nervously, glancing anxiously at Kaitlin.

"Kaitlin, this is Paul," Dr. Karanza grumbled.

Kaitlin curtly nodded in his direction.

Dr. Karanza softened a little, as she explained, "Paul has been Catherine's primary nurse for the last few years… her very own guardian angel of sorts."

Paul dutifully responded by saying, "Everyone is waiting Doctor. The medication is being administered. We're at one minute already."

"I'll be right in, go stay with the patient," Dr. Karanza dismissed him.

Paul glanced over at Kaitlin. In that instant, she felt a fluttering tickle that made her uneasy, yet excited, all at the same time. Seeing him made her feel like a giddy schoolgirl—a nervous butterfly wings inside feeling—that she hadn't felt in many years. In that time stopping moment as they stared at each other, a silent voice whispered to her, *I will be watching you.* As Paul slipped back inside the observation

room, his enchanting eyes stayed locked with hers until the door gently slid shut behind him.

"Did you at least bring the release documents with you?" Dr. Karanza murmured. Kaitlin barely heard the question. Her eyes remained glued to the closed door as if still looking longingly into his eyes. "Well... did you?"

Kaitlin quickly refocused on Dr. Karanza's angry stare. "Uh, well, yes... I think they ummmm... oh yes, I have them right in here." Kaitlin pulled the preprinted legal forms from the bottom of her large purse and handed them to Dr. Karanza to inspect. Like a *Pavlovian* conditioned dog, her mouth drooled a little bit when she caught sight of a loose cigarette at the bottom of her purse. It had slipped out of a long discarded pack, and had been hiding itself underneath the forms. *Oh no, not a good time to try and quit... again,* she groaned while envisioning lighting it up and taking a slow deep drag right there in the hallway.

"So, Doctor, is Catherine in the same condition as before?" She asked to try and forget about the cigarette.

Dr. Karanza ignored her as she shuffled through the papers in her hands like a deck of cards. Her eyes intently skimmed over the preprinted legal forms. The tiny printed lines blurred together as she frantically searched for each line that required Kaitlin's signature or initial. *I asked for these days ago... stupid bitch... ugh!* Finally satisfied that the paperwork was in order, Dr. Karanza returned her full attention back to Kaitlin who was now staring at her intently. "Well... this new medication is getting results... much better than anything else I've tried. She's gaining a little more lucidness with each session, every time we increase the new medication. There's no explanation as to why she's not aging. But we may finally be able to communicate with her. Then perhaps we could identify a cause."

Listening intently, clasping her hands together while anxiously shifting her weight back and forth, Kaitlin looked like a young child who was waiting to un-wrap a long awaited gift. "So it's actually working then?" She begged. Glancing down at her latex covered hands she was more excited about finding a cure for herself, than she was for Catherine.

"Yes, it appears to be… so-far-so-good," Dr. Karanza whispered, "with some manageable side effects of course." Looking Kaitlin straight in the eyes, she insisted, "But every risk is worth the price that has to be paid now, since nothing else we have tried has had any meaningful results."

"What about the smell?" Kaitlin asked, wrinkling her nose as if she had smelled something foul in the air.

"The same unfortunately," Dr. Karanza replied with a squeamish smile, "It seems Paul is the only one who has been able to get used to it, for a few minutes at a time that is.

The sound of clanging metal turned the women's attention to the end of the hall. The door had just slammed shut behind the figure of a man. His face was not yet recognizable. Dressed in a patient's white hospital garb, with a plastic identification band dangling on his wrist, he appeared to be a lost patient who had wandered in from another wing. Frozen in place, just inside the door, he stared down the hallway at the women as if he had unexpectedly found himself inside a cage, coming face to face with two lionesses.

Puzzled, Kaitlin and Dr. Karanza continued to watch him without moving or speaking, as if they didn't want to make a sudden move, one that would scare him away. Suddenly, as if making a run for it, he spun around and grabbed the doorknob—it was locked.

"Charles? Is that you Charles?" Dr. Karanza called to him.

Kaitlin spun herself around like a Whirling Dervish to glare daggers at Dr. Karanza. Through tightly clenched lips, she asked in a hushed yet stern voice. "You brought Charlie here?"

"Yes… I had to," Dr. Karanza answered. Her face became cold and hard once again as she emotionally retracted behind a hardened facade like a turtle inside of its shell.

Kaitlin tried to keep her voice to a low growl as she reacted to Charlie's surprise appearance. "He can't deal with this right now.

You should know that. He hasn't recovered from the accident. It's way too soon Doctor."

Charlie's foot shifted toward the door as his hand pulled it open slightly.

Not wanting to make eye contact with Kaitlin, Dr. Karanza peered down the hallway at Charlie over Kaitlin's shoulder. Seeing the door opening, she called out to Charlie again—while ignoring Kaitlin's angry ranting altogether. Her voice caught Charlie just in time to stop him from leaving. "Charles… down here!"

Pausing again—Charlie stood motionless in the open doorway.

Dr. Karanza looked back at Kaitlin who was still glaring at her with piercing eyes that could kill. Blue veins in her forehead bulged out and pulsed in unison with her pounding heartbeat as Kaitlin waited for Dr. Karanza to acknowledge her, and her pleas. "You know this is my last chance," Dr. Karanza whispered. "We won't get another opportunity to help Catherine. If we don't get results today it's over, they are going to lock her away for good. No one else will bother to try and help her… or you for that matter."

"So that's your plan then? You're going to use all of us like bait to try and lure her out?" Kaitlin snarled.

Dr. Karanza just nodded slightly, and said, "That's part of it, yes."

Kaitlin breathed deeply, in and out, utilizing the techniques she had learned in therapy. Ways to control her fear, her anxiety, and her overwhelming bouts of rage. She concentrated on listening to the air rushing in and out of her; while, at the same time, she could hear his footsteps approaching her down the long hallway. Kaitlin closed her eyes and breathed deeply, feeling her tension flowing out of her with each deep breath—in and out—in and out—each deep breath became synchronized with each step Charlie made. Kaitlin exhaled out one last long breath just as Charlie took his last step, as he stopped, just behind her.

"You don't have to be here. You don't have to do this Charlie." Kaitlin said softly without turning to look at him. She had not seen nor spoken with Charlie since they had both attended their father's funeral a few months earlier. Their father was laid to rest the day after the combined funeral ceremonies for Charlie's deceased wife and son—a ceremony she did not attend.

Charles had never provided a satisfactory explanation for any of their deaths. He was the only survivor that night, and Kaitlin remained bitter, and unable to forgive him for their deaths; even-though, she really couldn't find a good reason to blame him—not yet anyway. For now, it was just her way of dealing with the suspicion and the pain.

"Have you moved out of the house yet Charlie?" Kaitlin asked coldly, sounding more like a parent than an older sister. She turned slightly, just far enough so that Charlie was visible out of the corner of her eye. Charlie didn't respond. Not able to see his face over her shoulder, she assumed that he was just being his typical bratty self by not responding.

Dr. Karanza watched his reaction carefully. She saw Charlie's drooping eyelids that were sagging so heavily that he looked like he had been drugged. He had a vacant, soulless looking stare. Gloomy black circles around his eyes contrasted with the streaks of red inside his bloodshot corneas. A rough, pinkish, burnt scar tissue covered a small patch on the left side of his neck and lower face. Some of his chestnut brown hair was missing behind his ear. As if walking in his sleep, his arms dangled lifelessly at his sides. Both of his hands mir-rored his face, and what was not hidden by patient scrubs and gauze was covered with newly healed-over pinkish scar tissue. The tips of three of his fingers were missing entirely—burnt so badly that they had to be surgically removed.

Kaitlin began turning to confront her brother when Paul burst out into the hallway once again, blurting out frantically, "the medi-cation is taking effect. We have to get started, right now doctor."

Dr. Karanza abruptly turned and stepped through the door.

Kaitlin and Charlie followed Paul into the observation room. They found Dr. Karanza already positioned at Catherine's bedside.

A thick, black polyester blanket was draped over Catherine's body, covering her from the waist down. It drooped over the edges of the mattress, falling five feet to about an inch off of the floor. The only sound was the conspicuously loud noise of the antiquated ventilation system that had been installed to continuously suck the nauseatingly pungent air out of the tiny room.

Paul busily began to monitor the medicine filled I.V. bag, following the dripping liquid as it moved along the clear tubing to the needle that was secured to Catherine's arm with several layers of wrapped surgical tape. Her arms and legs were lightly fastened to her bed by thin leather straps. Kaitlin and Charlie silently watched Paul and Dr. Karanza working. Remaining near the door, unsure of what they should do, they silently waited for instructions. Paul seemed to be the only one comfortable with the situation, as he attended to Catherine.

Dr. Karanza was clearly less comfortable. It was evident by her slightly trembling hands and hesitant movements that she was not sure of herself, of Catherine's condition, or of what was going to happen.

"What should we do?" Kaitlin asked softly.

Not looking up, Dr. Karanza kept her eyes trained on Catherine's face, and raised her left hand slightly as a gesture, to let Kaitlin know she was interfering. Then, in a hushed voice, she said, "Just stay put, and be absolutely quiet... until she's ready."

Charlie squeamishly shuffled back towards the wall. He managed to nearly disappear entirely as he moved away from the light over Catherine's bed, back into the shadows, where his white clothing melded with the white paint on the wall. Only the sound of air rushing through the air-conditioning ducts filled the void of near absolute silence. Minutes ticked slowly past without anyone moving, speaking, or making the slightest sound. Everyone's eyes were transfixed on Catherine's face as they waited for any indication that the medication was working.

Paul glanced down at his watch, *9:23:11 a.m.,* and he leaned over, close to Dr. Karanza's ear, to whisper, "Past critical Doctor… time to call it?"

Dr. Karanza did not respond. She kept her eyes fixed on Catherine's face.

Paul looked up at Kaitlin. She was staring down at Catherine's face, like a young innocent child who was promised a miracle—a resurrection. It made him angry. *She has no idea how dangerous this is. Karanza didn't explain it to her. She never would have told her the truth.*

Looking back down at Dr. Karanza, Paul reminded her that they were running out of time. "We're past 15 minutes doctor… way past lethal. I suggest you pull the plug."

A droplet of sweat dripped down Dr. Karanza's forehead. "Pull the plug? No, no, no, there is no going back. I can't stop now. This has to work. It has to work now. I just need to increase the dosage," she started ranting. Glancing nervously around at the faces surrounding her, she suddenly realized that she must have the appearance of one of her own patients, who was desperately scratching at reality, in an attempt to remain within the realm of the sane.

Looking back down at her unresponsive patient, Dr. Karanza leaned forward, lightly touching Catherine's arm. Placing her quivering lips on Catherine's ear, she spoke to her softly. "It's time Catherine… time to wake up." Inside, she was screaming, *Wake up you damn bitch! Please don't do this to me Catherine. You are my star patient… you were supposed to save me… to get me the hell out of here!*

Paul turned and reached his hand up to the I.V. bag to stop the medication from dripping. As he began twisting the plastic lever to stop the flow of medication—Catherine's eyes popped open. A wave of imperceptible energy flowed through Catherine's body, causing goose bumps to appear on her skin, as every muscle within her responded as if suddenly hit by the energy from a powerful electrode.

Paul yanked his hand away from the I.V. and rushed back to Catherine's side.

Dr. Karanza was frozen, gazing down at Catherine in

amazement. *Yes, that's it Catherine, come on back to us.* Lifting up her shaking hand, she motioned for Kaitlin and Charlie to join them at Catherine's bedside.

Kaitlin hesitated, and then stopped moving. Her feet couldn't be moved another inch forward, as if liquid nitrogen had been poured over her, freezing her in place. Her desperate eyes looked up at Paul. His eyes encouraged her to continue. Fighting through her fear, she began to move slowly, like cold molasses across a frozen lake, shivering, as she edged up to the bed.

Catherine's lips quivered and her mouth moved slightly, as if she were trying to say something.

Kaitlin gasped as Catherine looked directly into her eyes. *This can't be happening*, she thought as her feet started to shuffle back. A hard, firm hand, pressed up against Kaitlin's back like a brick wall, stopping her. Looking up to see what was holding her there—Kaitlin saw Paul's face. He smiled and nodded with reassurance. Together—they inched back up to Catherine's bedside, and together, they touched her hand.

Dr. Karanza placed her fingertips on Catherine's vein to feel for a pulse.

Charlie drifted slowly away from the back wall and moved into the light like a ghost. Seeing Kaitlin's reaction, he followed her forward. Stepping to the end of the bed, he gently placed his fingers on Catherine's ankle.

Forming a semi-circle around the bed like the illumination of a crescent on the face of a waxing moon, each of them placed a hand on the person next to them. Knotting together, touching bare flesh, each of them was connected with everyone else, while all of them connected with Catherine.

Kaitlin hesitantly leaned down so that her mouth was close to Catherine's ear, and she began to speak to her softly. "Catherine. It's Kaitlin. I am here for you… to find you."

Catherine's eyes fluttered. Her fingertips twitched. Like a snake attacking its prey, her hand suddenly reached up and grabbed

Kaitlin's smock. With madman strength, she pulled Kaitlin's face towards her until they were nose to nose—wide eye to wide eye. Soft gurgling words whispered from her trembling lips, "I once was, where you now be, prepare with speed—to follow me."

As soon as the last word was forced out of her mouth, her eyes rolled back into her head as her entire body fell limply back down on the bed, seemingly dead.

Paul quickly turned off the I.V. feeding the medicine into Catherine's vein. Dr. Karanza directed everyone to move away from the bed. Paul took a white sheet and pulled it up over her morbid, lifeless face.

"What did she say?" Kaitlin mumbled nervously. "What did that mean?"

Dr. Karanza pointed at the door—directing everyone out.

Charlie was met at the door by an orderly and promptly whisked away.

Kaitlin and Dr. Karanza stepped back out into the corridor. They had to talk fast. Dr. Jenkins would be storming back into the hallway at any moment.

"What does this mean for me and Charlie?" Kaitlin asked.

"Nothing… it's nothing… we stick to the plan," Dr. Karanza insisted. "We will meet at your family's estate on Thursday, just like we agreed. There is still hope to find out what happened to all of you."

As Dr. Jenkins ripped open the door and stepped back into the hallway with a devilish look of self-satisfaction, Dr. Karanza was thinking; *and there is still hope for me.*

4

Inside the mind's eye, flashing ahead
The next Thursday, at the Whitcomb Family Estate
Twenty miles outside of Milledgeville, Georgia

"DAMN GATES… I always hated you and this whole damn place," Kaitlin muttered as she forced a key into the bottom of a padlock. Her hands were cold, and her fingers were already beginning to hurt as she twisted the key and jerked down on the ice cold metal lock that didn't want to let go. With a hard yank on the lock, its loop finally slipped free of the metal links at the end of a long chain. With the lock removed, her hands began working on untangling the chain that was wrapped around the two center bars of a large wrought iron gate.

The gate was erected at the entrance to her deceased father's estate. It was at the beginning of a long winding dirt and gravel driveway. On the other end stood a seven bedroom *Greek revival* that her grandfather had built at the turn of the century. At one time, the home was part of an expansive plantation that covered over one hundred acres of lush and productive farmland. Now, only this miserable tiny four acre plot surrounded the house.

A lonely country road passed in front of the gate. Those seldom travelers who now happen to pass by, and happened to notice the isolated and ornate gates, would be struck by an overwhelming feeling of *being out of place*. Thoughts of romantic bygones would float through their minds. Each person would initially paint a picture of a century old southern plantation, workers tending to crops on a hot summer day, as the carefree owners frolic about like a scene taken out of *Gone with the Wind*.

The family surname, *Whitcomb*, was written in twisted iron across the top of the gate—looming above Kaitlin's head as she struggled with the chain. She needn't look up to see it again, to know it was there, the image of her family's name had been forever emblazoned into her consciousness. Truly a love-hate relationship, she would love to get rid of everything associated with the house. If it wasn't for Charlie, the house would already be a pile of rubble. *I wish I had a bulldozer right now!*

Kaitlin had been forced to shed her soft leather driving gloves and expose her genteel hands to the frozen January air in order to retrieve the small key from her pocket and manipulate it inside the padlock. Her bare fingers ached as she anxiously pulled at the frustratingly twisted chain that now seemed to be fighting against her. Nearing the very edge of sanity, Kaitlin couldn't tell if she was about to start laughing hysterically about her plight, or if she should break down crying—or both—at the same time. But she was dead certain about one thing—it was all just another horribly ironic reminder of why she never should have come back here again.

"Damn!" Kaitlin yelped as a fingernail got pinched between two links. She let go of the chain just in time, before it twisted the nail clean away. The dangling chain fell back against the gate, rattling, making clinking sounds like laughter—directed at her. A light mist of hot breaths lingered over her fingers as she inspected the other nine finely manicured fingertips. Slowly, she took her time, examining each nail—one by one. To her relief, all the rest remained intact, smooth as silk, without a nick, chip, rough edge, or blemish.

Oh... hell? She thought, noticing the small black specks at the tip of every finger. Each of them was now a little bit bigger than

when she last looked at them. The dots looked like she had used a black ink pen to mark each one by jabbing the tip against her skin, tattooing herself. Her fingers on the other hand looked disturbingly the same way. *Whatever… it's nothing… just some rust off the chain or something*, she huffed, trying to pretend she didn't see anything. In the back of her mind, she couldn't ignore the idea that; *those black dots are getting bigger, exactly like they did on Catherine… just before that awful stench of death appeared.*

Kaitlin's overall appearance—dressed in a tailored Sassoon skirt and coat with matching black leather Prada shoes, accented by her luxuriously groomed wavy auburn hair that draped with soft curls over the neck of a full length mink coat. To accent her opulently wealthy appearance, her ring-finger was adorned with a four-carrot-diamond stone that sparked like fireworks being shot off when it was in the sunlight. Everything about her was a statement of her well-to-do cultured background.

With regularity Kaitlin enjoyed adorning herself in fashionable attire. Not only to make a fashion statement, but also to have her fashion make a proud statement about her Celtic heritage. Her Sassoon coat and skirt was custom made from hand cut tartan wool that she had personally selected while travelling in Edinburgh. She knew that the pattern woven into her clothing was that of Scottish origin, but she was completely unaware that the tartan pattern originated with the Clan of Urquhart. It had just appealed to her, in the same way that a certain scent arouses an innate passion.

Around her wrist was a silver rope bracelet. Dangling from the bracelet were tiny charms; a Claddagh, Thistle, and four Trinity Knots. A similar looking thin silver necklace draped over her shoulders. Hanging upon the necklace was an antique silver locket that was once owned by her mother. In her mother's arms a baby's fingers once tugged on it. On her mother's lap a child's eyes had looked at it with wondering admiration. Her mother took notice. And upon her mother's death Kaitlin finally received it—as a gift given to her from her father. Without explanation, on the day of her mother's memorial service, William placed the locket into her six-year-old hand. An intricately carved Celtic cross was etched onto the locket's oval face. Tucked inside was a black and white image of her mother, where it rested against her heart—always.

South-central Georgia had always been home to Kaitlin. However; she had never felt at home here, or anyplace else she had ever lived in her forty-one year life, including her professed hometown of Atlanta. Preferring to consider herself an orphan, she would often half-jokingly tell acquaintances just that—most often whenever she was inebriated—which in itself was something that was occurring more and more often. It became such a habit, that those who heard her repeat her joke would nearly believe she was telling the truth, even when they knew that she was lying.

I hope this is the last time I have to endure coming to this place, Kaitlin thought as she glared at the infuriating chain that was stubbornly holding the gate closed. Carefully, she manipulated the links, gently turning them, touching each thick link as lightly as she could to protect her nails. Groaning, *what the hell is wrong with this damn chain!* Her hot breaths misted in front of her face, forming a tiny swirling cloud, making it even harder for her to see her fingers *and* the chain.

"Aaaaaagh," she finally moaned, grabbing the chain without any regard for her nails. Leaning back on one foot, she pulled on it as hard as she could. The clanging links began to slide over the iron bars like a clanking slippery snake.

The sound of the chain moving across the bars forced a memory back into her mind—from when she was a young girl—not long after the day of her mother's funeral. She could hear it again, as if she were back at the hardware store with her father as he pulled a long section of chain from a spindle.

Her father, William, had taken her and Charlie with him to Johnson's hardware store in downtown Milledgeville. With rough calloused hands that were accustomed to the feel of tools, her father had pulled the eight feet of chain from a spindle. He eyeballed it for

a measurement before cutting. As he pulled the chain further, for another cut, it slipped over the lip of the sheet metal table, it made the same exact repetitious clanking sound that was once again ringing in her ears.

Kaitlin recalled asking him, "what you gunna do with that pa?"

William's dark brown eyes were trained on the links of chain in his hands as he estimated its length. He pretended not to hear.

Tiny Charlie was a few feet away, busying himself by examining slightly bent 10 penny nails that had been discarded into a metal bucket on the floor. Picking up one nail at a time with his tiny hands, he would hold it up close to his face, aligning the tip of the nail with his nose to simulate a bomb being readied to drop from an airplane, dropping it, he listened to it jingle as it bounced off the other nails and the sides of the bucket. Charlie made the deepest rumbling sounds of explosion that his little throat could muster as the nail hit the pile, "kaboooooooom."

"Huh... pa... what's it for?" Kaitlin repeated.

Four nails dropped from Charlie's hand before her father responded. His eyes never moved from the chain as he prepared to make another cut. "For the barn... keep you kids out... that's what for."

Kaitlin looked from his unshaven face, down to the bulging pocket of his tweed hunting jacket. The tell-tale bulge was where he liked to carry his bottle of whiskey. Reminding her of what she already knew. Daily, every day, all day, continuous copious sips had kept him emotionally blurred—making him more of a mirage than a man.

Kaitlin remembered him leaning against the metal table for support as he lazily gazed at the chain. He was wearing the same dirty overalls that he had worn for several days in a row. His clay stained work boots were strapped to his feet, and they would stay on his feet until he went to bed. His wooden cane rested against the table while he stretched the chain between his outstretched hands.

Greasy, matted black hair, unwashed for a few days, lay across his forehead like a heavily used mop.

Kaitlin understood that she and Charlie were not allowed inside the barn. But she never really understood exactly why. While peeking through the planks, they could see his liquor still. Making whiskey in the barn was not a secret he was keeping from anyone—not anyone—let alone, her and Charlie. Getting a hold of some of his hooch would not be a problem since he would leave near empty bottles of the stuff in almost every room. And whenever he drank too much and passed out, they could've had their fill. Kaitlin knew it wasn't booze in the barn that her father was trying to keep hidden and locked away.

His gruff voice was emotionless. His words were just as useless, as usual. Upon further reflection, Kaitlin recognized that the man who had cut this chain was not the same man who had placed the locket into her hand. He had already been changed. Her mother's death had changed him—killing something inside of him that spread throughout his life, slowly taking the life from everything he had, and from everyone around him.

Before her mother's untimely death, her father was the epitome of a polished business man. Up and going before the break of dawn. Spending every bit of daylight down at the Mill, no task was bigger or smaller than him, and none could escape his notice or immediate attention. His mind was always as sharply focused as his appearance. Usually wearing hip hugging belted trousers pressed with a crisp line down each leg, along with a stylish suit jacket or cardigan sweater, a tightly knotted tie, with a smart looking felt hat, one that never seemed to leave his head or his hand. And he absolutely never left through the front door without a freshly shaven face. Underneath his perfectly trimmed mustache resided an endlessly giving smile.

Kaitlin remembered her father standing there holding the chain for much longer than he needed to before turning to look at her through bloodshot eyes that appeared to be on the verge of tears.

He seemed broken. With lips trembling, he said, "don't you ever go into the barn again… understand me? Only thing in that barn now is death." Dropping his head as if praying, he closed his eyes. The chain slipped out of his fingers—scrapping over the edge of the metal table the chain rattled to the floor at his feet. A teardrop fell to the table top. It was the only tear she had ever seen fall from her father's eyes.

Looking down at the chain coiled at her feet, Kaitlin realized that the links of the chain used to secure the gate symbolized a simple metaphor for her life. She was unavoidably linked to this place forever just as her family was linked to her. Every time she had to come back to this place, to deal with her family again, another link in that chain was being forged. Soon—if she continued—the links would create a chain that was so lengthy, so thick, and so heavy, so tightly wrapped around her, that it would lock her up inside an emotional fence that she could never escape. In that moment Kaitlin suddenly felt that she was *Scrooge*, staring deeply into the hapless eyes of *Marley*, who was now doomed for all eternity, returning from the grave to warn her of a similar fate that was awaiting her.

Looking up, Kaitlin gazed through the iron bars. Her eyes drifted along the shallow ruts in the dirt driveway as they gently bent around a lazy curve before disappearing into the trees. Beyond the trees was her family's home. She envisioned herself going up the six granite steps, walking across the front porch, and standing at the front door. Seeing herself standing there contemplating what to do—not wanting to go through the door—her thoughts began to race backwards. Traveling back along the highway that she had just driven, her thoughts lead her back to her own home—back in Atlanta. *Just a couple of hours away, and I could be back for a match of tennis… or play backgammon… have some tea… or wine… all before Agnes serves dinner.*

But no matter how badly Kaitlin wanted to get back into her car and race back home to Atlanta, she couldn't escape the knowledge that Charlie was already waiting for her inside. *No. No. It's up to me. I am the only one. It's still my responsibility… It's what mother would've done… what she would have wanted.* Pressing against the cold bars, she reluctantly pushed the ten-foot gate open. The rust encrusted hinges squealed out their discomfort as they were forced to move once more.

Before returning to her car, Kaitlin looked down at her feet, and groaned, "Ooh damn." Her shoes were now spotted with sticky red mud. It was the perfect excuse to squeal herself, and vent off some built-up anxiety. *Shit! Look at this mess. Oh damn-it, not my new shoes. Damn Gregory, he should be here to do this shit. What am I doing here? I don't deserve this. Charlie… ugh… that selfish spoiled little baby… I'm so tired of having to take care of his ass!*

Kaitlin had never *actually* taken care of Charlie, not since they were very young. Now, they barely knew each other at all. They became distant in every way, barely seeing or talking to each other for many years. Her seething feelings of jealously helped to wedge them apart—beginning on the day she was forced to leave the house to live at the girl's academy. Ever since then, she could only think of him from a distance. Not a part of her life. He became that spoiled brat that got to do everything he wanted. Nothing was really expected of him, as far as she could tell. Especially since he eventually got to leave home on his own terms—without all the emotional baggage dragging behind him to torment his every waking hour—unlike her.

Kaitlin's right hand dipped into her coat pocket. She ran her middle finger along the stitching on the bottom. *Oh where is it?* She thought as her finger probed the bottom of the pocket. Half of her mind was hoping that her finger would touch the hard plastic container that held her pills—or at least one little loose *Xanax*. Nervously fingering the bottom of her pockets had become a frequent occurrence. It was now almost an instinctive reaction, whenever her anxiety reached a point of near full-blown attack. Her right pocket

was empty so she dug down into the other—with the same result. No bottle and no pill. *Knew I should've gotten a refill before I left Atlanta.*

Not being left completely empty handed, she did find a used tissue that she could use to clean her shoes. *I shouldn't have stopped taking my medication last year... Gregory was wrong... I wasn't ready... I should have listened to my therapist,* she thought to herself as she planted her right hand on the side of her car to balance herself as she began rubbing the sticky reddish clay from her shoes with the wadded up used tissue. *I don't need medication. It wasn't my fault. I shouldn't have to feel guilty anyway. The accident wasn't my fault. Their deaths weren't my fault. Charlie's condition is not my fault. There was absolutely nothing that I could have done to prevent any of this anyway. I couldn't have known what the hell was going to happen.*

Her guilt was sticking to her more than the clay on her shoes.

The sticky clay was too much for the tissue paper. It tore into tiny bits in her fingers. Picking up a small broken tree branch she tried to rake the mud from her fine leather shoes. This only made it look worse. Her black shoe was now decorated with brownish-red streaks. Giving up, she threw the stick to the ground next to the bits of muddy tissue. And while examining the mess that she had made—she turned her thoughts of frustration and disgust to the one person who made her feel the most frustrated, and the most disgusted. *Ugh... it had to be that good for nothing Daniel! It's his fault they are dead. He did this to Charlie... not me!*

Kaitlin opened the door and fell into the bucket-seat of the not quite a month old 1981 Jaguar Coupe. The purring engine was left running to keep the inside warm. She instantly felt better once she was back inside her new car. Such luxurious possessions instilled Kaitlin with a nearly-the-same comforting feeling that her anti-anxiety medications used to give her. Somehow, they allowed her to escape from the things that would usually make her feel upset. They, in some indescribable way, provided her with a means of escape, and made her feel peaceful, and safe.

All feelings of safety and peace vanished as the car rounded the last bend in the driveway and she saw the large house coming into view. Her eyes wandered up the granite stairs that lead up to an expansive wooden wrap-around porch. On each side of the stairs, there stood two white cornice topped marble columns as big as tree trunks. Eight evenly dispersed windows dotted the whitewashed wooden façade that had been added to cover the original red brick walls. On each end of the house, tall chimney stacks jutted up, pointing high into the air above the roof-line like two horns.

To Kaitlin, the two-story white house had always appeared to be like a cloud that floated above the ground. The dark tiled roof was the storm cloud's brewing storm. Inside the doorway, within the cloud, lived the raging storm. *The thunder cloud home in the sky*, she thought as the Jaguar rolled to a stop. A familiar crunching sound was heard as the weight of the wheels pressed down on the gravel driveway.

Kaitlin put the car in park, and then paused, taking a moment to sit quietly and look at the house where she had grown up. She then remembered a little saying, one that she would often whisper to herself as a young girl whenever she returned home: *My haven and my hell… my safety and my cell*. The line became a stanza incorporated into one of the many poems she had written inside of her journal.

As her eyes drifted across the front of the house, they landed on her father's bedroom window directly above the porch. It was framed by black shutters. A hand laced white curtain was visible through the dust covered glass. For an instant, she thought the lacy curtain moved, ever-so-slightly. A faint image of her father's face appeared as he moved back the curtain, just enough to peer out— keeping a sharp eye on her—just as he used to do when she was a child.

A turbid sensation of instantly maturing from infancy to old age swept over her as she looked up at the window. Her memories raced, from when she was a small timid child, up through the years, leading up to this day, where she finds herself as an adult. Now, hardened and tested, full of resolve, ready to do what she had to do

to help her brother and herself, she stepped out of the car, slammed the door shut, and walked briskly toward the front porch steps.

Kaitlin didn't make it more than a few steps before she began to notice the changes that had taken place since her father's death. As if the wind had suddenly changed direction, allowing her full sails to wilt, the sight of the neglected grounds began to deflate her renewed sense of passion. The lawn, the shrubs, and the house itself, were all abandoned and neglected—never having looked so bad. *That worthless bastard! Apparently Daniel has been drunk every day since father died.* Kaitlin thought as she made her way up the front steps. *I haven't even seen him since… well… it was way before father's funeral… after I was moved from Highlands Boarding School up to Atlanta… hell, really, now I can't even remember that last time. Fine with me… far as I'm concerned, I hope I never have to lay eyes on that no good worthless bum again.*

She envisioned a pickled Daniel passed out in his bed, sleeping off another bout of binge drinking. She could see him lying on his dirty mattress, wearing his filthy clothes that he couldn't get off before going unconscious. His deep rumbling snore shaking the thin, barely hanging on rotting boards, of his ramshackle old wooden farmhouse that was out back, on the far edge of the estate. The two-bedroom shack was built by sharecroppers before the main house was even conceived—a full century before. Situated on the edge of a large open field, his farmhouse was mostly hidden from view behind a thick stretch of woods that separated the two houses. Still, it had never been nearly far enough away for Kaitlin. *I'll burn his house to the ground to get rid of him if I have to*, she considered while looking over the unkempt grounds. *All he has to do is keep the yard. Hell… he can't even do that.*

At least I'll finally have the chance to fulfill my one long held fantasy while I'm here. Firing and evicting that no good piece of shit Daniel, once and for all! A sly smile appeared on her lips. With gleeful devilish anticipation, she could clearly see an image of Daniel's slack-jawed, dirty unshaven face, wearing that holey beat-up straw hat that never left his head, right in front of her as she slammed the front gate

shut. Him, standing there on the other side of the iron bars, looking back at her, utterly lost, without a home, now locked out from
all that he had ever known. He would be all alone, abandoned out
on the lonely country road, dressed in his dirty overalls and filthy
unwashed flannel shirt, covered in dirt from head to toe as always,
and reeking from the stench of sweating alcohol through his dirt
encrusted pores.

Kaitlin stepped up to the front door, and she refocused her
attention on what was waiting for her inside. *Oh, please don't let the
inside resemble the outside.* Hesitating, she stared at the doorknob. A soft
sound of loneliness seemed to blow past her, along with the cold
winter air. She couldn't help but pause, to look around at the old
front porch. She felt a queasy sensation of guilt and remorse—a
deep vibration, like harp strings being plucked inside her stomach—as she recalled why she abandoned this place, and her family.

Old-age, deteriorating health, and dementia, had slowly stolen
what was left of her father. Her contact with him had mirrored his
health. Waning as his health and vitality declined. Every visit Kaitlin
was forced to make brought more and more frustration. With each
visit, she found her father to be more frail, foul, and demanding. As
he became more demanding of her, she became ever more emotionally distant. Each visit became shorter. And the time between
every visit grew farther apart.

Soon, it seemed that every visit with her father inevitably
erupted into another regrettable confrontation. With a raspy,
half-inebriated voice, her father would take jabs at her expensive
clothing, expensive tastes, her wealthy "Doctor" husband, and her
lack of "gratitude". Sipping on his flask, his body and mind slowly
filled with alcohol, and he would become more and more belliger-
ent. Eventually, as always, whenever he had consumed enough, he
would drift off into a semiconscious haze. Then his hostility would
erupt into an uncontrollable drunken tirade.

Kaitlin could still see him sitting in front of the fireplace in
his favorite chair. Slumped forward watching the fire through his

droopy eyelids as his head bobbed like it was floating on water. Without ever turning or even looking in her direction—while she was pealing back his bedcovers and fluffing his pillows—he would start in on her.

"Kate; you wouldn't have shit without me. You know that, right? I sent you to that damn boarding school. Damn expensive! And then I paid for all those wasted years of college… or did you forget already? Sure; you don't need me now, do you? Not now. Not with all of your husband's money. Right Kate! Gunna turn your back on me now. When I need you? I worked so hard. Your grandfather worked hard. We worked hard for you, and for your brother, so you could have all this."

"Please father. How many times do we have to do this? You know I don't want any of *this*. Charlie could do it… ask him."

"Charlie can't do it. He doesn't have what it takes to run that Mill. You know he don't got what it takes. You know he can't do it. Kate, please… I need you."

Kaitlin's memory raced through the many arguments that she had with her father over the years. Till the last fight they had together. On the last day she saw him. The very last time she saw his face while he was alive. That moment, over ten years ago—when she could take no more—when she felt the last droplets of emotion evaporating out of her like she was a bone that was becoming brittle, lying in the drifting desert, exposed to a blazing midday summer sun. Kaitlin was drained of emotion, brittle, and near the point of breaking apart. That's when she decided to leave this house, and to leave her father, for good. Leave and never visit here again—before she shattered into pieces.

Kaitlin left William sulking in his room, sitting there in his favorite chair, in front of the fireplace. One hand held a metal poker that he used to stoke the flames—a bottle of whiskey in the other. Sipping from the bottle, he stared deeply into the fire that he was slowly stoking, along with his growing inebriated fiery rage. "I kept your secret alright… kept it safe… for you Kate," he slurred, in an alcohol induced haze—almost incoherent. "All these years… never told a sole. Neither did Charlie… I saw to that. We all got our secrets… don't you know. We'll take'em all to our graves… all the secrets and lies… all just for you Kate!"

Kaitlin did her best to ignore his drunken rant. It was too late to talk about anything else—there was nothing else he could say, or threaten. She had made up her mind and was leaving for good. "You hearing me Kate?" William's voice echoed through the house as she packed her bags. His yelling to her grew louder each time that she continued to ignore him. "I protected you for all these years… and this's how I'm rewarded?"

Before walking out the door and slamming it shut behind her, Kaitlin vowed to herself, and to God, that, *I will never come back here… never again.* This vow was unbroken for all those years. This was a solemn vow that she had only reluctantly broken once before, for one of the longest hours of her entire life—the less than an hour it took to bury her father in his grave in the small family cemetery out back.

Today, she was breaking it one more time for the sake of Charlie. But this time, she was also hoping to leave it all behind her, and finally bury everything else from her past—forever.

Kaitlin's thoughts abruptly jumped to the small family grave-yard behind the house. She could imagine their cold and lonesome graves. It felt as if they were all still alive. As if they were patiently waiting for reappearance—for a long awaited visit. And more regret seeped into her thoughts. *Dead family shouldn't be so convenient… it only makes it more painful when you don't bother to visit. Maybe I should just go. Can this really be worth it? I'm just grasping at straws here anyway. Charlie will be fine after he recovers.*

She hadn't gone to the graveyard since her father's dreadful funeral several months earlier. At the time, Charlie was still con-fined at the hospital under court supervision and wasn't permitted to attend. She was the only family member who bothered to show up in person. Everyone else, that was still alive, sent bouquets and

cards. Some even wrote something nice. Only a handful of friends came—Mill employees mostly. There was a smattering of towns-folk, who were merely morbidly interested. They included a couple of cops and a local newspaper reporter. Kaitlin remembered feeling awkwardly out of place, as if she was attending some stranger's funeral. The others in attendance only amplified her feelings of unease by the way they treated her. Everyone was cold and distant. All of them stoically drifted passed her, like cold air blowing across her face. *I'll be expected to clean up the graveyard as well, I suppose,* Kaitlin realized with a sick-in-the-pit-of-the-stomach remorse. She pictured the headstones covered with algae, dirt, and overgrown weeds. Neglected, just like the front of the house. *One more dreadful task, I get to endure.*

Kaitlin pulled a skeleton key from her purse and slid it into the lock. As she turned the key and heard the clunk of the locking mechanism letting-go, she thought of Charlie. He was supposed to be waiting for her inside.

Charlie, and his new wife Elizabeth, had dutifully returned to Milner at his father's reluctant request. They even agreed to move back into the house. Charlie managed the operations at the Mill, while Liz took care of the house, and William. Charlie had gladly jumped at the chance to prove his worth. Having struggled through-out his schooling, only managing to receive passing scores due to his family's local prominence, and the financial contributions made to his teachers each Christmas in the form of gifts. After being *assisted* through the University system, Charlie drifted from job to job, from one failed business enterprise to another failed business scheme, one after another, staying just ahead of the falling dominos, until he ran out of options, and cash. Year after unfortunate year, Charlie man-aged to fail. If not for the seemingly endless flow of money provided by his father, he would have been completely destitute well before leaving his early twenties.

Unfortunately for Charlie, his failures didn't end when he

returned home to live with his father. William, in his drunken stupors, would make sport of him, always eager to remind him that he was inept at business. Always managing to slip in a remark about how it was never his father's intention of letting him run the business at the Mill. The remarks stung Charlie like a bee sting each time his father's alcohol reeking voice hissed out at him. "You're incompetent. You shouldn't be running my Mill. It'll be the ruin of me and this town." The Mill had been floundering for years—slowly dying along with the rest of the cotton industry. Something William refused to accept—not while he was still alive. Charlie became an easy scapegoat.

Kaitlin's feelings of shame for refusing to return home to help her father eventually branded her psyche with a scarlet letter. A searing reminder of how she had failed him, Charlie, and her entire family. A constant pain that returned with thoughts of the home she had left behind. Ultimately that pain gave her reason to not visit them. She would pacify her pain with the thought that; *sometimes it's easier to feel ashamed for one's own actions, or inactions, than it is to, forgive others for theirs.* Unable to forgive her father for what happened she dealt with it by turning her back on him when he needed her the most—by refusing to take over the family business. She refused even when he broke down and swallowed his precious pride and pleaded with her for help.

The promise of a permanent job and financial security drew Charlie back home like a fly to filth. It was an opportunity that Charlie and Liz could not afford to pass-up. Even if it came with an emotional cost that was near to being unbearable. For Charlie, it meant that he would have to grovel at the feet of his father until the day he died. And it meant abandoning the tiny sliver of dignity he had left in him.

What happened to us Charlie? Kaitlin sighed. A powdery poof of dust erupted as the heavy front door swung open. *Smells like an old musty library,* she thought as she stepped inside. Taking just a single step

inside the darkened foyer, she stopped, to sniff in a big whiff of the stale air. The entire house was quite, dark, and uncomfortably cold. Taking two more cautious steps, she stopped again, to sniff the stale air. To her relief, there was no smell of decaying flesh in the air, but only the faint odor of smoke that was now a permanent reminder of the fire that killed Elizabeth and baby Matthew.

Kaitlin left the front door wide open. *Just in case.* An orange glow from the afternoon sun softly illuminated the space where she stood on the tile floor. The same soft sunlight filtered inside the rest of the house through the slits that opened up between the thick draperies hanging over the windows. Just enough light so that Kaitlin could see the furniture in the adjoining family room. *Well, it's all the same… everything looks just as I last saw it.* Her eyes darted around the dark room, lightly bouncing from a chair, to a clock, to a lamp, to a table—noting each piece of familiar furniture for only an instant— just long enough for recognition, before moving to the next. She intentionally avoided allowing her eyes to make direct contact with one spot inside the room. That spot on the floor near the fireplace where they had both burned to death in a horrible blazing inferno. It was something she needed to avoid, for now. *One thing at a time*, a hushed thought whispered in the back of her head.

A gust of wind blew in through the open doorway. The door creaked. Her skin crawled as goose-bumps raised-up on her arms, with a nervous feeling sweeping over her. Looking up the tall stairway going upstairs, Kaitlin thought about Charlie, and how it was his fault that she was back here again to be scared like a little girl. She could feel her face becoming warm as her blood pressure began to rise. Clomping across the floor she slammed the front door shut, before spinning around to face the stairs again, now thinking, *just where is that little bastard!*

With a pounding heart she glanced back and forth between the doorway to the kitchen and the staircase. *I need to calm down before I see him,* she realized as she slowly unbuttoned her coat. *No need to get off on the wrong foot… not this time… besides I came here to help. I'm the big sister and that's exactly what I will do. I will help him. I refuse to let my past, and his petty feelings of childish rivalry prevent me from doing what he needs me to do for him.* She tried to bring to mind images of her once happy, carefree, innocent younger brother, to help her calm down.

"Charlie", she called out timidly, "anyone here?" No one answered. Only the wind could be heard, blowing across the porch and breathing through the crack under the door. "Just get this over with," she muttered. Taking a few steps up the stairs, she had to continue pushing herself up to the next step, *like a fire-walker... keep on going... just go*! Every creaky step got easier as she marched up the stairs. *Go, go, go, don't stop*, she repeated as she turned and made her way down the long upstairs hallway.

Stopping at Charlie's closed bedroom door—she hesitated. Her shaking hand paused mid-reach as she started to grab for the doorknob. Pausing just a little bit too long, her momentum had been broken. A bright light seemed to pop inside of her head like a light bulb going bad. Instantly; the timidity, anxiety, and feelings of fear that she had managed to suppress, all came flooding back in. Recognizing the feelings holding her back, she knew that she had to act quickly. If she didn't do something now, she never would. *Just knock... do it already.* Forcing her fingers to curl up into a fist, it felt like a heavy metal sledge-hammer as she banged her knuckles against the wooden door. "Charlie," she called out softly. "Charlie... its Kate... can you hear me?" She called out a little louder. Again— there was nothing. Not a peep. As she had done in the foyer she tilted her nose up, lightly sniffing the air. *Just a little musty, nothing unusual... thank God... no smell of death!*

"Charlie... I'm coming in!" Kaitlin announced as she turned the doorknob and burst through the door. "Oh my God... get your lazy ass out of bed Charlie Benjamin Whitcomb!" she blurted out as she stomped across the bedroom floor to the edge of the badly disheveled bed. She tried to hide her deep sense of relief—to find her brother merely sleeping and not dead—by being a loud, obnox- ious, annoying older sister.

Charlie's half covered body lay stretched out in splendid hedonistic slumber. His chest was billowing up and down as he slowly breathed in deeply wheezing breaths just on the very edge of snoring. A sticky stream of drool flowed out of his gaping lips. Pooling below his mouth, a large wet spot was slowly spreading out across his pillow. *Yuck*, Kaitlin squirmed. Charlie tussled a moment beneath his sheets, only to quickly relax and become still again.

"Good morning Charlie," she said with disdain, "or should I say good afternoon? My Lord, it's after two in the afternoon!"

Charlie shifted his position on the bed once again. One of his eyelids reluctantly tore open slightly, as if being pried apart by invisible fingers.

Kaitlin stomped over to the window and similarly tore open the thick curtains, allowing the bright afternoon sunlight to spill in. "Can you move… why the hell are you still in bed… and where in the hell is that damn nurse?" She snapped, trying to rouse him.

But Charlie couldn't answer. Waltzing on the edge of consciousness, he struggled to open his eyes. Spastically opening and shutting independently of the other—his eyelids were randomly opening and closing at will. He began gurgling out slurred words like a half-awake drunken hobo. His numb, drool covered lips, could only create a stream of unintelligible mumbling sounds. His pitiful appearance nearly brought her to instant tears. At that moment she could only see the face of her young brother awaking from a nap—a boy six years old. The boy she once knew but almost forgot. *If only I could see him… the little brother… once again,* she thought, as a sense of being the protective and nurturing older sister, almost returned.

Kaitlin took a step towards the bed to help him, as Dr. Karanza's specific instructions rang out in her head—forcing her to stop. "*This is extremely important… you must only have very limited supervised contact with Charlie… and absolutely no contact with him until after I have arrived and we begin his therapy… and then… only if and when he is ready.*"

Swinging his feet to the floor and pushing himself upright, Charlie reached forward and pulled the bedcovers off of his legs.

Slipping off the mattress, he stood up. Swaying unsteadily on his feet he began to vigorously rub various parts of his anatomy with his hands as if he were seasoning a slab of meat. His weak legs moved in a zombie-like fashion as he tried to walk. Nearly stumbling over the blanket that was being partially dragged by his foot he struggled to get his semi-conscious body to the bathroom.

Kaitlin did not turn to look at Charlie's almost comical birthing from his bed. Her eyes followed the stony foot-path that lead to the family graveyard on the edge of the woods. *Grand-father Ben… grandma, father, mother, Liz, baby Matthew… all of them are still there. I'll pay my respects later… if I have time… perhaps?* Like an ashamed child she searched her thoughts for some excuse—for why she had not visited them sooner.

Old pipes groaned as Charlie turned on the hot water. Closing her eyes for a moment, she listened intently to the water cascading down from the shower head. It almost sounded like a soothing heavy rain, falling on a tin roof, on a slow Sunday afternoon. Until another faint, yet familiar sound caught Kaitlin's attention. Turning to face the closed door, a sound was coming down the hallway.

"Thump—shuffle; thump—shuffle; thump—"

Father! Is it? No. It can't be him!

"Shuffle; thump—shuffle; thump."

The sound suddenly stopped. Whoever was making the sound was now standing just on the other side of the door.

It is him. It sounds just like father!

Her father would make such a distinctively recognizable sound as he moved through the house—whenever he was alive. The thumping sound was made by his cane as it struck down on the wood floor. The shuffling sound was made by his partially paralyzed left foot as he dragged it along. The sounds of splashing water drew her attention back to Charlie.

Should I yell for Charlie… go in the bathroom? No, I have to protect Charlie… that is why I'm here. I won't run. No more hiding!

Her eyes watched the shadow on the floor beneath the door. It didn't move, as if to taunt her. With each tick of time Kaitlin's heart picked-up its beat—beating faster, harder, until it was pounding on her chest like an African drum. The doorknob slowly turned. Gasping, she held in a shallow breath—tensing as the door slowly opened.

"Are you decent Charlie?" called out a young man's voice.

Kaitlin relaxed and exhaled. A man in blue-jeans and a tight black T-shirt, with a large heavy suitcase dangling from one hand, stepped inside. "Oh… hello Kate," Paul said sheepishly, "wasn't expecting you so soon?"

"Oh, my God… you scared me!" Kaitlin gushed, feeling a little embarrassed. "You're that nurse from the hospital."

"Yea… we met in the hallway. I wanted to talk with you before you left—," Paul tried to say.

But Kaitlin lashed out at him instead—venting. "Where in the hell have you been! I have been here for over half an hour… and you… where were you?"

Paul tried to speak, but couldn't get a word in as she chastised him.

"Not watching Charlie… that's for certain! I'm paying your hospital a considerable sum of money to perform a simple task… to take care of my brother. He's suicidal! Doesn't that mean anything to you? He was not to be left alone… not for one single second!"

"Yes ma'am, I understand… won't happen again," Paul muttered back, standing up straight and erasing his smile, looking like a military grunt being dressed-down by a drill sergeant. "I just needed to check on my motorcycle. I wasn't gone very long. I thought he was sleeping. Hell, he's been asleep ever since the cops drug him in through the back door early this morning. And thanks for getting here in time to open the front gates for us."

"That's another thing," Kaitlin snapped back, "he shouldn't be sleeping all the time. You were supposed to have him on a regular schedule… not let him stay in bed all day. Haven't you been giving him the calea zacatechichi compound? Have you even reduced the Clozapine and Lithium like Dr. Karanza instructed?"

Paul tilted his head to the side like a puzzled puppy as he watched his owner pretend to throw a ball. He searched his thoughts, and then, he responded with a simmering anger of his own. "You do know that I have only been here for just a few hours myself. I'm not his regular nurse. This is a special assignment for me… one I volunteered for."

"What do you mean… special assignment?" Kaitlin groaned.

Paul explained that the other nurses and orderlies refused to come down to Milledgeville with Dr. Karanza and Charlie. Everyone else was too afraid. It was too dangerous. No one wanted to be locked up with a multiple murder suspect for several nights with nothing to protect them except a couple of women and his sedatives. Not to mention the fact, that Dr. Karanza was going to be supplying him with experimental medications in an effort to try and recover his lost memories, of the night when he may have killed his wife, child, and father.

And, as for where the hell he was, Paul further explained that when he arrived, the front gate was locked, so he proceeded to drive along the dirt road, following the fence-line, while searching for another way in. With a growing passion in his voice, he explained how there was no way in hell that he was going to leave his vintage 67 Harley Davidson Motorcycle on the street. It clearly held more value for him than Charlie. So he rode down the fence until he found the opening near the old farmhouse out back. Leaving his bike, he came inside through the back door and found his patient, sleeping, with a police officer guarding him. He went back downstairs and crashed on the couch—to get some rest for himself. After a few hours of restless sleep he awoke and went to check on his bike, and to get his things. That's when she must have arrived.

Kaitlin just stared at Paul. Her angry and skeptical expression didn't change. Paul gave up, getting annoyed with her, he said, "anyway… where do you want these bags?"

It was then that Kaitlin realized that he had brought in her suitcases from the car, and had lugged them all the way up the stairs—for her.

"How did you know those are mine?" She asked smugly.

Paul gave her a sly grin, and replied, "Obviously… they were so big… and there were so many of them… who else would have brought them?"

That's when Kaitlin noticed Paul was looking at her differently. Not as an employee should, but rather, as a flirt. She intuitively took notice of Paul's not-so-vague advances. She also took notice that Paul was tall, with a six foot two inch frame, a body that was slender, taught, and extremely muscular. Completely different thoughts were coming to mind as she took him in. *My, oh my… he's very attractive. Didn't get a good enough look at him at the hospital, with all the commotion and such. Nice, well-trimmed dark brown hair. I always loved a man with a mustache and beard—sexy. Oh, and, he's clever. Hmmm… thirty-three-ish, I would have to guess?*

Paul had already taken notice of Kaitlin's curly auburn hair and sleek figure. His attraction to her had been steadily growing—while he was explaining why he was gone. *Very pretty… got-ta-be in her mid-thirties*, Paul surmised. Kaitlin was in fact, nearly forty-two years old.

"I'm pretty strong," Paul boasted, "but I'll admit I'm not nearly manly enough to carry all of your bags. You must be planning a long stay?" There was clearly a crack forming in Kaitlin's frozen exterior, and he wanted to continue chipping away at it, hoping to get past it, and find his way inside.

Paul had always been good with people, bringing out their hidden agendas, and personality quirks, good or bad. It was necessary in his profession, as a nurse, to get past the personality barriers people erected to keep him, and others, at a comfortable distance. To provide the best treatment he would have to become an intimate partner in their healing. And Intimacy requires achieving a level of physical and emotional comfort.

"Oh no... I plan on leaving this place as soon as possible," Kaitlin smirked, cracking a tiny smile.

There was a silent pause where they looked into each other's eyes—just a little too long—before they realized how they were staring at one another. They quickly looked away from each other's slightly blushing faces—glancing around the room with nothing else to say.

A high pitch squeak yelled out from the faucet handle as Charlie turned off the shower. The sound of splashing water was replaced by a gurgling drain.

"Let's give Charles a moment of privacy to get dressed," Kaitlin suggested. "I'll be staying in the bedroom at the opposite end of the hall," she said as she lifted the large suitcase off the floor with a soft moan. "And you'll be staying in here. She nodded in the direction of the room adjacent to Charlie's.

"Who lives out back in that old shack?" Paul asked nonchalantly.

Kaitlin stopped abruptly. The suitcase fell out of her hand and dropped to the floor with a loud thud. She turned her head to look back at him.

Paul stopped behind her.

"Why... did you see him?" Kaitlin asked him nervously.

"See who?"

"Daniel... did you see him?" There was a sense of fear in her eyes as she waited for Paul to answer.

"I didn't see anyone."

Paul followed Kaitlin's eyes as they drifted away from his—as she became lost in her thoughts. She lifted her suitcase from off the floor, turned, and walked into her bedroom at the end of the hall, without looking back again. Paul lingered in the hallway, watching her, waiting for some reaction. But she just gently pushed the door closed behind her, as if Paul wasn't even there anymore.

Weird, Paul thought as he stepped forward and dropped the other heavy suitcase down right outside her door, making an intentionally loud—thud!

Kaitlin's mind was now elsewhere. *I'll call detective Thompson in the morning. I need to get settled in, and get Charlie ready for the doctor's arrival tomorrow.* Looking around the room her mind started to race—filling with images, places, things, people, ideas, spilling in, all at once, like a dam had broken open in her mind. *I need to unpack, and I have to call Gregory… did I lock the car? What will I wear tomorrow? Oh, I should wash my hair… what time was my appointment with O'Neal?* Like a telephone switchboard with every phone line ringing in all at once, her thoughts darted about like the nimble hands of the operator, pulling and replacing the phone lines in the proper place just as fast as her firing synapses could go. She could be occupied for hours by her own feverishly racing mind. Keeping her mind busy was a way of protecting herself. It kept her from obsessing over things that she had no control over—like Daniel.

Her randomly streaming thoughts abruptly ended when she began to think about what she would wear out tomorrow. There was only one bag in the room. *Oh darn, where's my other bag?* And only then did she remember that she had left Paul standing out in the hallway. Utterly embarrassed, Kaitlin burst through the doorway without looking down. Her foot tripped over the bag and she lunged forward, falling. Luckily she managed to grab the doorframe just in the nick of time. That's when she noticed with relief that Paul was already gone. Turning a bright red—she dragged the lonely bag inside.

Sifting through the neatly folded clothing she searched for something suitable to wear the next morning. It didn't take her long to come upon a favorite blouse, one that made her feel professional and confident (another way of saying secure). She held it up to allow the sleeves to fall away so she could inspect the wrinkles. *Not too bad,* she thought as she shook it. Laying the blouse flatly on the bedcover she looked back at the rest of her stowed clothing and began searching for a suitably matching skirt.

As her fingers flipped over a pretty white blouse that Gregory had bought her for a present the year before, Kaitlin felt a prick-ing sensation. That nagging feeling of guilt which felt like someone was poking her with the sharp end of a stick to get her attention. It forced her eyes to leave the clothing for a moment to glance over at the phone on the nightstand. The sight of the phone made the guilty feelings even worse. *I have to call Gregory first… before I do any-thing else. He may be worried.* Picking up the antique looking land-line receiver, her fingers nimbly jumped from number to number on the archaic keypad, as she dialed their home phone. Her thoughts briefly returned to her nails as she listened to the ring-tone. No one answered after several rings. Eventually the answering machine kicked on. At the sound of the beep, she lay the receiver down. *I'll try his office*, she thought while dialing the number, *hmmm… still at the office I bet… he's always working*, she imagined as she listened to the ring-tone—again.

A young female receptionist answered after four full rings, and recited, "Hello Doctor's Office… can you hold?"

Kaitlin managed to speak half of a hello in response before the receptionist hit the hold button. Nearly two full minutes of eleva-tor music played before the young woman picked up the line again to coldly inquire as to who she was and what she wanted—before abruptly placing Kaitlin back on hold. It was apparent that the receptionist was very immature, naïve, and uncaring. *Just like him to hire someone like that*, Kaitlin thought as she pictured a girl who was wearing a very tight skirt, one that was too short for a respectable appearance, and a blouse that could barely contain her heav-ing breasts.

Another five minutes passed. The young lady finally picked up the line again to glibly announce that, "Nobody seems to know where Gregory is at the moment ma'am… as usual."

Kaitlin slammed the receiver down. *That bastard… he must be out playing golf with his buddies… or just playing… as usual!*

Without really thinking, her fingers quickly punched in Gregory's new car phone number. The extremely expensive new gizmo that

he said he couldn't be without… in case of emergencies… or if she needed to get ahold of him. But, he didn't answer his car phone either. It didn't even ring. The first sound Kaitlin heard was the lifeless, machine generated voice, the one that answered in his stead whenever the phone was turned off. The soulless monotone voice informed Kaitlin that her beloved husband was not available—once again. *Why is his damn toy phone turned off?*

5

W HERE THE HELL *is Gregory?* Kaitlin fumed. Her fingers remained on the phone as her thoughts became more frantic, racing from place to place, along with the mental images of Gregory in different places that he frequented—off being his typical selfish irresponsible playboy self. She could just see him; laughing and drinking on the eighteenth hole with his golfing buddies, or at the clubhouse, drunk, playing poker while puffing on a pungent cigar, or staggering out of a bar, stinking drunk, with a young, busty blonde tramp clinging to his arm for stability; both of them giggling when he drops his keys as they try and find his car—with the phone stuck in the glove box—turned off. *Selfish, childish bastard! He only thinks about himself… never about me.*

He's supposed to be here with me. I knew he would do this to me again! She considered as she dropped the phone down onto the bed, so that she could reach up to wipe the single tear that dribbled down her cheek. Dabbing away the tear with her sleeve, she wished that she could wipe away her thoughts of Gregory as easily as she wiped away her tears. To be able to put him out of her mind completely—just as he had apparently done with her.

Putting on her pajamas she sat down at her vanity. While brushing her curling locks, her hazel eyes lazily inspected her

brownish-red hair. She couldn't ignore the glints of gray shining like strands of silver tinsel on a Christmas tree. Nor could she look past the dark lines on her face that seemed to suck in the light like deep dark caverns—deepening crevasses that were growing longer and deeper seemingly every day, requiring her to apply more and more make-up. The same thickly applied make-up that was now a day old, dry and cracking, like a hardened clay mask.

Seeing her aging face in the mirror sent her thoughts racing directly back to two nights ago, where she was sitting at her vanity on the second floor of her palatial home in Atlanta. She was slowly stroking her hair while talking with Gregory…

"Kaitlin, you must go. You've neglected your family's affairs for far too long. You can't just hide any longer. It's time to face that place again. Darling, you have to face your fears," Gregory implored as he manipulated his bow-tie with the fingers of the skilled surgeon that he was. Watching himself work in his own mirror, standing in an adjacent room, he slipped the ends of the silk tie around and through itself, nimbly pulling it up and around and forcing it through without any break in the flowing movements as if his hands were a pair of dancers waltzing in near perfect unison. Taking a final bow as the last notes of music faded, his long slender finely manicured fingers gently pulled on the ends making a crisp, taut, knot.

Gregory stood upright to inspect himself in the mirror from head to toe. He picked a speck of white from the lapel of his black tuxedo and flicked it away, before looking down to his pants, to follow along the sharp crease in his pants leg with his hawk-eyes, until he saw spots of white light reflecting up from the tops of his finely polished shoes. Lifting his nose up, while turning his eyes down and center, he flared his nostrils open wide so that he could look for errant hairs. Seeing that his nostrils were as finely groomed as the rest of the hair on his head he turned his face to get a look at his profile.

They were preening themselves in preparation to attend the annual staff appreciation dinner hosted by his medical practice.

Kaitlin was quietly applying her makeup before slipping into her sleek black dress. She pulled it up over herself slowly, moving with a methodical melancholy. While slipping her feet into her high-heeled shoes, she never looked back at the mirror that was reflecting back every inch of her. She could care less about her appearance right now—her mind was elsewhere. The prospect of spending a long night, mingling with a large group of mostly strangers—starting with an awkward greeting, that was followed by an equally awkward conversation that seemed to never end—made her cringe inside.

Kaitlin had always been painfully shy in a crowd of people. And she was painfully aware of it. Anonymity was her best friend, one that she courted, consistently. Shrinking like Alice after drinking a potion from a bottle is how she often felt in a room full of people— only wishing that she could shrink small enough to disappear completely. Or even better yet, to find a potion that would allow her to become invisible altogether.

In her youth Kaitlin had been diagnosed with having a persistent antisocial personality disorder. It was only treatable with limited success, manageable, and in most cases, somewhat controllable. An extraordinary sensitivity to other people, and what others thought of her, was just one of the symptoms. Physical contact only acted to exaggerate her resulting anxiety. She had even reported to the various school psychologists, counselors, therapists, and psychiatrists over the years that she would see things—strange and unexplainable visions—whenever she was too close to anyone else.

Inevitably, all of the experts would conclude that; "Kaitlin suffers from an acute case of reactive attachment disorder induced by the sudden and tragic loss of her mother at such a young and impressionable age. A condition that most probably was exacerbated by post traumatic disorder, as the result of sexual abuse trauma inflicted by close family members, or other person(s) closely associated with her immediate family. Trust in others shattered; with no sense of having a protector, support mechanism, or confidant, such

as a protective mother in the home, her only recourse is intense self-reflection and isolation".

Breaking her silence, Kaitlin couldn't restrain herself any longer. "We will not have this discussion again. Not tonight."

Oh great; here we go, he thought, turning away from his own reflection to look at the reflection of Kaitlin inside her mirror. He was the youngest general surgeon in the Southeastern United States. A Board Certified General Surgeon at the age of twenty-eight, he rose like a shooting star, up through the ranks at his practice, to become the youngest senior partner in his medical group. He had made full partner at the age of thirty-two. As handsome as he was smart, he was selected as the most desirable bachelor by the Atlanta Constitution Newspaper for two years running—just a year before he became engaged to Kaitlin. Those qualities, good-looks, charm, money and prestige, were all combined together by Gregory like molten led that he poured out into a mold to create an unstoppably heavy hammer. He would wield this irresistible hammer like persona to crack open Kaitlin's nearly impenetrably hardened social cocoon. Attacking her with Cary Grant looks, a perfect smile, impeccable attire, presented with almost fiendish whit. Blow after blow Gregory hit her with his irresistible charm until he managed to crack her protective shell, enough that he could get inside—close enough to touch her heart. A task no other man had been able to accomplish before.

Gregory always loved a challenge—until he got what he wanted.

After the wedding bells could no longer be heard, the home was lived in, the introductions became less enthusiastic, the conversations shorter, their time apart longer. He turned his interests to the more immediately interesting and satisfying. While she turned back, burrowing deeper inside of herself, retreating back inside the comfort of her self-protective hardened shell.

Gregory busied himself with working, playing golf, being off with friends, conventions, drinking, gambling, and always looking for ways to make more money. Not a second of his time was ever wasted, especially on his reclusive, boring, inhibited Kaitlin. Not surprisingly, he somehow managed to always be gone. And he became the master of convenient excuses.

They had met by chance when she was invited to a house party by a girlfriend who was dating a Doctor friend from Gregory's practice. They were introduced, dated, and married shortly thereafter. They had both made their careers, parties, and their self-indulgences their priorities, children and family could wait. At first glance, they appeared to be the perfect couple. Gregory was the hard working, well respected physician, ever vigilant in his studies, methodical, unrelentingly, and utterly demanding. Kaitlin epitomized the submissive loner; giving, conscientious, loving, unrequited supportive wife.

Her therapist first noticed the hairline crack inside their fairytale lifestyle. "If the metals don't completely meld, the best weld will eventually fracture at the weakest point when pressure is applied. You're welded marriage will be tested, put under great pressure," he would often tell her. "If you and Gregory are able to meld together, your marriage won't fracture. But if you continue to emotionally resist one another, your marriage will eventually fracture and break apart."

The largest crack appearing within their marriage—slowly cracking like an iceberg, shifting, flowing, and moving them apart—was her seeming inability to provide Gregory what he wanted most from his wife—a child. All of the specialists Kaitlin visited provided the same diagnosis, there was no physical impairment. Kaitlin could conceive. Gregory could impregnate. It just wasn't happening.

To Gregory it was as if there was an invisible force preventing their blessed unison. Kaitlin had created an emotional barrier forged by years of anger directed at her father that she had allowed to grow uncontrolled inside of her, which morphed into a generalized hatred of all men. Fear of a destruction growing within her womb. Fear of giving birth to death. "Eve's curse," Kaitlin's therapist would tell her, without further explanation.

Kaitlin eventually realized that he was staying away more, and for longer periods of time. His absences, and hardening cold of his emotional distance, played upon her worst feelings of paranoia—feeding her deepest and darkest fears. And soon her thoughts were preoccupied with visions of infidelity and divorce. *He obviously hates me. He's having an affair. He doesn't want me anymore. It's only a matter of time before he leaves me. I can make myself better… he'll want to be with me again. This new stronger prescription will help… it has to help. I've tried every damn prescription there is.*

The death of her father, her sister-in-law, and her baby, came at just the wrong time for Kaitlin. At the height of her paranoia, at the depths of their marriage, she was summoned back to the place where she was first mentally injured—back to her childhood home—where she was psychologically warped by the despicable acts of her father and Daniel. This was the place that made her *that crazy woman.*

Gregory on the other hand, thought it just may be the perfect opportunity to confront and conquer her fears. It was Kaitlin's chance to heal some wounds from the past. In her mind, she heard him saying; *time for Kate to see that it wasn't so bad… to get over it… to stop being so obsessed with her damn father and Daniel. Maybe then, she could be happy again, be the nice happy, loving, and giving. And finally, become the emotionally stable, sane wife that I deserve.*

Gregory continued speaking as he walked into the dressing room. "I need you back here as soon as possible. I have to pull doubles to cover for Michael."

"No!" She growled. "You're going to support me this time… if I do this… this is too important. My brother may spend the rest of his life in a god-damned straight jacket, or a jail cell. I need you to be there with me. You can be so damn selfish. Hopefully we will only be there for a couple of days. You can handle this little inconvenience… can't you?"

"Selfish… my wife is going to be sleeping in a house with a

possible homicidal psychopath, and I'm being selfish?" He scoffed at the idea.

"You know how afraid I am to go back there. This is what you want… not me. Still, I have to know what happened, my whole family, every-ones dead except for Charlie, and he's nearly comatose. Of course, you're right, as always. I should have been there a long time ago. This is my last chance to help. It will be good for him and me… that's what you want to hear me say… right?"

"You're doing so much already, and this is dangerous honey," Gregory said softly, consoling her. Working her like a serpent in the Garden of Eden, using the mastery of his passive aggressive skills, he pushed her to go home while at the same time made her feel guilty for leaving him. "You're the executor of your family's estate, you have to deal with the bankruptcy, and now you've been appointed by the court to act as Charlie's guardian… isn't that asking enough of you? Now you're going to take Charlie back to that mad-house and engage in some kind of voodoo ritual just to make you feel less guilty? I never should have replaced Dr. Barnes with that witch Doctor… what's her pet name Jenkins likes to call her… *crazy Karanza?*"

Kaitlin looked up to see Gregory looking past her to admiring himself in the full length mirror. She felt emotionally invisible to him. "Dr. Karanza is certainly unorthodox, but maybe she can actually do something. Dr. Barnes just filled Charlie with drugs keeping him in a stupor, so they wouldn't put him in jail instead of the hospital. He certainly wasn't treating Charlie. And it was you that convinced me to do this—for my sake. So we're staying as long as is necessary. Find someone else to take care of things while we're gone. Why don't you get one of your little girlfriends from the office to cover for you… as usual?"

Oh no, here it comes, Gregory recoiled, detecting that undeniable change in her tone of voice—the one he hears just before their conversations devolve into a heated argument.

"You know how much I regret not helping my father run his

business with all of his health problems," she continued with a firmer, louder voice.

Gregory quickly interjected, raising his voice to match hers, "you know you couldn't stand to be around your father, and that Mill had been failing for years, it was only a matter of time. There was nothing you could have done to help them.

Kaitlin continued speaking her thought as if she hadn't even heard him. "Charlie didn't have the knowledge or ability necessary to run that Mill. All of those employees were counting on us. Charlie just wasn't up to the challenge."

"You don't know if you could have made a difference with that Mill," Gregory implored, "just like you don't know if this little experiment is going to make a difference for Charlie."

Kaitlin began breathing deeply, trying to stay calm, as she was taught to do in therapy. "I know it will make a difference for me," she softly murmured, not wanting to spark his inevitable pompous, *have to be right all the time*, contemptuous anger that would end with a fight.

Gregory didn't hear her. Nor would he have cared. He was walking from the dressing room to avoid the same escalating argument. And he had already stopped listening—since he didn't want to argue with her before the party. That would only ruin his night.

Kaitlin refocused on the present, as her eyes focused on her face reflected in the mirror of her childhood dressing table. *Gregory is right*, she considered, placing the hair-brush lightly on her lap. She realized that she had not been debating for her husband's approval—she never needed that. Taking on so many burdens all at once was an attempt to relieve nagging guilt. This endeavor was her way of seeking forgiveness from herself, and from her dead mother. This was the best therapy, just as he told her it would be. *I don't need medication anymore. Gregory was right. I don't need anyone to tell me how to feel or how to think. I should be more confident in my decisions. I'm not crazy. Not anymore.*

Switching off the bedroom light and turning down the bedcovers, she crawled between the sheets, feeling a little of her childhood return as she settled on the lumpy old mattress. It was both comforting and disturbing at the same time. Looking up at the silver framed black and white photograph of her mother on the dresser, she mimicked the words, *I love you mom.*

6

K AITLIN FINALLY RELAXED—WITH a warm sense of security—tucked into her childhood bed under a thick quilted blanket. Slowly, she drifted off into a deep sleep—only to be pulled out of her dreaming by a man's pleading voice, as he called out in agony, "No… not again… please leave me alone! Leave me alone… not again!"

Kaitlin's head jerked forward off of her pillow and her eyes sprang open. *What was that?* Sitting up, she listened for the man's voice that woke her up. The house was eerily quiet as she glanced around the dark room. She slowly lay back down on her soft pillow. Pulling the covers up over her chin and rubbing her feet together as if she were stroking a purring cat—she started to relax again—believing that she was, *just dreaming… it was only a dream,* while slowly drifting back to sleep.

"Go away… leave me alone!" The man yelled out again—even louder.

Kaitlin shot straight up. Her eyes were wider and more focused than before. *Not a dream!* She thought as she peered through the darkness at her closed bedroom door. She couldn't tell where the voice was coming from, but from the sound of it, she thought that it must be coming from down the hallway. *It has to be either Charlie or Paul*, she puzzled, pulling her bed cover up to her chest as if to shield herself. *No one else is supposed to be here?*

"Not again! I can't do it again!" The voice yelled out again— only clearer and louder than before. For an instant the voice sounded eerily familiar to her. *Almost sounded like father?* Her heart began pumping harder as her mind raced for a reasonable answer. *Is that Charlie? Yes… it must be? It does sound a little like Charlie.* Tossing the warm covers away Kaitlin leaped to the cold floor and shuffled toward the dressing table. She groped for her silk robe until she found it on the seat of the chair. Cold air hit her like ice water and sent a nervous shiver up her back as her skin tightened. She quickly pulled the silk robe around her, lashing the sash tightly around her waist like a cowboy in a rodeo trying to make record time, while shuffling her feet across the cold floorboards towards the door.

Slowly pulling open the door, she peeked out. No one was in the nearly black hall. With a slight nervous shiver, she crept out into the hallway. Paul's bedroom door was wide open and his room was completely dark. Stepping down the hall she could see that Charlie's door was closed. Tiptoeing down the hallway, pausing just a moment to look inside Paul's room, she noticed that his bedcovers were thrown back on his empty bed. Continuing to tiptoe to the end of the hallway she stopped at Charlie's bedroom door. A small amount of light was glowing through the crack beneath the door. *Why was a light on in his bedroom… he should be asleep?* She considered as she began turning the doorknob. As the bolt holding the door closed let go and she felt the door moving in her hand—she thought, *I'm not a little girl. I'm not going back in here feeling like a scared little child as I did yesterday.* Emboldened, she pushed the door open and steadfastly stepped inside like a police officer making a raid.

Paul slowly raised his head to look up at her. He was sitting across the room next to Charlie's bed. Slumped over with heavy shoulders, his body was draped in the chair like a rag doll. His heavy eyelids were drooped down in his heavy looking head that was also sagging down. Charlie was lying in his bed, his eyes closed,

lips parted, his hands dangling over the edge of the bed, his body half covered, with one leg sticking out.

"Paul… what's going on… I thought I heard someone yelling?" She asked.

Paul put his index finger up to his clenched lips, blowing out a soft, "shhhhhh."

Charlie tussled slightly, and his face contorted, grimacing as if he were in pain, or feeling afraid.

"He's having bad dreams," Paul whispered, sitting up from his reclined position, wearing boxer shorts that were only partially covered by his thin cotton bathrobe that had been hastily pulled over his body. His bagging half open eyes were begging for sleep. Twirling up into points, his matted hair poked out all over the place like tiny horns. Slowly looking back over at Charlie, he quietly began to explained, "I was told that he would have them… nightmares… maybe even delusions. He probably won't be sleeping very well for the next few nights as the new medications kick in. It's that medicinal cocktail Dr. Karanza ordered for him. Hell, I don't know what half that stuff is, or what it's doing to him?"

Kaitlin stepped lightly across the room so that she was next to Paul, to where she could get a better view of Charlie's face in the dim moonlight that was streaming in from the window. "That's good… that's exactly what is supposed to happen," she whispered. "His mind is waking up. His memories are returning and they may be disturbing for him. I just didn't expect it to happen so fast, or to be so disturbing for the rest of us." Kaitlin smiled softly at Paul, and felt some sympathy for him. "How long have you been up Paul?"

"Half hour or so, I guess," Paul groaned. "I wasn't sleeping very well anyway. I just can't sleep in new places. He doesn't have a history of sleep walking does he?"

"You're kidding, right?"

"Hell no… I've had patients do some crazy ass things when they are supposed to be sleeping. It can scare the hell out of you sometimes. And I sure don't want him hurting himself, or me, especially during some experimentally drug induced nightmare."

Paul's coarse response forced Kaitlin to think. Blurry visions of her half-insane, drug induced brother, committing various dreadfully violent acts to her and Paul in the middle of the night started running through her head. Looking down at Charlie's contorted face—she quickly began to reconsider what she was getting herself into. *Maybe Gregory was right, maybe this is too dangerous? I just couldn't live with myself if Charlie, or someone else, gets hurt because of this experiment... one that I asked for... and paid for.*

"You should go back to bed Kate. Getting up in the middle of the night to watch Charlie is what I'm getting paid for... remember?" Paul said with a touch of sarcasm.

"Sounds good to me," Kaitlin whispered back, as she reached out and touched Paul lightly on his shoulder.

Paul looked up at her and their eyes met. His gaze beckoned for her to linger, for a moment longer. They smiled at one another softly, as if wanting more. Charlie suddenly twitched, opening up his eyes he glanced around in a haze, he mumbled something, before turning over and passing out again. Kaitlin yanked her hand away from Paul as if she had touched a hot stove. Her robe slipped partially open revealing her slender body. Paul's eyes jotted down to catch a sinfully fulfilling glimpse. Fumbling, she pulled her robe together and cinched the slipping sash. Blushing, she spun around and headed for the door. She couldn't stop herself from glancing back at Paul. His eyes were following her. He was smiling—warmly—letting her know that he very much enjoyed it. She paused, to bask in his comforting attention.

Fearing she may never want to leave—she forced herself to move towards the door. As she turned, a glowing spot of orange colored light shimmering on the glass of the window caught her eye—forcing her to pause again. There was a small spot of light in the window—glowing like the end of a burning cigarette. *That's no moonlight... what the hell is that?*

Paul watched her slowly walking over to the window. She pulled back the curtain and pressed her nose against the glass. The strangely glowing orb of light in the distant woods was steadily growing larger, like a fiery beacon, beckoning to her.

"Can you see that light out there?" She whispered, while pointing her finger at the window.

Paul slowly moved across the room. Realizing that he was exposing his boxer shorts, he tugged and pulled at his robe as he walked. He pressed his face up against hers—peering out with squinting eyes. After a few moments of straining, he replied, "no… can't really see anything."

"It's Daniel," Kaitlin muttered angrily, "got to be him."

"Out at that old house out there?" Paul asked, squinting harder—furrowing his brow to try and peer deeper into the dark woods. "Well if he's there… why the hell is he back there?"

"Supposedly he's the grounds keeper. My father kept him around because he couldn't do much work with his bum leg. Some family obligation… it's a long story."

"What do you think he's up to out there this late at night?"

"That's Daniel's burn pile… where he burns yard debris. I remember seeing him out there by his fire nearly all the time, day and night. That's the last place I saw him before I was sent away from here."

"Yea, well, that's a little too close to where I parked my motorcycle. Maybe I should go make sure everything's alright."

"No Paul, I'll go. I need to find out what Daniel has been up to anyway. You stay here with Charlie." Kaitlin tried her best to give Paul a reassuring smile.

Paul nodded with reluctant agreement. "I will be right here," he reassured her. He moved his hand to touch her arm, but she stepped away just before his hand could reach her.

Kaitlin returned to her bedroom for just long enough to slip into her tennis shoes. She had no intention on being outside in the cold for very long—only long enough to find Daniel and ask him why he was still living on her property.

Exiting through the back door Kaitlin followed along the familiar stone path that led up to the dirt path which passed through the woods, ending at the clearing where Daniel had his burn pit. Kaitlin glanced around nervously as she walked, darting her eyes back to the flickering fire light visible through the thicket of trees. Leaving the rock path behind her Kaitlin felt the softly giving dirt moving under her shoes. The glint of light coming off the sand along the path became harder to see as she passed deeper into the woods. As the pathway darkened, her feet moved faster, along with the beating of her heart. As if coming to the end of a long tunnel, soon she could see moonlit expanse of the clearing and her walking slowed— yet the beating of her heart was growing faster.

Reaching the edge of the trees she stepped out into the clearing and stopped. Kaitlin looked across the open field to where the roaring fire was lighting up the night sky off in the distance. Her own body seemed to glow in the moonlight contrasted against the darkness behind her. Cold air blew up under her robe. Shivering there in the cold darkness, she felt exposed, and alone. Getting colder her entire body was shaking.

Turning her head back towards the house, she could see a small glow of light coming from Charlie's bedroom window, and she yearned to be back up there—with Paul. Looking back over at the fire, Kaitlin said to herself, *No, I will not let him win… not again. It's time to end this.* She moved quickly through the tall grass and high weeds over to the edge of the fire. Circling the fire, her eyes searched the darkness. Fierce fighting thoughts repeated in her head. *C'mon Daniel, show yourself… where are you? Where are you Daniel? Stinking no good bastard… show yourself!*

Kaitlin moved closer to the warmth of the fire as she slowly circled it. It was inviting. Stopping, Kaitlin turned to face the heat. The flowing flames warmed her, slowing her shivering to a comfortable trembling. She swung her head from side to side like a nervous groundhog—searching the darkness for any movement. She could see Daniel's ramshackle old farmhouse that was about fifty yards away. It was as dark as the midnight sky, and just as quiet. *He's gone… he must be?* She reassured herself as she considered going over to the house to look for him. Her eyes stared hard at the dust covered windows, carefully watching the thin cotton curtains, expecting to see them move as he peeked out. A shiver ran over her spine. It was one thing to confront him out in the open, but the prospect of running into Daniel inside his dilapidated shack of a home, all alone in the dark, was a thought that was just too frightening.

With chattering teeth she inched closer to the fire content with the prospect of getting back into her warm bed. She began rubbing her hands up and down over the tops of her arms to help spread the warmth. She let her body absorb a little more heat before retreating back into the cold air. The flames were leaping from the large pile of timbers up into the air above the crown of her head. Watching the mesmerizing leaping flames as they swirled and curled up into the cold black air to disappear into the seemingly empty sky—a thought popped into her head. *Weird… it's so quiet?*

Although the fire was raging just a few feet away from her, she couldn't hear anything, no hissing, no popping, nothing, not any sounds of burning wood at all.

She leaned closer to the fire and strained her eyes to pierce the flames, trying to see what was fueling the large flames. Kaitlin slowly stretched out her arms and held her palms up to catch the heat. There was no sound—and now there was no heat. She watched dumbfounded as the flames rose up before her hands, twisting, flowing, billowing up and then disappearing into the invisible realm of the gases without giving off the slightest sensation of warmth. She moved her hands closer to the flames as her eyes were fighting to look past the bright red, yellow, and orange glow, down deep into the fire. Her vision was drawn deeper and deeper into the flames as the seductively dancing flames beckoned her cold body to come closer. Gazing into their silent rhapsodic rhythmic motion—she

rhapsodically flowed deeper and deeper inside the flames. The fire seemingly was coming alive, and the flames were somehow aware of her presence. And they desired her. A yearning; a feeling of needing to be within the flames so that she could feel the heat seemed to beckon to her to come closer—ever closer.

Suddenly within the swirling flames, a man's face seemed to appear. Desperately she tried to pull her hands back but found that she couldn't move at all. She stared with frozen eyes as the leaping flames inside the fire began to swirl tightly, circling around like a fiery cyclone, until they had formed into a twisting fireball. A fully formed head and torso appeared. And then eyelids formed on a fiery face—opening wide to stare back. Glowing fire-red eyes stared back at her and she felt as if he was flowing into her mind, consuming her. Frozen, held there by an invisible force, she couldn't move. Charring hands of flame formed beneath the fiery face—flowing out towards her like streams of red-hot lava. Bursting from the fire the flaming hands grasped out for her. Over and over again the fiery hands of flame burst out of the fire writhing like a mad-man—grasping for her—each time closer till they almost touched her face.

She started to scream for help—when the sound of cracking wood snapped her back to reality—as if breaking a spell. She spun around to confront a man who was stepping out of the darkness.

He had stepped on a fallen dried out branch close by. Before she could say or do anything, he said, "Well hello Mrs. Singleton. What the devil are you doing out here at this time of the night?"

Frozen with gripping fright, Kaitlin couldn't move her lips to respond. Wide-eyed she watched in shocked horror as the shadowy figure approached like a stalking animal—as he cautiously moved towards her. Agonizing seconds ticked past. Emerging from the darkness, he finally revealed himself in the soft moonlight.

"Oh my God… it's you," Kaitlin gasped with relief, recognizing Nick's face. Heaving with short breaths she couldn't say anything else. After a few more moments, she realized that her arms were still

sticking straight out in front of her, with her palms still raised up to catch the heat from a fire—that had somehow vanished.

An incredulous, half-cocked smile appeared on Nick's moonlit face. It filled him with joy, seeing her being so afraid.

Nicholas Thomas held the rank of Captain with the local Sheriff's Department, and was the only official homicide detective on their small force. And his investigation into the deaths of her father, Elizabeth, and baby Matthew were still ongoing. Whether they had been murdered, or died as the result of some bizarre accident, was as of that moment still undetermined. It was in fact his idea, to have Dr. Karanza join the investigation to help Charlie remember what happened—if it was at all possible.

Wearing a hunter-green jacket displaying an embossed shield which read Blackshear County Sheriff Department, Investigator Thomas epitomized the look of a small town Southern cop. With a thick, whisk like mustache with graying tips that were trimmed so carelessly that every hair appeared to have been cut at different lengths. A small scar was visible just below his left eye, where a small cancerous lesion had been removed. Sun spots and freckles blended with the two day old whiskers dotting his face—a face with skin that had the texture of alligator hide; dry, cracking, looking like the old brown leather boots on his feet. On the top of his head was a thin patch of pepper-gray hair, cut short enough so that his scaly scalp was visible.

Everyone that knew him, just called him Nick.

Nick ran his age-spotted right hand along his belt, moving his open jacket behind his revolver, and tucked his thumb into his pants. In his mid-sixties, he had a bulging mid-section that proudly displayed the fact that he was nearing retirement, and that worrying about diet and exercise were no longer part of his lifestyle. Placing his hand at the ready, next to his gun, he displayed his readiness to do whatever it took to make sure he made it to that retirement.

Embarrassed, Kaitlin dropped her arms to her sides and pulled her robe around her body as tightly as an Egyptian Mummy. He couldn't see how red Kaitlin's face became before she replied, "Well… hello Nick."

"Is everything alright out here Kate?" He asked, as if sensing something was wrong. His voice was dry, and as cold as the night air—not providing any comfort for Kaitlin.

"I saw this fire from a window up at the house," Kaitlin stammered, "and, well, I thought I should come out and check-up on things, and, I was still hoping to speak with Daniel… hoping that he might still be around here, so he could, well… so he could explain what he's up to." While she was trying to explain, she nervously glanced around, to see if Daniel was lurking off in the darkness.

Nick shifted his weight to cock back on one leg, and likewise began searching the area with his own keen eyes. Seeing only darkness in all directions, he muttered softly to himself, "Fire… what fire?" He eyeballed Kaitlin suspiciously. She was clenching her body tightly with wrapped arms, shivering like an embarrassed and scared teenager, who he had caught skinny dipping in a freezing cold lake. "Haven't seen nor heard from you since we last talked at the hearing last month Kate," he said, pointing out the fact that she hadn't been very helpful with his investigation.

"Right… that's right… been busy," Kaitlin stammered through chattering teeth.

"You were supposed to meet with me to discuss this," Nick responded bluntly, "You forgot I suppose." Starring at her with accusation filled eyes, he scolded her, "You know we've been getting nowhere since the night of the murders. And you're not being cooperative just makes it even harder to figure this all out."

He believes they were murdered? He probably believes I had something to do with it? Staring straight ahead, she fought to try and not look upset, or nervous—as he stared her down. It felt like a laser beam was probing her as his eyes searched her moonlit face for any sign of guilty nerves. "Well, exactly what are you doing out here… keeping an eye on me for some reason I suppose?" She tried to respond glibly, with an uneasy chuckle.

Her attempt at humor was lost on Nick. Spreading his feet apart a little more, he lifted his index finger to touch the cold metal of his revolver. In a firm, deep voice, that sounded even colder, he answered her. "Exactly right Mrs. Singleton. You think I'm gunna give y'all an inch after what happened here… no ma'am. I'm gunna be watching everything while y'all are here… understood?"

Kaitlin stared harder into the darkness, trying to ignore that he was even there.

Nick stepped closer to her—staring her down with eyes that looked straight through her. In a softer, less accusing voice, he told her. "You know I've been wantin' to have a little chat with Charlie for quite a while now." Leaning in even more to where it felt uncomfortably close, he whispered, "you know Kate… I don't want to see Charlie in jail. But someone needs to tell us what happened here. And someone needs to tell us soon."

Kaitlin's face flamed up red-hot as she growled, "you know that's why we're here Nick. I don't think you give a shit about what happens to Charlie… you just want your damn arrest!"

"Damn right I do!" Thomas snapped back. "I want justice for that baby."

They both stewed in their own body heat—Kaitlin staring into the darkness—Nick staring at her—neither of them able or willing to give up any ground.

Nick was the first to break their silent detente with what he thought would be an innocent and unremarkable question. "By the way… where's your husband… shouldn't he be out here in the dark… protecting you?"

Feeling a raging fire building inside of her, Kaitlin couldn't answer him.

So Nick tossed on a bit more fuel, "Well Kate… didn't Greg come with you?"

"No… he didn't," She finally replied, fuming, jerking her head around to stare daggers back at him. "I'm sure you already know that."

Nick just smirked—mocking her with his cocky grin.

Kaitlin stormed off into the darkness without bothering to say another word. Tearing off along the path with her feet moving as fast as they would move, steaming hot from her heated exchange with Nick, she couldn't feel the frigid cold January air blowing through her thin robe as she marched back to the house—completely forgetting about Daniel.

7

DR. KARANZA SPED along Interstate 75 in her aging yet still iconic Mercedes Benz. Swerving into the fast lane of the six lane freeway, her black four door sedan rushed passed a slower van, only to ride up on the dented and rust covered rear bumper of a V.W. Bug that was belching a stream of gray smoke out of its rusted tailpipe. As the toxins reached her nose she stomped down hard on the accelerator and veered back into the slow lane racing around the sputtering van. Like a NASCAR driver desperate for a win she began weaving through the thicket of slower cars damming up the freeway on the outskirts of Atlanta.

Glancing down at her watch, she took her eyes away from the bustling traffic for just a nervous second. *Shit! Oh… I need to get there before the meds take effect… before Kaitlin gets a chance to talk to Charles. Stupid bitch, I know she will screw this all up if given the chance. I should have left earlier to beat the traffic.* Dealing with the hectic Atlanta traffic was preferable to acknowledging her professional failure by relocating closer to the State Lunatic Asylum near Milledgeville. *It's just temporary*, she would remind herself every morning over her hour-long commute, *I'll get a position back in Atlanta soon enough.*

A typically frantic morning began replaying in her head like a video stuck on fast-forward: seeing herself leaping out of bed after being jolted from a dream by an alarm clock that was set too early, rushing out of her apartment without breakfast or her usual cup of coffee—black—before making the long commute, rushing to check on overnight emergencies, double checking charts, reviewing and writing out new scripts, briefly consulting with a family member while making her final rounds, racing up and down the hallway—pushing herself to finish a normal days work in just two hours. As her stress filled morning swirled around inside her head, muscles began to tighten like twisting springs all over her body. Her leg muscles tensed down along her slender calf muscle, tensing all the way down to her foot that was pressing down hard on the gas pedal, forcing her car to go faster and faster as she weaved her way down the freeway.

But this was no typical morning, since she had to get everything done at the hospital as usual, before rushing over to the Whitcomb estate to begin Charlie's treatment—making her even more stressed-out.

A bead of perspiration trickled down her forehead. The heater was still blowing on high from when she left home. She was too distracted by the strangling traffic and her preoccupation with work to notice that hot dry air was blasting out of the vents, making her hotter and hotter which made her heart pound harder and harder as the engine raced faster and faster—everything making her more and more nervous.

Realizing that she was nearing her physical and emotional limits, she wrenched her neck in a twisting motion trying to stretch out tight muscles and stiff joints that began to pop like popcorn. Opening her mouth and sucking in a breath of hot air, she ran her sticky tongue over her gummy dry lips. Shifting and twisting in her seat, she desperately tried, without much success, to ease the aching tightness that was quickly growing in her lower back.

Grabbing the rear-view mirror, she twisted it sideways so she could see her face. Her long straight black hair was parted down the middle, pulled firmly back, away from her face, held in place by a clip. It was the very same impromptu hairstyle that she had worn nearly continuously since childhood. No powder, just a dab of mascara, her lightly freckled face looked much the same way it had since puberty. Only now her skin was dryer, making the thin wrinkles more apparent. More makeup would hide them, but she didn't bother—she didn't really even care to try.

Leaning-in closer to the mirror, almost completely ignoring the other cars careening at high speeds all around her, she checked herself out. *Calm down Emily*, she told herself firmly, before darting her eyes back to see brake lights illuminating on the car slowing in front of her. Her foot lurched to the brake pedal just in the nick of time. Taking in a deep breath, she scolded herself. *Alright Emily… time to get focused… and just slow down. Just concentrate on driving for now, and try and forget about everything else… for just a little while.*

Dr. Karanza's unassuming appearance, for herself, was her unconsciously stated announcement to everyone that she was too busy for them. A slight passing glance in a mirror was all she ever needed. Emily didn't take an interest in vain appearances, hers, or anyone else's. Why bother? Her only interest and true obsession in life was her work. From her vantage point, being slightly more attractive provided her with no conceivable advantage. The stark realities of life including the unabashed bare naked appearance of people, was her truest attraction.

She lived a life that was as socially sparse as her unassuming appearance. Never seeming to deviate from her simple daily routine, nothing seemed to change in anything she did from day to day. Leaving her sparsely decorated downtown loft apartment, she would arrive at her sparsely decorated hospital office; perform the same routines like a figure skater that never deviated from a finely rehearsed program, only to return home in the late evening hours. Each day was numbingly identical. And every day she left home alone. And every day she returned home—alone.

Weekends also lacked any sense to true spontaneity or melodrama. Saturdays and Sundays were lived with the same type of fixed daily

routine as the rest of the week; only, instead of going to the office, which she would often do to *catch up*, she would typically spend her free time sifting through the latest medical periodicals, studying the articles for tidbits of information about recent studies, experiments, novel methods of treatment or promising new medications. Nothing made her happier than coming across a missing piece of a medical puzzle, one that she could incorporate into her treatment of a difficult patient. Proving her hypothesis—showing to everyone that she was more brilliant than Dr. Jenkins ever wished to be—was always a bonus that came along with such a rare find, and was nearly just as pleasing as the find itself.

Family life was as just as barren. Her only known relative was her mother, having been abandoned by her father before she was brought into the world. There were no pictures of family or friends to hang on her office walls. Only one reminder that she had any family at all was a discolored black and white photograph of her mother. In a cheaply made wooden dollar store frame, the photograph was placed on the top shelf of her overstuffed bookshelf in the corner of the office, as if stuck it up there to get it out of the way, along with the stacks of old files and forgotten papers that were piled all around it. It sat in a spot where a dark shadow would fall late in the afternoon.

Taken sometime in the forties, the photograph of her mother had begun to turn a hazy yellowish-brown with tiny spots, much like aging skin after decades of being out in the sunlight. Her hair was black and straight, pulled up and tied into a tight bun. Striking an austere pose, her emotionlessly black eyes peered off, away from the camera lens, as if looking into an undesirable and unwanted future. Loneliness was the feeling one would get while looking at her mother's solemn expression. She appeared to be worn down with life, out of hope, and devoid of any desire to live another day of life.

Dr. Karanza rarely took a moment of time to glance up at her mother's photograph. It was just there now—left there out of obligation. Because she hardly ever took a moment to really look at her mother's face in the photograph—or even her own face in a

mirror—she had never noticed that her appearance was slowly taking on her mother's forlorn gaze, more and more, with each passing day.

Breaking free of the gridlock, her Mercedes sped around the last remaining straggling car and broke out into a sprint along a nearly empty highway. A feeling of baptismal freedom washed over her as she watched the slower cars shrinking behind her in the rear view mirror. *Thank goodness*, she thought as she was finally able to relax a bit. Then a slow, tingling, feeling of excitement began to move over her body as she whizzed down the blacktop freeway into the wooded rolling hills of the South Georgia countryside. All of her attention shifted and focused on her patient Charles, and what lay ahead.

She finally felt some freedom from the infuriating myriad of hospital rules and regulations that hampered and restricted all of her efforts to advance medicine. Now; without the constant watch, evaluation, and criticism of the hospital staff and administration, she was finally free to release and utilize her smothered creative genius. Charles' treatment and miraculous recovery was going to be her greatest success, and her catalyst to medical stardom. *I will most likely be promoted to chief of staff... or even better, made a full professor at Emory University and head of clinical trials. Oh... what would I give to be out of that State Hospital... out of that dead end general staff position, and away from that dumb-ass, Jenkins!*

Charles was the perfect patient at the perfect time. The prime murder suspect of a triple homicide, suffering from apparent amnesia—feigned or otherwise—she was the best hope of a cure for him. It would go a very long way in buffering her credibility if she could find the pivotal clue to solving the mystery. And help Charlie in the process—of course.

She needed to use Charles to prove her hypothesis; that a synthesized extract taken from an ancient American Indian herbal remedy known as *Calea Zacatechichi* could be used to treat, and possibly cure, a person who was suffering from a lingering form of severe catatonic stupor. A powerful stimulant, *Calea* is used by Amazonian shamans to induce a hypnotic dream like state that forces the mind to open, revealing every hidden thought and memory. It was hoped that such a drug could force Charles' mind to jumpstart, waking him from his near coma like state, and force him to remember *that* night.

But to be successful, Dr. Karanza postulated, that the experimental medication would have to be given to Charles in such high doses, and in such a concentrated form, that it had the equally same chances of killing him as it did to cure him—just like with Catherine. Thankfully, Kaitlin still gave her consent to this experiment with Charlie, even after what happened with Catherine a few days ago. *I can't believe Kaitlin is still willing to go through with this?* She sighed.

This was absolutely her last chance to impress the Hospital Board. If she failed, her career would be over. The idea of being demoted back to the general staff, making mundane rounds, day after day, handing out pills to zombified patients, was all very frightening. But an even more disturbing thought, was the realization that her profession was all she had. Over the years she had completely ignored any and all chances at a social life. All of the possible relationships she might have enjoyed, she maliciously killed with impunity, just to remain entirely focused on her career. And now that seemed to be escaping her as well.

Even the used Mercedes, that she bought to help boost her self-esteem, had turned into another emotionally bruising antagonist. She wanted to own a symbol of prosperity—a crown of accomplishment for the world to see. But the fancy car quickly became just another millstone strung around her neck, pulling her down deeper into a sense of worthlessness. Each and every month she struggled to find enough money to cover the enormous payment—after she paid for downtown rent, student loan payments, credit cards, and hospital and doctor bills left for her by her mother.

When Dr. Karanza took the call from Investigator Thomas regarding Charlie's case, she felt a sense of relief so strongly that it was exhilarating. She felt as if she had been convicted of murder, sent to death row, eaten her last meal, was strapped into the chair, and

watched in utter despair as the lever on the wall was being lowered to send a jolt of electric current to end her life—when a phone call from the Governor rang in just at the last second—granting her a full pardon.

She could not afford to make any mistakes. Nor could she permit any unforeseen events, or people, to interfere. She had reviewed all of Charlie's medical history, was familiar with all of the facts surrounding the criminal investigation, and was familiar with the Whitcomb family history. Arrangements had been made to have Charlie isolated. He would be kept far away from the hospital where snooping staff and the controlling Jenkins would interfere. Investigator Thomas agreed to keep himself at a *reasonable* distance so that he would not be an intrusive influence—as his forceful personality usually dictated.

The only uncontrollable factor was Kaitlin. The presiding judge over Charlie's criminal case had reluctantly agreed to release him from police custody so that he could be transferred from the hospital back to his home. Charlie would remain in protective custody however; under the authority of his legal guardian—Kaitlin. She had total control while they were at the house.

Dr. Karanza understood this situation was both a blessing and a curse. She knew that no judge in Atlanta would have let the main suspect in a multiple murder case leave a psychiatric ward to return to the scene of the crime—to participate in her untried experimental treatment regimen. But, she also knew, Kaitlin held her career in her hands like a dangling marionette. A plaything that she could manipulate until she grew tired or bored, only to change her mind, and then drop Charlie's treatment along with her future, letting them fall lifelessly to the floor. Something a wealthy, spoiled, brat of a child would do—without a second thought or care.

8

THE MERCEDES SMOOTHLY navigated the curve of the exit ramp which flowed into a two-lane road that would take Dr. Karanza the rest of the way to Milledgeville. It was riddled with deep potholes. Every one of them was big enough to make even the best suspension bump up and down like an earthquake was shaking her. Each jolt made her flinch, and squeeze tighter to the steering wheel.

After navigating a long curve, and seeing no obstacles ahead, she let go of the wheel and reached forward to finger the small knobs on the stereo. Turning the tuning button slowly along the dial, she tried to find a signal for her favorite jazz station. Jazz was the only style of music she could actually enjoy. It was fascinating to her, how the musical notes danced on the verge of an ethereal disharmony, somehow always managing to meld together with musical perfection. Jazz was the embodiment of the elimination of the imperfect variables, those which distracted from the essence of a hidden truth. To her, it was emblematic of humanity—perfection emanating from the perfection of the imperfect.

Moving the tuning knob back and forth, she only managed to find a discomforting hissing static. The weather was not in her favor. Her station was lost in a mix of signals bleeding in from all of the other stations. She tapped the off button. The soft hum of the rough road under the wheels was not enough distraction to keep her from thinking about her patient. Her eyes glanced down at the stack of papers and the expanding folder filed with files and notes. With a little excitement she remembered the recording made during Charlie's court hearing—so she wouldn't miss any important details. *Perfect, if I can't read the reports, at least I can listen to the court hearing. Maybe I can find some useful information from the testimony on the tape?*

Reaching for her leather overnight bag she fumbled around inside, feeling ink pens, note pads, files, and a jumble of prescription bottles. The car jerked back and forth across the yellow lines on the thin country road as her eyes darted precariously back and forth from the roadway to the open pouch. Finally finding the cassette tape before crashing—she quickly pushed it into the player. As the tape began to play, she vividly remembered the feelings of angst that gripped her stomach as the hearing was conducted, a reaction to feeling helpless, without any means of control over her situation. Placing her future in the hands of this Judge, a despotic ruler, made her feel somewhat angry with jealous disdain. *He doesn't understand anything about what I'm trying to do with Charlie. I shouldn't have to answer to these idiot attorneys. Why the hell should they have the right to interfere with my work?*

The judge took his seat on the high bench, shuffled through the court's file for a few moments and then began to speak. His voice was emotionless and methodical. No indication of empathy or sincere interest in the matter could be detected—another day and another case. Feelings of bitterness returned as she again reconsidered the fact that the judge controlled her future, and he did so without any seeming care or concern, just another bothersome matter that needed a resolution. Any decision he made would not affect him in the least—he just had to decide.

She recognized the age roughened voice of County Judge Anthony Register on the tape recording as he began to speak. She adjusted the volume to make his voice a little louder. "Let's see, we are here on the Guardian's Motion, the case is 'In the Interest of Charles Whitcomb. Mr. O'Neal, you represent the Guardian Mrs. Kaitlin Singleton, is that correct?"

"Yes judge," Attorney John O'Neal responded as he stood up from his seat at the table, next to the seated Kaitlin.

"Mr. O'Neal, this motion is most unusual. But, the circumstances in this case are most unusual as well. As we discussed earlier, I am just not comfortable granting this request without some supporting evidence that it's the best thing to do for Charles, as well as this community. If you think it's appropriate to put Mr. Whitcomb back in that home… I need to know why," Judge Register demanded, is voice dripping with skepticism.

Attorney O'Neal gestured to Investigator Thomas who was sitting in the gallery, beckoning him to come forward to take the witness stand. "We would like for Officer Thomas to take the witness stand your Honor."

Thomas dutifully traced a path to the edge of the witness box and raised his right hand to the square, an act he had completed countless times before.

The court clerk asked in a robotic voice, "Do you solemnly swear to tell the truth, the whole truth, and nothing but the truth, so help you God?"

"I do."

"All right, Mr. O'Neal, you may inquire of the witness," Judge Register directed.

"State your name and occupation for the record please Officer."

"Investigator Nicholas Thomas… I'm the homicide investigator for the Blackshear County Sheriff's Department."

"How long have you been there?"

"Three years now with this Department."

"And how were you employed before that?"

"I was an Investigator for the Atlanta Police Department… uh… for about twenty-five years with them before I came here."

"How are you involved with Charlie's case?"

"I received a report of multiple deaths out at the Whitcomb residence. A patrol officer had already been dispatched to the scene. Whenever there's a homicide involved, I get called out."

"You mean suspicious deaths, right Investigator Thomas? I mean… the investigation hasn't been completed so we can't call it a homicide, not yet… right?"

"That's right Mr. O'Neal… but I don't believe it was an accident. It's still a homicide investigation as far as I'm concerned."

"So what did you do next, after you got to the scene?"

"I immediately traveled to the Whitcomb residence, secured the home, and assisted the paramedics who were already present on scene."

"If you could, please describe what you observed inside the home for the court Investigator Thomas."

Thomas shifted in his seat. His grimace was a reflection of his memories—as he detailed what he observed. "When I entered the front doorway, I could immediately detect the strong odor of smoke. Awful smell… sickening… it was the smell of freshly burnt human flesh. Unfortunately I'm too familiar with that smell due to the number of accidents and arson cases I have worked over the years."

"What did you see next?" Attorney O'Neal pressed him.

"O.K… well… when I entered the front of the home, I moved into the den where I could hear the paramedics. When I walked in, they were attending to Elizabeth Whitcomb and her baby boy Matthew. But they were already deceased."

"Could you determine how they died Officer Thomas?"

"Yes… apparently burned to death. A flammable liquid was poured on them before being ignited. I believe they got doused with homemade grain alcohol… moonshine… high octane liquor that would have lit up like gasoline."

"What else did you find?" O'Neal asked hesitatingly, as if afraid of the answer.

"One of the paramedics informed me that Mr. William

Whitcomb was in his upstairs bedroom with a gunshot wound to his chest… also deceased before my arrival."

"Was there anything strange about the condition of Mr. Whitcomb?" O'Neal asked, turning away from the witness as if shielding himself from the answer he knew was coming.

"Yes… he was covered with numerous superficial burn marks on his legs, torso, arms, and back. Burns that appeared to have been caused by the handle of one of his walking canes."

O'Neal turned back to face the witness, to ask, "How did you determine that?"

"Well… the burns matched the outline of the metal grip on his cane. A horse's head… looked like he was branded with it." Thomas grimaced again as he flipped through some photographs showing the burns covering William's body.

"So what killed Mr. Whitcomb… the burns… or the gunshot?"

"The gunshot to the chest penetrated his heart… that's what killed him. The burns were not severe enough to cause death.

"And where was Charles Whitcomb found?"

"Charlie was subdued at the rear of the property… out behind the house. He just took off running through the woods. I caught up to him as he tried to get inside the barn. He was burnt up pretty bad, out of his head and acting crazy."

"Did you find the gun that killed William?"

"No. We searched every inch… the house… the grounds… the old farmhouse out back, and the barn… found nothing. We never found where Charlie disposed of it."

O'Neal stepped up to the witness stand. Glaring at Investigator Thomas, he asked, "So you think Charlie killed them… don't you?"

"Yes I do," Thomas snarled, glaring back at him.

"And just why is that?" O'Neal asked flippantly.

"Charlie was the only person left alive… that's why."

O'Neal smirked, and asked, "Well… if you think Charlie killed his wife, son, and father… why haven't you arrested him?"

"He'd still be in jail if I had my way," Thomas fumed. "I

arrested Charlie that night… but the District Attorney ordered him released until they got a grand jury indictment. He said there isn't enough evidence to hold him. And since Charlie is pretending to be crazy, or have amnesia, or something, we had no choice but to take him to the hospital… where he's been ever since."

O'Neal softened his look, stepping back over to the where Kaitlin was seated, asking, "So I assume you are in favor of Mrs. Singleton's request to take Charles back home? So that she and Dr. Karanza can try and help him recover his memories about that night. Is that correct?"

"Unfortunately," Thomas remorsefully responded. "The D.A.'s right about one thing. There is no jury in this town that would ever issue an indictment against Charlie… let alone convict him of murder. Not until we get the evidence we need."

O'Neal lifted up his hands as if pleading with the witness, asking, "Now Officer Thomas… you do understand that this request is not intended to assist you in your investigation… right? His sister is just trying to help Charles with his *medical* condition."

This was a civil matter, and O'Neal knew the Judge was unlikely to grant the request to assist with a criminal investigation—knowing that he couldn't risk letting a murder suspect out of jail.

Thomas lowered his eyes and his voice, to respond in a calm voice, "I only want what's best for Charlie right now. And if this helps him recover his memory… so be it. My investigation can wait."

"No other questions Judge," O'Neal announced as he returned to his seat next to Kaitlin with a big grin.

Judge Register looked at Investigator Thomas with a look of concern. "Well… I have a few questions for you Nick. I need assurances that this community is going to be safe if I release Charlie for this treatment. Can you give me that assurance?"

Thomas stared hard back at the Judge, to reassure him in a firm voice, "I won't allow Charlie to step one foot off that property." Looking back over at Kaitlin, he added, "But I certainly can't assure any protection for Mrs. Singleton or Dr. Karanza… or anyone else staying out there with him."

"You do understand this is a civil matter Nick… a guardianship matter?" Judge Register reiterated.

"Oh, yes sir, your Honor."

"You won't be able to interfere," Judge Register pressed the issue. "This is not intended to assist your investigation. This is for Charlie's well-being. Whatever Dr. Karanza gets out of Charlie is confidential, unless he confesses, *after* being found to be competent, and with appropriate safeguards."

"Yes sir… understood."

"Very well, I'm going to grant the motion," Judge Register announced reluctantly. "Charlie can return home under the direction of his treating physician, Dr. Karanza. He must be supervised at all times and he is not to leave the house for any purpose other than emergency medical care—"

Dr. Karanza hit the stop button, turning off the tape recording.

9

D R. KARANZA FRUSTRATINGLY navigated the tangle of small back country roads on her way to the Whitcomb estate. As the trees grew thicker and the bushes denser, a feeling of being disoriented, isolated, and lost, enveloped her. In every direction she looked, it all had the same appearance—trees, trees, and more trees.

"Why the hell did they have to live so far away from town… and they could have provided me with better directions," she grumbled. "Oh… I hate this already. Absolutely everything looks exactly the same out here in the middle of nowhere!"

She wasn't able to relax until she came across the wrought iron fencing that ran parallel to the roadway—fitting the description Kaitlin told her to look for. *Thank God,* she thought as she drove through the open gate. Kaitlin had left the doors of the gate wide open, with the chain and lock dangling from the bars. She followed the winding driveway until she reached the house. She parked behind Kaitlin's *very* recognizable convertible Jaguar—the one that screams *I'm better than you.* She took little notice of the poor condition of the house, or the grounds. No time. All she noticed was Investigator Thomas reclining against his four-door, unmarked but unmistakable police cruiser, casually smoking a cigarette, as if he were on a break.

His face was all too recognizable. *Either too much outdoors, or too much smoking made that face. Definitely hard living in all respects*, she thought to herself as she got out of her car and walked towards him. "Hello Nick… you the welcoming committee this morning?" She quipped with a half-forced smile. Her warm breath made a mist in the cold air, which was mimicking the cigarette smoke spilling from Nick's mouth as he spoke back.

"Apparently so doc… but I have no present to welcome you with… just my ugly mug."

In unison they both smiled wide as they embraced for a friendly hug.

Kaitlin opened the front door and stepped out onto the front porch just as Dr. Karanza and Nick wrapped arms around one another. She stood there, watching in silence, as they hugged—along with light kisses on the cheeks. She quietly slinked down the front steps, as they continued with some friendly chatter. *That's an awfully pleasant greeting between those two. I didn't know they were so well acquainted. I've never seen either of them being so friendly with anyone else.* "Good morning y'all," she finally called to them—carefully watching for their reaction.

"Good Morning Kaitlin… how are you?" Dr. Karanza responded with a quick step back, away from Nick. She forced a nervous grin on her cold face. Sticking her hand out towards Kaitlin, she greeted her with a more customary, professional greeting.

Kaitlin shook her hand firmly, while thinking; *what… no kiss for me?* She then merely nodded her head at Nick, without a smile.

He replied in kind—tipping his head with a smug Cheshire cat smile.

"Is Gregory with you?" Dr. Karanza inquired.

"No doctor… he's not coming apparently," Kaitlin responded sharply, before quickly turning her attention to Nick, asking, "Well, did you talk to him?"

"Talk to who?" Nick replied, with questioning raised brows. His voice was thick and raspy, from too many years of smoking. Being early in the day, he hadn't coughed out much of the tar and it was still thick in his throat and lungs.

"You know I'm talking about Daniel. Didn't you find him last night?" She groaned.

"No ma'am. Why, did you really expect me to find him?" Nick scoffed, with a corresponding look of bewildered contempt. Starting to chuckle, the gunk in his throat forced him to cough a little.

Kaitlin's face blushed to a muted crimson. Her heart began to pound. She looked back at Dr. Karanza who was now staring at her with the same unattached look of bewilderment. With reddening eyes and steaming heated anger, Kaitlin was a boiling hot kettle—about to blow her lid.

"My, it's quite cold out here, let's go inside shall we?" Dr. Karanza blurted out, reaching to touch Kaitlin's elbow.

But Kaitlin quickly stepped away from her, turned, and strode off towards the house. She rushed through the front door and stopped in the foyer. An unexpected feeling caught her. She suddenly felt colder now—inside the house—than she had felt when she was standing outside in the near freezing winter air. Not cold on her skin, rather, deeply down in her soul. She felt utterly alone, with a morbid feeling of absolute isolation. Of being deserted by anyone and everyone that she believed she could have counted upon. It was not a new feeling however. It was the same feeling she remembered having when she was a young girl. That same inconsolable coldness seemed to be alive again—slowly devouring her.

Dr. Karanza and Nick noisily invaded the foyer. Their hands and arms were full of heavy luggage to the point that they each could barely walk under the strain. The sight was just comical enough to cause Kaitlin to grin with a sense of witnessing some devilishly designed karmic revenge.

"Doctor Karanza, you will be staying in my father's old room, up those stairs," Kaitlin announced, pointing at the steep staircase.

"Let me help with that," she said, taking the smallest and lightest bag before prancing up the stairway like a bratty child. She glanced back at Emily and Nick as they struggled up the steps, gasping at the air like two guppies. She waited for them at the top, with a big smile. Leading them down the long hallway to the bedrooms, she glibly announced, "This is it," as she strode into her father's bedroom and tossed the small bag onto the bed.

Dr. Karanza followed Kaitlin inside, moving across the floor like an inquisitive child. She casually set her things about the room, while carefully examining every detail with obvious fascination. "Is this how he left it?" She asked somberly.

"Nothing has been changed. Even his chair is still here," Kaitlin answered softly, pointing at the high-back lounge chair in front of the fireplace. She stepped over to the chair, swung it around on its swivel, and touched the small hole in the middle of the backrest. "That's where the bullet went through," she pointed out the blood stained jagged rim of the bullet hole in the fabric. With a distant voice, she whispered, "I'll get a blanket to put over this."

"No, that's fine," Dr. Karanza stopped her. "I don't mind. I think everything should remain the same as it was... if that's alright?"

Kaitlin nodded her unfortunate approval.

From the placement of the furniture and personal effects, Dr. Karanza could tell Mr. Whitcomb was an earnest, deliberate man, with a penchant for exactness. "You're father preferred the quiet, didn't he?" She suggested.

"What do you mean?"

"There's no television, no radio, no record player, there's nothing in this room that would make any noise at all... except for the fireplace, and that makes barely any sound at all."

"My father didn't allow televisions in the house. Father preferred that we read for entertainment," Kaitlin explained. "And work was his form of entertainment," she murmured under her breath.

Nick cleared his phlegm coated throat with a deep wheezing cough, before dismissing himself by saying, "I'll meet you ladies

downstairs." They could hear him hacking all the way down the stairs and out the front door—where he would light-up another cigarette.

Kaitlin rubbed the blood stained bullet hole on her father's chair—lost in deep thought. Dr. Karanza continued to peruse the unique items in the room. Neither of them could say anything else. Neither of them wanted to—at that moment—nothing seemed appropriate.

As the mood had turned awkwardly silent, Paul appeared in the open bedroom doorway, "morning ladies… how are we doing today?"

Dr. Karanza quickly replied, "Morning Paul. Good to see you."

Kaitlin watched as they shook hands. She couldn't help noticing that it was the same type of greeting that she had received, with no hug, and no kiss on the cheek.

"How is Charles?" Dr. Karanza inquired, sounding like a doctor on her rounds. "Have you been adhering to the medication regimen I ordered?"

Paul nodded.

"Where is he now? I need to see him."

"In his room," Paul replied, pointing down the hall.

Dr. Karanza brushed past Paul and strode briskly to Charlie's bedside. Grabbing his arm, she moved her fingers around his wrist to check his blood pressure. As she held his wrist she silently examined the patches of pink scar tissue covering his hands, wrist, and forearms. She released his arm and quickly pulled a small pen light from her coat pocket and began probing his sullen eyes. "How are you doing Charles… feeling OK… any nausea, discomfort, dizziness?" She darted the light back and forth between his eyes. Charlie slowly shook his head side-to-side. "Do you remember who I am Charles?" She gently prodded.

Charlie began to focus intently on Dr. Karanza's face. It appeared that it took every ounce of his strength to lift up his drooping eyelids, so that he could look out from his blood-shot, glassy, intoxicated looking eyes. "Doctor 'K'?" He slurred. "Yea I remember you. You're the crazy doctor from the hospital. Everyone knows who you are." A groggy-headed smile appeared on his lips as he talked.

"Good… humor is a good sign Charles. You're doing much better since we got you out of that dreary hospital," she replied, while softly squeezing his hand. Turning her attention to the prescription bottles on the night stand, she picked up each bottle to examine the labels, and to count the pills remaining. Turning her attention back to Paul, she asked him, "How's he been sleeping?"

"He seems to be getting more active," Paul responded. "Last night he didn't sleep well at all. I was up most of the night."

"Better get used to that for the next few nights," Dr. Karanza explained. "It's only going to get worse from here on out. Double his dosage of the Calea and reduce the dosage of the Diazapines by half."

Paul nodded.

Placing the last pill bottle back on the table, Dr. Karanza said sternly, "I need to get settled in tonight… need to get organized and get some rest… so let the new dosage take effect, then we'll begin his therapy tomorrow." With that, she marched from the room.

You'll have to use the fireplace if you get cold," Kaitlin called out to her as she disappeared down the hallway.

"What a bitch," Paul whispered with a grin.

Kaitlin broke into a sly smile. "Well, you're a naughty one. Keep that up and you just may get us into trouble."

Paul smiled wide—then winked.

Spinning around giddily, Kaitlin shuffled towards the door, whispering as she left, "just make sure you take good care of my brother… and me."

Kaitlin almost skipped down the hallway. She was feeling almost light headed, like a teenager with a crush. And for some reason, it seemed the opportune moment to call home and check-in with Gregory—while she was in such a good mood for a change. She

rushed into her bedroom at the end of the hall and picked up the phone. She nimbly dialed Gregory's car phone number on the keypad.

After two rings, Gregory answered with an abrupt and uninviting, "hello… this is Dr. Singleton."

Kaitlin was barely able to get out a "hello dear—"

Before Gregory interrupted her, saying pensively, "sorry dear, I can't talk right now. I have a patient waiting… call me later—bye."

The phone line went dead. With that silence—that dull, bitterly cold feeling of loneliness returned. The ground beneath her had suddenly given way, dropping her down into the depths of a freezing cavernous void—all alone.

10

A S KAITLIN ENTERED the downstairs den, she saw Nick standing by the fireplace. He was slightly bent over, staring down at the floorboards. Still fuming, after her short phone call to Gregory, she braced her nerves for another less than friendly encounter.

"This is where we found your sister-in-law and the baby," he said flatly, without moving his head to look at her. "It was not a pretty sight."

Kaitlin moved slowly around the couch to where she could see the jagged blackened stain burned into the wooden planks—looking like a spreading malignant melanoma.

"A horrible way to die," Nick mumbled. Glancing up at her, he asked promptly, "so did you know her well?"

"Actually no," Kaitlin answered in a distant whimper. Images raced through her mind as she reflected on the few times she spent any time with Elizabeth. *I never even laid eyes on the baby*, she suddenly realized. She had to imagine the photos that they had sent her to remember Matthew's face.

"We know that a bottle of your father's moon-shine caused the fire, but we don't know how the bottle got broken, or who broke it. Not yet anyway," he stated in a determined voice.

"Well what do you *really* think happened?" She asked with a hint of sarcasm, believing he would resolutely accuse Charlie of being the murderer without hesitation.

Nick turned and looked at her with contemptuous disdain—without answering. They just stood there, staring at each other like they were in a duel, each waiting for the other to make a move, making a misstep, one that would give the other an opening through which a fatal thrusting jab could be delivered.

"So, how long have you known Emily?" Kaitlin finally blurted out, revealing what really concerned her.

Nick was caught off guard by the question. His facial expression finally betrayed him as he searched for a way to answer the question, without saying too much. Sensing an advantage, Kaitlin prepared to pepper him with her own probing interrogation.

"I can't help feeling like there's something I'm not being told," she started saying, just as Dr. Karanza walked into the room.

"All unpacked… just need to retrieve a few more things from the car," Emily announced brashly as she walked up beside them. "I brought the painting supplies we talked about, and I think I left them outside." That's when she noticed the large black spot on the floor—and why they were standing there. "Is this is where they died?" She asked in a more subdued tone.

"Elizabeth was holding her son right here, as they were both burned to death by someone," Nick explained.

"You can't just say that," Kaitlin snarled. "Just how is that information helpful anyway?" Glaring at him, she pointed out, "it was an accident after all."

"It's OK, I need that information," Dr. Karanza intervened, "I need to know every detail of what happened. It will be useful for my therapy with Charles. It's alright to be angry about what happened. That's all a part of healing." She recognized this as the opportunity to invite Kaitlin to join the therapy sessions she had planned for Charles. She didn't expect it would be so soon, or so easy. "Healing is why we are here Kaitlin. Why don't you join me and Charles in our therapy sessions? I think it could do wonders for you, as well as Charles."

Kaitlin looked at Emily's sympathetic smile. At that moment Emily was just another woman offering her some help. The kind of help she desperately needed right now—just someone sympathetic to listen, like her therapist used to do.

"That sounds nice, thank you," Kaitlin agreed with a smile. The thought of recapturing some of that comforting interaction with someone who actually cares about her problems was more than she could resist. "What time did you plan to start?"

"Around four or five tonight would be good," Dr. Karanza suggested. "That would give Charles time to recover from his meds."

"Perfect... I'll have time to go into town and meet with my attorney about some estate matters. But I should be back well before Four."

"Guess I'll be going then," Nick mumbled, realizing he was being ignored.

Kaitlin wasn't going to let him leave without an answer, asking again, "Did you ever find Daniel?"

"I have a strong suspicion he'll turn up Kate," he smirked.

"Didn't you at least search his house?"

"Believe me, we've looked everywhere... but finding him is like trying to find a ghost or something."

Kaitlin huffed, turned, and stormed away—thinking, *asshole... why can't he just give me a straight answer?*

"I'll catch you later Kate," Nick remarked smugly as she stomped up the stairs.

Dr. Karanza was glaring at Nick, thinking, *idiot... don't screw this up for me!*

11

KAITLIN RETURNED TO her room and prepared for her meeting with the family attorney, Mr. O'Neal. As she shuffled through a small stack of legal paperwork, she overheard Paul cheerfully whistling as he passed by in the hallway. He was bringing Dr. Karanza's last remaining items that she had so opportunely forgotten in her car—including an easel, paint brushes, and a sundry of other painting supplies.

Charlie had enjoyed painting as a hobby since he was in elementary school. Dr. Karanza had become aware of that unique attribute about Charlie while interviewing Kaitlin, and she now intended to have Charlie paint during their therapy sessions as a cathartic way of expression. It was her hope that his suppressed memories could seep out of his subconscious, to be illustrated upon a blank canvas. She had worked with other patients using such projective drawing and painting with beneficial results. Especially with patients who were young children, very old, or those patients suffering from severe emotional trauma. Patients such as Charlie seemed to benefit most.

Glancing at the clock on the wall, Kaitlin realized how late she was running. Throwing the papers onto the bed, letting them scatter across the bedcover like falling leaves, she tore at her clothing to quickly change into something that she felt was more appropriate.

Pulling at the buttons on her blouse, her fingers moved erratically as she fumbled with the stubborn buttons. Her nerves were beginning to frazzle. Making it worse, her mind kept flashing back to images of the burnt floor and the burn pit—thoughts of Elizabeth and Matthew flaying in agony as they desperately tried to escape the tormenting flames as their flesh was slowly being flayed. The taunting voice of Nick was playing in the background as he provided a morbid play-by-play, as the horrendous scenes played out in her mind.

"Damn it!" She yelled as another button slipped out. Trembling, she threw herself down on the bed and grabbed the quilt with both hands and squeezed with all of her strength. "I hate this place!" She yelled, pushing the thick quilt into her mouth to muffle the sound. She imagined herself stuffing a handful of Valium into her mouth, before tipping back a large shot of vodka. Inside, she was screaming, *I just can't do this alone!*

For that moment, all she could imagine was crawling underneath the covers of her bed and fading off to an everlasting sleep. Only the sound of Paul's happy whistling as he passed by her room again forced her to remain rational. *Everyone out there is waiting for me. I'm the only one that can do all of this. They will never leave me alone until it's done.*

She looked over at the phone as if it were some floatation device that could be used to save her from drowning, and she tried to remember the phone number to her therapist's office. *I need help... some support. I can't do this all alone anymore,* she told herself. *He can call in a prescription for me... and when I go into town... I'll pick it up.* As her shaking hand began to dial, she thought, *No! Gregory would never forgive me if he found out. I can't disappoint him again.*

Squeezing twisting on the bedcover—with every muscle in her body squeezing to the point of near complete exhaustion—as if wringing all emotion from her body like water from a wet rag—she squeezed and screamed, *"AAAAAAAGH!"*

"Is everything alright in here Kate?" Dr. Karanza called to

Kaitlin through the door. She had overheard Kaitlin's muffled scream as she was passing by.

"Fine… I'm fine… everything is just fine," Kaitlin murmured.

"Mind if I come in?" Dr. Karanza invited herself, as she was pushing the door open.

Kaitlin sat up straight, doing her best to feign composure. Her fingers deftly finished buttoning-up her blouse, just as Dr. Karanza stepped into the room.

"You certainly don't sound alright," Dr. Karanza said softly.

"I'm fine… really I am… just feeling a little overwhelmed right now, that's all," Kaitlin muttered, while staring out the window, away from the doctor. She could feel Dr. Karanza's eyes moving over her, examining her like a patient.

"What you're feeling is good," Dr. Karanza consoled her. "You need to release those pent up feelings. Being here is going to be hard for all of us. But we're going to be better off by confronting what happened here and coming to terms with the pain."

Kaitlin could feel herself falling apart. Her entire body was aching to break down and cry like a lost child—crying out for help. Dr. Karanza's voice was a little too close to sounding like her mother, and it was killing her. Tears welled up and flowed out from the corners of her eyes, trickling down her cheeks.

"I think I have something that will help you relax," Dr. Karanza said with a soothing voice.

"What is it?" Just the mention of medication seemed to instantaneously change her mood.

Dr. Karanza walked to over to Kaitlin's side. While gently stroking her back, letting her nails scratch softly down her back, she pressed a pill bottle into Kaitlin's trembling hand. "Just some medicinal herbs that are somewhat similar to what Charles is taking. It should at least help you sleep better while we're here, and keep you from having to ride an emotional roller coaster."

Kaitlin's head bobbed slowly up and down. The caressing touch made her feel like she was melting. All of her emotion was draining away. With her eyes closed, she imagined that it was her mother's hand on her back, touching her the way her mother would do whenever she had been frightened as a young girl. Now looking like a fragile sick little child she looked into Dr. Karanza's reassuring eyes, to say, "Thank you Emily."

"Tell me how you are feeling."

Kaitlin's mind fumbled about within itself as she tried to find a focal point—a place to start—with so many feelings it was almost impossible to decide where to begin. "Well, I suppose I should tell you some things about Charlie."

"I know all I need to know about Charles dear. I know a lot about you as well."

Kaitlin's questioning eyes darted up to lock with Dr. Karanza's. "What exactly do you already know about me?"

"I think I know how you are feeling, because we have some things in common. My mother was an abusive alcoholic too… like your father."

Kaitlin's eyes fell away as she relaxed, and listened—her body softening under the spell of her soothing words.

"My father abandoned my mother when I was just a baby. I never knew him. My mother never forgave him. Her anger at him grew over the years as she struggled to raise me and my sister. Every passing year things got harder for her, for all of us, and her drinking slowly consumed her. I don't think I can remember a single day that she wasn't smashed out of her head. But it's because of my abusive mother that I'm now a psychiatrist."

"Why's that?"

"I wanted to cure her. But she couldn't be helped. You have to want to be helped. She just wanted to be dead. And she got her wish before I even got to medical school."

"What happened to her?"

"They found her putrid, half decomposed body in her house. The landlord found her when he came to collect the late rent. She finally overdosed on booze and sleeping pills."

"I'm so sorry," Kaitlin whispered.

"I went to her funeral, my sister refused to go. I don't blame her, or my mother for that matter. I've realized that we can't control people, and we can't let them control us either. We must control ourselves and everything around us… especially those around us. Never let anyone make you feel less important, helpless, or abandoned."

Yes… that's right, Kaitlin began thinking, *I won't let Gregory control me any longer. I know what is best for me and Charlie. I never should have stopped seeing my therapist, or stopped taking my medication for that selfish controlling know-it-all bastard.*

"So you'll be back in time for the therapy with Charles this afternoon?" Dr. Karanza asked excitedly, lightening the mood.

"Wouldn't miss it," Kaitlin smiled.

"Very well then… take two pills now… and then two at bedtime and in the morning," Dr. Karanza instructed before leaving the room to go check on Charlie.

12

WHAT WAS LEFT of the morning chill was slowly warming as the sun rose higher in the brilliantly blue cloudless sky. Kaitlin raced out the front door and rushed down the front porch steps on her way to her appointment with Mr. O'Neal—running late.

"Morning Kate," Paul called to her. He was standing near the corner of the house. A cigarette dangled from his lips which wiggled up and down as he spoke.

"Morning Paul," Kaitlin responded without slowing down as she walked to her car.

"Headed into town?"

"That's right… I have some business to take care of."

"Mind if I join you?"

Paul's voice froze her, just as her fingers touched the door handle.

"Don't you need to be here… with Charlie?" Kaitlin asked with a raised eyebrow.

"I got a break. Dr. Karanza thought I should take some 'R' and 'R'. She wants to be with Charlie *alone* for a few hours." He explained as the cigarette in his lips danced. It was still cold enough outside to force him to leave his hands tucked inside the warm

pockets of his dark-brown leather motorcycle jacket. With deeply hewn discolored lines and spots, the walnut brown leather jacket looked like it was a relic left to him from a World War I veteran. But it matched up well with his tattered blue jeans that appeared to be just as old—just as worn. With a purposefully cocky pose, like some James Dean imitator, he took on the appearance of a high school senior that was trying too hard to impress the popular girl.

She couldn't help but giggle a little inside. Biting down on the inside of her lower lip to hide her feelings—she considered his tempting offer. *He seems harmless. It may be nice to have someone like Paul to spend a little relaxation time with… someone to help take my mind off of everything.* His boyish smile was too much for her. Spinning back around to open the car door, she replied, "Sounds fine to me—get in."

"No. I have a better idea. Let's take the bike," he suggested, daringly—like a bad boy would. His lips stretched wide with the grin of indecent enticement.

A familiar feeling stopped her cold. Not breathing for a long pause, she stood in silence looking at the door-handle on her Jaguar. For just a brief moment she was struck by that old sensation of being young again. An electric feeling like she had back when she was that brave, daring, unstoppable schoolgirl—the one who only wanted to spend long summer afternoons on the back of a boyfriend's motorcycle. Together they would rebelliously tear off, heading out of town, going someplace, anyplace, anywhere away from here.

"Your motorcycle… you can't be serious? You want me to ride on the back of your motorcycle, with you, all the way into town, in the cold?" Kaitlin responded with feigned indignation at the suggestion. But she blushed, and that devilish smile slipped out, revealing her true feelings.

"What time is your appointment?" Paul asked with his own devilish grin.

"Not till eleven," she answered, releasing the handle of the car door. "Let's do this."

They walked together along the driveway heading towards the main roadway running in front of the house. Kaitlin wanted him to put his motorcycle inside the barn, for safe keeping. It should give him some peace of mind. They had to walk out of the way, following the fence line around to where they could cut through a patch of woods. Paul walked a step ahead of her intending to show her the way, but he wouldn't have made it very far. It was nearly impossible to follow the dirt path leading straight over to the barn now—with a thicket of thorny bushes and large vines with shark teeth daggers blocking the way.

She tapped on his shoulder to get his attention. "This way Paul… I'll show you a place where you can keep your bike indoors when we get back." Speaking boldly she strode past him while motioning with her hand—to follow her.

Paul had to pick up his pace to match Kaitlin as she raced off. She nearly disappeared into the thick brush ahead of him as she scampered off into the woods. He picked up his pace and fought to keep his eyes stuck to her back side. But she moved quickly through the thickets of branches. *Where the hell is she taking me? H*e thought as he repeatedly tried to grab the branches that were swinging back nearly hitting him in the face as she pushed ahead without slowing down.

They finally sprang out of the bushes, stopping on the edge of a small clearing.

"There it is," she said, while catching her breath.

Paul walked up to the double doors of the dilapidated old wooden two-story high barn. Its red paint was worn to a dull reddish-brown. Covered with rotting and half missing planks, it looked like a giant dying old tree that was losing its protective bark as it slowly rotted away.

"What's in here?" He asked like an inquisitive boy wanting to explore.

"You'll find out when we get back." She chuckled as she once again raced up ahead of him and tore off through the trees on the

other side of the barn. "You're motorcycle is over this way… follow me and please do try to keep up."

Now heading back in the direction of Daniel's house, they made their way through a dense patch of trees until reaching another large clearing on the south side of the estate property. In the distance they could see Paul's motorcycle. The sunlight glinted off the shiny chrome.

"There she is, over there," Paul called out to Kaitlin.

They ran hard, racing across the field. Kaitlin giggled as Paul ran passed her. Reaching the bike first, he threw his leg over the saddle and hit the ignition like some rodeo cowboy mounting his stead. Revving the engine, he grinned at her, motioning with his head for her to mount his stallion. Reluctantly, she climbed on, pressing her body against his, wrapping her arms tightly around his waist, holding on tight.

As the motorcycle roared and rolled forward, Kaitlin yelled in Paul's ear, "Wait, no helmets?"

Without responding Paul gunned the throttle and roared off down the winding country road toward Milledgeville. She ran her hands up underneath his leather jacket to feel his warmth. His body was as hard as the asphalt of the roadway beneath them. Her fingers caressed the smoothly bulging muscles beneath his shirt. Getting warm was all the excuse she needed—to take advantage of the situation.

The air was whipping Kaitlin's primped hair into messy knots as they picked up speed. She could only worry about her messy hair for the briefest of moments, before, the surge of adrenaline made her head feel dizzy with excitement—intoxicating. Suddenly her heart was racing, pumping renewed feelings of freedom and excitement into her. Instantly, she was overcome with feelings that she had repressed for too many years, and all of her concerns evaporated within the wind that was racing through her hair.

Looking at Paul's right hand gripping the throttle, she noticed his unusual ring. Yellow gold, carved with what at first, appeared

to be an image of knotted vines. She could make out the intricately carved lines that crossed and twisted around each other, just like the vines growing in the trees surrounding them.

"Where did you get that ring?"

"Scotland!" Paul yelled back over the sound of the roaring engine and whipping wind.

As the motorcycle rolled to a stop at the first stop-light on the edge of town, Kaitlin glanced at her watch and realized that it was nearly noon already. *Oh hell… I'm so damn late already… O'Neal will be out of the office for lunch. No matter, he'll make time for me after lunch. He owes me that.*

"We may as well get some lunch while we are in town," Kaitlin suggested.

"Sounds good… just point the way," he cheerfully replied.

"There's a pretty good Mexican restaurant right up ahead, if that's good with you?" Kaitlin mentioned as she pulled herself up hard against Paul's back, so that he could feel all of her. Her cheek pressed lightly up against his neck and her lips brushed across his earlobe as she spoke. All she could smell was his skin—more intoxicating. The rushing air pushed his scent deep inside her nostrils as she breathed. Her fingers spread out, feeling the movements of his muscles adjusting to the jostling road. She realized that she was behaving very suggestively—almost out of control—losing all of her inhibitions. She also realized that she felt absolutely incredible. "Just stay on this road into town, and turn left at the second light," she breathed into his ear.

"Just you two?" asked the flippant young girl at the front counter as she scooped up menus and utensils rolled up in napkins.

They both just nodded.

The girl led them to a booth near the back of the almost empty restaurant. She scampered off to get them the traditional glasses of water, chips, and salsa. An awkward silence fell over the table. Paul understood that Kaitlin was being emotionally distant—for good

reason. They were thrown together by necessity. Right now, she was in all respects his boss. And the last thing he wanted to do right now was to say something stupid that would make her angry or upset.

Play it safe, he thought, before he began speaking. "So you grew up here... must have been really boring?"

"Well, where did you grow up Mr. Excitement... in a circus tent?" Kaitlin shot back with a grin, upping the verbal ante.

"Yes I did as a matter of fact. You may have heard of the place—a little town called Los Angeles," he replied whimsically.

Kaitlin raised an eyebrow. "Well... you may just be surprised by what a girl can get her-self into, in this boring little town." She stated boldly back, not to be outdone. "In fact, you probably wouldn't have even recognized me back then. I was quite the rebel."

"Oh really?"

"Oh yea, you better believe it. I even had a boyfriend who rode a motorcycle, bigger than yours, and we tore up this little town."

"You're right Kate, I don't believe a word of that," Paul scoffed. "Look at you. You're the quintessential spoiled little rich girl. This is probably the longest time you've ever spent with a guy like me, except if you needed something fixed, that is."

"Oh yea... well I have proof." She almost yelled—nearly jumping up out of her seat. "Uh, never mind," she reconsidered, realizing she was in public.

"What is it? Aw, c'mon, what is this proof? I won't tell... I promise. C'mon Kate," he childishly goaded her on.

"Only if you promise to never tell anyone—I mean never."

"I promise. Now out with it already."

Kaitlin sheepishly scanned the nearly empty restaurant to see if anyone was around. Sliding out of the booth, she moved around to the end of the table, positioning herself directly in front of Paul. Reaching to her waist, she unbuttoned the top of her pants and then moved the zipper down just a couple of inches, low enough to reveal the top of her silky black panties.

Paul looked up at her, and asked, "Is that all... black panties?"

Kaitlin whispered, "Take a peak."

He peeled down the top of her panties, revealing an elaborate Celtic Knot that had been artfully inked into her skin.

"A tattoo, oh you're a real rebel all right," he smirked. He let the top of her panties snap back against her skin.

Turning a bright red, she quickly zipped up and quietly slid back into the booth, to hide her face behind the menu.

"I thought you're family owned half this town… so what made you turn so bad?" He chided her from the other side of the menu.

Kaitlin slammed the menu down on the table. His stomach turned as he realized that he had done exactly what he was afraid he would do—say something stupid.

"It's a very nice tattoo… as tattoos go… you know Kate—" Paul mumbled before she interrupted him.

"Lots of things made me want to be bad, I guess? I think I just needed to escape."

"Escape what?"

"Everything," She said in a numb voice. "Growing up in my family wasn't as easy as you seem to think it was. Having money isn't everything. And we were not that rich anyway." Kaitlin paused, leaned back and relaxed, her eyes wondered along the table top, as her thoughts navigated along the long crooked path of her past.

Paul watched her in silence as she retraced the events that led up to today. Slowly, her eyes seemed to fade out of the present and then come back into focus on the moment, and she said, "My mother was killed in a car wreck when I was only six, and my father was just a no-good drunk. I was pretty much forced to take over for her… taking care of them… my little brother and father."

"Sorry for that Kate… so how did she die?"

"My father killed her. Well, his drinking killed her. He was drunk as usual when he ran off the road, running straight into a tree. Mother died in the accident."

"Wasn't he arrested?"

"Arrested, are you kidding? They were on their way home from a big party at the mayor's house. Everyone was there, including the Sheriff. Hell, they were all friends. Rich daddy, you said it yourself. A few people in town spread some gossip about how he staged the whole thing, to kill her. Some wanted him prosecuted. But as usual, all his friends, the Sheriff, the District Attorney, the mayor, they all protected him. Everyone knew that if my father was gone, the Mill would go under. Back then that's all they had. If the Mill was gone, this whole town would go with it."

"So what happened?"

"District Attorney said there was insufficient evidence. The local press just reported it as a tragic accident." A look of utter disgust came across Kaitlin's face like she had sucked on something sour. "Memories last a long time in this town. But nobody ever mentioned the accident again—damn cowards! I wasn't even allowed to ever talk about the accident. I still feel uncomfortable even bringing it up with my own brother—like I'm violating some bond of secrecy."

"Sounds like you and your father didn't have much of a relationship," Paul interjected sheepishly.

"Not after mother died."

"How did your father deal with losing your mother?"

"Don't know, since he never dealt with it. He made it clear we were not to talk about it—mother was dead—car accident—end of story."

"So that's why he walked with a cane?"

"Yea, all he got out of the whole thing was a bum leg." She smirked. She leaned forward to rest her chin on her folded arms—peering intently into Paul's eyes, and then said, "But I don't think his leg was even hurt. I think he was faking so he wouldn't have to feel so bad about killing mother. And just so that he could get some sympathy for himself."

"You sound pretty bitter… understandable of course."

"Damn right I'm bitter. At six, I lost my mother. I had to become a mother for my young brother. And I had to deal with my father's drunken bullshit until I couldn't take it anymore and left.

He wouldn't even stop drinking. It just got worse and worse. Him and Daniel, they can both just rot together in hell!"

"What does Daniel have to do with it?"

"He's the bastard that taught my father how to make moonshine. That's when their drinking really got bad. Out in that barn I showed you. Damn still is there to this day, I'm sure?"

"Wow, real-life old-fashioned moonshiners?" Paul chuckled.

"Yea, they drank every day—all day."

"Oh my," Paul whispered with a nervous grin.

"Of course I would have left home a lot sooner, but I couldn't leave Charlie there all alone with those louses. I can't count how many times I fantasized about killing both of them in their sleep—" Kaitlin caught herself, and abruptly stopped talking.

Paul's amused grin vanished. He was now looking at her as if he was almost afraid. Afraid for what she had just said, might say next, or what she had actually done.

Time to change the subject, she realized, before quickly reaching for a chip. "Enough about me… let's talk about you for a while."

Paul leaned back and slumped down on the wooden bench seat. "Not much of a story really, born in Carmel California, spent most of my time on the beach… a surfer dude… you know. Went to college—dropped out. Couldn't decide what the hell to do with my life, so I bummed around for a while doing odds and ends jobs before going back to school to do emergency medical services, drove an ambulance for a few years until I almost lost it from the stress and the crazy ass hours. But I didn't want to leave the medical field completely so then I decided to become a nurse."

"Must be exciting driving an ambulance?"

"I'm an adrenaline junkie as you can tell."

"Oh yea," Kaitlin winked.

"I really enjoy the medicine part, but the stress of the L.A. accident scene was making me insane. You couldn't imagine the horrible stuff I've seen. It got to the point where I didn't want to leave my house knowing what was waiting for me."

Kaitlin's face turned sour again as she tried to imagine the bloody carnage. "I wish you would have been there for my mother Paul," Kaitlin said softly as she reached across the table and touched his hand. He clasped her hand, giving her a reassuring smile. "But how in the hell can you ride a motorcycle after seeing what you had to see?"

"I'm a junkie remember?" He responded resolutely while chomping down on another chip. "I can't give up everything I love. Hell, life would be way too boring."

Kaitlin sighed, nodding.

"I did manage to settle down a little. Working at the State Hospital with mental patients sure keeps me on my toes though. But the hours are perfect for my freewheeling bachelor lifestyle, so I can't complain about that."

"Don't you get lonely?"

"Sure, sometimes," Paul replied, with a flirty wink, "but I get over it when I meet someone interesting, like you."

Kaitlin blushed. And she bit her lip.

13

"WOULDN'T BE RIGHT of me to make the *help* pay for my lunch," Kaitlin snickered as she snatched the bill from Paul's fingers. "Besides, I'm the spoiled little rich girl, remember?" Traipsing over to the counter Kaitlin paid the bill with a credit card that had a credit limit that would have allowed her to pay for the entire restaurant if she were so inclined. Paul relented, an easy choice, since he didn't even have a bank account, and no credit cards. All he had to live on was just a little cash that would buy him some food and gas for a few more days. Before Paul could pull out his keys, Kaitlin suggested, "O'Neal's office is just down the street—let's just walk it."

"Fine with me, I need to walk off this lunch anyway," he replied, pushing the keys back down into his pocket. Gallantly stepping out in front of Kaitlin, he pulled the heavy glass door open and held it for her. Bright sunshine greeted them as they exited the darkness of the restaurant, walking out onto the sidewalk that ran along a desolate side street.

"This way," Kaitlin said as she scampered off, leaving Paul a few steps behind.

She headed towards Main Street that was a short block to the North. Every century old building they passed by was constructed

using the same red bricks that had been fired in the same kiln in a neighboring town. The red brick façade was very popular at the time, and it was widely used. So much so that small towns for hundreds of miles around all now looked almost identical. With the only noticeable differences between them being the names on the signs advertising their respective businesses—all of which were of the same type themselves; hardware store, apparel, attorney at law, and the ubiquitous antique store. The red clay bricks unintentionally filled one's senses with an undeniable feeling of both stability and obsolescence—both at the same time.

People glanced at Kaitlin and Paul as they passed by. The towns-folk appeared to be right at home in their little isolated oasis of small town charm. New faces such as theirs received pensive smiles and reserved nods of the head as a greeting. It made them feel a little uneasy—the way they were being looked at—as if they were intruding on someone's private party.

Kaitlin brushed up against Paul each time they paused to peer inside a store window. He noticed how she would lightly touch his arm or back whenever she had the opportune moment. And he did the same—a way of flirting without obviously showing affection. She was even toying with the idea of taking his by the arm under the pretense of hurrying him along, when she was stopped in her tracks by the sound of a familiar voice.

"Well, hey there Kaitlin!" A woman called out. "Over here Kate," the woman called out again from behind the open trunk lid to a new shiny silver convertible Mercedes Coup. A large plastic bag dangled from her slender arm—from the maternity clothing store.

Kaitlin turned her head to see a very pretty young lady shuffling towards her on heels that were high enough to make it difficult for her to step up onto the curb. Kaitlin and Paul felt transfixed for a moment as they watched the stunningly beautiful young woman sauntering towards them like a model down a runway. She had perfect gleaming white smiling teeth surrounded by luscious red lips. Her tall slim frame was supporting a pair of voluptuous breasts with dimensions that were still easy to make out underneath her knee length black coat. Silken locks of swirling blonde hair cascaded over her shoulders. Her enormous diamond earrings, rings, and studded bracelets, sparkled in the bright sunlight, making her appear even more stunning.

Who is she? Not from here… that's for sure, Kaitlin thought as she looked her up and down, trying to remember how she may know her. She glanced over at Paul's admiring eyes. An instinctual jealousy swept over her as she turned her eyes back to watch the young woman daintily stepping over cracks in the sidewalk. "I'm sorry, have we met?"

"It's me Cynthia. You don't remember?" The young lady asked, making a pouty face. Kaitlin twisted her eyebrows in deep thought—drawing a blank. "From your husband's office, remember?" She said gleefully, providing her a clue as if it were a game.

"No. I'm sorry. I just don't remember you," Kaitlin huffed as she shrugged her shoulders and turned to walk away.

"I was a receptionist at his office for a couple of years up in Atlanta? We met a few times when you came by the office. It's me, Cynthia. Remember?"

Kaitlin turned back and looked at her with a forced smile, and said. "Oh yes, now I remember. Cynthia. Of course, how could I forget? You were so young. You've changed your hair, right?"

"Maybe, well, oh yea, I that's it. I always wore it up at the office. I always did that when I was working with Gregory, since that's the way he liked it," Cynthia said playfully while lifting up her hair and squeezing it into a bunch. "Gregory told me you were from around here. Well so am I—small world right?" She giggled and let her hair fall back down over her shoulders.

Kaitlin spun her head around and glared at Paul with eyes that could burn holes in him. Her hands were clasped and pressing against each other to the point that her arms were trembling, as if she were wresting with herself. "Paul—" She groaned through her grinding teeth.

Cynthia glanced over at Paul with a flirting smile—expecting an introduction.

"I'm Paul, nice to meet you," he awkwardly offered along with a tepid wave.

"Hello, it's so nice to meet you too," Cynthia smiled wide, waiving her hand back at him like a celebrity would do while riding on a float in a small town parade. The trio stood for what felt like an eternity, staring at one another in silence—Paul was grinning uncontrollably—Cynthia smiling all innocent and sweet—Kaitlin was grimacing.

"How is Gregory anyways?" Cynthia finally burst out.

"Fine I guess? You'd probably know better than I," Kaitlin growled.

"Well—I—I—uh," Cynthia began to stammer.

Kaitlin cut her off. "Oh my, we really have to be going. So nice seeing you again—Cindy wasn't it? Say hello to Gregory *if* you see him." Turning, she briskly walked away, leaving Cynthia and Paul standing flat footed, and stunned.

"Good seeing you too?" Cynthia said hesitantly, as if questioning herself.

Paul gave Cynthia an awkward shoulder shrug as if to say *sorry*, before he skipped off to catch up with Kaitlin.

"Nice meeting you too Paul," Cynthia called out to him as he was jogging away.

Paul caught up to Kaitlin and they walked briskly down the sidewalk in silence. They didn't slow down until Kaitlin abruptly turned and stopped in front of her attorney's office.

"This is it," Kaitlin noted solemnly while staring at the old wooden door. She took hold of the door handle, and then paused. "This may take a while Paul."

He understood this was a private matter, so he made an excuse to leave. "I have some shopping to do before we head back. I need to pick up a few things."

"Good idea—you'd just be bored in here anyway."

Paul strode off down the sidewalk. Kaitlin paused with her hand on the doorknob, just long enough to watch him walking across the street. As she opened the door a small bell rang out.

"Kaitlin, it's so good to see you again, how are you dear," Evelyn greeted her with arms reaching out for an obligatory hug. As the long-time secretary for the family's attorney, she may as well have been a part of Kaitlin's family, since she knew everything about them—all the odd little details that only family would know—both good and bad. Kaitlin responded with a forced smile and a half-hearted hug, like the greeting you would oblige a distant relative.

As if not a day had passed since they last saw one another, Evelyn began to tell her about the most current news that was floating around town. Feigning interest in the sordid gossip, Kaitlin just smiled, nodding her head as if she were paying close attention. Inside, she was yelling through the partially opened doorway for Mr. O'Neal to hurry up and come out and end her suffering.

As Evelyn talked, Kaitlin looked around the small room. The office was exactly how she remembered it from many visits over the years. She would frequently accompany her father here to conduct family business. Sometimes they would bring little Charlie along as well. She and Charlie would spend their time running around the office getting into trouble as they waited for what seemed like eternity for father to reemerge from O'Neal's private office. They would crawl about on the floor, snaking themselves around the furniture and hiding behind chairs and plants. Their tiny fingers couldn't resist fiddling with all of the neatly arranged books and periodicals. Evelyn would do her best to entertain them while juggling phone calls, typing, and helping other clients that were frequently popping in wanting information or just some attention. As Evelyn chattered on, she sauntered over to her desk and stealthily took a piece of candy from the jar. Evelyn winked at her to let her know it was o.k.—just as she would do when she was a child.

Nothing about the office had changed. Even the pictures remained unchanged, including the one she hated—the one of her

family. Still hanging exactly where it had always been. Up on the wall, prominently displayed like an honorary plaque for the entire town to see. Her family had been Mr. O'Neal's longest lasting and most lucrative client. The picture was hung there to let everyone know that her father was his client.

It turned out to be the last picture taken of Kaitlin's mother. The black and white photograph showed her mother standing next to her father who was seated and holding baby Charlie on his lap. Kaitlin was posed at the side of her mother holding her hand. She was too young to remember having the picture taken, but it made her feel angry to see it hanging on O'Neal's office wall nonetheless. *Mother wouldn't have wanted to be used this way. Father is gone now, and everything he did should be leaving with him,* she thought as she crunched down on the hard candy. She desperately hoped this would be her last visit, and the very last time she would ever have to be reminded of that picture.

Gregory had encouraged her to hire another law firm from Atlanta. Although she desired to do so Kaitlin just couldn't let Mr. O'Neal go. O'Neal had aged along with his dusty books and furniture, and everyone was concerned that he had lost the mental and emotional acuity to continue to perform the complex duties necessary to provide adequate legal representation. She often considered that replacing him may in some small way help relieve her emotional strain. The extra worry of having to always second guess his decisions, having to explain everything to Gregory, and try and justify everything he did. Removing another reminder of her youth would also be a welcomed extra blessing.

Things seemed to be going well so far. Gregory insisted on retaining the services of a reputable accounting firm in Atlanta to verify every financial transaction. Anyway, the Federal Bankruptcy Conservator appeared to have matters well in hand. O'Neal would merely handle the local probate transactions and prepare deeds. Besides he was good friends with the local judge, insuring that the local wheels of justice would stay greased, as long as he remained on the case.

"Is that Katie?" O'Neal finally hollered, "Come on in here young lady." He always kept his door slightly ajar so that he could overhear any conversations in the rest of the office. Over the many passing years, Evelyn had developed a unique manner of speaking, just to compensate for his eavesdropping. "How are you doing? How's Charlie? Everything treating you well? Good to see you dear, please grab a chair," O'Neal rattled on without giving Kaitlin time to say anything. He just flashed his big white dentures and slumped back in his tall leather chair.

"Fine, we're all fine," Kaitlin muttered underneath his loud voice.

O'Neal didn't seem to be hearing her anyway. He glanced up at her as she walked into his office, momentarily lifting his droopy eyelids that fell over bloodshot eyes that never seemed to focus directly on her face. Remaining seated, he waived a hand gesturing for her to sit in a side-chair as he began shuffling through a pile of papers that littered his desk.

"You're husbands not with you Kate?" O'Neal asked as he glanced passed her to the open door as if expecting Gregory to walk in behind her.

"No," Kaitlin coldly responded, "does he *need* to be?"

O'Neal suddenly remembered that Kaitlin had a very short fuse. Seeing her pouting face reminded him of when she was a stubborn and bratty little girl who would do anything and everything within her power to interrupt his meetings with her father. And now that snotty little brat was his biggest client.

"I sure miss your father Kate. This town lost a great man," he continued speaking while leafing through legal documents, while she glared at him. His speaking highly of her father, only made her even angrier.

"What did you want to see me about this morning Mr. O'Neal?"

The casual but warm smile left O'Neal's face and his eyes returned to the documents. "Let's see, there's some good news and bad news of course. First, let's deal with the bad I suppose," he suggested. His voice lowered in pitch as he began delivering the bad news. "That accountant's office in Atlanta that is assisting with the estate sent me this report they prepared. I've reviewed it carefully. It doesn't bode well for your family. Based upon the numbers they came up with, it would appear that the Mill was hemorrhaging money for the past several years. There are many, many, discrepancies in the bookkeeping that was provided by your brother. The purchase orders, sales, and expenditures are all out of sorts. They just don't jive."

"And exactly where doesn't it jive?" Kaitlin asked in a breathless voice.

"Apparently the correct amount of income has been under reported, that is to say that, the amount of money the Mill generated over the past several years was not correctly reported to the I.R.S.," he continued explaining without looking up.

Kaitlin sucked in a short breath—feeling like she had been sucker-punched in the gut.

After a long silent pause, O'Neal raised his eyes up from the papers on his desk, looking at Kaitlin with a forlorn gaze, he added, "now the I.R.S. wants your family's estate to pay a large amount of back taxes they say are owed."

"How much are they saying we owe?"

"The initial estimate is well over a couple of Million Dollars."

Kaitlin started to tremble and the room began to move underneath her as her head started to spin. Clenching onto her purse in her lap she tried to maintain some composure. "Oh, my, God; my, God," she repeated softly. "Everything I'm trying to do is going to be ruined, I can't pay for all this—oh no, Gregory—he is going to kill me," she continued to mutter.

O'Neal looked back down and continued to nervously flip

through the paperwork as if to be searching for something good that could make things, *not so bad.*

As she watched his fingers nervously flipping the pages she knew that he was just avoiding her. Her eyes darted nervously in all directions without really focusing on anything. On the verge of hysteria, she opened her purse and frantically scrambled the loose contents on the bottom searching for her pack of cigarettes. She pulled out the half empty pack and pulled out a cigarette and placed it up to her puckered lips. Catching herself—she realized where she was. O'Neal had stopped looking at the papers, and was now glaring at her with contempt.

With a huff, Kaitlin took the cigarette and dropped it back inside her purse. As it landed inside, the cigarette bounced off of a pill bottle that had shuffled up to the top. Inside was the medication that Dr. Karanza had given her. She grabbed the bottle and twisted the top off. Three pills spilled out into her hand as she shook the bottle. Without any hesitation she tossed them into her mouth and tried to swallow the chalky oblong pills.

"Evelyn, can we get a glass of water in here," O'Neal called out. Moments later, Evelyn dutifully whisked in through the door and handed Kaitlin a plastic cup filled with cold water.

"Thank you," Kaitlin gushed before gulping down four of the pills.

Evelyn patted her softly on the back and said, "You're welcome dear." As quickly as she had appeared, Evelyn disappeared from the office to return to her desk.

Kaitlin gave O'Neal a reassuring smile and then asked, "Well then—just what the hell is the good news."

O'Neal grinned a little and said, "Well Kate, apparently the bankruptcy conservator that has been managing the Mill believes she can temporarily turn a profit. In the very short term, perhaps long enough to forestall a seizure… until the Mill can be sold off that is."

"O.K., so we have to sell the Mill, no problem, but what about the house?" "The conservator believes she can manage to make a sufficient short term income from the Mill to satisfy some of the tax debt they claim is owed. And the profits from the sale of the Mill should pay off the remaining debts. So if all else goes well the estate, including the house, would be free and clear for you and Charlie."

Kaitlin sunk back in her chair like a deflating balloon and sighed, "So we can keep the house." A small tear welled up in Kaitlin's eye and trickled down her cheek.

O'Neal was quick with a tissue and a promising response. "Yes, of course Kate—you should be able to save the house. I think most definitely. The house should remain in the estate, don't worry, I'll do whatever I can to save the house from the creditors and the revenuers—damn vultures."

"What about the rest of the land?" Kaitlin asked softly as she dabbed the tissue on her swollen eyes.

"Well, again, the conservator believes that we can negotiate and settle most, if not all of the estate debts, and the house and land would not have to be mortgaged or sold, but that's all that would remain from your family's estate. It looks like everything else will have to be sold."

Kaitlin continued rubbing her eyes, silently pondering the prospect of losing almost everything her family had built.

"Everything will be fine Kate," O'Neal said reassuringly, but sounding like an aging fighter in the last round of his last fight—about to go down for the count.

Kaitlin leaned forward and said, "Very well, is there anything else for me to do?"

His eyes rose up from his paperwork to meet hers. Like a Doctor examining a patient, he paused for a moment in deep thought, and then said, "No, not today. That's enough for today Kate. All I need is for you to sign these documents here. This updated inventory, proof of service on creditors, and this beneficiary disclosure—right here, and here, and one more here."

Not taking time to read anything, Kaitlin scrawled her

unintelligible signature across the black lines and laid the pen on the desk.

"Tell Charlie I said hello," O'Neal said smiling—not remembering that Charlie was nearly comatose.

Kaitlin strode across the lobby. She wanted to make a hasty exit without having to speak with Evelyn again. Out of the corner of her eye, she could see Evelyn giving her a slight wave and gentle smile. Evelyn was holding the phone receiver—her attention was divided—between her conversations with the friend on the phone and wanting to say her goodbyes to Kaitlin. Covering the receiver with her hand, she whispered to her, "goodbye Katie… say hello to Gregory." Without disrupting her conversation, Evelyn lifted her hand from the receiver and continued speaking with her friend.

I'm barely a person, a tool, used and dismissed. I now have nothing of my own, and only do for others, Kaitlin thought as she reached for the doorknob. Her feelings of being used, and her loneliness, made her think of Gregory, until she pulled the door open and the bright rays of sunlight hit her eyes. Squinting to see, in front of her she saw the grinning face of Paul who was patiently waiting to greet her. All thoughts of loneliness disappeared—along with all thoughts of Gregory.

14

P AUL WAS IMPATIENTLY milling around like a vagrant on the sidewalk, just outside of O'Neal's office door. Three cigarette butts lay at his feet. As he pulled the fourth from the pack, he heard the familiar sound of Kaitlin's heels clicking on the concrete. Everything he needed to know about her meeting was visible in her eyes. "Bad news huh," Paul said sympathetically. Her eyes were swollen and bloodshot, with swaths of smeared mascara. He felt forced to say something, but he didn't want to intrude.

"You could say that," Kaitlin replied sharply with a sniffle, dabbing her eyes with a tissue. Walking straight up to Paul, she moved up close, to where she could feel the warmth of his breath. Her eyes looked deeply into his. But her mind was distant, with the glazed-over blank stare of someone at a funeral. Paul hesitated, caught off guard, and completely unprepared, he searched for something that might be appropriate to say. Continuing to dab at her welling eyes, she was on the verge of crying. Paul stared down at her, afraid to say something wrong, and yet, even more afraid of not saying anything at all. He smiled reassuringly—the only thing he could do. It was enough. His smile said everything he needed to say.

Kaitlin relaxed and smiled back. More of a pouting smile; as if to say, I don't want to smile, and you shouldn't be able to make me

smile, because I shouldn't feel happy right now. Without any more words needing to be spoken, Paul threw his arm around her shoulders and together they walked down the sidewalk. Reaching the motorcycle, they climbed on the long black seat. Kaitlin squeezed Paul's waist as the bike rumbled to life. He threw the metal stallion into gear, throttled up, and they thundered down Main Street heading for the highway leading out of town.

As they passed the last stop-light she leaned in close to place her face softly up against his ear, and yelled, "Go faster!"

Her arms and legs squeezed on him tightly as he obliged.

Paul grinned and twisted the throttle as far as his wrist would go. Everything around them became a blurry green and brown collage as they flew down the winding country blacktop. Kaitlin closed her eyes, allowing only a sliver of daylight inside—she smiled—her whole body seemed to be melting into the blurring scenery as her cares blew away along with the whipping wind in her hair. The cold air couldn't get to her body that was melting into his warmth.

Brushing her lips up against his ear, she whispered, "Please don't ever stop."

Time flew by as fast as the wind in their hair, as they spend the rest of the afternoon riding up and down small country roads, stopping at small antique shops, or for a slice of homemade pie in some quaint country Inn.

All too soon they arrived back at the house and entered the property through a small gate on the far side of the estate. They slowly rode along a winding dirt road that dead-ended in front of the old wooden barn that they had passed by that morning. The two-story wooden barn was completely hidden from view from the main road. It had been intentionally built behind a wall of trees and large bushes. It was not meant to be seen from the roadway, and Kaitlin understood why, and she wanted Paul to know why too.

Paul lowered the kickstand and turned the key to the off position. An uneasy quiet greeted them as the rumbling engine died.

Kaitlin quickly dismounted and strode over to the doors and

grabbed the end of a dangling chain that was laced through the handles. *Daniel must have broken in,* she silently speculated when she saw the cut padlock lying on the ground. *Good thing, because I don't have a key anyway,* she remembered as she pulled the chain from the handles.

Paul stepped forward to help her swing the creaking old wooden doors wide open. A powerful odor of corn mash and burnt wood met their nostrils. The daylight streamed in and illuminated the dust that hung thick in the air like a very fine smoke. Various hand tools along with some cobweb covered landscaping equipment lined the walls. A large stack of burlap sacks full of corn were neatly stacked. On the far wall they could see a mound of split logs, dried out, and ready to be used as kindling. Yellow and white kernels of corn made a speckled mosaic on the dirt floor. They both coughed to clear the dust that was gagging them.

The streaks of sunlight also reflected off of a large metal drum that was sitting in the middle of the barn's dirt floor. Four feet in diameter, the copper still had a smooth golden colored metal skin, giving it the appearance of a giant copper teardrop. Kaitlin froze in place for a moment—appearing to be lost in deep thought. As if possessed, she suddenly yelled out, "There you are!"

Rushing across the barn, she scooped up a piece of firewood and heaved the log high above her head. With both hands, she slammed the split log against the still. As the log bounced off the still it flew out of her hands. She crashed down onto her knees, landing in the dirt along with the piece of wood. The copper drum vibrated and rang-out, giving off a deep resounding tone—a penetrating sound that vibrated them to their core. It was ringing with the sound of resilience. A mocking sound that reminded Kaitlin that it was stronger than she was.

Gasping, she sucked in more dust. Face to face with the still, she screamed at it, as if it were a monster, "I hate you! Why are you still here?" Her fingers dug deeply into the dirt. A thick cloud of dust swirled over her head. "You killed my mother," she moaned softly, sounding defeated. Tears ran down her face, dripping to the dirt floor like a soft rain.

Paul leaned down and placed his hand gently on her drooping shoulder. He examined the still, wondering what had caused her to snap. "What's the matter Kate?" he asked quietly.

"My father built that thing with Daniel. They loved making shine and getting wasted—stupid bastards." Kaitlin muttered. "This is what really killed my mother. Booze destroyed my family's business, and now it's destroying the rest of my family. It looks like Daniel is planning on making him some more of that poison— unless I find him first," she snarled.

"Destroyed your family's business? How did making shine do that?" Paul asked with a puzzled look.

"Before the accident the Mill ran smooth as silk. Father was a true businessman. Everyone loved him around here.

"So what happened?"

"After mother died, he started drinking more and more—always with Daniel. It got worse and worse the better they got at making the shit. The booze kept getting stronger and stronger and they drank more and more. Over the years his heavy drinking began to take its toll. Pain and Dementia took him over. It got so bad he just couldn't continue to run the Mill. That's when he finally relented and decided let Charlie move back home and take over the business. Charlie's not like father, he was over his head the second he started. O'Neal just told me that the Mill has been losing money for years. It has to be sold off to pay the back taxes and debts."

Paul's hand moved across the top of her shoulder, his fingers moved her hair, rubbing lightly on her skin.

She felt his fingers on her neck, and she shrugged. "Stop it!" She half yelled, throwing up her arms to push his hands away. "Please don't touch me now. It's not right… I'm not right."

Memories of what Daniel had done to her flashed through her mind.

"What's wrong?"

"Never mind… I just have to get out of here," she blurted out while leaping up onto her feet. "You go get the motorcycle and park it in here. I'll meet you back at the house." Patting the dirt from her clothes she headed for the door.

Stepping outside, she paused and stared into a thicket of overgrown Hydrangea, Juniper, rose, and Azalea bushes. It was the only direct way back to the house. And her father had planted thorny shrubs and prickly vines all along the path to keep them from using it. The now completely overgrown army of thorn covered branches, vines, and weeds, all did their intended job well. The old dirt trail was nearly eaten away by them, almost completely hidden.

Bam! The door slammed shut behind her—swung shut by a gust of wind. Startled and feeling panicked like a race horse hearing a starter pistol, Kaitlin felt an overwhelming desire to run—run fast. With her hands raised up like shields she pushed her way into the outstretched branches that were spliced together like a sticky spider's web across the pathway.

As she pushed deeper into the darkened trail, the limbs and thorn covered vines seemed to be growing larger, thicker, as they wrapped her up within their tentacles, clinging to her clothes, scratching into her skin. On the verge of panicking, the memories of what happened here when she was twelve years old began to resurface, reaching out at her, poking, scratching, and tugging at her mind—just as the menacing, long, thin, jagged branches, that were reaching out to catch, scratch, and pull at her clothing and hair.

I'm not afraid of him, Kaitlin fought back against her fear. But she couldn't escape the feelings of being isolated, alone, helpless, and lost, that all welled up inside of her again as she tried to move faster down the trail while fighting with the limbs as they grasped at her like long bony fingers. And she could feel his clawing fingers tearing at her shirt again, and his filthy broken fingernails digging into her flesh. As she tripped on the vines tangling on her legs, she could smell the disgusting stench of Daniel's breath in her face, as he grabbed her, fell on top of her, and began to rape her—on this very path.

I won't be afraid. I'm not a child anymore! Kaitlin yelled at herself to keep moving as she pushed deeper into the nearly impassable thick morass of branches. Every step became harder to make as she struggled to move faster, with her shirt and hair being caught, pulled, and twisted. *You don't scare me anymore Ed. You better be afraid of me now!* With one last agonizing push, she finally broke free and stumbled out into the open field covering the back of the estate.

Scampering towards the back of the house, she spied a dark silhouette moving off in the distance near the family cemetery. Seeing the back porch light up ahead, she prepared to make a mad dash for the back door. Just as she started to run for the house, the image came into view, and it wasn't Daniel. It appeared to be an old woman covered in a long black dress. She was standing at the family grave-site, motionless, and looking down at the ground. *Oh, thank the Lord. It's just Karanza looking around.*

"Wait up!" Paul called out from behind as he tore himself free of the tangled thorny branches. Quickly turning back toward the graveyard, Kaitlin started to call out to Dr. Karanza—but the woman was gone.

Paul scampered up next to Kaitlin, and asked breathlessly, "Why'd you take off on me?" She didn't hear him. She was staring off into the distance with a lost, puzzled look. "Well?" Paul demanded a response.

"Did you see that woman?" Kaitlin finally responded, without looking at him. Her eyes peered into the distance, cautiously scanning the tree-line.

"No." Paul replied as he spun around, looking in all directions.

Giving up, she connected eyes with Paul. "Never-mind… I thought I saw someone… just my nerves playing tricks. Guess I just need some more of Karanza's *crazy* pills," she murmured sarcastically, with an awkward grin.

Paul stared at her, thinking, *is she joking? Why in the hell would she be taking Karanza's medication?*

15

"I NEED TO GO check on Charles," Paul said, motioning for Kaitlin to follow him. They slowly made their way across the back lawn, weaving through the last remaining old oaks that had not been cut down or killed by lightning.

As they approached the back porch they could hear Dr. Karanza speaking to Charles with a nasally sounding voice. The cold moist air was thickening in her sinuses. They were seated on rusting metal deck chairs out on the back porch all wrapped-up in thick blankets, as Dr. Karanza softly recited poetry—reading from a small notebook.

An easel holding a canvas was in front of Charles. He was seated directly across from Dr. Karanza, but they couldn't see one another, as he made slow methodical strokes with a brush in his left hand. And neither of them noticed Paul and Kaitlin as they approached in the sun falling twilight. Dr. Karanza stopped reading and spun her head to look as they stepped onto the porch.

"Oh, hello Kaitlin," Dr. Karanza blustered, "You startled me— how about a warning next time?"

"Sorry," Kaitlin replied snottily, before adding, "isn't it a little cold for Charlie to be outside tonight? And what are you reading to him—sounds kind of weird?"

"Therapy… you know my treatments are unorthodox."

"Is that why you were in the cemetery a few minutes ago… for some unorthodox therapy?"

"I've never been in the cemetery."

"I just saw you over there."

"You're mistaken."

Kaitlin turned and glared at Paul, expecting some support.

Wanting to avoid being caught in the middle, Paul stepped over to Charlie and looked over his painting. It appeared to be the expansive clearing out in front of them, with the trees on the horizon, and a flat triangle, resembling the roof of a house. The very top of the roof was just visible above the trees. Looking up over the top of the canvass, Paul peered at the dark gray skyline just above the tops of the trees, and tried to make out what Charlie was painting.

"Looks like you're feeling a little better Charles?" Paul whispered to him. "Are you painting the old farmhouse over there?"

Charlie did not respond. He continued to paint with slow methodical movements as if he were half asleep. He tilted his head upward slightly to gaze across the woods, then, his eyes slowly drifted back to his canvas, where, he would very slowly lift the brush to smear on another stroke.

Paul followed Charlie's eyes as he looked up—to try and see what Charlie was seeing. The trees were there, but not the rooftop. But Paul knew the house was out there where Charlie was looking—hidden behind the trees.

"You look absolutely frazzled dear," Dr. Karanza gushed, as Kaitlin stepped into the light.

"I got some bad news from the attorney." All she could think about was what Gregory was going to say and do to her whenever she got back home—now knowing that the estate is bankrupt and she will not have the funds to pay for Karanza's *unorthodox* treatment. *Gregory is going to kill me or divorce me for sure now. If he has to pay an enormous bill for Charlie's treatment… my stupid attempt to help my loser brother… someone Gregory never liked in the first place.*

Dr. Karanza slipped up next to Kaitlin and took her hand, wrapping a supportive arm around her waist. It was just what Kaitlin needed in that moment. With masterful technique Dr. Karanza used her skills to sooth Kaitlin. In a soft reassuring voice, she whispered into Kaitlin's ear, "Charles is not ready to talk about things just yet. We need a little time to let him adjust to a level of comfort, where he can feel safe, where he can confront those memories."

"I know. I'm just stressed out right now… please ignore me," Kaitlin apologized, before asking. "So what are you reading to him?"

"Something that I believe helps patients to relax, to focus their attention. I read poetry to them while they paint," Dr. Karanza explained. "It seems to distract them from the fact that they are being treated, or being analyzed." With a little squeeze on Kaitlin's waist, she suggested, "Kate, why don't you go take some of the medicine I gave you, get into some comfortable clothes, and come back down and join us in our therapy session. It may just do you some good too."

"Sure," Kaitlin said as she stepped toward the back door. "I've got to do something to help me relax right now. I'll be right back." She paused just inside the doorway, and listened for a moment, as Dr. Karanza dismissed Paul,

"Go get some rest Paul. You'll be needed later. It's going to be a long night I think?"

Kaitlin pulled the door shut and walked down the hall leading to the stairs. She could still feel the lingering remnants of dust that had pasted inside her mouth and throat. Instead of heading straight to her room, Kaitlin detoured into the kitchen to find a bottle of wine. Not wasting time to find a clean glass she popped the already loosened cork and guzzled straight from the bottle. It was some of the best red wine she could remember tasting as the crisply-tart refreshing liquid washed over her tongue. Before she realized it, she had guzzled over half the bottle. *Best medicine for a sore mind,* she thought as she tipped the bottle back.

She carried the bottle with her up to her room. At her bedside, the feelings of loneliness crept back in. The absolute silence that was filling the empty house was overwhelming. As if looking for a life-line, Kaitlin looked down at the phone and thought of her husband. *I should call Gregory before I go back down. I need to let him know what's going on.* After taking another gulp of wine, Kaitlin dialed. Her back tensed up as she listened to the familiar ringtone. Almost instinctively, she slammed the phone down when Gregory's prerecorded voice on his answering machine began to speak. The same message she has endured a thousand times before. *Asshole!* She screamed to herself. *Thinks he's so witty and charming… lousy bastard… he's never ever there for me.* Taking the pill bottle from her purse, Kaitlin shook four more pills into her hand. Tossing them to the back of her throat she emptied the bottle and swallowed hard, almost choking herself as she forced the medicine down.

As Kaitlin turned and walked along the hallway leading to the back door, an image in a photograph hanging on the wall caught her attention. A cold shiver moved over her skin as she leaned in close to the black and white photograph held in an antique wooden frame. It was a family photograph of her grandparents taken when they were young—a picture she had passed by, only glancing at, for many years without giving it any real attention at all. It was her grandparents, standing on the back lawn, about where Charlie was now sitting. They were standing together, posing for a family portrait while dressed in formal attire. And standing behind them, in the far distance, there was a woman. With noticeably darker skin, she had long straight black hair that was pulled up and wrapped into a bun. She was wearing a long cloth turn of the century dress that covered everything except her hands, neck, hair and face. Her hands appeared to be covered with black gloves. Not posing with the family, she appeared to be working out in the field, looking down at the ground with a tool in her hand. A shudder swept over her as the realized, *oh my Lord that looks just like the woman I saw by the graveyard.*

"What are you looking at?" Paul blurted out behind her.

Kaitlin nearly jumped out of her skin, saying loudly, "Damn it Paul… don't do that! You scared the hell out of me."

"What's got you so jumpy?" He asked while looking over her shoulder at the picture. "Oh wow… now that is scary," he snickered.

"It's her… there… that's the woman I saw in the cemetery a few minutes ago," Kaitlin insisted, pointing at the small dark image in the photograph.

"You're starting to get me worried Kate," Paul chuckled, as he turned and walked down the hall toward the kitchen. She continued to stare at the picture—now questioning herself, thinking, *Oh just forget it… it's just a maid or groundskeeper, or something.*

Walking out the back door, Kaitlin joined Dr. Karanza and Charlie outside. She took a seat in one of the uncomfortable rusting metal chairs and braced herself against the cold air. Hoping to put every problem out of her mind, she jokingly said, "Think I'm ready… so work you're magic doc." Now, she smiled wide—half-inebriated.

Dr. Karanza didn't respond to Kaitlin's whimsy, she just opened up her book of *poetry,* and flipped to a bookmarked page. The bookmark attached at the top of the binding was a slender metal chain. On the end of the chain there was attached a silver medallion that had a Kabbalah diagram etched inside. Glinting in the moonlight, it gently swayed back and forth in front of Kaitlin as Dr. Karanza read aloud. She deliberately pronounced each word slowly, and precisely:

Like ants in a line
One by one
Front to end they move
Only trusting the one ahead
Stepping only in tracks leftover
Their destination yet to be discovered
Obstruction finds the path divided
Scattering in all directions toward destinations each they alone
will discover

actions follow instinct
nature calls for reaction
thoughts cause hesitation
wisdom forces contemplation

There are no maps to plot my way
I can only follow those who have crossed before
Yet they all followed the same path
one by one
only trusting the one ahead
the destination yet to be discovered

Like bees flying to flowers
One by one
Following the invisible trail
Only trusting the one ahead
Searching for nectar discovered but not yet savored
Their destination yet to be discovered
Obstruction finds the path divided
Scattering in all directions toward destinations each they alone
will discover

actions follow instinct
nature calls for reaction
thoughts cause hesitation
wisdom forces contemplation

There are no maps to plot my way
I can only follow those who have crossed before
Yet they all followed the same path

one by one
only trusting the one ahead
Your destination is yet to be discovered

Dr. Karanza repeated the poem two more times—each time repeating the words more deliberately. With each spoken word, Kaitlin and Charlie became more relaxed, tuning to her vocal trance inducing persuasion.

Pausing, Dr. Karanza stared at Kaitlin intently. With an accusatory sounding voice, she asked her, "Are you an ant… a bee? Do you know how to find your path to your own destination?"

Kaitlin looked at her blankly, unprepared for such a strange question.

"We're all like the ants and bees," Dr. Karanza explained. "We're all searching for the same thing. We are all doing the same things… imitating each other. Each of us wants to follow a clearly defined path through life. A path defined by the lives of others who lived before us. A path that leads to expected happiness. But things always happen to us as we travel along that path, forcing us to rethink our course, to reconsider what it is we are truly trying to find, and how we should try to find it. Ants and bees just react instinctively. We are different. We are forced to retrace our steps each time because of our intense memory recollection, constantly reliving and reconsidering all of our prior choices that led to our current situation. Those are just stumbling blocks that keep us from progressing.

Kaitlin just nodded her head with the same blank expression as Dr. Karanza continued talking. "Sometimes the things that happen to us are so disturbing and so terrifying, that we abandon our journey all together. If those memories are too disturbing, we may suffer a psychosis, forcing us to relive those destructive events over and over again. Those disturbing images become so ingrained in our thoughts that they begin to distort our sense of reality. Charles has abandoned reality to escape the memories of the horrific events that are constantly replaying inside his head. Do you understand?"

"Yes, I think so," Kaitlin mumbled with a shrug.

"Good, then you are still on your journey," Karanza said smiling. "Now you just have to get back on your right path."

Right path… my path… this isn't supposed to be about my path?
"Now, listen closely to this poem," Dr. Karanza continued:

Faith guides my action
Blind to the world in front of me
Moving through thought
Finding my way without physical traction
I live to complete my journey
Forward to the end
Mindless of reaction

Circles mark my path
Moving forward yet never learning
Traveling towards myself
Yet farther away I keep moving

Obstacles that block my way
They look so familiar
Placed there some other day
Images seen and forgotten again
I move on
Searching for myself in vain

Circles mark my path
Moving forward yet never learning
Traveling towards myself
Yet farther away I keep moving

Looking back it looks the same
Turning nothing changes
Keeping up seems the thing
Faster I keep pacing
Faith is showing the way
The end I am seeking

Circles mark my path
Moving forward yet never learning
Traveling towards myself
Yet farther away I keep moving

Changes follow movement
Having faith that things move
I have faith I will find myself changing
As long as I keep moving

Circles mark my path, moving forward yet never learning, traveling towards myself, I only move farther away from myself and towards a new beginning.

Charlie continued to paint. Kaitlin had begun to slump over in her chair a little, leaning forward with glazed over drooping eyes, still listening—as Dr. Karanza stopped reading and looked up at her, to say, "You're moving in circles Kaitlin. You are not progressing. Something is holding you, keeping you from finding happiness. You should open up Kaitlin. Tell me what is holding you back. What are you hiding?"

Like a spring welling up from the ground, Kaitlin's mind opened, filling with long lost memories of her family—even memories that were long forgotten.

16

AS KAITLIN'S MEMORIES filled up her mind—her mouth spewed them out. "My grandfather moved to this area along with the railroad," she spoke slowly, methodically, her warm breath misting.

Charlie continued making slow methodical paint strokes, oblivious to anything else around him.

"His name was Benjamin Whitcomb. His father was a wealthy doctor from Atlanta. A hospital was named after him. Gregory does surgeries there still."

"Yes I know... I've been to that hospital many times," Dr. Karanza whispered back. Tell me more about your grandfather Ben."

Kaitlin's head bobbed slightly, her eyes refocused.

"Well... according to my father... Ben and his father started investing in property where the railroad was going to lay down tracks. They bought up large pieces of property all over this area of Georgia. They were always hatching schemes, business ventures... with most of them ending up miserable failures. But then Ben met two local families who owned and operated the local cotton Mill here in town. Have you seen it doctor?"

"No, but I intend to soon. Please continue," Dr. Karanza urged her.

"As fate would have it, they needed Benjamin's help badly, and that's why they invited him to become a joint owner in the Mill. At that time, they were not able to transport the cotton and textiles to the bigger cities. They couldn't compete with the other, larger, more established Mills. The ones in the towns closer to the cities had reliable rail links that poor little ole Milledgeville didn't have. They needed a rail spike. Without it, they had to continue transporting everything by horse drawn wagons… until they started using trucks. They were on the verge of going under when Benjamin arrived. Saved their asses," she giggled, "saved the Mill… an answer to their prayers. They never would have gotten a railroad line built way out here without him. Ben convinced the rail company to build a short line that would run right past the Mill. It was just a few more miles of track to connect to the main North-South line leading all the way up to Atlanta." The ends of her lips curled up with a devilish grin. "They could make a fortune out of that Mill now." Gesturing her hand in a circle, she explained, "This whole area is surrounded with some of the best cotton fields in the country. And full of some of the poorest people too… dying for any steady paying job. They would take anything, even for the lowest wages they could find—like what we pay at the Mill."

"Oh, I see," Dr. Karanza whispered.

"Benjamin and his father invested a large amount of money to retrofit the old machines… new looms, modern feeders, spindles… new everything. They completely modernized the old Mill. It was like new again. For his share, Benjamin got a one-third ownership interest. Plus, he made the other two owners sign agreements that if they died, he, and the other surviving owner would get their share outright. They all agreed to pay their surviving families some support money if they were to die of course. So Ben moved here and fell in love with this place. He enjoyed the country life… tired of the bustle of the big city in Atlanta… and tired of his father controlling him. So… he bought this house along with over a hundred acres.”

Kaitlin nearly nodded off—her voice lisping.

“Very interesting… please tell me more,” Dr. Karanza whispered some more encouragement.

“Ben never intended to own and run a cotton Mill. My father said he felt tied down by it, made him feel trapped here, smothered, eaten up with responsibilities he never intended to take on. This little community relied on the Mill for most of the work, taxes, and all that shit! Now I know how he felt… with all the pressure… everyone expecting you to take care of every god-damned thing!”

“Kaitlin,” Dr. Karanza chimed in, “try and focus on your family dear. You were telling how they improved the Mill.”

Kaitlin leaned back in her chair and paused. Her eyes rolled back in her head a little as if she was forcing her eyelids up. As her eyes rolled back down to look a Dr. Karanza, she smiled softly, and continued talking.

“Turned out Ben was the youngest by far of the three owners… probably his plan all along. It wasn’t long at all till the first owner died in an accident. He was actually crushed by one of the new rail cars—totally ironic right?” She chuckled. “He needed the railroad to save his Mill… and it ended up killing him… so he lost it all anyways. Apparently the railcar got unbuckled somehow and it rolled. He was in between the two cars. They say he lived for a few days… being all crushed and mangled.” Her eyes shut and reopened. Scrunching her lips, she said, “The other owner who was the older one… well… he died less tragically… plain old heart attack. Just fell over dead.”

“So that’s how your family became the sole owners?”

“Yep,” Kaitlin smirked tilting her head on her lilting neck, “By mere coincidence. And he ran it for over thirty years till he died… left it to my father to run—” Her eyes were nearly shut as her voice trailed off.

"Go on," Dr. Karanza pressed her to go deeper. "Then what happened?"

"He tried hard… working so hard… late at night… almost every night," Kaitlin slurred, before she suddenly stopped talking.

She drifted into a dreamlike state where she remembered being a young girl, all alone, standing in the darkness on the work-floor of the cavernous cotton Mill. Wandering through the machinery on the floor of the Mill waiting for her father to finish for the night, a hulking middle aged man appeared in front of her, lurking in the shadows. He was dressed in dirty, oil stained overalls, with sweat running down his dirt spotted, unshaven oily face that was hidden behind a shadow cast by one of the looms. All of the lights in the Mill were turned off for the evening. His enormous torso was barely visible in the little bit of light escaping from her father's office doorway, and the soft moonlight that was seeping through the windows high up near the roof on the second story.

He stepped closer, staying hidden in the shadow. Tipping his dirty fingers, he beckoned for her to follow after him. Pointing with a finger, he gestured to the large wooden double doorway that opened up to the loading dock. Without making a sound, he motioned again for her to follow him outside. Grimacing, he appeared to be suffering in terrible pain. With wild starring bloodshot eyes, his black-stained rotting teeth were visible between his trembling lips. As if pleading, his jaws clenched down as his eyes widened with glaring impatience—as he anxiously gestured again with his outstretched hand for her to follow him outside.

Her tiny frame quivered as she took a step back, with her fingers squeezing deep into the squishy cotton stuffed doll in her arms. As she turned to run, the man lurched forward, reaching out to grab her, as his face flushed red with angry rage.

Bursting into tears she ran screaming into her father's office and leapt into his arms. She desperately tried to describe what she saw. He immediately jumped to his feet and left the office to investigate.

Tired, angry, and disturbed, her father soon returned, telling her that no one was there, and it was just her imagination running wild—once again.

"You're becoming as crazy as you're damn mother was," he scolded her. "I'm busy and it's late. Don't bother me again," he grumbled before returning to his paperwork. She stayed right there, cowering on the floor next to his desk until he was done—with her eyes glued to the office door.

"Kaitlin… come back to us. What are you thinking about?" Dr. Karanza called her back from her blurry haze.

Kaitlin pried open her drooping eyelids. She was looking at Dr. Karanza as if she were a frightened child again, waking up from a horrible nightmare. With quivering lips, she tried to say something, but couldn't.

"That's enough for tonight," Dr. Karanza said bluntly—replacing the dangling amulet book-mark inside the pages and snapping her book of poetry closed with a pop.

17

KICKING OFF HER shoes at the back doorstep, Kaitlin slid her bare feet across the slick wood floorboards—staggering like her father used to do when he was finished drinking for the night—heading for his room upstairs to sleep it off. Hardly able to lift her limp-noodle legs up, she managed to climb up the twenty blurring steps. Slipping out of her clothes, falling into bed, she collapsed, and drifted off to sleep in an instant.

As everyone else settled in for the night—the house was dark, silent, and cold.

"Mommy, why did you leave?" Kaitlin mumbled in her sleep.

"Don't you worry sweetheart, mommy is always nearby. Just sleep now. I won't ever leave you princess. I'll always be here sweetheart, waiting for you." Her mother answered softly while gently stroking her hair.

"I love you mommy," Kaitlin whispered as she reached over to touch her mother's arm.

Kaitlin's eyes cracked open to look up from her pillow. In horror, she saw that her hand was resting on the arm of a recently deceased person—with gray rotting skin covered in oozing sores. Her jagged fingernails were cracked, gray, and black. Looking up, she could see her mother's face smiling down at her, with rotten black and green teeth and grayish pale skin that was covered with thousands of black streaks as if all her veins and capillaries were filled with ink. Her rotting skin was covered with the same oozing pustules of puss as it decayed and peeled away.

Clamping her eyes shut Kaitlin covered her face with her arms. Squeezing tightly, she hoped it was a bad dream—that it would *just go away when she woke up*. The mattress lifted beneath her as someone got off the bed next to her. *This is not a dream!* She screamed inside with her eyes still shut. Jerking her arms back she bolted up straight. Her frantic eyes darted around the room. A shadow drifted along the far wall near the closet. The floorboards creaked. Glancing at the closet door, she could only see her coat hanging on the door-knob—gently swaying. A foul stench lingered in the damp air.

Shaking her head, Kaitlin tried to refocus. Very little moonlight could get inside her bedroom through the one window. Thick curtains covered it. They had hung there since she was ten years old. And she never opened them. The curtains were not there to dampen the light. They were hung to block out her view of Daniel's house. Heavier, thicker curtains—those made out of steel—would be hung over the window, if she could have found them. She couldn't ignore the eerie feeling of being watched through the veil of darkness as she lay her head back down on her pillow. Nor the stench of death that slowly left her. Gently running her hand across her arm, she attempted to replicate the feeling that woke her up—hoping it was just her imagination. *I knew this place would give me nightmares.*

With a glance at the clock on the bedside table (3:22 a.m.), she rolled over and shut her eyes. *Oh, why didn't I stay at the motel? And why the hell isn't Gregory here with me?*

"Kate." A woman's voice softly whispered to her. A creaking noise came from the bedroom door. She sat up again to see that her door was now ajar. *I shut it… I'm certain I did.* The floorboards in the hallway began creaking with the distinctive sounds of footsteps— moving down the hallway, just outside the room. Slipping out of

bed she slipped into a robe and scampered to the door. Slowly pulling it open, she peered down the dark and empty hallway to see only blackness.

I should check on Charlie. Walking quickly to Charlie's door at the end of the hall, she turned the doorknob—it was locked. She shook it again—gently—trying to jiggle it open. It still wouldn't open. Another creaking sound came from behind her, near Paul's room. Kaitlin spun around but couldn't see anything. Tip-toeing back down the hallway, she stopped in front of Paul's room. His door was slightly ajar. Again, she heard the distinctive sounds of footsteps on the creaking floorboards inside Paul's bedroom. *Asshole! Not funny, scaring the hell out of me again*, Kaitlin thought as she pushed the door open, expecting to catch him sneaking around like a naughty little boy playing tricks.

"A-ha," Kaitlin bellowed as she burst inside. Her feet were planted firmly on the floor with her arms sticking straight up in the air and the door banged loudly against the wall.

To her utter dismay and absolute horror, the room was dark and quiet. Paul was in his bed—snoring. Half his face was peeking out from underneath his covers. One of his bare legs was sticking out, and it twitched a little as the door slammed into the wall.

Oh… shit! Kaitlin cringed. Making herself small, she started to shuffle back out of the room, quietly pulling the door shut behind her.

"Kaitlin… is that you?" Paul mumbled lifting his head with one eye tore open.

Caught—she stood straight up and whispered. "Yes, it's just me. I heard noises, and I thought I saw someone come in here. Is everything alright?"

"Yes, I'm fine… come-on in," Paul requested politely, batting both eyes awake.

She hesitated, but not for long. *I don't really want to go back to my room… all alone.*

"Mind if we talk for just a minute Paul?" Kaitlin asked shyly while shutting the bedroom door. Before he could process the proposal and answer her, she gingerly walked over to the edge of his bed. Sitting on the edge, she leaned closer to him, so that he could see her face in the soft light, and said, "I'm really glad you're here with us Paul. This has been terribly emotional for all of us. I'm having a hard time dealing with all of this stress right now." She covered her face with her hands, as if to hide.

"Just relax," Paul said reassuringly. Sitting up, he began massaging Kaitlin's stiff shoulders and neck. Kaitlin exhaled a deep breath and moaned. Her hands, arms and shoulders dropped, going limp at once, as her body melted beneath his healing hands. An overwhelming feeling of release swept over her as his strong hands caressed her cold, tense, hard muscles, slowly kneading them into warm, melted, soft, putty. Moving down her neck and over her shoulders, his fingers slowly drifted down her back, deeply rubbing every muscle that begged for attention.

She silently moaned, shifting her body to make herself more available to him. *It's as if he is part of me… knowing just where to touch me… making me feel so incredible.* Like a genie being coaxed from her bottle, his amazing hands were rubbing her just the right way, igniting a passion that was building with pressure, building and building, until she couldn't stop herself from escaping the emotional cage that was holding her. "Oh God, that feels sooooo good," she purred. She could feel herself letting go—giving in.

"Should I stop," Paul whispered in her ear. His hands froze on her lower back, as he waited for her permission.

Turning her head, Kaitlin looked deeply into his eyes, to let him know, "No, Don't stop. I need you."

Moving in close, they began to breathe the same breath as they stared longingly at one another—until she could not restrain herself. She pressed her lips hard against his mouth—kissing him with unrestrained passion. Their desires flared into a raging burning flame as they tasted one another. With her body burning with a feverish

yearning, she tore her lips away from his mouth, just long enough to stand up—letting her robe slip away from her naked body.

Paul's heart was now pounding, his chest heaving with heavy breaths, as he flipped back the bed covers like a toreador facing a charging bull—revealing his nakedness.

Kaitlin climbed on top, straddling him, completely giving in to her passions, kissing him hard and deep thrusting her body against his with wild abandon.

Both of them were feeling electricity moving through every inch of their bodies as their excitement grew into a roaring flame of ecstasy. At the point of full arousal, each of them wanting to explode with anticipation, she maneuvered herself so that he could enter her. With waves of exhilaration moving through her body, her heart pulsed violently inside her chest, pounding with growing, aching—anticipation!

Paul slowly pushed himself up, deep inside of her, and then slowly pulled himself away, over and over again—moving faster each time—until he was thrusting into her with fast pounding repetitions—filling her with his pulsating manhood until her entire body began quivering uncontrollably as her entire mind and body became enraptured within a cascading euphoric orgasm that seemed to never end. Gasping for air, she squeezed down hard on his clenched chest muscles as he continued to thrust himself inside of her—rolling her eyes back in her head.

Slowly Kaitlin began to return to reality as rolling orgasmic waves slowly relented in their intensity—with tingling sensations crawling over every inch of her body. Catching her breath she was able to realize what was about to happen—she pushed hard against Paul's chest, trying desperately to lift her body up and away from his pulsing erection before it erupted inside of her. It was too late. His face strained with pleasure as he continued ramming himself deep inside of her at the point of exploding—he was lost in his own orgasmic rapture—with his hands grasping her hips, holding her

firmly in place on top of him. Quivering uncontrollably, he released his seed deep inside of her.

An image of Gregory lying under her suddenly popped into Kaitlin's mind. *No; this isn't right… I have to stop this now.* Overwhelming feelings of guilt replaced her orgasmic delight. Paul's gripping hands relaxed as the waves of ecstatic contractions subsided.

"No! Forget this happened… this shouldn't have happened!" Kaitlin groaned.

Pulling herself away from Paul's embrace, she leapt to her feet and grabbed her robe from off the floor. Cinching it tightly around her, she headed for the bedroom door. Without looking back, she said to him, "Just go back to sleep… I'll see you in the morning," before closing the door behind her.

Idiot! What the hell were you thinking… you seriously screwed up! She scolded herself on the way back to her room—while almost simultaneously another voice in her head was telling her, *you deserved it… you shouldn't feel guilty… Gregory has screwed a million little whores… he's off fucking pretty little Cynthia right now!*

As Kaitlin was scurrying passed her father's bedroom door, she noticed a strange glowing light underneath the doorway. *The fireplace… it looks just like when father would have a fire going?* Kaitlin thought as she stopped to watch the flickering glow. An acrid whiff of smoke hit her nostrils as small puffs of white smoke wafted into the hallway. *Shit… she probably didn't open the flue… she's going to fill the whole damn house with smoke!*

The doorknob was hot. Flinging the door open there was a roaring fire in the fireplace. Glancing over at the bed, it was empty—Emily was gone. Her father's high-back lounge chair had been pushed across the floor so that it was positioned directly in front of the fireplace. She could just make out the faint outline of a person seated in the chair. *What the hell is she doing?*

"Up a little late… aren't we Doctor?" Kaitlin growled her disapproval. Stepping closer to the chair to confront Dr. Karanza—she froze in place—seeing that her father was sitting there. He was

holding his cane in one hand. She instantly recognized the gold ring with a garnet stone in the finger of his emaciated and liver spotted hand. He lifted the handle of the cane that was made of brass and formed into the shape of a horse's head—pointing it towards the fire. She couldn't move, or speak, as her father's trembling hand move the brass handle into the raging flames inside the fireplace. Her gaping eyes watched as the brass handle rapidly heated until it was glowing, red hot.

Forcing her feet to slide on the floor, she moved in front of the chair—to where she could see all of him. The firelight made a glowing dance on his oily unshaven face. His eyes drifted deeply into the leaping flames with a maniacal, piercing, stare.

"Father?" She muttered.

He kept his eyes looking straight into the fire, staring intently at the horse-head handle as it dangled in the flames. Droplets of sweat beaded up on his balding scalp as the flames grew higher, the room getting hotter. Swaths of perspiration soaked onto his pajama top that was torn open, exposing his gray-haired chest.

"Father… what are you doing?" Her shaky voice whispered.

His hand swung the cane up, putting the handle right up close to his eyes. Staring hard at the glowing red-hot brass handle, he grimaced and said, "She tricked me Kate. She tricked all of us." His trembling hand slowly moved the scalding red-hot handle down—stopping at his sweat dripping, heart pounding chest. Singed hairs sent up a small puff of foul smelling smoke. Forcing the horse-head handle against his skin, his jaws clinched with his teeth grinding to the point of shattering. His flesh bubbled and flayed away as the scorching handle pushed in, sizzling up a foul smoke. The veins in his neck bulged out to the point of exploding as his back wrenched into an agonizing arch—every inch of him fighting back the pain—swallowing back his agonizing scream.

Kaitlin felt herself becoming dizzy, nearly fainting. But she couldn't turn away as she watched him in horror.

Sweat poured from almost every pore on his body, running down his scalp, saturating his clothing, moving down his body and dripping to the floor like a small flood. Sticking to the handle, his skin peeled away as he pulled the cane away—leaving him scarred—with the branded image of the horse-head handle. Looking down at his charred flesh clinging to the metal handle—he smiled. Staring into the leaping flames once more, his shaking hand slowly moved the cane back to the fire, returning the brass handle to the flames—where it began to glow red hot once again. The rank scent of his burnt flesh filled the air.

Kaitlin's eyes followed the handle back inside the licking flames. A face suddenly appeared, leaping about, moving from side to side. Its flaming eyes glared up at her, before leaping across the fireplace to face her father. Tiny fingers of flame reached out to grasp the brass handle—swirling around—until it began to glow red-hot again. Her father looked up at her smiling maniacally, and whispered, "She'll find you too… but don't let her trick you too Kate."

With one quick motion he swung the cane over at her—sticking the glowing red-hot brass handle just an inch from her face—singeing the tips of her eyelids and eyebrows. Jerking her head back she swung her arms up violently, swatting the cane away just as the scorching handle lightly touched her cheek. It flew out of her father's hand and landed on the floor.

In a blind rage, she screamed, "go to hell you bastard!" Charging at him, she reached out for his neck with both hands. Grasping him around the throat, she squeezed with mad-man strength, cinching her fingers like a vice. With his old decrepit body, he feebly fought back, desperately prying at her chained-together fingers that were tightly wrapped around his neck. As they fought, his chair tipped backwards. "I'm going to kill you!" She screamed. Filled with a sudden surge of adrenaline she threw all of her weight against her father, flipping the chair back. With her hands still firmly wrenched around his neck, they spilled out onto the floor.

"Kaitlin… Kaitlin… Stop it… Kaitlin… please—" Dr. Karanza chocked out of her clamped throat.

Finally hearing her voice, Kaitlin opened her eyes to find herself straddling Dr. Karanza—both of her hands firmly gripping her slender neck.

"Please... let go," Dr. Karanza gagged.

Kaitlin released her grip and threw herself across the floor—backing herself up against the wall like a cowering animal.

Dr. Karanza sat up, rubbing her throat, and scooting back up against the bed, eyeballing Kaitlin as she readied herself to make a run for the door.

Kaitlin wrapped her arms tightly across her body and started quivering. Her eyes were darting erratically around the room.

To Dr. Karanza, she had taken on the appearance of one of her old patients. An army private suffering from PTSD—he was shell-shocked out of his mind from having been tied down in a fox hole for hours as bombs pounded his buddies to pieces all around him—now avoiding most human contact, he was constantly afraid, unsure of where he was, and expecting to be attacked and killed at any moment.

"Is everything all right in here?" Paul called out, as he stepped inside the room.

Kaitlin was staring at the overturned chair. She didn't even seem to notice him.

"Yes... I'm fine... everything's fine?" Dr. Karanza responded as she pulled herself up onto the bed. "I fell asleep while reading... sitting in front of the fire," she explained in a raspy voice. "Kaitlin was choking me. I woke up and she was on top of me. We struggled and fell over. She must have been sleepwalking."

Dr. Karanza and Paul simultaneously looked over at the overturned chair, and then back over to Kaitlin. Watching her silently—her eyes were still darting back and forth across the room, until she noticed them staring down at her, with looks of suspicious bewilderment. The expressions on their faces brought back a flood of bad memories, and there accompanying ill feelings. It was that same exact expression of suspicion and judgment she had seen on the faces of her father, brother, teachers and classmates, on almost a daily basis since when she was a child.

"No… no… everything is not alright! It's fucked up, is what it is!" Kaitlin lashed out at them, looking like a wounded and cornered animal. "It's happening all over again. You don't understand… you can't understand… I never should have come back here!"

"What's happening again?" Dr. Karanza demanded.

"My insane visions… it's all happening again just like when I was a girl… before my father sent me away," Kaitlin mumbled, lowering her head down so that her hair fell over her face.

"No… this is good… I believe this is a breakthrough dear," Dr. Karanza tried to console her as she slipped off of the bed and knelt down next to her. "We need to explore your thoughts… these visions." She gently wrapped her arms around Kaitlin and gave her a reassuring hug. "Kaitlin… Its O.K. to be afraid… use this experience… let me help you. Tell me what you saw Kaitlin."

"Tell us," Paul suggested softly, trying to help reassure her without intervening.

Kaitlin lifted up her head slightly, peering through her dangling knotted hair with red tear stained eyes, and she began speaking like a sullen child. "I saw him… my father… in his chair—" She paused to look up at Dr. Karanza and Paul. *They'll think I'm crazy… just like everyone else. Gregory will find out I'm having those visions again. No one never really believed me. Now, they will all be right… I am crazy.*" Her lips quivered as she held back the words she desperately wanted to say.

"Please Kaitlin… it's very important that you tell us. We must know," Dr. Karanza insisted.

"He was there… right there… my father… I saw him in that chair… holding his cane," Kaitlin muttered, pointing over to the overturned chair. A large round blood stain was still visible on the back cushion of the chair. Stained at the point where the bullet had torn through her father's body. "He was burning himself with the handle of that cane," she said, pointing to the corner of the room.

"He tried to burn me too." Tears welled up in Kaitlin's eyes and flowed gently down her cheeks as she spoke.

Paul and Dr. Karanza glanced to the corner of the room— nothing was there.

"It's O.K., you're safe now. Help us understand what's happening to you," Dr. Karanza said in a soft, comforting voice while rubbing her back. "Everything you saw is important. Trust me dear, you need to explore each and every thought, every event, every detail, nothing is unimportant."

"It started when I was young… six… seven… I'm not sure. All I can remember is that something terrible happened to me in the barn. Ever since then, I had visions," she continued, sniffling and fighting back tears as she spoke. "I barely remember. I was lying on the floor inside the barn. My parents leaning over me, kneeling down next to me, holding my arms and legs, and my mother… she was pouring a foul tasting medicine into my mouth from a glass vile. Daniel was there, standing in the back, in the dark, watching us. I blacked out right after. They said I drank something poisonous when I was playing around inside the barn. They said I was in a coma for a few weeks. Mother said she gave me the antidote that saved my life. Soon after that I started having visions."

"Yes… go on dear," Dr. Karanza urged her, rubbing up and down on her back.

Kaitlin paused to wipe her runny nose and weeping eyes with the sleeve of her robe, before she continued. "That's why father sent me away to that boarding school. He didn't believe me. He didn't want to hear about my problems… my insane visions. He said I was crazy."

"What did you see?"

"I saw my mother mostly… after she died. It wasn't long before I had a reputation in this little town for being a freak. I didn't have any friends growing up. I hid myself in this house. Charlie was my only friend. The only person who I think actually believed me… I think? Eventually I would only tell Charlie what I was seeing and hearing. He was the only one that didn't judge me, or call me names, or make me feel like I was crazy all the time."

"Why did your father send you to boarding school?"

"That disgusting bastard Daniel is why," Kaitlin moaned. "He tried to rape me in the woods out by the barn. And of course, when I told my father, he didn't believe me… no one ever believed me… just another vision." Throwing her arms up, she almost began yelling, "He said that was the last straw… he couldn't take any more of my lying and making trouble for everyone because of my mental illness. He said it was for my own good, that I needed help… professional help!"

Dr. Karanza was silently analyzing her; *inherited Schizophrenia traits exacerbated by extreme panic attack disorder induced by physical assault.*

"Now it's starting all over again." Kaitlin lowered her head and began sobbing.

"Let's just get to bed dear," Dr. Karanza whispered. "We have a lot to get done and we need our rest."

Paul stepped over to her and put out his hand to help her stand. Kaitlin took his hands and he pulled her up. Without looking him in the eye, she quickly, and quietly, slipped through the open doorway and disappeared down the dark hallway. Paul and Dr. Karanza stared at each other in silence as if looking for clues, or for answers in the other's expression. It was obvious that they both wanted to speak—but they held their tongues until they heard Kaitlin's bedroom door latch.

"This is good… she is responding just as I expected," Dr. Karanza whispered.

"How was that good?" Paul responded fighting to keep is voice down. "Just what the hell are you doing to her doctor?"

"Treating her is what I'm doing," Dr. Karanza snapped back, "exactly what I'm supposed to be doing. And I suggest you stick to what you are supposed to be doing. And stay out of my way."

"I thought you were brought here to treat Charlie—not Kaitlin?"

Dr. Karanza glared up at him, without an answer.

"And I know you have been giving her Charlie's medication."

She looked away from his accusing stare. "Yes… that's right… it seems appropriate under the circumstances."

Paul leaned closer to her, and whispered, "I was listening to your little *therapy* session. I could hear you through Charlie's window. Poetry my ass! I know enough about hypnotic suggestion to know you were putting her under some kind of mind altering spell."

Dr. Karanza ignored him. She silently stared into the fireplace, watching the flames slowly dying.

Paul poked at her to try and stoke a response. "You're using some kind of mind control… so you can manipulate them… right?"

After a few tense moments of silence, Emily looked up at him, staring him straight in the eye. "You're one to make accusations. Apparently you certainly know a thing or two about taking advantage of someone. It appears that you and Kaitlin are getting along very well—very well indeed. Should I say more?"

Paul's eyes dropped to the floor like a scolded puppy.

"Tend to your patient nurse," Dr. Karanza curtly dismissed him.

Paul turned and left the room.

18

KAITLIN THREW HER bedcovers away. She couldn't stand to be in the bed for one more second. Constantly tossing, her mind relentlessly racing, it was impossible for her to get any sleep anyway. With frantic thoughts spinning around as if a needle was stuck in a scratch on an antique record player—continuously skipping back to the beginning of the same old song which played over and over again—tormenting her.

As the first rays of sunlight fell through the window, she stood in front of her full sized dressing mirror to examine herself. It was time to face who she was, and what was really happening. Accepting that she was having delusions was the first step, before considering that there was something else, something more; *Maybe Charlie is having visions like me? He could be hiding it? Of course… he saw what happened to me, so he would be too afraid to say anything. It has to be true? He wouldn't kill his wife, his father, or his own child!*

Her eyes were swollen and bloodshot. Deeply set dark circles under both eyes. Matted hair sticking out in all directions, wrapped up in a white robe that looked like something an inmate would be forced to wear in an insane asylum. It was her reflection forcing her to face the realization that; *Dr. Karanza won't ever believe me, or Charlie. She will think that we're both just crazy. She'll say that we both must have killed*

them. *They'll medicate us until we can't think at all, and then she'll just put us both away… case closed.*

Just stop it! Get a grip! She yanked herself back. *I didn't kill anyone… and neither did Charlie.* Tearing off her depressing robe—a change of plan was needed. *I've got to find some answers… since no one else is going to help us. I won't let that conniving bitch lock us away in prison or some nut-house.*

While getting ready; she noticed that the words of Dr. Karanza's poems were being repeated in the back of her mind, like the words of a memorable song that won't stop repeating inside your head until you have started singing the song out loud.

> Changes follow movement
> Having faith that things move
> I have faith I will find myself changing
> As long as I keep moving
>
> New beginning.
> Moving forward yet never learning
> Traveling towards myself
> I only move farther away from myself and towards a new beginning.

That's it! I have to stop running away. Stop ignoring my problems and face them once and for all! She considered as she hastily buttoned up her blouse. *Something happened to me here. Now it must be happening to Charlie too. There has got to be some reason, some rational explanation… because I'm not fucking crazy!*

Wracking her brain while applying a little make-up, she recalled that; *Mary wasn't the first… neither was mother. My first vision was… of… it was a man… the man in the Mill… yes… it was that man who was trying to get me to follow him outside onto the loading dock. That's it! I'll start at the Mill.*

Finished getting ready, she headed down the stairs, hoping to leave without anyone else taking notice of her departure. Stepping lightly as she made her way down the stairs, she glanced in all directions, peeking into the living room, kitchen doorway, and down the hall, making sure nobody else was around, before slinking across the foyer towards the front door.

She couldn't help but take notice of Charlie's easel and canvas propped up against the wall of the foyer. And she just couldn't resist the appeal of seeing what Charlie was painting for Dr. Karanza. *This should be good?* She chuckled. Tilting her head slightly, she squinted a little, trying to make out a clear image in the roughly applied smeared strokes of paint, made in poorly blended shades of blues, grays, dark greens, deep browns, and black—all melding together into an indescribable near monochrome mess.

Then, an image began to appear—slowly growing clearer the longer she stared into it; *Kind of Looks a little like the family graveyard… and, is that the outline of Daniel's house over there?* As her eyes moved across the canvas, back over to the graveyard, she noticed an oddly shaped dark-gray image that she hadn't noticed before. A woman, dressed in a black dress, standing in the graveyard, looking down at the ground—down at one of the graves. *It's her—not just my imagination.*

The sound of a thump and the floorboards creaking above her head caused Kaitlin to look up at the ceiling. *Karanza's up?* Her eyes immediately dropped back down at the painting. When her eyes landed back on the canvass, all of the images in the paint blurred together again—beyond any recognition. No graveyard, no house, and no woman—just smeared paint. *Wow… I really need some coffee. I'm still dreaming,* she considered as she stared at the picture. After a minute of staring at the picture she gave up. *Hell… what am I doing? This isn't even clear enough to be considered an impressionist painting,* Kaitlin thought with a dismissive smirk, before heading out the front door.

The parking lot at the Mill was completely empty, except for one very old blue Ford truck that was parked near the employee entrance at the far end. It was covered in large dents, with rust eating away

the metal where the faded paint had peeled away. Looking broken-down that old truck appeared to have been abandoned there. *Nobody's here yet*, Kaitlin pondered as looked across the empty spaces. *It's not that early?*

Getting out of the car she walked towards the white painted wooden door marked OFFICE in bold black letters. The door was locked. Then she realized that it was Saturday and the Mill was closed. It wouldn't be reopened for regular working hours till Monday morning.

Then, she remembered the spare key, left back at the house. *I just had to pick Saturday of all days. Well… I'm not going all the way back to the house… just to get a damn key!* Undeterred she began banging on the door. No one answered.

It was cold—getting colder with a thick wet morning fog drifting in. Shivering, she paced down the side of the building heading around the back corner over to the employee entrance. It was locked. Another few steps over was the loading platform. With a large concrete ramp, it allowed trucks to pull directly up to the over-sized double doorway—that was also locked. Now fuming, stranded in the cold, she remembered; *the emergency exit! I used to be able to pry it open just far enough to slip through… when I was younger… and much smaller.*

The emergency door was supposed to be left unsecured during working hours, but her father had never let the law get in the way of his business practices. He kept the doorway chained shut to keep out vandals and thieves. *It's probably still open?* Kaitlin thought as she grabbed the door-handle and tugged. Just as when she was a little girl, the door opened a few inches until the thin chain that was wrapped around the inside door-handle pulled taught—holding it closed. Yanking on the door only made the opening in the doorway an inch or two wider. That was just enough for her to slip her leg through. Sucking in a deep breath she squished into the opening—until her entire body finally popped through—where she flopped down on the floor like a marshmallow that had been forced through the tiny opening of a bottle.

It was very dark. Most of the light was coming through the crack in the door and the small windows on the second floor. And most of those had been boarded over after being repeatedly broken by thrown rocks by bored small-town delinquent boys. The remaining windows were covered in a thick film of dust. Precious little light got through for the cavernous sized Mill.

Kaitlin quickly made her way over to the closest light switch. Flipping it up, nothing happened. She flipped it up and down a few more times before she remembered; *Oh… that's right… they kill the breakers when nobody's here to prevent electrical fires.* Clear across the workroom was the door to the manager's office. *Father had said the office was on a different switch so he could keep his lights on to work late,* she recalled.

Inside the office she shut the door and flipped on the light switch. "Thank the lord above," she whispered as the florescent bulbs above her head flickered, slowly humming to life.

Oh hell, she thought as she looked around, seeing stacks of cardboard banker's boxes covered the middle of the floor like a small white mountain. *They're already shutting us down.* All of the boxes stuffed with financial records. The new temporary manager, the bankruptcy custodian, the I.R.S., along with the F.B.I., had all been busily piecing together the business records—all of it negative—showing an unexplainable precipitous fall in revenue over the last few years. Red streaks of ink underlined the declining numbers.

Flipping through the last remaining open ledger journal that had been left on her father's desk, it was quite evident that the Mill was in desperate financial condition, and getting progressively worse by the day. *It would have gone under anyway. Charlie couldn't have helped father turn it around. Hopefully the bankruptcy conservator can squeeze enough money out of selling the Mill to save the house for him.* Everything they had worked for was now stored in the characterless white cardboard banker boxes that were all neatly stacked in rows—waiting to be removed.

Her frustration grew as she opened each paper stuffed box. *It would take years to read all this meaningless shit! I'm looking for a needle in a haystack. No… worse… I'm looking for something, that I'm not even sure yet, what the hell that is, inside a haystack!* Kaitlin scolded herself, flopping down in an old squeaky swiveling office chair. *Ugh,* she groaned, flipping the lid off of another box. *Oh God, please let me find something… anything… any clue… anything that would lead me somewhere… anywhere… just some small sign.*

A distant banging sound rang out inside the Mill—metal clanking against metal.

Not moving, she listened for the sound. *It's probably my imagination… or some animal… another goddamned cat most likely. Or… heavens forbid… a rat.* Moments passed in silence. "Yuck… I can't handle seeing a nasty rat right now," she whispered as she glanced around the room, scanning the floor for any signs of the scampering fury rodent. Thump! Another banging sound rang out—this time closer to the office door. She jumped to her feet and quietly tiptoed to the door. Cracking it open, she peeked through the slender opening. *That was no rat,* she thought for a second before her thoughts turned to something more sinister. *Oh lord… what if it's a security guard or a cop? I don't want to go to jail… shit!* It took another few seconds before she realized; *Wait a second… I can be here if I want. We still own this fucking Mill. What an idiot I am.*

Throwing open the door she marched fearlessly out onto the work floor.

An eternity seemed to pass as she waited, staring out into the Mill that was shrouded in darkness—until something moved—casting small shadows as it moved towards her. She could hear the shuffling sounds of lazy footsteps, half-sliding over the dirt covered concrete floor. "Hello," she called out softly.

The shadowy figure stopped moving.

"Who's there?" She called out with a shaky voice.

The darkened figure started to move toward her—remaining hidden in the shadows.

A fearful realization gripped Kaitlin. She was standing in the exact same spot where she had encountered the angry beastly

man. And she suddenly felt as if she was that tiny young girl again. Standing in the light of the open office doorway—frozen—staring into the dark. Her stomach sank with her head starting to spin. *It's him… but what does he want?* Taking in a deep breath she tried to steady herself as the figure moved slowly closer to the light. "What do you want with me?" She muttered.

All she could see was the image of the man beckoning to her—wanting her to follow him outside—replaying in her mind. *He wants me to go outside… to see something? He's trying to help me?*

Then, a man stepped out of the shadows.

"Oh my God," Kaitlin gasped with relief. "It's just you." She recognized Fred, the head custodian.

With his graying afro and stubbly beard on his dark chocolate skin—his body completely covered up by a black long-sleeved janitor's jumpsuit. It kept him camouflaged in the shadows until he was right in front of her.

"What the hell you doin' here miss," He asked in his deep, rustic voice, seasoned over seventy-eight years.

"I'm sorry Fred… oh my… you sure scared the hell out of me," Kaitlin muttered.

"No shit lady… you scared the hell out of me too," he bellowed. "Now, you gunna tell me why you're in here before I call the police."

"Fred… it's me… Kaitlin Singleton… remember? She leaned forward to try and get more of her face in the light. "Charlie's sister… from Atlanta… William's daughter? I'm here to deal with the estate… closing the Mill and all that," she stammered to explain.

"Oh yea, you, we heard you'd be round here soon enough. Picked a damn fine time to show up… aint no one here sep't for me. Hell, I'm bout the only one that works around here anymore anyways," He grinned and chuckled. Now that y'all goin' to sell the Mill, most people done left… quit… moved on… mostly up to Atlanta where you is I expect. They done packed everything up. Gettin' ready to close this place for good… course, you know that now, don't you?"

Kaitlin just stood there—speechless—nervously smiling.

"Can I help you find somethin' miss," Fred asked, seeing the lost look on her face. "This place show aint gunna clean itself. I need to get back to work since they want everything out by Monday."

"Uh, well, yes, I do need some help locating some personal belongings, but all I could find in the office were stacks of business records."

Fred furrowed his brow, and said, "Yep, them bankruptcy people been here goin' through everything—boxing and stacking all day long. There's so much stuff been kept round here for years. You know what it is—exactly what you're lookin' for—cause I don't got no time to be rummaging around, looking through all them boxes with you."

"No, not really, just personal items—family stuff I guess?"

Scratching at the brittle gray stubble on his chin for a moment, Fred thought, and said, "Oh yea... I think I might know what you're lookin' for. They been puttin' all the old pictures and such in a locked closet so nobody would walk off with them. All that stuff been boxed up and waitin' for somebody to show up and get it... come on, follow me, I'll show you."

Kaitlin followed Fred as he slowly shuffled through the Mill, over to a small wooden closet door. Reaching into his pocket he pulled out a key chain ringed with jingling keys. "This is the only door in here that still uses a skeleton key. Makes it easy to find," he said with a generous smile. "They been storin' stuff in this little closet for years, like some kind of museum," he explained as he turned the lock, pulled the door open, and switched on the single light-bulb that was dangling from the ceiling on a bare wire.

Kaitlin pushed her way past him to get inside. "Thanks Fred," she said without looking back at him. "That's all I needed for now." She immediately started her rummaging as if he wasn't even there.

His smile drooped along with his demeanor with the abrupt dismissal. "Let me know when you're done so I can lock this door," he grumbled before shuffling away, disappearing back into the shadows of the Mill.

There were stacks of older cardboard boxes of differing sizes, browning with age, and covered with dust. Old photographs, litho-graphs, portraits and prints that had been removed from the walls and desks in the office, were all neatly stacked against the boxes on the floor. Most of them were lying in small lose stacks like paper, but a few, like the very large exquisitely done portrait of her grandfather in oil had been kept within their original ornately carved wooden frames. A sampling of odd diplomas and certificates of award were mixed in with the family paintings and photographs. Most of the cardboard boxes were filled with an assortment of envelopes, hand-written letters, personal notes, Birthday and get-well-soon cards, and hand-made gestures of good-will—kept as reminders of the generations of people who had worked at the Mill.

Kaitlin excitedly started sorting through the treasure trove of memorabilia, like a young child jumping into a sand box, digging her fingers through the piles of lose sand playing a pirate in search of lost gold.

Six hours quickly passed by and she had found nothing but lost memories—mostly of people she never knew. *What a waste of time this is*, she thought as she pulled another letter from another old tat-tered envelope, and began to read. *Oh… yea… I'm learning a lot about all these old dead people… and absolutely nothing about me… or what I need.*

"Ma'am… you almost finished in there… cuz I need to lock up," Fred's raspy voice echoed through the crack in the door.

Kaitlin glanced at her watch. *Oh shit… it's getting late.*

"Just a few more minutes… please?"

"Ten minutes—then we got to go," he grudgingly groaned back, "I got better things to be doin'."

She ignored the newer looking boxes, pushing them aside, to get at the oldest and most worn looking boxes that had been shoved way back into the corner of the room. Tearing feverishly through the

dusty brown boxes, she picked through the papers and photographs as fast as she could go, looking at each one for a mere second before tossing them onto the floor. Each empty box on top was thrown across the room—getting it out of her way—until she was looking down at the last remaining box.

She could hear the sound of the janitor's shuffling footsteps walking towards the closet door as she peered down inside the box. She readied herself for the prospect of being forced to abandon her search. *I'll just have to come back later if I get the chance.* Then the outline of a face caught her eye. It was a very old, black and white photograph, spotted and yellowing. Half of his face was sticking out, half-hidden beneath a pile of other old photographs, near the bottom of the box. *That's him… that's his face!*

It was a photograph of a group of people posing in front of the Mill. The Mill looked newly built and the people were dressed in turn of the century factory worker's garb.

She snatched it up and held it closely to her face. Squinting a little, she stared at his face. *Oh my God… he looks just like Daniel… when he was younger? That's the man I saw in the Mill that night. Maybe it's his father? But that is definitely his hat. It can't be him… it just can't?*

"Time to go ma'am," Fred grumbled as he pushed the door open and stepped inside.

"Who is this man—do you know him?"

"Well, let me see," Fred squinted and stared at it. "No ma'am, I don't know who that is. I aint been here all that long—little over twenty years is all now. Hell, that picture looks to be a hundred years old. You don't think I'm that old now—do you?" A large smile returned to his face.

"Of course not, but who do you think it might be then?" Kaitlin insisted, gesturing for him to take another look.

Fred relaxed his smile, took the photo from Kaitlin, furrowed his brow, and stared earnestly at the man's blurred face. "Hmm… well, I don't know who that man is, but I sure do know who that little girl is standing next to him. Maybe she can tell you who that man is?"

"Yes… I suppose… if she is still alive. Who is she then?"

"Louise Kimbrell, that's who that is," Fred answered, smiling even wider. "Longest working employee this place ever had, so I understand. Ever-time I seen her, she never would shut up bout this place. Always tellin' stories, and showin' us pictures. She really loved this place—she sure did. So sad… it nearly killed her when she found out we was closen' down. Louise was like the resident historian for this here Mill. I'm sure she knows that man alright. If she don't know him—nobody does."

"How do I find her Fred?" Kaitlin anxiously furrowed her brow—bracing for the answer—thinking that she was already dead.

Fred furrowed his brow too, to reply, "Funny thing though. Louise never showed me no picture of that man. Don't recall her ever speaking about him neither. That wasn't like Louise. If that man would'a worked here, she would'a said somethin' bout him. Aint no doubt in my mind, she would'a said somethin' bout him."

"Please, Fred, do you know where she lives? Just tell me."

Fred looked up at her with puzzled eyes, as if she shouldn't have to ask. "Same place she always was livin' at I suppose. Over on Willow Avenue—clear out on the other side of town."

"Thanks Fred, you've been a big help," Kaitlin said as she brushed passed him again—heading for the exit.

"Hope you find whatever it is you're lookin' for," Fred half-heartedly mumbled as he watched her disappearing into the dark shadows of the Mill.

19

IT WAS NOW late afternoon as Kaitlin sped down the winding two lane country road on her way to Louise Kimbrell's home on the other side of town. The day had passed quickly while she searched for answers at the Mill. Now, much like Charlie and Dr. Karanza, she too was running out of time to find some answers.

Kaitlin pulled into the driveway of the small unassuming forties era wood framed home. A brisk breeze made the January air was bone chilling as she stepped out of the car and walked towards the front door. She felt a little like a lost child as she knocked, standing on the doorstep, clutching the lapel of her coat to keep it closed while fighting with her wind-teased hair—trying in vain to keep it out of her face.

A woman's face appeared in the small window in the door. Hard and weathered, she had the skin of a sandstone boulder, rough and pitted from unrelentingly bracing against the elements for many years—making her appear much older than her fifty-eight years. Looking out at Kaitlin suspiciously, she cracked open the door just wide enough for Kaitlin to peer through. The woman's voice was as rough as her face. "What do you want?" She snarled.

"Hello, I'm Kaitlin and I need to see Louise Kimbrell… is she home?"

The woman's eyebrows and forehead furrowed, squishing her loose skin giving her the likeness of a Shar-Pei Dog. She paused in thought, and then asked, "Are you sellin' something?"

"No ma'am, I'm an old friend. Please, I really need to see her," she pleaded as she began to shiver with the frigid air blowing up underneath her overcoat.

"Come in quick then!" The door opened just wide enough for Kaitlin to squeeze through. "Got-ta keep the cold out," the woman said as she slammed the door shut. "I'm Tonya. I'm here looking after Louise right now. Sorry... I didn't catch your name... miss?" The hag of a woman informally introduced herself. She didn't offer a handshake, clinging to a damp rag in her hand. Her head was covered with frizzy graying hair that was pulled up in a bun. The apron was stretched around her Buddha-belly which poked way out underneath her soiled nylon floral pattern dress, that was worn and outdated—that should have been discarded many years ago.

"I'm Kaitlin Whitcomb... is Louise home?" Kaitlin asked again, just to make sure she was in the right place.

"Yea, she's still with us, if that's what you mean?" Tonya answered sarcastically. Her face remained void of any emotion, like a poker player, as if still waiting for Kaitlin to play her hand— revealing her true intentions.

"Where is she then?" Kaitlin asked sheepishly while rubbing her hands together to ward off the lingering chill.

"In her bedroom of course... where she always is," Tonya curtly nodded towards an open doorway. "But she's not well. She may not want company." Her hairy plump hands began to wring the dish-rag, as she looked Kaitlin up and down skeptically. "But you would know that... being her old friend and all?"

"Who's there Tonya?" Louise called out from her bedroom. Her voice was weak, dry, and raspy—in desperate need of a drink of water.

"It's me... Kaitlin Whitcomb... William's daughter." Kaitlin called back to her, before Tonya could open her mouth.

Tonya's brow drooped, wrinkling deep with resentment—but she held her tongue.

"C'mon in dear… let's have a look at you," Louise's cracking voice invited her.

Tonya rolled her eyes and sauntered back into the kitchen.

Kaitlin followed the voice and walked through the open doorway.

Louise was lying in her bed, covered from her toes to her chest with a thick hand-stitched quilt. Used crumpled-up sticky tissues littered the bed and night stand like big discarded cotton balls. A recently read and refolded newspaper lay on the bed next to her. Her glass of water, crackers, old rotary phone, and an antique lamp adorned the night stand, along with a half-completed crossword puzzle book with a pencil stuck inside the pages to mark her spot.

Louise's face was gaunt, white as bleached paper, and dotted with age-spots, moles, and fading freckles. What was left of her brittle white hair was unkempt and very thin, exposing parts of her scalp. Her hands and arms were thin and frail, barely wrapped beneath thinly stretched emaciated skin, making visible her bones, joints, and veins that shown through. The index finger on her right hand had been severed at the knuckle. On her left hand, the tip of her pinky finger was missing.

"Oh my look at you… just how old are you now child?" Louise asked with a warm smile, showing her unnaturally white and straight dentures.

"Forty-one," Kaitlin smiled back.

"No daughters then?"

"I don't have any children."

"You do have your mother's eyes though," Louise said softly, adding, "you look just like her—when she was your age."

"I understand that you worked for my father down at the Mill for many years?"

"Oh, where's my manners, go on, sit yourself down," Louise pointed to a chair in the corner. Kaitlin slid the chair over next to

the bed and sat down, not thinking to remove her coat. "I heard a little rumor that you were home. I was hoping that you would pay me a visit. Wasn't sure I could hold on too much longer."

Just who would have told her I was in town? Kaitlin wondered.

"Terrible what happened to your family Kate," Louise mentioned somberly. "I'm so sorry. I loved your mother and father very much."

"Yes, well in fact, that's part of the reason I'm here Louise."

"You're still havin' them visions... aren't you dear?" Louise interjected.

"What are you talking about—what visions?"

"You're father told me about you and them visions long time ago. No need to pretend with me. He told me all about how he tried to find a way to help you dear."

Kaitlin sat straight up, balling her fists. "Help me—by sending me off to that girl's prison?"

"He was out of options," Louise explained, "you were hysterical by that point... terrified by all of them visions and nightmares you were having most every night. You barely slept at all. He was frightened you would hurt yourself, or someone else, if he didn't send you there, away from all the stuff that reminded you of your mother. He said she wouldn't... uh, well, her memory... it wouldn't let you alone, not as long as you lived in that house."

Kaitlin looked down with folded arms and a pouting face—not wanting to remember.

Louise spoke sympathetically, "you know he came to me in tears. He was a beaten man by the time he decided to send you away. Broke down and told me he was sending you to that school. He was an emotional and physical wreck, with all the stress of running the Mill... with all us employees countin' on him... him working 12 to 16 hours a day without sleep with you keepin' him up. All he did was worry—all the time." Kaitlin fought back the urge to cry as she listened. "He loved you so much. It was so hard for him to watch you falling apart before his very eyes, with nothing he could do."

Nothing he could do? He could have believed me, instead of giving up on me and sending me away! Kaitlin thought as she thrust her hand down inside of her coat pocket to pull out the old photograph from the Mill. Shoving it in front of Louise's face, she bluntly asked, "Well what about this? This is no vision. Tell me, who is that man standing next to you?"

Louise stared at the face in the photograph for a moment, and then said, "I knew someday you would come back here lookin' for answers."

Kaitlin's eyes widened. "Yes, please, tell me, what's happening to me and Charlie?"

Louise gave her a stern look, and said, "You know your father and I worked together for many years. He came to trust me as a friend. He told me some things—bad things." Staring at the man in the picture, her voice softened as she recalled, "Oh yes… that is me alright. Such an innocent little thing I was. And that man is Daniel Collins, one of the original owners of the Mill, and a partner with your grandfather."

"That can't be?" Kaitlin muttered, shaking her bewildered head.

"Oh yes dear, that's Daniel all right. But he died in a freak accident at the Mill. Run over by a train car is what I was told."

Kaitlin leaned forward—staring intently into Louise's eyes, to say, "That cannot be Daniel. That's the man I saw in the Mill. He only looks like him. Daniel is not dead. He's still alive. He's been living behind our house since I was born."

Louise looked up at Kaitlin as if thinking; *Oh, you poor delusional girl.*

Kaitlin pointed at the man in the photo—pleading, "That's the man that has been tormenting me since I was a little girl. Now, I need to know why? You have to tell me everything you know about him and my father. Please Louise—you must help me."

Louise stared off into the distance in thought, and then said solemnly, "When you stir up the ashes, don't be surprised if you uncover some red hot embers down in there—ones that may burst up with flame to burn you dear."

Kaitlin leaned in close to Louise, shooting flames out of her eyes, and demanded, "No more damn secrets. Now—tell me everything you know."

Louise began talking in a distant, almost trance like voice, "Some-things people ignore—some they forget—and some things just aren't spoken of. After some time, those things not spoken of— they are both ignored, and then forgotten. Everyone chose to not speak of Daniel Collins after his death at the Mill, for good reason, and he was soon forgotten."

Looking back off into nowhere, Louise explained about how Daniel's family helped found this town. His father Osric homesteaded most of Blackshear County. Daniel was an only child and did not acquire his father's talent for farming, or anything of much use for that matter. But his father's cotton and the land needed for the Mill provided the perfect opportunity for Daniel to become a partner with the original financier of the Mill. His father was given half ownership in the Mill in exchange for the land to build it on. And they got a guaranteed cheap supply of cotton. Illness took Daniel's father soon after the Mill was completed. So, as it happened, Daniel was forced to give the remainder of his miserable life to its endless demands.

Louise smiled softly as she remembered being just a child when his father hired her to work in the Mill—her first job. Her own father was also a cotton farmer, and he knew Daniel's father—naturally. She spent the rest of her working days in that Mill. Working every job there was to do there at one time or another; slubber, drawing-in girl, spooler, twister, weaver, until finally her body had given its all. She recalled that her last position held at the Mill, "Was an office secretary for your father. These hands didn't get this way from punching a typewriter and answering a phone, no dear, these are the hands forged of hard labor. I gave a lot to that Mill." She poked

up her crooked and mangled fingers—showing that her pinky finger was now just a nub.

Louise took a heavy sigh, before telling how Daniel had lived such a sad life—one of his own making. "We all make mistakes in life dear, and Daniel, he made a life out of making mistakes." A large burly man, he was utterly devoid of social graces, raised-up by his farmer father with no woman around. Naturally he was just an uncivilized farm-boy that stayed that way the rest of his life. "Just look at him," she said pointing at the photo. That's just how I remember him being every day of his life; filthy overalls, unshaven and dirty, stinking of hooch."

Louise went on to explain how he had spent most of his time in the opening room, poor wretch, where the bales of cotton got dumped when they brought them into the Mill from the fields. They'd tear open the bales, pull out the cotton, and get it all moved on to the lappers on the floor. It was hot, dirty, miserable labor, reserved for those with Daniel's special mental acuity and temperament—like a stubborn ole mule.

He seemed to enjoy the work though. He certainly could out-work anyone else, no doubt about that. But he enjoyed making deliveries to Atlanta and Savannah much more. Not because it got him out of the opening room, oh no, he enjoyed the prurient pleasures that a big city could offer to such a hedonistic man.

The *wages of sin* was not idle preacher talk when it came to Daniel. His sinning cost him everything. To pay for his drinking, and gambling, and whoring, he petered away everything his father left him. He started selling his ownership interests to Andrews, who was all too willing to finance Daniel's insatiable appetite for debauchery, as long as he could get ownership away from Daniel. By the time Benjamin arrived, Andrews had acquired almost all of Daniel's remaining farmland and cotton crops.

Benjamin came along just at the right time for everyone. Daniel was out of land and money, and Andrews was desperate to turn a profit. Profits and sales were dropping like rocks to the bottom in a pond. They had plenty of cotton—that was certainly not the problem. No, they could weave the hell out of those looms night and day, and lord knows they had plenty of cheap labor to run them. What they didn't have was a way to transport the finished products to the bigger cities, where they could get a much better price—all because there was no rail line running into town. They were still relying on the old fashioned mule wagons, and later an old truck, military surplus supply wagon. Of course any day it rained hard, all these old clay roads round here turned to mud, making impassable bogs of sticky red clay.

Louise showed her awkward dentures again, smiling big as she remembered, "Those big city boys must have been laughing there asses off when they saw Daniel coming into town on that old horse drawn wagon, sportin' his overalls and spittin' chew, like some big dumb country bumpkin. Yep, your grandfather breathed new life into the Mill, and into this community. Everyone was so happy when we got the rail line built—it was truly a blessing."

In return; Benjamin got Andrews to sign away his inheritance rights to the Mill, including all the fixtures and machinery that Ben had bought. Andrews knew he could continue making money off his cotton, as long as the Mill stayed open. So, when Andrews died, which was soon after their deal was struck, Benjamin owned it all.

"Are you going to tell me what happened to Daniel Louise?" Kaitlin butted in, stating impatiently, "I already know all about my family history—what about Daniel?" "I am dear," Louise grumbled. "But it aint him you need to know about—it's Gitana."

20

L OUISE SNATCHED-UP A tissue from the bed cover to wipe her nose. Her eyes wandered the room. Kaitlin sat silently next to the bed, tensely waiting for Louise to give her something useful—anything. A clock ticking on the wall taunted her—tick-tock.

Louise finally continued speaking in her raspy dry voice, telling of how she remembered Daniel was gone on one of his deliveries to Savannah. Benjamin was talking in the office with the door open, complaining about him being gone for far too long, as usual. How they were losing more money because Daniel was probably off drunk, in some juke joint, gambling, or laid up with some whore, all while his deliveries were piling up to the roof. The rail line wasn't finished being run because of some political maneuvering over in Macon—they had to line the right politician's pocket to get the final permits they needed. So, for the time being, they had to rely on Daniel to keep making deliveries. And when he finally got back from Savannah, the real reason for his delay shocked everyone for miles around. Nobody could believe their eyes whenever they saw him sporting around town with a young girl by his side.

"Gitana Baillie is what she told everyone her name was. We didn't know what to believe. She couldn't have been much older than eighteen. Real ethnic looking—not like any girl you'd find living round these parts," Louise pointed out with a smirk. "Looked like an Indian girl to us, with thick long straight black hair reaching all the way down past her waist. She had deep chocolate brown eyes and dark olive skin. We knew she wasn't no Mexican by the way she talked, with a kind-of funny European accent of some sort. Wasn't no Spanish accent we ever heard? Why she was with gruff old Daniel, we just couldn't imagine. Talk was, he won her in a game of poker or bought her straight off a boat. But soon after they got to town, she just kind of disappeared for a while. We didn't see heads-or-tails of her for several months. He kept her pretty much hidden at his house, away from the pry-in eyes of the towns-folk and everyone at the Mill. If we asked about her he would just grunt, make some sarcastic remark, or just plain ignore us. He never did give anyone a straight answer bout how he got her to follow him home."

Soon the rails were laid right up to the loading dock at the Mill. Everyone acted like little children on Christmas. They had a write up in the paper and ribbon cutting by the mayor. What it really meant was more work, and more money for the business-men. Never-the-less, it was a very exciting time for the whole town. Nobody was more pleased than Benjamin, this was his baby, his creation, and he intended to make it pay.

Daniel was the only person in town that was unhappy. Oh no, he was not pleased a bit. The rail meant he was no longer needed for making deliveries. He would still make a run every now and then in the truck, but he spent most of his time in the Mill, slaving in the opening room day after day without a break. No more trips to the city. And unfortunately for Gitana, that also meant Daniel would be spending a lot more time at home—all alone with her.

Glancing over at Kaitlin like a child, with wonder still left in her eyes, Louise fondly recalled the day Gitana showed up at the Mill to work. She just seemed so out of place, like a fragile porcelain doll being sat out in the center of a bull ring.

"All us girls snickered and laughed behind her back, no one

thought she would last very long in the Mill. She soon proved us all wrong. Everyone was surprised watching her work, tough as leather, working in the summer heat like the devil himself—tough girl. And she caught on quick, eventually turning out to be one of the best weavers we ever had, hell, one of the best workers we ever seen, period."

The only reason Daniel let her leave the house was because he was so damn greedy and so damn bad with his money. Business at the Mill was booming when the rail was finished, just as Ben predicted. It was so good that there was plenty of work, but not enough people in town to keep up with it, so Daniel allowed Gitana to work at the Mill. He pretended he was just trying to help out with the worker shortage, but everyone knew he just needed the money for all his boozing and gambling. It wasn't long before we found out just how tough she really was. Daniel was such a horrible man. He treated her so badly. Constantly drunk, dirty, and full of anger at something, or someone. He would berate her right in front of all of the employees, pull her hair, pushing and kicking her like some mangy ole dog. She would show up covered with bruises, scratches, torn clothes, all from his regular beatings. And lord knows he was jealous. No man had better be seen looking at her, let alone talking to her, if he was around. He would go into such a rage if he even thought that she might be thinking of another man.

"Gitana was as quiet as a church mouse for a very long time, didn't seem to want to talk to no one. We didn't know if she was so quiet because she was embarrassed about Daniel, bout her bad English, or just plain unsociable. We kept at her till she opened up. Then she was talking up a storm—whenever Daniel wasn't around that is. And oh the stories she would tell, keeping us girls entertained for hours upon hours while we worked. It was a blessing having her stories. Tedious work in this small town, that's all the life most of us ever knew you know; wasn't any television or radios going all the time to keep us distracted. At least we weren't constantly reminded of what we didn't have."

The most amazing story Gitana ever told, was the one about how she came to live in this little town. Gitana talked about how she was born in a horse drawn carriage, on a dirt road, on the outskirts of Paris, France. Her whole family were gypsies. For generations they had roamed from town to town, moving all across Europe. Vagabonds—miscreants—they were endlessly wondering in search of food and money, always feeling alienated and afraid without a true home to call their own. Earning money anyway they could, mostly by entertaining people in the small towns, like this one, using trained animals to do tricks, telling fortunes, selling magic coins and beads, or just plain ole stealing like drifters—if the right opportunity presented itself. Making camp for a few weeks at a time until the towns-folk would grow tired of them, and run them off.

Gitana would sing and dance for the town-folk who gathered up around a big ole bon-fire at their camp after it got dark. All done-up in hand-made dresses, covered up from head to toe in jingling trinkets, bright linen scarves, and tiny bells, they glittered chimed as they swayed and swirled around in the firelight, dancing all night long as the men played and sang. Gitana said it was her favorite time of all, when she could dance underneath the moonlight, let herself get lost in the music and forget about the cares of the world.

Louise looked at Kaitlin with a little frown, and said, "Oh we girls would beg her to dance and sing for us down at the Mill, but she never would. She was always too afraid. There was only one time that she dared to show us some of her strings of coins, jewelry, and a beautiful dress, that snuck to the Mill in a tiny box. Gitana made us swear that we would tell no one, especially Daniel. He threatened to beat her good if she showed any of her stuff to anyone. In fact, she was not even supposed to tell us who she actually was, or where she came from. But Gitana just couldn't resist telling us girls."

Her mother, Lala, would tell fortunes and do magic tricks. People would be coming from all over to hire her to break a dreaded curse put on them, or to put a hex on someone that crossed them.

Or, she would make for them a special potion to cure illnesses and such.

Gitana's father had no interest in their gypsy ways. He was a horse trainer from when he was a child. His own father taught him, and he became exceptional at training horses; so much so, that he was very sought after. He was constantly being requested by wealthy families, dignitaries, even royalty, to help them train their horses. He started training horses for a very wealthy man named James Urquhart, who lived up in Scotland. So, they all moved to the small town sitting right up on the edge of the highlands. A place called *Rock Bridge.* Where there was nothing but a bunch of simple farmers and sheep herders, trying the best they could to just eke out a meager living.

James Urquhart was the descendant of Scottish Nobility. Inheriting a castle built sometime in the Fifteenth Century. He remodeled and expanded it, turning it into a lavish manor house that dwarfed all the other homes. James was a large boisterous, pompous man. His wife, Margaret, was as vicious and spiteful as she was beautiful. Together with their only daughter, they enjoyed a lifestyle as big and imposing as the manor house they lived in.

James had his hand stuck deep down in all the goings-on in *Rock Bridge.* Most of the townsfolk worked either directly for James, or they, in some way, owed their livelihood to him. He controlled nearly everything.

Kaitlin's fidgeting grew worse when she glanced up at the clock, realizing how much time had passed. "This is a nice story Louise," she grumbled, "but what exactly does this have to do with me seeing Daniel at the Mill?"

"You youngen's aint got time for living… runnin' here and there… like chickens with their heads cut off," Louise scowled. "You'll find what you're lookin' for—if you can just be patient child. I'm telling you everything you need to know. You're gunna have to just sit there and listen."

Kaitlin's head drooped down in submission, whispering, "Yes, I'm sorry… please forgive me Louise—please continue."

Before Louise could say another word, a familiar voice called out to Kaitlin, very softly—as if coming from a far distance.

"I see you… Craaazeee Kateee."

Kaitlin shuttered and lurched back in her chair. Her head spun hard toward the open bedroom doorway—*Mary?*

"Is everything alright dear?" Louise asked nervously

"Did you hear someone?" Kaitlin replied, glancing around the room.

"No dear. Probably just Tonya getting on-ta the cat again… they truly do hate each other with a passion."

A shadow drifted past the open doorway. Kaitlin stiffened and clenched down on the seat cushion of her chair.

"Oh my… you are as jumpy as that cat," Louise snickered.

As the room quieted, they could hear Tonya clearing her dry throat over the sounds of the clinking dishes that she was washing in the sink.

"Tonya just startled me, that's all," Kaitlin murmured, "I forgot she was here—please continue your story Louise."

Louise cleared her throat and gathered her thoughts, trying to remember where she left-off—as Kaitlin's eyes nervously darted back and forth between Louise and the doorway.

A girl's voice screamed out again—from right outside, "Crazy Katie—I see youuuuu!"

Kaitlin jumped to her feet—breathing heavy she stared at the open doorway.

With Mary's voice taunting her. "Hey Crazy Katie… guess who's back?"

It is Mary! Kaitlin raised a clenched fist to burst through the doorway expecting to find Mary.

A calico cat lurking in the foyer arched its back, hissing with angry surprise up at her—before scampering off into the kitchen.

No one else was there.

"Oh Katie—don't leave. Come back and let me finish. I'll try to finish quickly, I promise," Louise called for her to stop.

Tonya burst into the foyer gripping a broom handle firmly with both hands to confront Kaitlin. Eyeballing her, she called out, "Everything alright Lou?"

"Everything's fine Tony… just some touchy nerves is all," Louise cackled back.

Tonya squeezed her grip on the broom handle, while murmuring to Kaitlin. "You'd best not be makin' her upset. She's dyin' of cancer and she aint needin' to be upset right now."

"No; I, I, I just—," Kaitlin fumbled back, looking startled and lost.

Tonya didn't give her time to explain. "She don't need to hear about your ghosts right now." Her nubby fingers squeezed the broom handle even tighter—like a batter readying to swing.

Oh no… oh God… she thinks I'm insane, Kaitlin realized as she stared blankly at Tonya's angry glaring eyes.

"It's alright Tonya… ask Kaitlin to come back in here," Louise feebly called out again, "She needs for me to finish telling her—"

"No," Kaitlin blurted out, "I think I had better just go home. I'm not feeling well Louise, and I need to get back to Charlie."

Tonya grabbed the doorknob and pulled the door open—just wide enough for Kaitlin to squeeze back outside—back out into the frigid air.

21

KAITLIN SHUFFLED QUICKLY to her car. A late afternoon shadow swept the cold ground. The horizon skimming sun barely made any warmth at all. Climbing into the frigid car-seat she shivered while searching for some gloves. As she opened her purse, the pills Dr. Karanza had given to her made a rattling sound, and she thought; *Oh, I could use some of those right now.* Scooping up four pills she gagged a little as they rubbed down her dry throat. Cranking the engine the heater knob was spun to max-heat as her foot stomped on the accelerator pedal. Almost instinctively she turned down a familiar road—a makeshift shortcut that only a person who grew up in Milledgeville would know.

Without anything to distract her other than the sound of the air flowing through the heater vent—her thoughts reluctantly returned to Charlie and what was waiting for her back at the house. *I don't know if I can go back. I shouldn't go back there.* The events of the past two days replayed over and over again in the back of her mind. *Daniel killed them… I know he did. Charlie has gone crazy because his wife and son are dead. Father killed himself out of grief. And there's nothing I can do to help any of them—not now. I'm only making myself sick again by being here… that's it… I'm not going to make myself go back.* Lost in thought, at each cross-road she spun the wheel without thinking—before she

realized it—she had driven completely off course, speeding down a small country rode in the wrong direction. *I'll just find the freeway back to Atlanta,* she began to concede.

The farther away from Milledgeville she drove, the more relaxed she became. And she let her eyes wander across the rolling grassy hills spotted with black cows that were lazily grazing. *Lucky mindless beasts,* she silently envied. Lazily her own eyes watched as the scenery slowly passed by her. A humming from the engine, and the soft massaging vibration of the tires on the roadway, acted upon her like a soothing tonic. The empty fallow fields slowed down time—for the moment—where nothing was in a hurry. Nothing was needed to be done—nothing at all. Only time needed to pass by at its own pace.

Her eyes began to feel heavy as the car's interior became a warming cocoon. Sunlight was flowing through the window and covering her like a thick blanket. Like in a dream, images of Gitana swaying in her long cotton dress drifted into her sleepy head. Gitana danced on the moss covered granite rocks. Gently swayed to the sound of her humming, as the jewelry dangling from her ears, wrists, waist and neck, all jingled in time with her motion. She sparkled like a Goddess in the streams of sunlight that filtered down through the thick canopy of highland forest above.

"Crazy Katie!"

Kaitlin jumped in her seat and grabbed the steering wheel tightly with both hands. Mary was standing in the middle of the road, directly in the path of her speeding car.

There was only time to make out the devilish grin on Mary's freckled face—under her reddish hair—dangling over her monogrammed sweater and tartan skirt. Looking exactly the way she looked, on the day she died.

Mary! Kaitlin clenched her eyes and stomped down on the brake pedal. The Jaguar lurched forward as its tires dug into the asphalt—screeching to a halt right at Mary's feet.

Blood rushed to Kaitlin's spinning head. Gut sickening churning in her belly made her eyes blur. Shaking, she gasped for air. A few dizzy seconds passed before she could twist her eyes back up—to see that Mary was gone. A pumping heart beat against her heaving chest. The steering wheel bent in her tensed grip. Bulging eyes frantically searched outside of the car. But Mary was nowhere to be seen.

Slowly she relaxed her grip, taking in deep breaths. She wanted to stomp down on the accelerator and tear out of there. Only she couldn't will her arms and legs to move. As if detached from her physical body, her mind raced around the car scouring the ground for any sign of her. *Why are you back… why won't you leave me alone?*

An old sign on the right side of the roadway caught her attention instead—forcing her eyes to abandon the search. *That's why she stopped me here!* The car idled at a cross-road, and turning right would take her back to her old boarding school—where she had first met Mary. Unknowingly, her hand slipped the transmission into park as her mind drifted away.

The time worn sign with peeling paint was now leaning gently to one side, like a very old man that had enough of life, it was almost ready to give up and fall to the ground. Its cracking black and green letters were barely legible. She could still make out the school's crest and name Georgia Highlands School for Girls. A pointing arrow showed the direction to turn. Staring down the road, Kaitlin remembered how the old school looked when she last saw it. And she began to recall all of those disturbing events. The ones she could not force herself to forget—even after years of therapy and every medication imaginable…

Her father frequently turned at the sign, to drive her down that road, taking her back to that school. No matter how many times she had managed to escape, briefly by running away from the tiny dormitory room that she was forced to share with two other eighth grade roomies. He always managed to find her and bring her back

again. Her mind followed the fading lines on the road as she drifted back there—again.

Sara would always be waiting with open arms and a patient *I'm glad you're back* smile. A shy and timid girl, Sara had long straight strawberry-blonde hair that softly curled up at the ends. Thin and wispy her hair was usually full of static electricity and sticking out in all directions being pulled out of place with the slightest of breezes. Her thin wire-rimmed glasses sat uneasily out on the tip of her nose and would constantly slip down—to the annoyance of everyone around her—unless some of her hair happened to get caught up in the hinges. She would cringe with pain—while everyone else would giggle.

Preferring to be alone, away from the tormenting jeers, Sara spent most of her time indoors reading books. She loved curling up with a good read inside the dorm, the library, or any other semi-darkened room where she could hide away.

Mary Covington also shared the dorm room. Slightly chubby, and slightly above average in every other way, her mere presence was intimidating to all of the other girls. Mary's personality was just as imposing and brash as her physical appearance. Her favorite past-time was tormenting everyone else, and she was very gifted at zeroing in on a person's weakest point, combined with the unenvied ability to inflict the worst possible physical and mental pain that possibly could be inflicted by a mere mortal. Being a first rate bully, she assigned everyone at the school a distinctively cruel nickname—ones that she used incessantly for her sadistic pleasure. Sara became an abbreviated *Wormy*, as *Book Worm* didn't seem diminishing enough. But for Kaitlin she found a very special moniker. Not due to its simple harshness as a foul word or description, no, it was much worse because it was so insidiously insightful—*Crazy Katie.*

Mary was able to craft such a devious nickname due to all the rumors that had preceded Kaitlin's arrival at the school. And they spread like a virulent disease throughout the school, passing from person to person by the sound of whispering voices—as if rustling

leaves. Stories about Kaitlin and her ghosts arrived at the school before she had even entered the front gates, and she was welcomed by her classmates with whispers and strange looks. Mary easily picked up on the fact that Kaitlin was the only girl at the school who was regularly excused from class, and provided with a special hall-pass, to go meet with her therapist. Her medications were also hard to hide in the tiny dormitory room.

"Does that keep you from going completely *crazy… Katie?*" Mary loved to ask whenever she heard the rattle of the pill bottle being opened.

Each time Mary taunted her with it, *"Crazy Katie"*, embarrassing her in front of the other girls and the teachers, yelling it at her in a high pitched shrill voice, it struck a flat cord that reverberated inside Kaitlin like she was striking a gong, filling her with the rage of a fearsome animal that wanted to leap on top of Mary—instinctively attacking the source of her pain—tearing, biting, destroying and finally killing. But like a caged Lion, she kept her silence, forcing back the rage as she waited, paced, and watched.

It wasn't long before Kaitlin would get the chance to get her revenge.

It had rained continuously for nearly three straight days and everyone had been forced to remain cooped-up inside, frazzling there already frazzled nerves. Their headmistress needed some peace, so all of the girls were sent on an outing to a close by park, one that was situated next to a large creek. The creek was one of many that fed into the very large, Lake Sinclair. It was a pleasant little park where the town's folk would gather to swim and picnic. They had been instructed to stay near the park, *in sight*, and to stay far away from the creek altogether—with absolutely no swimming allowed. All the rain had swelled the creek into a swift moving river full of swirling rapids.

Mary seemed to be unusually nasty that day. She had managed to anger many of her classmates, even taunting one of the younger girls to the verge of tears as they walked the four-mile trek from the

school down to the lake. Along the way Kaitlin and Sara devised a simple plan to exact some vengeance on her. Just a small amount of embarrassment, a slight retribution, something to remind Mary that she was not liked.

"There's a mother alligator down that trail… with several babies that just hatched too," Kaitlin shared with Mary, while sneaking a shared grin with Sara, when Mary turned to look down the muddy path going off into the tall reeds.

"There aint no gator in there *crazy*… you can't scare me," Mary said snidely.

"My daddy brings me and my brother up here all the time," Kaitlin boldly responded. "He was just up here the other day, and he told me so, and he aint no liar. You're just chicken is all?" Kaitlin shot Mary a snotty pout, before stomping away, disappearing into the tall reeds and bushes.

"Wait up!" Sara called to her.

Sara and Mary raced up behind Kaitlin along the creek. Their shoes pressed deep into the reddish clay mud. The mud became wetter and deeper the closer they came to the water, making squishy sucking sounds as their shoes pushed and pulled—up and down. With each sticky step the reeds and bushes thickened around them, making it harder and harder to see the edge of the stream.

"There's one!" Kaitlin said excitedly, pointing down at the water's edge.

Mary and Sara pressed up beside Kaitlin and peered down into the dark swirling water.

"I don't see nuthin'," Mary grunted, while leaning over to peer into the water. "Your crazy people pills makin' you see gators *and* ghosts now Katie?"

"Take a closer look!" Kaitlin yelled in Mary's ear as she pushed hard on Mary's back. Mary tried to take a step forward to stop herself from tumbling forward, but her feet were stuck firmly in the mud. Before she could utter another sound, she flopped, falling face-first, hands out, straight down into the brackish water.

It wasn't clear how deep the water actually was until Mary's entire body sank down deep, until only her sock covered feet were sticking out. Both of her shoes remained stuck in the muddy bank. Kaitlin and Sara watched in stunned silence as Mary's stringy red hair floated along the top of the water until she was pulled out of site by the fast moving stream—sucked down by a whirling-swirling suction between two boulders where there was a whirlpool in the rapids.

Sara turned and ran for help, losing one of her own shoes as she tramped through the clinging clay that stuck like thick red glue.

Kaitlin became faint, her head swirling and sucking into her own black hole—passing out and falling in the mud on top of Mary's shoes.

"It was an accident… how could I know… she couldn't swim… not my fault—," Kaitlin mumbled to herself. As if waking from a nightmare, she slowly began to realize that she was still sitting in her car—at the intersection.

Mary popped-up just outside of her window. Her piercing green eyes were glaring in at Kaitlin, visible through her wet dangling hair that fell over her face in stringy tangles. Her face and hands were grayish blue, wrinkled, and pruned, as if she had just crawled out of the cold creek. Raising her hand, Mary gently tapped on the window.

Kaitlin slammed her foot down on the gas-peddle, pressing it all the way down to the floorboard. The engine roared—flipping the tachometer into the red until the engine was close to blowing. Black smoke billowed from the exhaust pipe.

But, the car was in park.

"You alright Kate?" Nick bellowed to her through the window.

She couldn't quite hear him over the roaring engine. He rapped on the window with his knuckles to try and get her attention. Glancing over, Kaitlin saw his waist line through the window.

Slightly bent, he peered in at her and continued to tap the window. His other hand stayed at his side, fingering the holstered pistol on his hip. Jerking her foot off the accelerator the engine quickly revved down to a nearly silent idle.

Lowering the window, she chuckled nervously, asking, "You following me Nick?"

Nick leaned in, glancing around inside the car.

Clenching tightly to the steering wheel, Kaitlin glanced around behind him, watching for Mary.

"Maybe?" Nick finally responded. "I haven't seen you since I caught you sneaking around outside, out in the dark, all alone, in the middle of the night."

"I told you, I was looking for him," She moaned. "He made that fire for some reason. Isn't that important?"

Nick paused. Bent down a little lower, to where his mustache could almost tickle her cheek. Staring intently at Kaitlin's face, with an expression of disbelief and caution, he replied, "Kate, I don't know no Daniel—and there was no fire."

Kaitlin bit her lip. Silently venting, she clenched down hard on the steering wheel. Staring through the windshield at the taunting sign, she couldn't control her raging thoughts that were racing out of control. *There was a fire… I saw it… I felt it… Daniel is there… he's playing with me… I saw a man's face in the flames… he thinks I'm crazy. Damn bastard. Why is he screwing with me? Does he think this is funny? I'm now part of his damn sick joke!*

"You got any idea how long you been sittin' here Kate?" Nick scoffed. He watched her straining eyes—pointing straight ahead. "I was watchin' you for a while now, till I got concerned," He mentioned while slowly moving his head through the opened window—just far enough so that he could conspicuously sniff the air. He moved his eyes deliberately, yet, discreetly—as if he were a carnivore on the hunt, stalking, finding, then freezing, remaining hidden within the tall swaying grass, not wanting to alarm his cornered prey before he pounced. Slowly moving his head back to where he could stand up straight, he just stood there with his fingers tapping on his holstered pistol.

Kaitlin remained frozen—fully expecting to be captured and taken back home, just as her father had done to her many times before.

"Charlie's missing," Nick casually blurted out. "And it looks like you're headin' out of town for some reason. You got something you want to tell me Kate?"

"No," she snapped. "I don't know where he is."

With a stern calm voice, Nick suggested, "Maybe you should get yourself back home to help us find your brother… before there's more trouble."

He sounded just like her father. Dropping his hand away from his gun, he took a step back, turned, then walked slowly over to his car.

Kaitlin's steaming-hot breath was fogging up the windshield. Caught again!

22

THE DRIVE BACK to the house was all just a hazy blur. Kaitlin's mind was lost in a dense fog—much like the thick patches of fog that the car was passing through as she drove along the winding country back roads. The driveway was barely visible, and she had to hit the brakes when Dr. Karanza suddenly stepped out of the mist.

Looking agitated, Dr. Karanza strode over to Kaitlin's window, to ask in an accusing voice, "Where's Charles… is he with you?"

Kaitlin lowered the window, but didn't answer fast enough.

"Well, where the hell is he?" Dr. Karanza demanded to know.

"I don't know… why does everyone think I should know?" Kaitlin groaned while putting the car in park and turning off the ignition.

"He's gone. He's run off someplace," Dr. Karanza muttered, before shouting off into the mist covered trees, "Charles… Charles… you must come back home Charles!"

Kaitlin watched Dr. Karanza calling out to Charlie, and she suddenly felt somewhat bemused by the whole situation. She cracked a little smile, not knowing if she should join in the search or just go inside and crawl into bed. *Why the hell would Charlie run off now? This just can't be happening. I'm done… this has got to be it… I really don't think*

I can handle anymore drama. Feeling like a bag of wet sand, Kaitlin lumbered across the driveway and tugged her aching cold body up the front steps until she was onto the porch.

Paul burst through the front door and raced up to her. He was flush and breathing hard like he had just run a marathon. "Found him… I found him… ," he mumbled between deep breaths.

Dr. Karanza jogged back to the house and skipped up the stairs. "Where is he?" She asked before even reaching the top step.

"Back… back… back in his room," Paul answered breathlessly.

Dr. Karanza flew through the front door and raced up the stairs to Charlie's bedroom.

Kaitlin looked at Paul as he tried to catch his breath, and smirked, "Well…What the hell happened now?"

"He escaped and ran off—outside," Paul gasped. "It's my fault. I fell asleep reading. I thought he was sleeping. Karanza went to check on him and he was gone. I got to be more careful. I'm sorry Kate… it won't happen again… I promise."

"Where was he?" Kaitlin asked with a wide grin. She almost laughed out loud as she watched Paul squirming—looking like a pitiful schoolboy in trouble.

"The barn… I found him out in the barn."

"He was in the barn?" Kaitlin's smile vanished, replaced with rigid concern.

"Yea… out in the barn… where we parked my bike. He was down on the floor, kind of digging around on the ground, like he was looking for something. And he sure didn't want to leave either," Paul smirked. "He struggled hard… fighting with me… all the way back to the house. Until I got him in his room… then he finally settled down. He kept mumbling something about a fire—seemed kind of scared. Reminded me of some of the trauma victims we would pick up after bad accidents—half out of it you know—hallucinating, fighting with demons in their minds, some crazy stuff."

"I need to see him right now," Kaitlin insisted grabbing Paul's arm and pulling him back through the front door.

As they moved across the foyer, Kaitlin noticed Charlie's unfinished painting resting on its easel against the wall where she had seen it earlier. She noticed that Charlie had finished painting the bare spot in the center of the canvas. There was now a large bonfire painted there, with billowing yellowish streaks of flame leaping high up into the air. Yanking hard on Paul's arm, she forced him to stop. She stared at the painting, noticing what appeared, at first glance, to be the outline of a man's face, delicately painted inside the lines of the flames. Other images slowly emerged from within the lines of the leaping flames; the body, the arms, the hands, of a man—as if they were reaching out of the fire, grasping at her—reaching out at her. A cold chill ran over her body.

Paul leaned in close next to her. He looked over the painting, searching for whatever she was so interested in. Before he could figure it out, she tugged on his arm, urging him forward. Squeezing tightly to his arm she nearly lifted him up the stairs. She didn't let go until they were inside Charlie's bedroom.

Charlie was sitting in a chair with a blank detached stare on his face. Staring straight out, his eyes were wide and wild. Grayish black soot covered his pajamas. It was thick on his lower arms, as if he had shoved his arms into a pile of gray plaster all the way up to his elbows. Small bits had stuck to the sweat on his face making little gray spots. Almost his entire body was dotted with dirt, dust, and soot.

Dr. Karanza was sitting on the edge of his bed. She was holding his right hand, softly whispering into his left ear. Charlie's lips quivered as he tried to form words in response. "That's it Charles, you can do it. Talk to us," Dr. Karanza encouraged him.

"Faces are in the fire," He mumbled.

"You saw faces in the fire?" Dr. Karanza asked softly.

Slowly rotating his head, opening his eyes wider, Charlie stared straight at Kaitlin, and said, "They are all still here—in the fire."

"In the fire—in what fire Charlie?" Kaitlin quivered.

"You see them too, don't you?" Charlie snapped with an accusatory tone, turning his glaring eyes directly at her.

Dr. Karanza and Paul both looked at each other in disbelief.

"See who? Who do you see in the fire Charlie?" Kaitlin begged, as if she already knew the answer.

"All of them… Liz… Matthew… Daniel… father!"

"Why are you seeing them Charles?" Dr. Karanza interjected.

Without turning his head, maintaining his fixated stare on Kaitlin's face, he answered, "They want me to tell what happened to them."

"Tell me Charles—what do you know?" Dr. Karanza asked excitedly.

Moving his detached gaze back to meet the eyes of Dr. Karanza, Charlie paused, and then answered in a soft voice, as if he were telling her a secret, "Nothing yet, but I think they already told Kate, because she already knows what happened to them."

Paul and Dr. Karanza's heads swirled in unison to look at Kaitlin's face.

Kaitlin took a small step back. She could feel their eyes probing her.

"Know what? How would I know?" Kaitlin seemed dazed.

"Are you having visions again Kaitlin?" Dr. Karanza demanded of her, catching her off guard.

Kaitlin's eyes locked with Dr. Karanza. "Just what the hell have you been giving us?" She asked, "This isn't about me… right… we're here for Charlie… not me, right?"

"What's she talking about?" Paul chimed, as he stepped between them. "Have you been giving Kate medication—is there something I should know about doctor?"

"Hold on now—let's slow down," Dr. Karanza requested as she slipped over to Kaitlin's side like a cat, taking a gentle hold on her hand, "That's a private matter Paul. Why don't we talk about this in private?"

"It's O.K. Everything is alright," Kaitlin whispered to Paul as

she followed Dr. Karanza out of the bedroom into the hallway, pulling the bedroom door shut behind them.

Before Dr. Karanza could utter a word, Kaitlin launched into a tirade, "Those aren't fucking sedatives you've been feeding me—well are they?"

"Please, calm down Kaitlin."

"And just how in the hell do you know Nick? What do you know about me, and how in the hell did you find out about my visions?"

Dr. Karanza took a deep breath for composure, before answering her. "Gregory hired me because he knows I'm the best psychiatrist in the country, and possibly the only person in the entire world who can help Charles."

"That's not an answer."

"Nick and I are colleagues. We've worked together on some cases in the past—mostly criminal—when he was up in Atlanta. If you had bothered to check my credentials, you would have discovered that one of my primary practice areas is doing forensic psychiatric evaluations of criminal defendants to determine their competency."

"What exactly has Nick told you about me?" Kaitlin demanded, clenching her fingers tightly together, forming tiny white fists.

"Everything I needed to know. I have to know everything. I needed to review your mental health history to know if you were somehow influencing Charles, or if your family had some unique inherited trait, or had some other predisposition."

"Well, did he also tell you about Daniel, and what he did to me—what caused my visions in the first place?"

"Of course he did dear," Dr. Karanza said softly, in a comforting tone. "But, is there something that Nick doesn't already know about—anything else you want to tell me—tell me now?"

"Well, it wasn't a lie if that's what you think?" Kaitlin shrunk back, lowering her arms. "He did attack me that night. He did try to rape me."

"I read the police reports," Dr. Karanza whispered, "I know

what you told them happened dear." To try and comfort Kaitlin, she reached up to softly stroke her upper arm.

"Then you don't know shit Doctor! They said I lied! The police didn't do anything. They said I was just crazy and made the whole damn thing up!"

"You told them it was too dark to see—that you couldn't see who attacked you for certain. What did you expect them to do?"

"My own father didn't believe me. He let that bastard stay here, and then sent me away to that school."

"You hated your father, and you hated Daniel, right dear?" Dr. Karanza asked sympathetically.

Kaitlin began to tremble, her eyes puffed up, tears trickled down her cheeks—her head nodding up and down to say, *yes*.

"You hated this Daniel so much, didn't you? What happened to him Kate—where is he now? Tell me what happened to him—tell me what you did to him?"

Kaitlin looked up with fiery-red, scorching eyes, "What I did—to him? As she forced Dr. Karanza's hands away from her—spewing through her gritting teeth, "Go to hell!"

Dr. Karanza took a step back, glancing over to her bedroom doorway for a quick escape.

Paul opened the door and stepped out into the hallway between them, to say, "What the hell are you two doing out here?" He sounded like a disappointed father scolding two misbehaving children. "Charlie can hear everything," he reminded them—speaking in a softer voice while rolling his eyes back in the direction of his room.

Kaitlin immediately stormed off, heading down the stairs. Paul and Dr. Karanza listened to her footsteps as she made her way down the stairs, across the foyer to where she snatched up her coat, before storming down the back hall. They both exhaled—finally relaxing as the back door slammed shut.

23

ULLING A CIGARETTE from her coat pocket—with a quick flick of a lighter—Kaitlin lit up. On the back porch, the billowing puffs of smoke drifted up into the cold black air. The warm smoke glistened like a ghostly apparition for a split-second, before it disappeared. Her heart pounded hard and fast, along with her heated thoughts; *I'm not going to let them get to me. I won't let them stop me this time.* Sucking in deeply, she inhaled as much as her lungs would hold in without coughing. Then she held it all inside until her head was lighter, with a spinning carnival ride sensation, before blowing out a euphoric breath, *Ahhhhhhhh.*

As the burning tobacco got closer down to the butt of the cigarette, Kaitlin became more and more relaxed. The disturbing events of the day finally began to slowly drift away from her like the swirling smoke. Her eyes gently drifted across the yard along with the smoke until they fell upon the foot-path that led to the family cemetery—over near the edge of the woods. *I never did visit mother.* It was the least she could do now. Taking one last quick drag before flicking the butt onto the patio—with a quick step and a twist of her foot she put it out. Bracing herself against the cold and her nerves, she scurried off into the darkness heading for the cemetery.

Paul reopened Charlie's bedroom door. Dr. Karanza gingerly followed him back inside. She watched as Paul placed two capsules in Charlie's hand before retreating to the far side of the room. He leaned against the wall, out of the way.

Kneeling at Charlie's side, Dr. Karanza encouraged him to swallow the medication while handing him a glass of water. He swallowed the pills and handed the glass back to her. She leaned over close to Charlie's face, to stare deeply into his bloodshot eyes, and then asked, "What are they telling you Charles? The people in the fire—what are they saying to you?"

Charlie raised his burn-scarred finger to point at the door.

"You want to go out Charles?" She asked, while glancing skeptically over at Paul.

Charlie nodded his head—*yes.*

"Very well Charles," she grinned nervously, "We'll follow you out this time. Go on, show us what's out there."

Charlie climbed from his bed and began walking towards the open bedroom door. Paul walked directly behind him—ready to grab ahold of him if he tried to bolt. Dr. Karanza clung to Paul's hip. Together, they all walked slowly down the hall.

Charlie stopped in front of his father's open bedroom door. Paul reached up and put his hand firmly on his back, just to let him know he was there, and ready to take control. Charlie pointed inside.

"He wants to go in there," Paul whispered to Dr. Karanza.

"Let him take us where he needs to go," she whispered back.

Charlie slowly walked inside the room, shuffling over to his father's chair to sit down—facing the fireplace.

Paul positioned himself directly behind the chair—right where he could finger the small circle of fabric in the backrest where the bullet had passed through.

Kaitlin stopped at the short metal fence surrounding the cemetery. The rusted metal gate squealed as she forced it open. It was tangled-up by thick vines. Tall overgrown weeds and long twisting vines

had devoured most of the tiny burial ground. She stepped gingerly, trying not to trip in the dark, searching for her mother's headstone. The inscriptions on the granite slabs were almost impossible to read now—especially in the dark.

Kaitlin knelt down next to her mother's marble slab and tore away the tangle of vines. Running her finger over the etchings on the stone she tried to envision her mother's image of when she was still alive—when they were together—both of them still so happy and full of life.

"Can you tell us what they are telling you now Charlie?" Dr. Karanza asked, kneeling down beside Charlie in the chair. She and Paul leaned forward, staring at Charlie's face with morbid fascination. He didn't speak. Charlie merely raised his hand slightly to point a finger down at the fireplace. Dr. Karanza and Paul looked at each other, puzzled, and then, they looked at the fireplace.

"A fire… you want us to make a fire?" Dr. Karanza guessed.

Charlie nodded—*yes*.

Dr. Karanza looked over at Paul, and then nodded—telling him, *you do it*.

Paul walked around the chair and kneeled in front of the soot covered brick fireplace, and neatly stacked some fire-wood. He rolled up some newspaper that Dr. Karanza had brought with her from Atlanta and slid it up underneath the wood. Striking a match he lit the paper. The small fire illuminated Paul's face with an orange glow—his eyes full of uncertainty as he gently blew on the growing flames.

Kaitlin flicked her lighter to get a better look at her mother's head-stone. The small fire-light made the headstone glow. And not to waist the flame, she put a cigarette between her lips and torched it up. A soft glow of the cigarette replaced the light from the lighter. *Those happy good ole days didn't last long did they mother? Oh no, you had to leave me here to deal with Daniel… a father going mad… and now Charlie. So,*

what else is there mother—any more surprises for me? The cigarette quickly melted down from her deep drags until the heat was burning her fingers. "Thanks for nothing mother," she whispered as she flicked the still burning butt up into the air.

When it landed a few feet away, the burning ember lit up a patch of ground. Kaitlin's eyes fixed on the small circle of smooth reddish clay where all of the leaves and vines had been recently cleaned away. With a quick flick of her thumb she ignited the lighter again—as she stepped over to get a better look. There was writing on the ground, scratched into the dirt by a finger. Her body shuttered as she read the words:

I once was,
where you now be,
prepare with speed,
to follow me.

The metal tip of the lighter burned hot and her thumb let go again. It was suddenly pitch dark again.

Paul continued to blow on the fire as it spread over the stacked wood inside the fireplace, and the flames began to grow. He was forced to move back as the heat poured out. Charlie sat silent, staring into the flames. His eyes growing wider as the flames grew higher.

Kaitlin nervously blew on the lighter to cool it down. She ran her thumb across the metal spindle hoping to spark the flame. "Oh, c'mon—," she groaned as she flicked the lighter with her thumb over and over again. It wouldn't spark. Looking around in the dark, she spied another glowing light off in the distance. A light that looked just like the fire-light she had spotted through Charlie's bedroom window. It was the bonfire over by Daniel's house.

The rolling heat from the fire reached Charlie's face. His eyes were wide and staring into the fireplace as the flames grew higher. Paul and Dr. Karanza watched his eyes as the reflection of the flames

danced in them. Charlie began to speak in a slow, hushed, methodical voice, saying, "He wants me to tell you what happened."

"Who wants you to tell us Charles?" Dr. Karanza whispered in his ear.

"The man in the fire," He answered coldly.

"What man—what did he tell you Charles?"

"Daniel is in the fire."

"How's that Charles?"

"Kaitlin knows why," Charlie answered, grinning. She's been drawn back to the flames like a moth. The flames beckon for her now. Beckon for her—to torment her."

"How does Kaitlin know he's in the fire?"

Charlie turned his head to look her straight in the eyes. With wild burning eyes, he said, "Because, she put Daniel in the fire." An ember cracked with his last word, sending out a spark that landed near his foot.

Kaitlin stared through the darkness at the glowing fire off in the distance through the trees. It was getting larger with each passing moment. *Bastard is back again*, she thought as she headed towards the gate. "It's time to end this once and for all," she murmured as she marched down the path through the trees, heading towards Daniel's burn pit.

"She hated him," Charlie groaned. "You know that, don't you doctor?" Charlie turned his face back to the flames, to explain how, "She just went wild one night after having a run-in with him out back. It was late at night. He was drunk as usual, coming out of the barn. She had run away again from that school again and was trying to sneak into the barn, again, for some reason—to hide from father most likely. Daniel caught her and chased her towards the house. He snatched at her clothing trying to hold on, but she tore away."

"Oh my Lord," Dr. Karanza muttered.

"She told father that Daniel was trying to rape her… but father called her a no-good liar and trouble maker for going back in the barn after he'd told her so many times before to stay out!" The heat from the fireplace was sweltering as the flames shot up. Charlie's face contorted with burning pain—with droplets of sweat beading up on his forehead and dribbling down his face.

Kaitlin slowed her pace and nervously approached the fire-pit. Just like the other night, a roaring bonfire was raging in the pit. But no one was there. She yelled out towards his house. It was dark inside— about forty yards away. There was a raging fire inside of her and she let it out—screaming at the top of her lungs, "Daniel Collins! You can come out now, and show yourself, you fucking bastard!" No response—not a sound. Kaitlin spun around in a circle, nervously scanning the darkness, and saw nothing—no one. "Where are you, you fucking bastard, come out and face me!" Still nothing—his old wooden shack was silent and dark just like the woods.

As if the fire was coming alive, a presence was felt coming up from behind her. Spinning around she gazed into the flames and could see a face emerging in the fire. Flames leaped out towards her like outstretched arms, with fiery hands and clawing fingers, they scratched at the air in front of her—frantically grabbing at her.

Charlie stopped talking and seemed to stiffen as he starred into the flames dancing inside the fireplace. Their rhythmic motions drew him in deeper, and deeper, and deeper—until he saw him. "You see—there he is. It's Daniel. Crying out, he pushed himself back— tipping the chair backwards until it was falling over. "He's come for me too!"

"There's nothing there… everything is OK Charles… no one's there!" Dr. Karanza said loudly with her hands pressing down on the armrest to stop the chair from falling over. Paul grabbed Charlie's arm and pushed against the back of the chair keeping it upright.

Charlie yelled, "No… let me go! He's come back for me

now—he wants to kill me too!" Pushing frantically with his legs, he flipped the chair over, sending himself and Paul tumbling to the floor. Breaking free of Paul's grasp as they fell, he sprang up from off the floor like a frightened cat, leapt across the bed, and bolted out the door.

Kaitlin's eyes were transfixed on the image of the man that was emerging within the flames. *It's Daniel!* She realized, as his facial features took shape, and she could see his angry eyes glaring back at her. Frozen in place, she watched in horror as his hands reached out for her, tearing at the air in front of her like a crazed mad-man.

"What-cha look-in at *crazy*," Mary cackled from behind her.

Kaitlin spun around to find Mary standing inches from her—smiling maniacally.

"Well, looks like you finally have a friend," Mary said as she stepped closer. Kaitlin stepped back, moving closer to the fire. "Well, aren't you gunna introduce us?" Mary snickered. A devilish smile appeared on her face, just as she raised her clawing fingers and leapt at Kaitlin—pushing her back towards the fire. Kaitlin spun around, coming face to face with Daniel. His arms of flames leaping from the raging bon-fire—now just close enough to touch her face. Sizzling, the ends of Kaitlin's hair puffed, singing away into pungently-sweet white smoke.

A fist of fire flew past Kaitlin's face as she braced her legs—stopping her from flying face first into the fire. She could feel the blazing heat as it evaporated on her skin. Another finger of fire flew up in her face, just as Mary's hands slammed against her back again, sending her a few more inches closer.

Feeling herself falling forward, Kaitlin jumped with all of her might, leaping-up as high as she could—catapulting herself through the flames. She could feel Daniel's hands of flame wafting over her skin, grabbing and pulling at her, as she passed through the raging fire—just above the cracking and spitting embers that were glowing like bubbling lava in the mouth of a volcano. Landing on the other side, she rolled out onto the ground—just out of the reach of Daniel who continued to throw himself against the air, grasping at her in a burning rage. As she rolled across the ground to put out her smoldering clothes, his fingers of fire agonizingly stretched out to try and pull her back in.

As she rolled around, she could still hear Mary taunting her from on the other side of the fire.

"Where you going crazy Katie?" Mary cackled as she bent down to pick up one of the burning limbs. She held out the torch with both hands, walking fast towards Kaitlin.

Kaitlin jumped to her feet and ran down the path. Time seemed to be slow, like moving through molasses, slowing her with each step, no matter how hard she tried to run. Mary's giggling voice followed her into the woods. "Don't' leave us now Katie—we're just getting warmed up!" Everything was blurry and dark, and Kaitlin's feet kept stumbling and tripping on the tangled limbs, roots, and vines. She could see the lights of the house off in the distance. But no matter how hard she ran, each time she glanced back, Mary was right there, right behind her. Falling to the ground, Kaitlin rolled out of the way just as Mary took a swipe at her with the torch, barely missing her. A trail of sparks sprayed over her.

Kaitlin sprang to her feet and rushed through the metal gate of the cemetery, slamming it shut behind her. Without looking back at Mary she ran across the cemetery to jump over the fence on the other side. She only made it half-way when a thick vine became tangled around her foot, tripping her up, sending her sprawling onto the ground—falling with such momentum that she wasn't able to get her hands out in front of her face before her head slammed down upon a marble slab. Stars swam in her head as her eyes rolled back. She could still hear Mary giggling someplace off in the distance—as she drifted away into unconsciousness.

24

PAUL CHASED AFTER Charlie. Dr. Karanza tried to keep up with them. Down the stairway and out the back door they all went.

Charlie was running hard and fast. He quickly outran Paul, vanishing into the inky black darkness covering the thick woods. Paul tried to follow him, but lost sight of him as he sprinted into the trees—darting around the bushes like a scared rabbit. Dr. Karanza stopped at the edge of the trees—afraid to enter the darkened woods—she watched Paul moving around in the dark like a blind man.

The night sky provided the perfect cover for Charlie to hide.

A deep sensation of impotence swept over Dr. Karanza as she watched Paul up ahead, zigzagging haphazardly through and around the shrubs and trees as he continued his futile search. *He knows every inch of this place… he could hide anywhere out there*, she mused. It was obvious to her that the only way to reach him now, was with her voice. Sucking in a deep breath, she yelled out to him, "Charles… Charles! Don't run… come back! You need to come back so we can help you!"

Paul kept up his pursuit, keenly searching around every bush, watching for any movement, and listening for the slightest of sounds of crunching leaves or breaking twigs. The futility of the situation was beginning to sink in with every passing second—along with the danger. *He could be hiding anywhere. I could walk right past him and never see him… got to watch my back.* Walking out into a clearing, he could see the silhouette of Daniel's farmhouse in the distance. The open field in between was empty. Charlie was nowhere in sight. *He must have gone in there?* He gulped, before heading towards the dilapidated old house.

Stepping onto the porch, the rotting wood planks creaked as they shifted under Paul's feet. He stepped gingerly as the insect riddled, rotten boards, sunk in like wet sponges, giving way a little, cracking without breaking. As he reached out to turn the tarnished doorknob, he paused, listening for any movements inside. He sheepishly called out, "Hello… hello… is anyone there?" Nobody answered. He slowly turned the knob. The door cracked open. Before he could push the door open a biting realization struck him cold—he was about to enter a completely dark house, in pursuit of a suspected murderer, alone, while being completely unarmed. *Who knows what Charlie is thinking? He may really be insane? He may have a weapon and be waiting just inside? Was this all planned… some kind of trap?* Frantic visions of an untimely gruesome death started racing through his mind.

Creaking floorboards behind him and the feeling of fingers touching his shoulder caused Paul to shudder and wrenched his neck around while blurting out an embarrassingly feminine sound-ing, "*Aaagh!*"

Doctor Karanza had silently tip-toed up from behind. "Did he go inside Paul?" She whispered.

"I don't know," Paul's voice quivered a little, "I lost sight of him in the woods."

"Well then—you first," She suggested, with a gentle push on his back.

Paul steadied himself and walked through the door. Dr. Karanza

stepped in behind him—hugging the wall she felt for the light switch. Paul stepped out in front of her as if standing guard while scanning the room. Flipping the switch nothing happened. "Damn it—no power," she said softly.

"Of course not," Paul smirked. He could feel Dr. Karanza's hand on his back again, pushing harder this time, urging him on like a retriever—to go search—*to go fetch him boy*. Paul didn't move. He called out instead, "Charlie… you there? Come on out… Charlie."

As their eyes adjusted to the darkness, they could make out a living area filled with the usual furnishings; a couch, a few chairs, an outdated black and white television adorned with a useless broken rabbit-eared antennae. Tiny particles of dust swirled in the soft moonlight. Everything was old and unused, like a bunch of discarded items after a yard sale. Dr. Karanza ran her fingertip across a bookshelf—it was turned a dark gray by a thick layer of settled dust. *Nobody has lived here for a very long time*, she surmised. A pungent odor of dust and mold was almost overwhelming. Paul shuffled off down the hallway to search the two bedrooms as Dr. Karanza peeked into the kitchen. In hushed voices, they both called out, "Charlie, are you in here? Come on out Charlie—."

Paul reemerged into the living room, to report, "No sign of him."

"Check around the outside then," Dr. Karanza instructed. "He may be hiding underneath the house."

Paul scampered back outside, leaving the front door open.

Dr. Karanza plopped down into a soft chair, to relax and gather her thoughts, while her inquisitive eyes continued a search of the room. A beam of moonlight fell on an open metal lock-box. About the size of a briefcase, it was sitting conspicuously on the couch across from her. Unlike everything else around her, there was no dust on the box. And the dust on the seat cushion beneath the box was smeared away, where it had recently been moved. It was also left open. Inside, there were a number of scraps of crumpled papers—nothing of apparent importance. Similar looking papers were strewn across the coffee-table, with some of them falling to the floor. It was clear to Dr. Karanza that; *someone has recently been in here… that's for certain. Someone opened this lockbox and sifted through these papers looking for something. Perhaps Charles was looking for something?*

Shifting over to the couch, she began sifting through the loose pages. But she couldn't read the words on them—they were written in an unrecognizable language. All handwritten, it looked like some type of instructional manuscript, littered with symbols and diagrams that were drawn between the lengthy notations. On most of the papers, it was a jumble of hastily scrabbled notes, jotted down observations, and formulas, that were written, erased, and rewritten, as if the writer was involved in some scientific testing of chemicals. *This looks like it was written by a woman,* she surmised, *like something I would have done.*

Quickly leafing through the loose pages, Dr. Karanza was astonished to find that she recognized some of the strange looking symbols. Each of them identified various chemicals, elements, and chemical compounds. She had learned about variations of each symbol while in college and med-school. It suddenly donned on her, that she must be looking at notes made by a medical practitioner of some sort—perhaps a pharmacist, biologist, or some type of chemical engineer. *What the hell is this doing here?*

A tingle ran up her spine when her eyes ran across something intriguing. It was a symbol that only a very few people even knew of—a specific chemical compound—one only used in alchemy. *What the hell?* As her eyes scanned down the page, even more of the secretive and elusive alchemical symbols appeared. *They don't teach this in any school I know of,* she pondered. *Someone's got to be playing with me?*

Dr. Karanza had been introduced to alchemy by a fellow med student, and friend. But, being a by-the-book student of science, she never considered their impromptu alchemy experiments to be serious. It was purely fun-and-games from Emily's point of

view—nothing real or worthy of serious endeavor. It was merely a game to be relegated to that of childish distraction, like playing with a, *Ouija Board*.

At first, she did it more for social reasons anyway. Never having achieved any meaningful relationships in her life, Dr. Karanza saw this as an opportunity to network and find friends outside of the classroom. Studying was always her passion, and learning about anything, even the art of alchemy, could help her master the intricacies of chemistry, and allow her some social life, as a small bonus.

It was after med-school that she really began to delve into alchemy. Frustrated by the conventional medications that she was forced to use on her patients by the stifling bureaucracy of hospitals, the F.D.A., and the pharmaceutical empires, she forced herself to embrace the untested, the forbidden, the forgotten, and all the things that everyone else told her she couldn't do—or try. Inspired by her study of Kabbalah, she melded her unconventional practice of medicine with alchemy, and began to try anything and everything—especially those things that no one else would dare.

Her excitement grew as she read. Carefully reading, she searched for any clues to who the author was. The alchemical recipes had been mixed together with personal notes and letters, so she expected to find a name—someplace. "Ah ha," she gushed, finally spotting a simple name at the bottom of one of the letters: *With all my love, Gitana.*

At the bottom of the metal box, lay a leather-bound notebook. The notebook was out of place, even within the out of place documents. It was altogether different. She snatched it up and flipped through the yellowed pages. To her astonishment, its contents read much differently than the other loose pages. It was hand-written— with the hand of a man—very masculine, with hard lettering that was penned straight across even lines, with no scratches, smudges, or corrections. And there were no alchemical symbols of any kind, just words in plain old English. *It's a man's personal journal?* She speculated.

Flipping back to the front page, Dr. Karanza read the introduction: Zerzura; An expeditionary account by Adrian Forth.

Before she could turn to the next page, Charlie burst through the front door, saying in a loud emphatic voice, "Here it is Doctor… I found it… its right here!"

Dr. Karanza jumped up and dropped the journal to race over to Charlie's side. He had a crazed expression of satisfaction—staring at the object he was holding up. She could barely make out the object in the moonlight—a small, bumpy, gray object that looked like a stone.

"Now I have proof. I found it… now you'll believe me… everyone will—," Charlie stammered on excitedly.

Paul appeared in the doorway—grabbing Charlie in a tight bear hug around his chest.

"No, wait, its O.K… look I found it!" Charlie pleaded as he held the gray object up for them to see.

Dr. Karanza snatched it from his hand. She spun it around in her fingers, moving it around in the low light, examining it carefully at every angle.

"What is it Doctor?" Paul asked.

"It appears to be a human bone… perhaps a vertebra?" She muttered.

"I told you… she killed him… and now you have proof," Charlie blurted out.

"Where did you get this Charlie?" Dr. Karanza demanded, holding the bone up to his eyes. "And just who does this bone belong to?"

Paul squeezed Charlie even tighter—just in case.

"The burn pile," Charlie answered, with relief. "Kate burned him alive in the burn pile."

Dr. Karanza noticed the black ash marks Charlie's hands and arms, and the gray soot that was covering his pajamas. "So, you found this in the burn pile out there Charles?"

"Yes, it's him… Daniel. I told you," Charlie insisted, squirming in Paul's grasp. "I couldn't find anything last time, but I knew he was still in there."

"You saw her kill him?" Paul asked sternly, with another hard squeeze on his chest.

"I told you I did," Charlie pleaded while squirming to get free. "I followed her out the back door after I heard the gunshot upstairs in father's room. I saw Kaitlin run out the back. I watched them. It was dark, but, I saw them both standing near the burn-pile… she was standing over him… hitting him. He was bent down on his knees, pleading. She just kept hitting him in the head, knocking him down. Then she rolled him into the fire to finish him off. I swear—I saw the whole thing—now let go of me!"

"But why Charles… why would Kaitlin kill him?" Dr. Karanza demanded.

"She hated him for what he did to her."

"What exactly did he do to her?" Paul interjected.

Charlie grimaced and he hesitated in thought, and started to answer, "He—,"

"That's enough!" Dr. Karanza interrupted. "Get him back to the house and get him cleaned up. I have to call Nick before you say anything else."

Paul spun Charlie around, and with one hand on his shoulder and the other on his wrist, he led Charlie like a prisoner back to his room.

Dr. Karanza gathered up the loose papers and the leather bound journal. She carefully placed them back into the lockbox and took them with her as she left. Paul and Charlie had already vanished into the trees before she got out of the front door. Afraid to find her way through the trees, she followed the dirt path past the cemetery. Passing by the rusted metal gate, she didn't notice Kaitlin's unconscious body.

Kaitlin's face was glowing in the soft moonlight.

Dr. Karanza rushed inside the house, going straight for the phone to call Investigator Thomas. A wave of excitement swept over her. Her medicinal techniques had worked just as she had envisioned. With giddy anticipation she waited for Nick to answer.

"This is Nick," his gruff, just-woken-up voice answered the call.

"I did it… it worked… just like I told you!"

"What happened… what worked?" He grumbled, with his half-asleep mind trying to focus. Sitting in front of the television with a half-empty bottle of whiskey nestled between his legs, he had dosed off early while watching another big-city crime saga—the kind he loved to hate. Especially when he was drinking—watching them just so that he could point out all the inaccuracies—slurring out comments about how it was all so unrealistic before pointing out *exactly* how *he* would have *really* done it.

"Charles is talking, and he told us who killed Daniel!" Dr. Karanza gushed, sounding like a school-girl that had just been invited to the prom by the most popular boy in class. "You were right all along—it was Kaitlin! And you owe me an apology Detective. My medicine did exactly what I told you it would do. And you doubted me this whole time—," She rattled on without giving Nick time to think, or respond.

"Hold on now Doctor!" Nick finally blurted out—silencing her. "Let's just slow down a little bit. Now, tell me exactly what Charlie told you, word-for-word."

"The night of the murders, he said he heard the gunshot upstairs and then saw Kaitlin run out the back door, so he chased after her, and she attacked Daniel out by his house. He then saw her hitting Daniel out by the burn-pit. After knocking him unconscious she rolled him into the fire, burning his corpse."

"There's no proof of any of that—no physical evidence at all," Nick huffed, completely unimpressed.

"Well, there is now," Dr. Karanza replied arrogantly. "Charles found what appears to be a human vertebra in the burn pile,

underneath the ashes. We just need a DNA analysis to make sure. There's your proof."

"That's not proof of anything Doctor," Nick scoffed.

"Well, its proof that Kaitlin's a cold blooded killer," Dr. Karanza chided angrily. "That's proof enough to convince me that she killed her father, then killed Elizabeth and her baby. She has a long history of mental instability with obvious psychosis exacerbated by paranoid delusional behavior. What the hell else do you need Detective—Daniel himself to tell you face-to-face?"

"There's something you need to know Emily," Nick spoke softly into the receiver, "Something I should have told you before all this got started."

"What? I thought you told me everything—that's what you told me?"

"Well, I never imagined this would be happening again, because I don't buy into all this psycho mumbo jumbo that you thrive on. I deal in cold hard facts—period. Not ghost stories and delusions."

"What exactly *didn't* you tell me Nick?"

"Daniel died almost a century ago, down at the cotton Mill. He worked there for Kaitlin's grandfather. His head was crushed-in by a rolling train car—in an accident—not by a crazy woman."

"That just can't be right," Dr. Karanza muttered under her breath. "She and Charles talk about him as if he is still alive, like he's still living here out back in that old shack. They've both seen him here, as recently as the funerals. He's been their family care-taker here since before they were born—," She rambled on trying to make sense of it.

Nick cleared a frog from his throat, before explaining, "Believe me he's dead. He died many years ago down at the Mill. I double checked the county records, found his death certificate along with the obituary that ran in the paper. I visited the city cemetery and found his grave. The headstone says he died well before Kaitlin or Charlie was even conceived. So there is no way in hell that Kaitlin managed to kill him—not when he was already long dead."

A long empty silence fell over the conversation as Dr. Karanza tried to piece something together—to make it all make sense—anything. Her moment of elation was evaporating, along with her future.

"C'mon Emily… you said it yourself," Nick chimed, trying to reason with her. He could feel her becoming frantic on the other end of the phone line. "Kaitlin is certifiably insane. She must have imagined Daniel being after her all these years and Charlie just went along with it. Or, he is using her to distract us from what really happened. Remember, we are investigating the deaths of William, Elizabeth, and Matthew, not Daniel. So I would strongly advise you to be very careful—very careful—about everything they tell you. Especially about whatever line Charlie is feeding you."

There was another long uneasy pause—with the sound of soft breathing in the receivers, as Dr. Karanza puzzled over everything—still unconvinced. *He's still not telling me everything… still holding back?*

"Just don't try and do anything else, and don't let anyone talk to them until I get over there—understood?" Nick demanded before abruptly hanging up the phone.

Placing down the phone receiver Dr. Karanza could feel the weight of her body slumping down, like that of a scolded child, with heavy hapless thoughts of feeling utterly unprepared, impotent, and professionally inadequate for the situation, all suddenly pressing down on her at once. *What does he expect from me? He was supposed to tell me everything. I told him how important that was. I'm not a cop. How the hell was I supposed to know all of that about Daniel? If Charles is pretending, then my treatment had no affect at all. I'll look like a fool!*

25

K AITLIN'S BODY SHIVERED violently. Her teeth started to chatter, knocking against each other, vibrating with uncontrollable rattling violence. Opening her eyes, she found herself lying on her back—still in the graveyard—on top of her mother's grave. *Just a dream… it was all just a horrible dream*, she told herself while trying to wrench her shaking body upright. Slowly getting her body off the ground like a decrepit old woman, she forced her numb trembling legs to start moving. Stumbling through the darkness she staggered in the direction of the house. Still caught in a dazed fog from hitting her head hard on the slab—everything was a blur. Physically numb from head to toe, she could only really feel her emotions—a deeply felt aching—an overwhelming sense of being utterly abandoned by everyone, especially by her husband. Gregory… *why did you leave me here all alone?*

Opening the back door Kaitlin was surprised to be greeted by Dr. Karanza who was standing in the hallway—there to greet her with a cold stare that was as frigid as the freezing air outside. "Welcome back Kate," she sneered.

Bitch—she has no respect for me or my home! Kaitlin groaned as she stepped inside the door. *Where's all that feigned sympathy now?*

Dr. Karanza crossed her arms, looking like a mother who had

just caught her teenage daughter sneaking in long after her curfew, drunk, and dirty. She watched with glaring accusing eyes as tiny bits of dry leaves, dirt, and dead grass fell off of Kaitlin as she stumbled towards her. Sticky dried on clay spotted Kaitlin's clothes—with thicker and darker patches covering her knees and elbows. Her hair was matted and speckled, sticking out in every wind-blown-direction, clinging to crushed leaves and twigs.

"Nick is on his way," Dr. Karanza muttered snidely as Kaitlin brushed past her.

Kaitlin didn't respond. She didn't even want to hear what she was saying. She was making a bee-line for the living room, hoping to find the fireplace ablaze with a roaring fire to warm her bones.

"We know what you did," Dr. Karanza cunningly jabbed, as if verbally stabbing her in the back. "You killed him—didn't you Kate? Don't try to deny it," she stated resolutely like a prosecutor in trial, adding, "Charles has told us everything."

"Killed who?" Kaitlin moaned, spinning around and glaring daggers back at her.

"Daniel of course," Dr. Karanza answered with a look of smug satisfaction, as if she had just called *check mate*.

"Go to hell!" Kaitlin burst out, "All of you! You can all just go straight to hell!"

Her anger jump-started her adrenaline and helped to warm her up a little, and in that small indiscernible way, it made her feel a little better. She hadn't even realized yet that her body was no longer quivering.

"Have you been outside getting rid of evidence?" Dr. Karanza inquired as she was slowly running her eyes up and down Kaitlin with a look of disgust.

"What the hell are you talking about?"

"Did you kill the rest of them too, Elizabeth, Matthew—your father? It will be much better for you if you just tell me now Kate."

Kaitlin's head started to spin as she tried to make sense out of what was happening—but all she could hear was the brash voice of her father scolding her again, calling her a no good liar for making false allegations to get attention—for acting crazy. *You's nothin' but a liar. Daniel aint never tried to rape you or hurt you in any way fashion or form. You're just imagining things! You're crazy… just like your mother was crazy! You aint seen your mother neither cuz she's dead and buried… just like you're gunna be soon if you keep this up!* As his voice was thrashing her, she staggered backwards—catching herself on the armrest of a chair before falling all the way to the floor. Pushing herself upright, she turned and staggered towards the front door, just desperately wanting to escape—from everyone and everything.

"Won't do you any good to run and hide. It's too late for that," Dr. Karanza said firmly, "Best to just stay right here and face the truth."

"Oh, you've helped out quite enough already Doctor," Kaitlin mumbled as she closed the door, walking back out into the chilling air. *This is what I get for trying to help that little bastard,* she thought as she shuffled to her car. As she started the car's engine, the only thing that was clear to Kaitlin now, was the cold harsh realization that she could no longer trust anyone—not even Charlie. Once again, just as when she was as a child, she was utterly abandoned, deprived of anyone who she could rely upon for protection, or anyone who would even believe her. And once again, she was just—*crazy Katie!*

Everything around her was a blur that passed through the fog of her headlights until she found herself back in the parking lot of the Mill. Lowering her head she wept like a lost child, sobbing, with snot running out of her nose. She could only imagine; *Gregory will leave me. This is what he was waiting for anyway… he had left me emotionally years ago anyways. Hell, he may have even planned this whole thing… wanting to get me back here… knowing I would snap! This will be his perfect opportunity to make it all official. Divorce me… marry her… oh so convenient… so perfect. He's probably been with her this whole time. It's understandable I guess… I mean, my God, I've lost everything that would make him want me… the Mill, the house, my families money, my youth, my looks… it's all gone. They may as well put me away now, there's nothing left to live for!* Slipping deeper and deeper into a state of paranoid hysteria—abandoning all hope, she pleaded for some relief from the only person that could not abandon her now, "Please mother… please help me… mother… help me—."

After hitting emotional bottom, where one gives up, or finds a way to start climbing back up, Kaitlin finally found some courage with thoughts of her mother, and she began to wipe away the wet tears left on her cheeks. Her eyes were now empty and dry. *No… mother would not let me give up now. She is helping. Just like she did when I was young… she's protecting me. I just haven't been letting her this time. She's leading me to an answer. I can't give up on her… or me.* Shutting the car door, Kaitlin stood in the parking lot of the Mill for few moments while wiping the last bit of wetness from her face with her coat sleeve.

As she stared up at the large looming building that was cold, dark, and empty, something moving caught her eye. A person had walked out of the shadows, only to disappear around the corner of the Mill, heading towards the loading dock. A chill ran up her spine. She thought of her mother and muttered to herself some encouragement. "C'mon Kate… you can to do this… you have to do this," she repeated as she strode across the parking lot, over to where the image had vanished.

Rounding the corner Kaitlin began to feel warm—very warm. The night sky dispersed and a bright hot sunshine filled up the sky. Hot humid summer air flowed over her hands, arms, feet and legs, until her entire body was so warm she could feel the droplets of perspiration squeezing through almost every pore. Her back was suddenly soaked with perspiration. Heavy beads of sweat dribbled down her forehead. An unfamiliar pain swept over her body. Aches and pains erupted in nearly every joint, muscle, ligament, and limb—crying out for relief after suffering from years of hard manual labor. *What is wrong with me?*

Looking down at her arms and hands, they did not appear to

belong to her at all, covered in scratches, scars, on top of rough calloused skin that had been darkened to a deep brown from exposure to the sun. Her sleeves were different also, her clothes had changed, and she was now wearing an old turn of the century, plain, ankle length cotton dress. *Oh my god! I'm having a vision… right now!*

"Gitana, get your ass over here… NOW god damn it!" A man yelled at her from a few feet away—deep, gruff, and angry—his voice was thick and scarred from many years of smoking and boozing. Looking up, Kaitlin saw him standing by the rail-cars. It was Daniel. He appeared to be younger, but still wearing his dirty overalls and a sweat soaked filthy undershirt matted with dust. His whiskers peppered his sweat dripping unshaven face. All of which only exaggerated his slack-jawed half-drunk scowl. "Well you stupid bitch… what the hell you waitin'fer?"

Kaitlin stood in place, frozen, unsure of what to do.

"I gotta get this damn train loaded b'for three, so get your ass a-movin'," Daniel jeered. Kaitlin turned her head to see if anyone else was there. No one else was around, but her eyes caught the reflection of a woman in a nearby window. It was her own reflection—of a young woman who appeared to be in her twenties, with long straight black hair that was pulled back and tied with bailing twine into a make-shift ponytail. Droplets of sweaty dust clung to her forehead. She had deep olive skin, dark brown eyes, and was wearing the same exact ankle length cotton dress that she saw herself wearing.

Looking around, the entire Mill itself looked very different, almost new, with unbroken windows, fresh paint that wasn't sun-bleached and peeling away, and metal railings that were still unscathed, unbent and free from dents and rust. Underneath her feet was a perfectly formed concrete loading ramp without the familiar lightning looking jagged cracks running up and down, caused by bearing the years of all-too heavy loads.

Oh my god… it's me! Kaitlin screamed inside, staring bewildered at her reflection in a window. *I am Gitana!*

"Don't make me have to *encourage* you *again*, now *git'* your ass over here!" Daniel sneered again, while wiping a dirty sleeve across his dripping face.

An uncontrollable rage welled up inside Kaitlin. She knew the feelings rushing through her body were not just hers, not now, they were the feelings of hate she now shared with Gitana. And now, it felt so undeniable, so right and so good—it was now too uncontrollable.

Startled by his bark, she quickly turned and walked slowly down the loading ramp, moving towards Daniel like a lioness. He was standing at the bottom of the loading ramp peering up at the cargo hold through the sliding doorway of a rail car—deep in contemplation on how best to stack the pallets inside. She bent over and picked up a sledge hammer that Daniel had dropped on the ground. A hammer he used to assist in decoupling or coupling the cars, or forcing the tracks to switch over so that cars could be moved onto another line, whenever needed. Positioning herself behind Daniel while holding the heavy sledge hammer in her aching fingers, she watched the back of Daniel, intently, with feelings of intense hate and anger growing stronger inside of her with each pounding heartbeat. It was becoming a delightful lust—like finally getting to consume her drug of addiction, filling her body with an ecstatic relief as her arms raised the hammer above Daniel's head. He glanced back, just as the hammer slammed against his head, tearing open a few inches of thin skin, cracking his skull like an egg-shell.

Kaitlin felt a morbid feeling of joyful relief as Daniel slumped to the ground at her feet. It was just something that had to be done. And it was finally over. His body shook violently with convulsions as blood gushed from the large gash.

Standing over his body beneath the scorching sun, she suddenly felt dizzy and faint. The heat from the hot humid day, along with her out-of-control adrenaline, had sapped her strength. Her grip on the sledge hammer went slack, slipping it back down to the ground. Her knees buckled and she fell down beside the dying body of Daniel. A tickling sensation of butterfly wings fluttering inside of her tiny-bulging belly brought her hands to her womb—along a worrisome thought, *Oh… my baby… everything is fine… you're going to be fine now.*

Breathing deeply, she forced herself up. Dirt and blood speckled her dress with spots of brownish-red. Stepping over Daniel's barreled chest she straddled him. She looked down into his dying eyes. He had one open wide, and the other nearly closed—both were lifeless, like buttons sewn onto a rag doll. Reaching down to his side, she placed her fingers across his wrist and squeezed down gently, feeling for a pulse. *It's not too late… he's not dead yet,* she considered, before pulling a small vile from her pocket. Holding the clear glass vile up to the sunlight, she examined the thick dark-red liquid inside—some partially coagulated blood. Quickly putting the vile up to her mouth, she pulled out the cork stopper with her teeth. With her other hand, she pried open Daniel's mouth. Tipping the vile, the purplish, nearly black liquid slowly ran along the side of the vile and poured out—with small droplets dripping down onto his tongue. Her eyes watched intently, making certain that it flowed all the way down his throat, till it was swallowed up. Gurgling sounds bubbled up as the bloody liquid filled the back of his throat. Grabbing his thick jowls tight, she held his mouth shut as he choked the concoction down. *That's it… swallow it all, my pet. Now you will know what it's like to be used like some animal.*

"Gitana… Gitana… are you alright?" Another man called out to her.

She looked up to see Benjamin coming towards her—running along the railroad tracks from the front of the train. She hastily corked the vile and slipped it back inside a pocket. Leaning over Daniel's face, she snorted to draw mucus up from the back of her dry throat. Puckering up, she spewed what little spittle she could get up, out onto Daniel's distorted face—as a last farewell. *Welcome*

to your own personal hell I created just for you, she thought, as her slimy spittle spewed out of her mouth and stuck to his cheek.

Ben pulled her away, embracing her. "What have you done to him?"

In a whimpering voice, she whispered into his ear, "If he ever found out, he would have done much worse to us."

Ben gently placed his hand on her belly—a sign of silent understanding and agreement. "Is he dead?" He asked solemnly.

"In a way," Gitana whispered with hesitant lips. Looking deeply into Ben's eyes, she said, "He will be alive in his own way for you and me… but he must be forever dead to everyone else."

The ground began to tremble and a gust of wind blew a thick spray of dust into Kaitlin's eyes. She snapped them shut and covered her ears as a thunderous rumbling sound enveloped her—shaking her entire body. Loud squealing sounds of clanging and screeching metal pounded her eardrums. Covering her face with her hands, she peeked through her fingers to try and see what was happening. Metal boxcars in a long train were racing past the Mill along the tracks. It was dark again, and the warning lights along the tracks were flashing crimson-red.

26

D R. KARANZA RETURNED to her room to await Nick's arrival. She wanted to spend that precious little time reading from the leather bound notebook discovered inside Daniel's house. On the inside cover the author had inscribed his name in dipped black ink, **Adrian Forth**. She hoped to find some morsel of information, a tiny tidbit or clue, anything that would lend itself to help explain the truly bizarre events that were now transpiring all around her—hoping most of all to find something linking Kaitlin to murder.

Her finger flowed over the hand written words along the neatly pinned lines, zigzagging down each of the time-worn yellowing pages. There wasn't much time, and she desperately did not want to be forced to turn the book over to that smug asshole, Nick. Not before she could discover its purpose, along with an explanation for the loose pages covered in alchemical symbols. *He couldn't relate to such a relic. And he certainly could not understand its importance... might as well throw it on the trash pile as to give it up to him. It's up to me to figure this out,* she told herself while reading intently.

Knowing there was little time for her to devour the entire journal, her eyes nervously jotted about, skimming over each turned page, quickly scanning for relevant words, consuming important facts while discarding the rest—just as she'd learned to do while cramming for med school exams.

15, October, 1897...

    ...brilliant news today! With much hard won luck I have managed to persuade a wealthy Scottish gentleman by the name of Allister Urquhart to provide the necessary financial backing to fund my life-long dream of a trek through the great western dessert of Tripoltania to search for the lost treasures of Zerzura...

    ...He was finally convinced to back my venture when I read to him from the 15th Century Arabic treasure-hunters' guide, 'The Book of Hidden Pearls.' The ancient city of Zerzura is described within the book as a whitewashed city in the desert where many treasures can be found. He was most fascinated with the passage describing the method of entry. 'Take with your hand the Key in the beak of the bird, then open the door to the city. Enter, and there you will find great riches'...

    ...Finally my years of preparation have won the chance to find one of the greatest finds in antiquity. Having departed from service with the Department of Lands, working as a surveyor for nearly 20 years, I have spent the past 6 years scouring the Egyptian delta for lost antiquities. Over those years I have managed to Procure all manner of fascinating antiquities from ancient cities such as Thebes and Memphis. I have supported myself by acquiring and selling artifacts of significance to museums throughout Europe. Due to my efforts in that regard, I have become quite adept and skilled in the process of procuring pieces of worth from indigenous families

who have made a long standing family business of sorts—plundering relics and dispersing them to people devoted to their salvation such as myself. Museums and curators across Europe will pay handsomely for most anything of ancient Egyptian origin. It was on one such memorable occasion...

...It is becoming more difficult to escape the sticky grasp of the authorities however. The Egyptian Government has retained the services of some very well trained and seasoned mercenaries of sorts to end my career, and the family traders as well. While I have been responsible for saving thousands of items of historical importance, the Egyptian authorities now view my existence as nothing more than a black market thief...

...I have set my sight upon an unexplored, and unexploited region, in order to defray my incarceration whilst I continue to pursue the hidden treasures that have enslaved my passions. Over the past several years I have made contacts with both criminals, as well as men of considerable respect, amongst the learned gentlemen of Europe and across the Mediterranean...

...An avid reader of the 'Journal of the Royal Geographical Society', I have pieced together information regarding the fabled lost city of Zethura (a.k.a. Zerzura) which is said to lie near the Oasis of Siwa, out in the far reaches of the deepest parts of the Great Western Desert of Tripolitania. From one of my less than respectable, and even less reliable, contacts in Cairo, I have been kindly provided a copy from an ancient text written by Osman al-Nabulsi. The translated 13th Century transcript provides a detailed description of the lost city and its grand temple of the Oracle of Ammun. A map of limited use, it portends to provide directions to finding the lost temple of the Oracle of Ammun and possibly the relics of the lost army of Cambyses II. It is certainly not as reliable a map as one would dream of possessing; however, it is of sufficient quality and detail as to make it worthy of interest, and worthy of my pursuit. Such a find would most certainly return a substantial fortune in both wealth and fame...

...The directions provided in the translation appear somewhat vague and cryptic. I have surmised that by following a strict course leading through the expansive Western Desert one would assuredly perish if a path between the chain of small oasis' is not strictly adhered. The translation cannot be relied upon; however, the dire warning appearing within the text is noticeably striking in its predictions. Eternal damnation amongst the sand awaits anyone who attempts to disturb the restrained army of Cambyses. Such warnings are familiar and not alarming. Warnings of doom are discovered with nearly every ancient Egyptian tomb that is uncovered...

...From my limited abilities to translate the ancient text, it would seem that the Oracle of Ammun is able to summon the word of God, or possess the powers of divination, by using the 'fire upon the bones of knowledge'. The bones of knowledge (a.k.a. Oracle Bones) having the word of God upon them. The Oracle by accepting the Word is sustained within the fire, and therein, as a Seraph, she is able to reveal the words or prophecies of God, (pronouncements of future events, fortune telling, etc.) to her followers...

...Plans have been made to depart in the spring and I will begin procuring the necessary provisions at once. Mr. Urquhart has kindly provided a handsome sum necessary to begin preparation for the journey. I will be traveling alone. Most provisions shall be acquired once I have made arrival in the port of Tripoli. I have arranged two guides to assist in my transport by camel, and to act as translators with the local inhabitants. Being not familiar with the local Berber dialects and other languages spoken by the Siwans living across the vast and mostly uninhabited desert terrain...

...Transport by camel will be taxing, and not allowing for maintenance of much in the way of water or food. One must preserve life sustaining supplies at all costs. Based upon my research into the area to be covered, it is well known that many nomadic thieves and robbers make the area their home. Tales of shadowy spirits and blood thirsty raiders roaming across the Western Desert prevent most from attempting such a journey into the area alone. Much like pirates of the old Caribbean Seas one can imagine, harmless nomads, gents of my own sort, is my hoped expectation...

...26 day of March, 1898, having arrived in the Port of Tripoli, all provisions necessary are speedily being secured. I expect to make contact with my guides, Omar and Hakim at first light...

...Damn camels are a most nasty and foul creature indeed. Best suited for desert travel, I have no other choice but to endure their torment for the next several weeks...

...The desert is vast and unrelenting in savagery

toward human existence. This sea of sand is as treacherous to traverse as any stormy ocean that may cover this earth. I internally rejoice resoundingly as each tiny oasis of salvation appears on the horizon. Must maintain appearance of assuredness, my guides cannot be made aware of my hidden concern...

...One week into the desert, I am completely reliant upon my guides to see me through. They seem congenial enough, and appear to be most competent in their abilities in using both the barren terrain and the stars of the night sky to keep us on track. We are following the ancient rout once travelled by the greatest of all kings, Alexander the Great, whenever he ventured here himself in pursuit of ancient wisdom, and counsel from the fabled Oracle. According to Omar we are nearly to our destination, only a few more grueling days until we should arrive at the Siwa Oasis...

...Dreams and hopes of finding unrivaled rewards help to keep my spirits up. This is most assuredly my most daunting expedition I have ever attempted. If I were to have a wife and child to concern myself with, I do believe I would have already returned a beaten man. Thankfully I have no immediate family to write to, or to be at all concerned about. Perhaps that's why I have chosen to be a vagabond of sorts, a nomadic pirate of my own making...

...16 April, 1898, we have made our arrival at the Oasis of Siwa. Sadly I am most disappointed to find that the famed city and the Temple of the Oracle of Ammun are mere mud brick ruins. Any treasure that may have been found has long been looted by time and grave robbers. I have decided to scout some of the outlying areas of interest before we

abandon altogether this quest and begin the long journey home. Perhaps some of the local families have made good, and have saved something of value...

...18 April, 1898, Omar and Hakim have related a most interesting story told to them by members of a passing nomadic Siwan tribe who make this desert their permanent residence. They told a story which has been passed down through generations of tribesmen wandering this forbidding terrain. They tell of how the temple of the Oracle Ammun was built before 1300 B.C., in honor of Ham, a descendant of Noah, of biblical fame. The tale is quite fantastic indeed. I only hope that I can translate my guide's limited English into an accurate recitation.

To my best understanding, the story states that the bones of Cain had been dispersed throughout the known world by the original, Seraphim, or for lack of better word to describe, the original 'illuminate', or keepers of the flame, referring to the words of God as described in the text that helped lead me here.

It would seem that the Oracle's were the keepers and protectors of the remnants of the bones of Cain, which when placed within a flame, the bones would reveal the words of God, that being the past and future foretold and revealed. The Oracle of Ammun was the possessor of the most important remains of the Oracle bones, namely the skull of Cain. Upon the skull was inscribed the word of God which when revealed provided an alchemical recipe that would sustain life. But if the word of God was breached, any person who had consumed the concoction was eternally damned, as was Cain.

Apparently, this bizarre story begins when

Lucifer beguiles Cain into slaying his own brother Abel in exchange for the promised gift of returning to a state of eternal life (promising to allow him to consume the fruit of the Tree of Life, allowing him to pass by the Cherubim and flaming sword, and thereby being permitted to return to live in the Garden of Eden, of sorts). Cain gladly consumed a concoction produced with the crushed bones of Abel, (some kind of alchemical medication) which did give him eternal mortal life.

But as always, with Lucifer, there is a catch involved with every deal. In this case, in order to return to the pristine condition of the Garden of Eden, Cain had to have his mortal flesh consumed by fire (fiery sword of the Cherubim as decreed by God). He literally had to jump into a flesh scorching bon-fire to have his imperfect mortal body consumed away, thus dying in what is described as the "Seraphim Death". Once the mortal body is dead, and perfected by passing through the fire, it can be reborn into immortality as a perfect being, like an angel, or Seraph, otherwise known to the ancient historians as creations of the Nephilim.

Cain immediately built a large bon-fire with flames as hot as molten lava from the pits of hell. But every time he approached and tried to throw himself inside the flames, he couldn't take the pain. As his skin and hair sizzled and blistered, he would pull away and withdraw. Ultimately he abandoned his attempts to pass through the Seraphim death. Because he could not face being burned alive, to die in order to be resurrected anew, as does the phoenix, he was instead eternally cursed. He was cursed to die for an eternity.

As part of the curse, Cain's flesh slowly began to die, slowly decaying upon his bones, as an extremely slow progressing form of gangrene spread over him, feasting upon his flesh for centuries. His flesh rotted and turned a form of green and black, all the while naturally becoming very foul smelling due to his rotting flesh. To make it even worse, Cain was able to witness his fate at all times, having the dubious ability to see into the hearts and minds of everyone around him. With a simple touch, he could read their very thoughts. Thus he was able to see their utter disgust and hatred of him in his own mind.

Cain of course was despised due to his cursed condition and was not permitted to live amongst any other persons. It was believed that God had commanded that none shall kill Cain, or they themselves would fall under the same ravages of this curse. Cain could not escape his eternal damnation by the hand of another, and he soon found that he could not take his own life. He was immortal as Lucifer had promised him, but he found himself living in his own personal hell.

Lucifer, or one of the Nephilim of the time, found Cain after nearly 800 years wandering in the desert. Cain pleaded for mercy and a means by which he could end his mortal torment. He was mercifully provided the key to his release from the curse. Cain was told that he must surrender himself to death by burning within flames of a fire until his entire body was consumed to nothing. Cain, unable to continue his existence on Earth, finally capitulated to his fate and leapt into a bonfire so that his flesh could be consumed by the flames. Cain was again tricked, for his flesh had become to rotten and decayed, so corrupted that he could not pass through the resurrecting fire. The Seraphim were unable to repair him, in his fallen state. The flames burnt his corrupted flesh until his body was merely a pile of ashes. The only part of him that remained was his bones. And his soul continued to live on within his scorched bones. His spirit was captured in the only thing left of his mortal body, since the Seraphim would not allow him to pass on to the afterlife.

Cain's bones were given to his son, Lamnech. Upon the skull of Cain, Lucifer had inscribed the recipe for eternal mortal life with the ashes of Cain's own consumed flesh. By crushing a portion of Cain's bones and mixing it with the blood of an innocent person, and drinking the bloody concoction, Lamnech readily took upon himself the curse, believing that he would attain immortality. Lamnech sought to rule over mankind, and he believed he could live eternally, building an army of followers, and create the greatest empire in the world. But, he did not know that he must pass through the "Sephirah Death" to actually attain immortality.

Lamnech was also cursed with slowly rotting flesh. He was cursed to die over a thousand years. Condemning God, Lamnech wished to spread this curse to all of mankind. To accomplish this evil task he anointed his likewise evil followers to spread the bones throughout the entire world, and along with them, the curse. From that day forward, the most noble, virtuous, and wise men have been appointed the task of finding, taking, and hiding the bones to prevent the spread of the curse. The bones Lamnech sent out were located and secured. The bones were eventually hidden separately in disparate lands throughout the far reaches of the world, in an attempt to hide them from the likes of Lamnech...

...The Oracle bones of Cain were to be protected, and watched over by the anointed priestesses, known as Oracles. They were the females who were able to withstand the burning of their flesh, and able to pass through the "Seraphim Death" thus being reborn as perfected immortals. Oracles were able to read the hearts and minds of those they came into contact with, and they would use the bones to foresee the advance of evil doers who would seek to use the bones for power, those who sought to conquer and to kill.

A descendant of Ham brought the skull to a hidden place in the vast desert, to the Oasis of Siwa, to prevent the curse of eternal death from spreading again across the earth.

A woman of pureness of heart was appointed to guard the skull of Cain. The skull was the most valuable of all the Oracle Bones. For only the skull, when placed inside flames, would permit the spirit of Cain to speak aloud for all to hear...

...Many leaders of great civilizations sought to capture the skull of Cain, for to possess its powers would certainly allow them to gain great wisdom, wealth, power, even the ability to conquer the entire world...

...Around 550 B.C., an evil descendant of Lamnech, Cambyses II, captured one of the Oracles who possessed one of the 'oracle bones' of Cain. That oracle lived in Persia, within the ancient city of Babylon, and she was captured when the great city was sacked by Cambyses. She was the oracle of the Zoroastrian's. Knowing of the prophecy of eternal living damnation, Cambyses imbibed the sacred concoction, took the life of his own infant son, and as Lamnech had done, invited the curse upon him-self.

At the same time he was told of the remaining oracles which had spread across the world, each possessing a bone of Cain. He raised an army with the intent of finding and destroying every oracle, in order to possess all of the bones of Cain. He believed that with all the oracle bones that he would be invincible against any army of the known world. Cambyses desired to rule the entire world for all eternity...

...Cambyses was successful in destroying the army of Egypt and securing his powerful domain in the City of Memphis. From that city he sent an army of 50,000 men out into the vast Western Desert to take the skull of Cain from the Oracle of Ammun in Siwa. After learning of the fate of Osiris from the Egyptian captives, Cambyses did not make the journey with the army, and in his stead, he sent his evil daughter Malaika to capture the skull of Cain...

...The inhabitants of Siwa observed the approaching army across the Great Western Desert. The people asked the Oracle why the army had come to Siwa. They were afraid, and wanted to determine if the army was peaceful, if they journeyed to Siwa merely to consult with the Oracle, as had many armies done so in the past.

The Oracle's response was not what they were expecting to hear. Not the reassuring words of comfort. No. She provided a dire warning of impending death, and many fled the city. The Oracle even sent her own son out of the city, with a trusted servant, fleeing into the North countries...

...Raising the skull of Cain in her hands, the Oracle walked up the marble stairway leading to a platform. Upon the marble alter there was created a large bon-fire. The Oracle stepped into the flames and was not burned. As she stood within the leaping flames, the skull began to glow brightly as the image of Cain's face appeared. With Cain's head in the Oracle's uplifted hands, together, they began speaking prophetic words to all the gathered inhabitants of Siwa exhorting them to either flee, or die...

...Upon Malaika's arrival she found the City of Siwa to be without any army, or any weapon for defense, or any other means of defense whatsoever. She was confronted with a city comprised of approximately 10,000 souls who worshiped the word of God in peaceful harmony. Entering into the Temple of the Oracle of Ammun, Malaika found it to be abandoned. No Oracle was to be found, and no Skull of Cain...

...The army set up camp, in, and around the city. The entire army shared the same well for drinking as there was only one source of water, a small well at the Oasis. The water tasted extremely bitter and had the reddish appearance of blood. After a few days without any success of finding the Oracle, or the Skull of Cain, Malaika grew violent with rage. Malaika took a young woman into the Temple of the Oracle and held her by her hair. She ordered her army to gather together every resident of the city at the Temple of the Oracle.

Placing a dagger at the throat of the young woman, Malaika demanded that they reveal the location of the true Oracle of Ammun, and the skull of Cain, or she would kill everyone in the city. To demonstrate her intent, Malaika slit the throat of the young woman.

When the people of Siwa refused to do her bidding, Malaika ordered her army to kill every living thing within the city walls. The blood thirsty army rampaged through the small city, killing everyone they encountered. As the last person's throat was cut open, the city streets ran red with innocent blood.

To Malaika's surprise, another young woman appeared from underneath the marble alter upon which she sat, as she watched the rampaging army. In her hands, the true Oracle held the coveted skull of Cain, offering it up to Malaika and pleading for her to end the carnage.

Malaika took hold of the skull and raised her dagger to strike the woman. Unafraid, the Oracle lifted her face toward the heavens allowing Malaika a clean blow. Malaika swung her blade, cutting clean through her outstretched neck, severing her head which rolled across the marble floor. Malaika began laughing maniacally while holding the skull high above her head for the surrounding soldiers to view her prize. That is when Malaika heard the gargled voice of the Oracle speaking up to her from the ground.

Malaika turned her face to look at the severed head. The hair of the young woman was tangled, matted, and sticky with her freshly spilt blood. Her face remained alive, her eyes moving, looking back up at Malaika. Then, the Oracle's mouth began moving.

From her blood oozing mouth, she cried out, "hear me Malaika! I am the Oracle of Ammun. The word

of God is eternal round. Within his weaving you are bound. You have tied the eternal knot. Only eternal damnation, have you found. I once was where you now be—now prepare with speed to follow me!"

Malaika became afraid, and angry, due to the spoken curse. "You cannot curse me, you are dead, and I am alive, to live forever!" Malaika screamed. As she yelled out her last word, Malaika grabbed the severed head by the hair and threw it into the well. Looking back at her army, Malaika ordered, "fill every vessel with water for our journey home! We are departing before the sun sets!"

Examining her prize (the skull of Cain) Malaika puzzled over the fact that several teeth had been removed, as well as some small pieces from the back of the skull.

Neither Malaika, nor her army, took notice that the well water was saturated with the blood of the city dwellers that they had just slaughtered. The blood of the Oracle had also mingled with the well water, along with finely ground bits of bone, from the skull of Cain.

Malaika and the army departed Siwa, plunging into the Great Western Desert, believing they would return to Memphis in glory. Malaika believed that now, along with her father, they would rule the world forever. However, after only two days journey through the desert, an enormous sand storm arose before them. Attempting to find shelter, the entire army fled toward the only place of available refuge, the mountain of Aghuri.

The sandstorm blew incessantly for many days. Malaika and her army were forced to hide within the caverns underneath the mountain. Over a hundred feet of sand blew onto the foot of the mountainside, covering every possible entrance, or exit, to the caverns in which the army sought refuge. Malaika and the entire army were forever trapped by the sandstorm, eternally entombed within the mountain, or buried deep underneath the sand.

The mountain is now referred to as the, 'mountain of the dead,' by the local nomads. They call it that because of the dreadful smell of rotting flesh which seems to emanate from the desert sands surrounding the entire mountain...

...The nomads also provided along with their fascinating, yet, unbelievable story, a clue to finding some remaining antiquities in the desert. They related that some strange artifacts of warfare, as well as many valuable antiquities from ancient Egypt, had been discovered over many years within the deep desert. Supposedly artifacts from Egypt that had been looted by the army, were discarded, or abandoned, as they fled the sandstorm near the base of the mountain. Now, many of those artifacts are being uncovered by the blowing winds that continually shift the dunes around that surround the mountain.

They also provided a warning when I displayed an interest in searching for artifacts in the vicinity of the mountain. Omar has related that the nomads spoke of wandering demons, skeletal monsters with dried flesh, who, seem to emerge from the sands, digging themselves out as if escaping up from hell to attack and kill anyone they may encounter...

...The nomads provided very detailed directions to a location which is approximately two days travel across open desert to the mountain of Aghuri. Possibly remains of the lost army of Cambyses? Omar and Hakim are not familiar with that area of desert and they are most reluctant to travel in that direction, primarily due to the nomad's dire warnings and their susceptibility to superstitions...

...21 April, 1898, I have convinced Omar and Hakim to continue our trek home by way of the mountain of Aghuri. It has been my most satisfying experience in the past to find hidden treasures based upon such fantastical stories. I believe that such stories have some element of historical fact to back them up, and I dreadfully desire to not return empty handed. This very well may be my last expedition to recover artifacts in this region. My age and the shrinking world will most certainly bring an end to my impassioned pursuits...

...23 April, 1898, we can see the mountain of Aghuri looming before us in the far distance. The nomads were definitely correct about one disturbing fact; the smell of rotting flesh is becoming nauseatingly strong, and almost unbearable, the closer we get to the mountain.

We are short on water and Omar believes that a spring will be found at the base of the mountain. It is our unfortunate lot to be forced to make camp there...

...24 April, 1898, the smell of death pervades every breath to the point of making us sick. No

water can be found at the mountain. We have made camp for the night and will depart quickly at first light. No artifacts have been found, most disappointing...

...25 April, 1898: During the night the strongest storm I have ever encountered in the desert raged. Wind and heavy rain destroyed our camp. The camels have fled without us, taking nearly all provisions with them. There is very little water remaining. A small cave opening in the side of the mountain Aghuri has revealed itself with the shifting sands. We have no choice, and we are forced to take shelter within the small cave. We will wait within the protection of the cave in hopes of passing nomads discovering us...

...27 April, 1898: The stench of death is growing seemingly with every breath we inhale. Omar and Hakim have resigned themselves to death and both are pleading with me to depart into the desert. They feel we would be safer in the open desert, rather than staying within the protective bowels of this 'mountain of death,' as they call it. Our water is almost completely gone and my will to remain is weakening...

...29 April, 1898: I awoke this morning to find myself alone. Omar and Hakim have made a stealthy departure during the night. I fear they will perish in the desert heat before the sun reaches its highest position in the sky. Unwilling to follow them, I have decided to go in the opposite direction, down into the bowels of the cave, in search of a source of fresh water...

...?, 1898: I have lost sense of time, the going is

slow, and the temperature has cooled considerably the further I move away from the mouth of the cave. No water yet, I will continue a bit further before returning to the surface. The cave continues into the mountain without any sign of ending. To my utter dismay, all that I have managed to find is piles of bones. The interior of this cave is littered with the remains of what appears to be hundreds of corpses. All that is left is their dried bones, with the flesh having been completely stripped from their bodies...

...It is impossible to walk upright the further I go, crawling and slithering like a worm is the only means of negotiating most sections. Hard to write by lighted matches, my oil lamp is nearly depleted of fuel. May not make it back to entrance...

...I'm going mad, or I have reached the far side. I can clearly see a light source ahead, some sort of strange flickering light, possibly a fire far off in the distance?...

...I have been rescued, or damned, not yet certain? A nomadic woman has found me and provided water, or some liquid, hard to tell in this dark chasm. Still weak, I can only drink. I do not feel pains of hunger anymore. Strangely, I have no desire to eat. I cannot communicate with the woman as she does not speak any English. Her manner of speech sounds nothing like any Arab dialect I have encountered.

Wearing what appears to be a black burka covering her entire body and face, I dare not ask her to reveal herself to me, as such is their

custom. I have not seen her eat or drink for some time, she merely tends the fire. The fire casts a strange light. There appears to be no kindling or any discernible source of fuel...

...Many days have passed I believe, time has lost meaning in this tomb. The Arab woman is eager to learn my native language, and she is a very quick pupil. I have realized that the horrendous stench of death has departed. I am feeling much stronger and can now move about with relative ease...

...The woman continues to provide a liquid to drink, on further examination, it does not appear to be water, hard to tell, its black, oily to the touch, no discernible taste...

...I feel that I am slipping into madness. There is no rational explanation for my continued survival. I believe that we have possibly been in this cave for many weeks now, and neither of us has eaten. Worst of all the woman's thoughts seem to be entering my own. I am beginning to believe that the woman is in fact merely a mirage created within my own mind. Some hallucination as I pass into death's cold grip. I may have only been here a few days...

...I continue to drink her potion that sustains me. The more she speaks to me, the less I am able to distinguish myself, apart from her thoughts...

27

P AUL CRACKED OPENED the front door to see who was there—as Nick pushed it the rest of the way open walking inside. Wearing his coffee-stained trench-coat, an opened collared shirt, wrinkled, with no tie, half tucked inside an old pair of slacks that he pulled from a pile of laundry, he meant to get right down to business.

"Evening Detect—" Paul tried to say, as Nick brushed past him heading straight into the living room.

"Where is he?" Nick asked curtly, only making eye contact for a second before looking up the stairs.

Paul knew who he meant. "Charlie's upstairs, in his room," he answered dismissively, being just as rude.

Nick headed up the creaking staircase as fast as his tired legs would take him, enticed by the prospect of hearing Charlie's story, only briefly pausing at Dr. Karanza's room to peek through the door that was slightly ajar. She was sitting on her bed, with her eyes glued to the pages of the leather-bound notebook. She didn't notice him there. He gently rapped on the door, pushing it open. "Is Charlie still awake Emily?" He asked, in a surly voice, doing his best to impress upon her the idea that, *she had better not be wasting his time,* without outright saying it.

Dr. Karanza sprang upright and shuffled the papers out of sight. Quietly sliding into her slippers, she shuffled past Nick as if he wasn't there—letting him know that, *she thought he was a jackass*, without saying it outright. He followed her to Charlie's bedside without either of them uttering another sound.

She gently pushed on Charlie's arm, saying, "Investigator Thomas is here Charles—you need to wake up."

Charlie opened his eyes, bloodshot, drooping, completely drugged-up looking, as he tried to focus on the blurry image of a gruff stout man walking toward him. Dr. Karanza slipped back out, wanting to continue reading. She already knew what he was going to say. Charlie didn't move or speak, or even let out a soft groan. His head was mushed deeply into the goose-down pillow much like a corpse in a coffin.

Nick pulled a chair up to the bed. He leaned in close to Charlie, getting his face up close—only a few short inches from the tip of Charlie's wheezing nose. Waiting a few seconds, he watched Charlie's eyelids going up and down, moving so slowly, along with his chest, slowly rising and falling, as he took shallow breaths. Nick spoke softly. "I hear you're doing better Charlie… that's good… real good. They tell me you found something in the burn pit out back… that right Charlie?"

Charlie's face was molded clay, pasty, white, and soft, with dead eyes, unmoving. Nick continued speaking, more energetically, "You don't have to talk to me Charlie, hell you know I don't give a shit about you. Don't matter to me—not a bit—where you spend the rest of your sorry ass life. Way I see it now—you can spend the rest of your life back at the loony bin where I found you… along with the rest of your crazy ass family—or—you can spend it in prison. Cause we already got plenty enough evidence to put you away and keep you locked inside—one or the other. No matter what you say now. Kaitlin done told us everything. About how you killed Daniel… you're piece of shit father… you're pretty young wife… even your sweet little baby Matthew."

Dr. Karanza slinked back inside the room, her eyes still glued to the pages of the journal. She couldn't resist hearing what Charles was going to say—proving her right.

Charlie's eyes flickered nervously. His lips quivered as he started sputtering out words, "No… that's not it… that's not what happened… I didn't kill them. I didn't kill no-one. It was Kaitlin who killed Daniel… put him in the fire pit… I, I, I, tried to stop her."

"When did she kill him Charlie?" Nick grumbled with disdain—with the bitter-sweet smell of sour whiskey mixed with strong black coffee lingering on his breath.

"That night… that night… out back… I saw it all," Charlie stammered with his eyes welling up.

"The same night the others were killed… is that the night Charlie?" Nick cajoled, moving closer to Charlie's face, clenching hard on the arm-rests of his chair.

"Yes… that same night," Charlie muttered as a tear trickled down his cheek.

"You're absolutely certain about that Charlie?"

"I was in horrible pain. Got the fire put out on Liz and Matthew… heard the gunshot upstairs and saw Kaitlin running downstairs and straight out the back door… I didn't know what the hell was going on?" After a pause, Charlie stammered out what he remembered, "I chased after her… out back… she went after Daniel next… they fought… she was hitting him with something… an axe or sledge hammer… I saw the whole thing—I swear I did." Then he broke down sobbing as if vomiting up poison.

Nick sat back in his chair, forcing himself to slow down—to calm down—allowing the blood to flow back out of his angry flush face.

"Perhaps we should take a moment—," Dr. Karanza started to say, as Nick threw his hand up—silencing her mid-sentence.

"So, how do you know it was your sister who killed him?" Nick asked softly, giving Charlie a little breathing space, to recompose himself too.

Dr. Karanza huffed, cocking her eyebrow—thinking; *of course it was her, idiot, who the hell else could have been?*

"Well—," Charlie paused a moment in deep thought, before saying, "I saw her… a woman… she looked just like Kate… she was hitting him with something." Sniffling, he fought hard to keep his composure, while recalling every tiny detail.

"Then, why is she saying that she still sees him out there?" Nick blurted out full of skepticism. "And why she's saying he's still living out back there in that old abandoned farmhouse?"

"Father ordered Daniel to stay away from us after the incident with Kate… when she got sent to that boarding school. Nobody saw him often after that. He stayed around his house—staying out of sight. Especially after we moved back—father wouldn't let him get near Liz or the baby. None of us ever went back there, but we all knew he was out there. Maybe she believes he's still there?"

Not giving him time to think, Nick asked coldly, "Who killed your wife and baby Charlie?"

Charlie recoiled—the question bringing back the repressed pain. He could only close his eyes, and turn his face towards the wall—not answering.

"And how did she kill the others—huh Charlie? What did she do to them?" Nick snarled—urging him to keep talking.

"She didn't kill them," Charlie mumbled between sniffles, with another teardrop escaping his eyelid and dripping down his cheek. "Father did it… the fire… it killed them. It was the fire… a man in the fire… he killed Elizabeth and Matthew."

"How did the fire kill them Charlie?" Nick asked sternly—his anger returning to a soft boil.

Dr. Karanza stopped her reading, turned her head slightly, focusing all of her attention, she listened intently for Charlie's answer.

"Father was drunk… drunk and angry… again. I was up in my room reading. He was yelling and hollering at someone, downstairs, in the front room, near the living room. Little Matthew was on the floor on a blanket… by the fire… just sleeping. Father must not have known he was there, when he threw his bottle of whiskey at the fireplace—he was in a drunken rage. I was walking into the room when the bottle hit the mantle, bursting, splattering whiskey all over. Then—that's when it came alive. The fire… it came alive, crawling out of the fireplace like some sort of demon. He, it, whatever it was, it's fiery arms reached out and grabbed ahold of Matthew. It was holding on to him, burning him—it just wouldn't let go. Liz got to him first and tried to pull little Matthew away, but then it grabbed ahold of her too. Her clothes caught on fire and it just enveloped her. It looked like he, something, was on her tearing at her with flaming arms, until she couldn't take it anymore, and she died. I tried to pull her out of the fire, but it was too strong—it had her—it wouldn't let go." Charlie's voice trailed off as he broke down, sobbing uncontrollably.

"Then who killed your father? What happened to him Charlie—tell us—who did it Charlie?" Nick implored with his unrelenting face turning a bright red.

Between gasps, Charlie spoke, "I saw her, for just a moment, running past me, following after father, going up the stairs."

"Who did you see Charles?" Dr. Karanza asked intently—expecting the answer.

Charlie paused, squeezing his eyes tightly shut, as if trying not to see his own memories—before he revealed. "I had given up trying to save Matthew and Liz… the pain was too much… they were burned-up… already dead… I was burned so badly too. I turned to run… I had to get out of there, but I saw her, the woman, it had to be Kaitlin—it looked just like her."

"Yes, and then what did she do to him Charles?" Dr. Karanza encouraged him on.

"I heard a gunshot… right after… she ran back down the stairs and ran straight out the back door," Charlie whimpered as he pulled the bedcovers up to his eyes.

"That's enough… he's had quite enough for tonight," Dr. Karanza announced, urging Nick to end the interrogation.

Nick pushed the chair back and walked to the door, motioning for Dr. Karanza to follow him out. They quietly exited Charlie's bedroom and walked swiftly into Karanza's room without speaking. The door was shut so that Charlie couldn't overhear them.

"Congratulations Emily. You did it again," Nick said with a slight grin. His scruffy face displayed a rarely seen look for him— pleasant satisfaction.

"Are we finished then? Are you arresting Kaitlin?" Dr. Karanza asked, with a similar looking, satisfactory smile.

"Sorry, but no," he answered sharply. "You got Charlie talking, but that's all. We don't have enough yet."

Dr. Karanza scowled, huffed, and crossed her arms.

Nick realized she didn't like his answer, and she would be hard to convince. So, he turned it up a notch, intentionally rubbing her the wrong way, saying with a contentious smirk, "His story's bullshit doctor. You aint about to start believing that bunk now are you doctor? We know ole Daniel wasn't killed the same night as the others. Hell, he'd been dead for quite a few years prior—best we can figure."

Dr. Karanza turned away from Thomas, slowly looking around the room—stewing—with the sound of his overly twanging, controlling, good-ole-boy small-town smug voice, twisting her nerves into a tightly wound up ball. But she listened to his seasoned cop logic, as he explained.

"He doesn't know where and how Daniel was killed. Now, Matthew and Elizabeth, they did die in that fire, but, Charlie says it was an accident. And how he described it fits with the evidence. He says Kaitlin followed her father upstairs, and he heard a gunshot. But, he didn't see who fired the gun. It very well may have been suicide. William could have put a bullet hole in his heart to get out of this nut house. And hell, ole Charlie is plum crazy to boot… aint no doubt in my mind about that. And aint nobody in their right mind gunna buy that story about the fire crawling out of the fireplace and grabbing hold of them, like some demon crawlin' out of the fire-pits of hell itself."

Stupid Asshole, what an ignorant bumkin'! Dr. Karanza fumed inside as she started to tune him out. *He has no appreciation for what I've done, and will do. He either doesn't trust me, or thinks I'm an idiot, why else would he be keeping important information from me.* "So, why didn't you tell me that Daniel had apparently been killed years ago?" She finally snapped—having heard enough of his hillbilly logic.

Her angry question caught Nick off guard, causing him to pause to reevaluate the situation. He wasn't prepared to be on the defensive, a position he always attempted to avoid. Going back on the offensive, he scowled and raised a pointing finger to push into Dr. Karanza's chest like a knife, saying, "Remember Doctor, I'm the Investigator here—not you. I decide what information you need to know, and when you need to know it. Don't meddle in my investigation Emily. You got Charlie talking… that's great and all… even if it is all a bunch of lies… but there's a lot more we need to know before this is over, and I can't let you, or anyone else, corrupt this investigation by tipping off Charlie and Kaitlin. Just keep doing your job Emily, and let me do mine. Got it?"

Dr. Karanza couldn't speak, almost biting through her lips to keep them shut. She knew all too well that he had the authority to end the investigation, anytime he wanted. And if he did, Charlie would be returned to the hospital, and she would be forced back there too—right along with him. *Well, I can play that game too,* she thought, glaring at his ugly mug. *Guess I don't need to let him know about the documents I found out in the farmhouse then either?*

Paul opened the bedroom door and casually walked in. The pair did not realize that Paul had been standing in the hallway, listening to them through the door.

Nick turned his attention away from the smoldering eyes of Dr. Karanza, to ask Paul, "where is Kate?"

Paul paused with a puzzled look. A relaxed smile appeared on his face, and he said, "You know, I actually haven't seen her in a while. I think she left the house a couple of hours ago. Probably headed into town to get a drink… and I'm thinking we all could use one right about now."

Nick and Dr. Karanza stared at him cold-faced.

Nick slowly raised his pointing finger again, and ordered them both to, "Keep Charlie and Kate apart, and do not let them talk to each other—not until I get a chance to talk to her first—understood?"

They both nodded as Nick brushed past Paul again as he headed downstairs.

"Whoa, a little uptight wouldn't you say?" Paul snickered.

Dr. Karanza was still fuming and she turned her back to Paul, ignoring his whimsical remark entirely. Whisking the journal and documents from off the bed, she carried them out of the bedroom, telling Paul to, "Just go find Kaitlin," as she passed by—just as dismissively as Nick.

Dr. Karanza slipped back into Charlie's bedroom. He was still awake, and calmer, having had time to recover from Nick's interrogation. Slipping into the chair at his bedside she shuffled through the pages in her hands. Putting them up to where he could see the writing on the pages, she asked him in an almost desperate voice, "Charles, take a look at these papers… tell me… do you recognize any of them?"

Charlie studied the papers for a brief moment, before cracking a smile, as if reading a memorable joke.

"You do know… so what is it Charlie? Who made this, and what do these symbols mean?" She begged for an answer.

"It's nothing… just some of mother's magic spells," Charlie grinned fondly.

"Well, what do you know about them Charles?"

"My mother… somehow she became obsessed with that black magic shit before she died. They weren't just making moonshine

out there in the barn. They had built a whole chemistry lab, like some mad-scientist movie. Turned into some kind of bizarre hobby I guess? The best I can remember… I was so young then… Kaitlin told me about most of it… how they would be out there all night long playing with some magic spell book and making all kinds of magic potions and such. I can't remember much myself—just a lot of blurry images—lost memories.

"What book?" Dr. Karanza blurted out.

"The book they got from William's father… after he died… that he left for him. That's what Kaitlin told me anyway. I never saw a book."

"Where's the book now Charles?" Dr. Karanza demanded to know.

"It's still out there in the barn someplace. I never bothered looking at it… stupid nonsense. But Kate seemed to be obsessed over it. She just wouldn't stay out of the barn. She even tried to burn it down once."

"Yes, go on Charles, tell me everything—everything you can remember," Dr. Karanza prodded.

"She kept telling everyone crazy stories about having visions… mostly seeing grandmother and mother… always seeing them around the graveyard, in the barn, in her room. No one believed her. In fact, it seemed like the less we believed her, the worse she got. At one point she even accused father of keeping our mother locked up in the barn—man she really lost it."

"Just what exactly was going on out there Charles?"

"I never found out exactly what they were doing, but me and Kate figured they were doing séances—you know—trying to communicate with dead people, dead relatives, that kind of stupid shit. Black magic shit. We did sneak in a couple of times… and they had all sorts of bottles, vials, containers of powders, all kinds of weird stuff… most of its still out there all boxed up in storage. Father cleaned the rest out after he sent Kate off to that school. But, he still kept the barn locked up for years, till I finally convinced him to let me store my stuff in there—after I agreed to move back in."

"But what about all these symbols here? I recognize many of them, related to alchemy, but do you know what any of them mean, and how they were used?" Dr. Karanza asked redirecting his attention to the papers that she was holding up to his face.

"Hell… I don't have a clue doc? They put those same symbols all over the house—if you haven't noticed. Charlie pointed at the fireplace, saying, "See, the symbol is on the corners of every fireplace mantle, and up in the corners of every doorway. Grandfather Ben and his insane wife Catherine had them put there when they built this place, for some reason."

Stepping over to the fireplace, Dr. Karanza looked at the intricately carved knot in the mantle above the fireplace—with the same pattern—matching the symbols on the pages, exactly. *That doesn't look like a Celtic Knot… looks more like a Sanskrit eternal knot… or like knots I've seen on sixth century Pictish stones from Scotland, or even more like a Solomon's Knot?* She wondered as she ran her fingertip along the carved line that flowed along an intersecting, never ending circular pattern.

A flashing glint of light reflecting off of a small shiny object caught her attention. It was down in the ashes, tucked back into the corner of the fireplace. She knelt down and reached inside to sift through the puffy gray ashes with her fingertips. It was the size of a small stone, *hard and bumpy but not a wood chip or piece of coal, and certainly not glass*, she pondered as she tumbled the strange object around in the tips of her blackened fingers while rubbing away the sticky layer of soot. Rubbing away the last bit of soot she could see the hard white enamel. *What the hell?* She suddenly realized that it was a *human tooth.* A molar, with a large cavity, filled with a gold filling that sparkled when the light hit it at just the right angle.

"What is it Dr.… what did you find?" Charlie asked lifting his head to see.

Dr. Karanza acted as if she hadn't heard him as she examined the tooth, while thinking, w*ho's is this… and why the hell is it in the fireplace?*

"What did you find doctor?" Charlie asked again, impatiently.

"It's nothing Charlie. Just try and get some rest now… and I'll check up on you later," she muttered while walking toward the door. She clutched the tooth so that he could not see it. Pushing the tooth into her pants pocket she raced back into her own bedroom—stopping in front of the fireplace. There were two eternal knots just like the others in Charlie's room—carved into the mantle with one on each side.

Falling to her knees at the hearth, she searched the top of the dark gray ashes with her eyes. All she could see were bits of charred wood, coals, and ash. *Well, here goes nothing*, she said to herself as she slowly slid her fingers deep into the ash, pushing the burnt chunks of wood out of the way so that she could run her fingers along the bricks lining the bottom of the hearth—carefully sifting, and feeling, for anything unusual.

Every time she felt something small and hard, she pulled it out and rubbed away the soot and ash to examine it closely. Over and over again she plunged her hands into the ash, blackening her hands and arms up to the elbows. And, each time she wiped away the soot, she was disappointed. Soon, she had made a small pile of discarded lumps of wood and small stones. *What the hell am I doing? Now I'm losing it too*, she started thinking, just before her finger touched something small, hard, and unusual.

Her frantically rubbing fingertips removed a thick layer of soot—revealing another human tooth. "What the hell is going on here?" she muttered, rolling the tooth around in her fingers as if she had found a priceless gemstone. *Clearly, this is not just some odd coincidence.* Jumping to her feet she pushed the tooth down inside her pants pocket with the other one. *There's only one way to find out*, she considered, *since there's another fireplace in almost every room in this house.*

It was much easier to find the tooth in Kaitlin's bedroom, sitting in the corner of the fireplace with very little ash covering it at all—almost as if placed there for someone to discover. *This is getting downright disturbing*, Dr. Karanza told herself as she placed the tooth in her pocket along with the others, and then headed down

the stairs. Reaching the bottom of the stairs, she was unexpectedly greeted by Paul. "Thank God it's you," she gushed.

Paul looked her up and down. Black and gray smudges of ash dotted her face and covered her arms. Her blue-jeans were grayed at the knees and around the pockets. Ash was smudged up and down her legs where she had patted her hands. Thick, sticky black-tar soot blackened her fingers. *Oh, my… what the hell has she been into… she looks just like Charlie did whenever he pulled that bone out of the fire-pit,* Paul puzzled. "What the hell have you been doing doctor?" He had to ask.

"I can't explain right now Paul," she responded, pushing past him and storming into the front room, "just go keep an eye on Charlie. And whatever the hell you do—do not let him leave his bedroom!"

Paul didn't bother to try and get an explanation—he was too stunned. Moving cautiously to the bottom of the stairs, he stopped, lingering just long enough to see Dr. Karanza kneel down in front of the fireplace. His jaw dropped as he watched her thrust both of her hands inside to start frantically kneading the pile of ashes with her fingers.

"Here's another one," she muttered while jumping to her feet.

"What's going on Doc?" Paul asked nervously.

Startled, Dr. Karanza spun around to face him. She opened up her hand to show Paul the soot covered tooth resting on her palm. "I don't know yet," she responded resolutely, "but I have found a human tooth in the ashes of every fireplace in this house."

"We should call Detective Thomas," Paul suggested.

"No!" Dr. Karanza snarled, closing her fist tightly around the tooth, "he doesn't need to know anything about this."

"But isn't that considered evidence?"

Dr. Karanza glared at Paul as if he had just slapped her across the face. She slid the tooth into her pants pocket. Not answering, she sauntered past him with an icy stare—slinking like a cat down the hallway—to disappear out the back door.

28

A S THE FINAL boxcar of the long train flew past Kaitlin along the tracks that passed by the loading dock of the Mill—the night sky fell silent once more—all except for the sounds of the groaning rusted hinges of the large wooden delivery platform doors. They had been blown open by the rushing wind as the train whished by. As the air settled, both doors swayed gently, giving off a soft voice that called to her—a white picket fence gate blowing in the breeze on a summer afternoon—inviting her to come inside. It was just all too familiar. *I've been here before… this has happened to me before,* she felt as she walked up the concrete loading dock. She couldn't resist accepting the invitation. She walked through the doorway into the vast expanse of the dark Mill.

As her body passed across the threshold, moving from the moonlight outside to the near blackness of the interior, everything seemed to change at once. She found herself walking into the barn back at home. There was a lighted lantern up ahead. A hand brushed up against hers as her mother appeared next to her, taking her hand. She looked up to see her mother's face that was partially hidden in the dark. It was then that she realized that she was a young girl again, about three years old. Across the barn she could make out an image on the floor, drawn with a white and gray powder on the wooden floorboards where the dirt had been cleared away making a circle. It was a hexagram, with smaller symbols drawn inside the corners of the triangles and within the center. The barn was softly illuminated by a small lantern burning a few feet away in the corner.

Her father was standing at a table near the wall with his back to them. He was busily working with twisting glass, bottles filled with powder and liquids, and a small flame from a gas torch. He finished what he was doing, turned, and walked over to them, handing her mother a small glass vile. Camilla looked down at her and smiled, asking in a soft voice, "Are you ready my little miracle?" Pointing down at the floor, she told her, "Go ahead, lay down in the circle like I showed you."

Kaitlin did as her mother asked, and she lay down on the floor inside of the pentagram. Camilla and William took their places, kneeling down on the floor, one on each side of her. They put their hands on her arms—holding her in place. "Now, open your mouth and swallow all the medicine dear," her mother whispered, placing the glass vile to Kaitlin's trembling lips. The black liquid tasted rancid, and she gagged as she tried to swallow the vile substance. Her stomach wrenched and her throat burned as if she had swallowed a strong acid that bubbled up as it mixed with her saliva.

As the concoction entered her bloodstream and took effect, her entire body began to convulse. Her parents pushed down harder on her arms and legs as she began to shake all over. The looks on her parent's faces frightened her as they looked down at her. *They were not right anymore… not her parents at all… not anymore*, she thought.

The convulsions subsided quickly, and Kaitlin began to feel a numbness sensation—a tingling that was moving up her fingers and toes—slowly moving up her arms and legs and travelling over her entire body. Soon Kaitlin had no feeling in any part of her body. Everything around her was moving extremely slow. Even her mother's voice was distorted and slowing, as if they were all underwater, "It's alright… just relax dear… the medicine is working. It will be all better soon," Camilla whispered in her tiny ear. She could tell from

her parents wild eyed looks and devilishly amused smiles that they were pleased. They were enjoying watching her under the influence of their *medicine*.

That is when she could remember first seeing Daniel's disgusting face—as he lurked in the shadows. Barely visible, he lingered near the lantern in the corner of the barn. Straining to look up at him, she could just make out his gruesomely distorted face underneath his straw hat, with thick sweat stuck to him like hardened wax that was running down the side of a candle, looking exactly the same, from the time he was pictured with Louise at the Mill, until the time she last saw him, chasing after her in the darkness when she was a teenager—a disgusting appearance that never seemed to be changing. Daniel leaned over the lantern and blew. The barn went completely black. Tiny Kaitlin squeezed her eyes shut and began screaming, fighting against her parents hands, until she finally gave up and opened her eyes again—only to find herself as an adult once again, still standing just inside of the double doorway of the loading dock, just inside the Mill.

A nauseating feeling swept over her, realizing that she was remembering what actually happened to her when she was a small child. Remembering what her parents had done to her. It wasn't merely another vision, or another mad hallucination this time, no, this was all too real. *Did they poison me… father… Ed… my own mother? No! It couldn't have happened. Why would they do that to me? Why am I being tortured like this?*

Behind her, the sky glowed yellow and orange with the first rays of morning sunlight breaking over the horizon.

29

KAITLIN BRIEFLY CONSIDERED returning to the house for a hot shower and change of clothes, but she couldn't escape the lingering thoughts of Louise's voice and her bizarre story. *Louise was telling me what I needed to know I think… about my family history… about Gitana… what my mother and father knew about her… and what she did to them… and what they did to me*, she puzzled, as her feet stumbled back to the car, where the keys were still dangling in the ignition switch.

Instead of going back to the house, she raced back to Louise's home along the empty early morning country roads.

The interior of Louise's house was still dark as Kaitlin crept up the slender concrete sidewalk. *She's still sleeping, I'm sure?* With a wimpy tap on the door, she called out in a hushed voice, "Hello. Louise. It's me, Kaitlin. Toni, Louise, is anyone up?" There was no response before she grabbed the cold brass doorknob and turned it, opening the door. Stepping halfway inside, she called out again into the dark home, "hello, anyone up?" No one responded—she only heard the soft hum of the old refrigerator running.

Tip-toeing past the kitchen into Louise's bedroom, she could barely make out the silhouette of Louise's slender body underneath

a quilt that had been tossed over her to ward off the night chill. Discarded tissues were piled up on the night stand, with a few littering the floor where they fell off. Lying on her back, Louise's hands were laying gently crossed on her stomach as if she had been readied for her final resting place. Kaitlin daintily slid a chair up to her bedside and sat down.

"Louise it's me Kaitlin. Louise, please wake up."

The room was still so dark that she couldn't see Louise's face very well at all. She could see that Louise didn't open her eyes, or turn her head to look over at her, before she began to speaking, in a dry, forced, congested voice.

"Kaitlin my dear, I knew you would come back. You need to know the rest of the story, don't you?"

Kaitlin nodded—*yes*.

"Where'd I leave off dear?"

Kaitlin thought for a moment, and whispered, "You were telling me about Gitana."

"Well then, you were listening… good girl," Louise said softly, before continuing with the story. "All was well until Malaika arrived in Rock Bridge. Her name meant *the angel*. Townsfolk called her the, *the black angel*. She was some kind of gypsy all-right, but she travelled alone, never associating with the others. And she always wore a long black dress and veil, never showing her face to anyone."

Louise went on to explain that Malaika was not like the other women. She didn't use cards or read palms. She didn't even tell fortunes. Oh no, she *made* people's fortunes, by telling people their futures as if she knew it already. Malaika would talk to their dead kin folk, telling them what they wanted and such. But most folks wanted her to conjure up healing potions, or to cast a curse on someone that had crossed them. But no one could just call on her like the other gypsies. Oh no, Malaika had to invite you to meet with her, in secret. And she wouldn't accept money. She would make people perform tasks for her in exchange for her special fortunes, spells, cures, or curses. It was rumored that she was hundreds of years old, perhaps even immortal. Many believed she was the daughter of Lucifer or some unholy demon.

Malaika was always guarded by her man-servant, Mr. Forth. He was a tall lanky fellow, never saying a word, with a most distant, empty, lost look about him. Like a loyal guard-dog, he would always be at Malaika's side, at her beckon call. No one got past ole Forth, unless Malaika permitted it.

Mr. Forth grabbed Gitana when she wandered close to Malaika's home one day—way on out in the woods. He dragged her kicking and screaming inside the house, where Malaika was waiting for her. The house stunk to-high-heaven with the smell of rotten flesh. Gitana nearly fainted-there-and-then it smelled oh-so bad. And the house was only lit up by one tiny candle. Gitana could barely make out Malaika's body in the darkness, covered from head to toe in a black veil. Even her hands were covered up by long black gloves that ran all the way up to her elbow.

Malaika told Gitana that she was in need of someone who could venture out in the daytime—out into the woods—to find the special ingredients needed to make her potions. Malaika knew Gitana had a keen knowledge of the woods, she could find everything she needed, easily. So, Malaika promised Gitana that if she did what she asked, then she would teach her many incredible and marvelous things, such things that were ancient secrets, things she could not reveal to anyone else, ever, including her mother.

Gitana reluctantly agreed, fearing for her life if she didn't, and once she was let out the door, she raced back through the woods to her home to tell her mother exactly what had occurred—just as Malaika knew she would, of course.

Gitana did what she was told. It wasn't long before Malaika was having her drinking some of her foul tasting potions that made her feel different after she drank them. Her personality began to change. She became less sociable, less friendly to others, always feeling tired, not being able to sleep, having horrible nightmares all the time

where strange people would visit with her—spirits—pleading with her to get away from Malaika and to stop using her black magic.

Day after day, Gitana would collect the strange ingredients Malaika would send her out into the woods to collect. Malaika would silently read from a large book, that she kept locked up when she wasn't looking at it—an ancient *Grimoire*. She would read out of if like some magical recipe book, then scratch out a list of ingredients that was needed for Gitana to fetch—frogs, bugs, mosses, barks, and all kinds of mushrooms, all that crazy stuff witches use to conjure-up something. After collecting them all, Gitana would have to cut, crush, grind, mix, measure, cook, and sometimes taste the nasty potions they would make together. Malaika would sometimes say some strange words, casting spells in some foreign language that Gitana couldn't understand one single word at-all. After it was done, Malaika would put it in a little bottle and send Gitana off to deliver it to whomever it was intended.

But one day, Malaika sent Gitana out to a graveyard. An ancient burial ground used by the Urquhart Clan. She was to collect something altogether different—something all-together special.

On this list of ingredients, there was written; 'a knotted rope that was growing up from out of the ground'. Gitana paid it no mind, believing it was some sort of root she was after. But it was indeed an old knotted rope sticking right up out of the ground—right up from where someone had just finished digging up an old grave. There was a very old headstone sticking up where the rope was buried. The headstone was so old that you couldn't even read the name. It had worn nearly completely off. Only thing left was a Pictish Knot carved deep into the face of the stone. And Malaika had drawn that same exact symbol next to the words on the list, *'knotted rope'*.

So, Gitana reached down and pulled on the rope, pulling it up out of the loose dirt like some long earthworm. Up popped an old sack from out of the ground—tied shut by the rope on the other end. She did what she was instructed to do, and she toted the bag, rope and all, back to Malaika. She never looked inside the bag, fearing for what she might find inside.

Malaika told her to put the bag on the table and open it. When Gitana untied the knotted rope and pulled open the dirt covered burlap bag, she saw a naked newborn baby boy, his body was cold, gray, and limp, but she could see that he was breathing, just a little, and he was barely still living. Gitana begged Malaika to save him. And that's when Malaika finally took off her veil—showing her deep green and black skin that was covered up with cracking sores, puss oozing sores, with rotten flesh that stank of death. She had horrifying black eyes, with pupils that was, a piercing bright white. Then she took off her long gloves—showing that her entire body was covered with rotten flesh just like her face. Gitana tried to run right out of there, but Forth grabbed-hold of her, holding her tight.

Malaika told Gitana that she wasn't always a horrible monster. Over two-thousand years ago, she was once just like her, a beautiful young girl—a princess in Egypt. She said that she was cursed by an evil Oracle who was jealous of her, taking everything, her beauty, her empire and her power—took everything from her. And with the blood of that child she was going to cure herself. She told Gitana that the child's blood alone was of no use to her. She needed a girl like Gitana to consume her concoction and then conceive a child of her own. A child who was sired by a man descended from the direct blood-line of the Oracle—one of pure blood that could withstand the purifying heat of a flesh cleansing flame. Within her womb this pure blood-line would mingle with the blood of the unborn child. And the Oracle's blood would be her cure. While the unborn Oracle was still growing within her womb, they together would be placed inside the hottest flames of the largest bonfire—to be refined.

Gitana gasped and struggled to escape, but Forth gripped her firm.

Malaika then stabbed a knife deep into the baby's chest, puncturing its tiny heart. She placed a glass vile up to the gushing wound to catch the blood. Then, she proceeded to mix some of the crushed

bones into the freshly spilt blood. Malaika turned and pressed the vile to Gitana's lips before she could move away. Forth grabbed her mouth, forcing her lips apart. Malaika poured the blood right down her throat, watching carefully to make sure the foul bloody concoction ran all the way down into her belly.

Gitana was told that she was now cursed with the everlasting death, just as Malaika. And the only way to escape her fate was to allow Allister Urquhart to lay with her, and to conceive his child. And, if she were to deliver a daughter, she would be the Oracle. With her blood, she would give them all, immortal life.

Malaika had tried many times in this way to bring back the Oracle's pure bloodline—with no success. And with her flesh now quickly decaying she was almost out of time.

Gitana ran straight home that night to tell her mother all the things that Malaika had shown and done to her. In so doing, she broke her solemn vow that she had sworn to Malaika, to not reveal anything. Lala decided then and there that they must flee from that place. But Gitana was now under the same curse as Malaika. If they were to run off now, she would never know how to cure herself. She didn't want to wind up like a living corpse, like Malaika. So they devised a plan to try and steal the ingredients they needed to help them find a cure before they would flee.

Gitana knew the comings and goings of Malaika. She knew that Malaika would be resting during the next day. Her servant Forth would be up and about keeping watch. So they decided that Lala would distract him long enough for Gitana to sneak inside the house with Malaika, get the book of spells and the bone powder, and make a run for it.

Gitana crept inside and tossed the grimoire and bone powder into a cloth sack that held a skull and other bones. The same ones Malaika used to make her concoction. There was another book too, a journal, a leather-bound notebook that once belonged to Malaika's man-servant, Adrian Forth.

They knew Malaika would come looking for them as soon as she realized what they had done. It wouldn't take her long to figure out who it was. So they grabbed up what they could carry and headed out of town, hoping to find a caravan of gypsies headed for the coast. They fled to America, boarding a ship headed to Savannah Georgia.

30

D R. KARANZA SLAMMED the back door shut. She was headed for the barn. The idea of finding a laboratory out in the barn was just too irresistible for her to ignore, and she certainly wasn't interested in waiting for Nick or Paul to accompany her. She was done being hampered by them.

Walking carefully along the dirt pathway through the woods she pulled her coat tightly around her waist with wrapped arms—as her entire body began to shiver. The cold misty morning was still thick with dew that was just beginning to be lifted up into the air by the slowly warming sunlight. Tip-toing, she slowly pushed through the thicket, trying the best she could to avoid being caught in the thorny branches. But nearly every step got her caught-up on some thorny briar, vine, or branch. Catching on her coat sleeves, pants and hair—frustrating her so badly that she just wanted to scream. Her head swung nervously from side to side as she followed the tiny, barely visible, dirt path. The eerie sensation of not being alone pricked at her thoughts.

She reached the dilapidated wooden barn as the sun crested the treetops. Soft rays of light cast long jagged shadows across the wooden frame. Stopping at the threshold of the open door, she peered inside. It was dark. Only a tiny bit of sunlight got in—not enough so that she could see what was waiting for her to find. *This better be worth it*, she thought as she stepped through the door. Nighttime air lingered inside the barn—still, cold, and damp. A musty smell, with a hint of oil and gas vapors tingled in her nose. Paul's motorcycle was there, parked and leaned over on its kickstand, just a few feet away. Its chrome engine sparkled in the morning sunlight coming through the door, enough to draw her attention down to the small spot of oil that had slowly dribbled out onto the dirt floor.

Looking back at the wall, she quickly discovered that there was no light switch. There was no electricity at all. Standing in place, she patiently waited for her eyes to slowly adjust to the low light, while thinking *I'll look like a real fool, if I'm discovered out her looking for Charlie's fantasy lab… especially if it never even existed.* She strained her eyes to see what else was in the barn. All she could see were various old rusting yard tools, rakes, trimmers, shovels, and a pitch-fork, all hung up, lining the walls on equally rusted nails. There was a wooden bench littered with other hand tools, hammers, screwdrivers, wrenches, saws, and boxes of nails and screws. Along the walls on the dirt floor, she could see scraps of wood, an outdated lawn mower, and an assortment of buckets and boxes. Only the metal tear-drop alcohol still and the stacked burlap bags of grain seemed completely out of place—but not a surprise.

Relaxing, she took a seat on the stacked bags of grain just inside the doorway, bathing in the warm morning sunlight—taking advantage of this brief time alone before returning back to the house. *Coming out here all alone shouldn't be a complete waste of time*, she mused, appreciating the soft comfort of a morning out in the countryside, with no patients, no hustle and bustle city traffic, and most of all, no Jenkins breathing down her neck. A glint of sunlight reflected off the chrome on Paul's motorcycle, catching her eye once again. But as she gazed at the motorcycle this time, she felt herself drifting away in a fantasy, as the gleaming metal stallion floated across a deserted desert landscape, with her, straddling its leather saddle like a cowgirl, gripping tightly with both legs in skin-tight jeans and

leather jacket as she flew down the highway with the hot air blowing her hair straight back—blazing off to nowhere. With her shoulders relaxing and falling, her eyes slowly drifted down the engine, appreciating the long slender chrome exhaust pipe, hearing it roaring in her head as she throttled, spinning the rear tire like a tornado, spitting up the desert sand into a dust cloud behind her.

That's when her eyes caught sight of the floorboards beneath the back tire. It had spun in place when Paul parked, throwing away the dirt on the floor exposing the wooden planks that had been hidden underneath. Shooting to her feet, she nearly jumped over the motorcycle to get a better look. Falling to her knees she used her hands to push the dirt away, revealing the outline of a doorway. Pushing her thin body against the heavy metal machine she heaved the motorcycle upright. Veins popped out in her neck as she struggled to roll the thousand-pound beast just a few feet forward. With the motorcycle out of the way, she grabbed a shovel from off the wall and began scraping away the rest of the compacted reddish clay covering the wooden doorway in the floor. Using a metal pry bar, she cracked it open, high enough for her to slip her fingers underneath the boards, so that she could pull it up and swing it over. It creaked loudly as its weight moved on its rusty hinges, crashing onto the floor with a loud reverberating thud that made the entire wooden floor vibrate beneath her feet. *There's a basement room under the floor.*

As the door slammed into the ground it sent up a plume of throat choking, eye irritating, cloud of dust. She covered her mouth and nose, squinting, until the dust cloud dissipated. Peering through the opening, down into the pitch-dark cavern below the floor, all she could make out were the first few wooden steps of a stairway, going down into blackness. Bracing her nerves, she slowly moved down the wooden staircase. Her eyes adjusted again as she cautiously descended, lightly stepping on each creaking step, with her hands scouring the wall—desperately feeling for a light switch. From the middle of the stairs, just beneath the floor, she could begin to make out the dimensions of the basement room. It was nearly as large as the interior of the barn above. The walls were plastered and smooth, painted a stark white. The floor was just as smooth. A concrete slab—painted white. *It's so clean down here*, she quickly realized, it was nearly completely free of dirt, dust, or clutter, everything that littered the barn above, *like an operating room, almost.*

A large, barren, metal table was positioned against a far wall. Against the opposite wall she saw four large metal steamer trunks, with no locks dangling from the latches. On the wall at the foot of the stairs, directly in front of her, was a single light switch. *Thank the Lord*, she thought as she flipped the switch, lighting up the room. Two rows of florescent bulbs flickered and hummed. *That's odd*, she wondered, *why no lighting upstairs, but lights down here? No electrical lines outside either. They must be buried in the ground, running from the house.*

Seeing nothing else of interest, she walked with a light step across the concrete floor and opened one of the large steamer trunks. Just as Charlie had described to her earlier, inside the trunk was an elaborate display of items that would be used to construct a chemist's laboratory; beakers, glass vials, rubber and plastic tubing, specimen jars, mortar and pestle, scales and weights, all neatly arranged and stored away. *Wow*, this *looks just like my first lab back in college.*

Opening a second trunk, she discovered that it was completely full of neatly arranged plastic containers. Each one labeled to identify the chemical compositions they contained. Most names and symbols she instantly recognized, but many she did not. Her eyes slowly mover across each label as she tried to decipher the contents—identifiers for chemical compounds, alchemical symbols, and the strange looking symbols that seemed out of place, or completely unrecognizable. Most of the seemingly bizarre symbols were exactly the same as the ones that she had seen written on the papers discovered inside Daniel's shack.

As Dr. Karanza moved toward the third steamer trunk, she heard a faint noise behind her, from across the room. The quiet

creaking sound, like metal hinges on a doorway, stopped her cold. She glanced around the room. But all she could see was a slender bookcase, about as wide and tall as her shoulders, positioned flat against the wall underneath the staircase. It was painted white—same as the wall. Walking over to the bookcase, she read the covers of the few books arrayed on its wooden shelves. They were mostly out of date chemistry textbooks. Emily chuckled while looking at them, being forced to fondly recall her schooldays. *These are all relics,* she thought as she ran her fingers across the spines of the old books, *but no dust on them?*

On the next shelf down she found books of a very different subject altogether—an odd array of books addressing various aspects of the occult, human physiology, human anatomy, and psychology, next to two other out of place texts on ancient mythology and biblical histories.

A large thick book with a tattered leather cover stopped her eye. On its cover was a demonic looking pentagram with the reddish flames of fire burning in the center. In the corners of the pentagram, and along the stem of the book, were some of the symbols she had seen on the plastic containers and on the papers at Daniel's house. No title. No words at all on the cover. There was nothing to indicate what the book was about. *A Grimoire… could it actually be, an ancient book of spells?*

She couldn't resist taking a peek. As she lifted the heavy book—the entire bookcase moved, ever so slightly, making that same faint noise that first drew her attention. *What the hell?*

While still holding the heavy hardback book in one hand, she reached out and gently pushed on the shelf with her fingertips. The entire bookcase moved slightly back, swaying, it moved forward slightly, coming to a rest again. She pushed again, a little bit harder, watching in amazement as it rocked back and forth, making the faint noise as the hinges squeaked, until it stopped moving again. Reaching to the back of the left side of the bookcase she ran her fingers down the sliver of an opening between the bookcase and the wall. She could feel four small hinges. Peering behind the bookcase, she found what appeared to be a small metal latch. It was attached to the back of the bookcase through a small hole. The book fell from her hands, falling to the floor with a loud thud. She anxiously pulled the other books off the shelf until she could reach her slender fingers through the opening, to get to the latch. Using a fingernail to lift up the latch, it sprung free, allowing the bookcase to slowly swing away from the wall.

The bookcase swung open as far as it would go—only to expose another door—built flat into the concrete wall. A small metal door with rounded corners that didn't reach the floor, painted dark gray, it looked just like a hatch on a submarine. Only this door was flat, without a handle, and without a spinning-wheel locking mechanism, or even the cliché small circular window. Its hinges were on the other side. It could only be pushed in. Running her hands around the edges as she had done with the bookcase, she quickly came to the realization that the door could only be opened from the other side. Feeling frustrated, she pushed on the metal door gently at first, then harder, and then she gave a hard shove with her shoulder. The door did not budge. It seemed to be as secure as a bank vault. She turned away and rubbed her shoulder that was now throbbing. Giving up her notion of opening the metal door, for now, she turned her attention back to the unopened steamer trunks.

Striding back across the room she grasped a metal latch on the front of a trunk and hoisted up the large lid. Inside the trunk was a thick woolen blanket that was being used to cover up the trunk's lumpy contents. Lifting up the front edge of the blanket with her fingertips, just high enough to see what was underneath—her heart skipped a beat—as she gazed wide eyed, down at the neatly wrapped and stacked, bundles of Twenties, Fifties, and One Hundred Dollar bills, that filled almost the entire trunk. *There must be well over a million dollars in here?*

31

A HIGH-PITCHED SCREECH OF sliding metal—sounded from the metal door behind the bookcase. Dr. Karanza spun her head around. Her eyes focused on the metal door, watching, as it opened up, just a little. *I must have knocked it open?*

Lowering the lid of the trunk, slowly, she gently moved the latch back into place—trying to not make a sound. Every muscle tensed-up and she mentally prepared to run for the stairs.

A soft voice called out to her through the metal door. "Dr. Emily Karanza at last… please join me won't you?"

"Who's in there?" Dr. Karanza answered tepidly.

"Please join me Doctor," the woman asked again.

She had a friendly voice.

Dr. Karanza couldn't resist. She forced her reluctant body to move towards the metal doorway. Gently, she pushed on the door—pushing it open into the room on the other side of the wall. Before she could get her face up close to the hole—a wave of stench rushed out—with a putrid, rotting human flesh smell billowing out of the dark opening. Grabbing her nose and turning away, her stomach heaved, forcing acid and bile up into her throat. Clasping her fingers over her mouth and nostrils, she stopped the erupting vomit from spewing. Standing up straight, moving her head away from the

opening, she gasped for fresh air, sucking and puffing with billowing cheeks like a blowfish—until her nausea slowly subsided.

"I'm sorry about the awful odor, but it can't be helped. I have forgotten how horrible it must be. Much worse now, I would imagine. But please try and come inside," the woman beckoned through the black hole in the wall.

Dr. Karanza slowly stepped through the tiny entrance. It was nearly pitch-black inside the room. Her fingers were covering her mouth and nose. As her eyes adjusted in the dim light, a black silhouette of a woman appeared standing in the middle of the small room. With her back to the doorway, the woman was dressed in a long flowing dress that draped down from her neck all the way down to the floor. Spreading her fingers just enough, she asked, "Who are you? And what is this place?"

"Please, take a seat. I will explain everything to you," the woman requested. Her voice was calm and reassuring, as if she was an old acquaintance, and was expecting her arrival.

Dr. Karanza slid her feet across the floor to the closest chair—keeping her eyes trained on the woman like a skittish cat watching a dog. Feeling the cloth armrest of the chair, she slowly sat down. Her only comfort was the tiny sliver of light streaming through the small doorway.

"Who are you?" Dr. Karanza asked again.

"I once was known as Camilla Whitcomb, William's wife, and the mother of Kaitlin and Charles," she answered somberly without moving. Standing a few feet away, she kept her face turned away.

"Well, that just can't be... Camilla Whitcomb is deceased... she died years ago."

"That is partially correct," A remorseful sounding Camilla responded, "I no longer have a mortal body as you know it. Sadly, it's true that I am deceased in most respects. Unfortunately, here I am, still alive none the less."

Dr. Karanza began to look around the room as her eyes became fully adjusted to the darkness. She could now clearly see the floor,

the walls, and the roof of the small room. Everything resembled the interior of the main house. The entire room was decorated as if it were another bedroom. There was a bed, chairs, pictures, and even a faux fireplace. "So then, what is this place, and why are you here?"

"I cannot satisfactorily explain my condition, or why I'm here… not without showing you," Camilla said as she slowly began to turn her body, "Please try not to become upset."

Dr. Karanza gasped, pushing herself back into her seat while clenching down hard on the armrests—as Camilla's face slowly came into view. "Oh my god," she muttered, not being able to restrain her disgust—gazing in horror at Camilla's greenish-gray complexion, black veins, arteries, and capillaries, that ran up her black pustule spotted lower neck, moving up over her face like fine roots of an upturned plant—the fine black lines slithering like fine black hairs growing beneath her skin. Her eyes were completely black, except for her piercing white pupils that seemed to stare straight through one's soul. She appeared to be nothing more than a rotting corpse. The only evidence of life inside her was her thick black hair, hanging straight and long, flowing over her shoulders all the way down to where the frazzled ends nearly brushed the floor.

Dr. Karanza caught herself, holding her composure—just like a well-trained professional. She could not let the patient know her true feelings. And with an almost instinctive reflection, she began searching her memory for clues to what disease could possibly create such bizarre symptoms. *Even with the greenish-gray skin tone she looks somewhat healthy… and young… perhaps even younger than Kaitlin… much too young to be the mother of Kaitlin and Charles… as she claims to be. I need a better look.* "Come closer Camilla… I want to see your arm," she calmly requested.

"As you wish Doctor," Camilla readily agreed. She walked over to Dr. Karanza and lifted her arm, pulling back the long black sleeve of her dress.

Gently prodding Camilla's wrist with her fingertips, Dr. Karanza ran her bare fingertips over her cold clammy skin, avoiding the oozing pussy sores. Pushing down on her vein she could feel a faint pulse. *Hearts beating a little, but her skin looks like a disgusting corpse, drug out of the woods after a few days in the summer.* "Do you have some light down here?" Dr. Karanza mumbled through clenching jaws. "I can't see you very well."

"Just some matches, right now," Camilla answered in a distantly soft voice, pointing down at a box of matches sitting on the wooden table next to Dr. Karanza's chair. "I have a bad reaction to light anyway, so I haven't had much use for any. It seems to hasten my condition, and it is very painful to be exposed to direct sunlight, so I have learned to appreciate the darkness."

Dr. Karanza lit a match. Holding it up, she motioned for Camilla to bend down closer to the flame. By mimicking a wide open mouth, she wanted to examine the inside of Camilla's mouth and throat. Camilla bent down and opened up her mouth—as wide as she could. Placing the small flame up to her gaping mouth Dr. Karanza peered inside. Camilla's throat was even more disgusting. Oozing green and black pustules dotted her tongue and the sides of her slimy black throat. Green and yellow fluids gelled on her gums where her teeth had rotted down to small pitted decayed nubs. A whiff of Camilla's pungent smelling breath gagged Dr. Karanza, forcing her to throw herself back in her chair—jerking her face to the side to avoid the putrid odor.

Camilla stepped back.

"Sorry—my fault," Dr. Karanza groaned through tight lips. Not to be deterred—wanting to complete her examination—she motioned for Camilla to move back, up closer, so that she was within arm's length. Camilla complied, this time, keeping her mouth shut tightly. Dr. Karanza reached out and placed her hand on Camilla's chest. Waiting, expecting to feel a heartbeat, she waited some more, shifting her hand a little, probing, searching for a pulse. *Very shallow breathing with almost no discernible heartbeat at all... she shouldn't be alive?* Lighting another match, Dr. Karanza peered deeply inside

Camilla's black eyes. *Her eyes shouldn't even be functional in this state. They appear to be completely full of coagulated blood, like bruising.* Camilla's eyes followed Dr. Karanza's hand as she moved the small flame from side to side.

"I call it the mark of Cain," Camilla whispered, seeing that familiar shocked, distant, almost lost expression on her face as the flame died out.

"Are you in any pain?" Dr. Karanza asked.

"At first the pain is excruciating," Camilla answered as if she were reliving it, "Like a fire burning inside of you, that slowly moves up from your fingertips and toes, moving slow, a constant burning, a tormenting flame that eats you alive inside as your dead flesh begins to go numb—slowly decaying with the horrible, inescapable, wreaking, constant smell of death."

"Are you suffering now Camilla?"

"Terribly so, but it's something I've come to terms with over the decades, living in this dark dungeon. The light aggravates the pain—makes it feel like you are standing inside a bonfire," Camilla explained, with that terrible reverberating sound in her voice— heard when one is recalling moments of sheer terror.

Dr. Karanza could see the loathing and fear on her face. "How did you get this way Camilla? I mean, I've never seen or heard of anything like this before. I'm still not sure all of this is even real?" Dr. Karanza dubiously pointed out, obviously not yet willing to accept what she is seeing—as if questioning her own sanity.

"Gitana brought this curse to our house… along with that book," Camilla snarled, motioning to the leather bound Grimoire sitting before the two women on the coffee table.

The Grimoire… it is real? Dr. Karanza's eyes grew excited, peering down at the book with the same expression she had when she looked down at the trunk filled with money. A feeling of being that fresh faced college student washed over her, with an overwhelming sensation of newfound desire—a passion lost, then rediscovered. It was almost sexual, as she reached over to run her fingers across the rough cover, like the touch of a lover.

Camilla noticed the look on her face as she gazed down on the ancient book—remembering her own rousing desires felt, when she first laid eyes on it. "Daniel brought that gypsy girl here many years before I married William," Camilla explained, "she was running away from something. That book, and her bag of bones, they all came here together—bringing this curse along with them."

Dr. Karanza tore her eyes away from the book to look up at Camilla, to say, "Kaitlin keeps saying that he's still alive… that he's still living here. But he was reported to have died years ago in an accident and was buried in the city cemetery… so which is it… is he dead or alive?"

"Oh, Daniel is very dead Doctor. But he never died in any train accident as they pretended. And nobody bothered to attend his funeral… so it was easy to have his body removed from his casket before filling the grave."

"Then he is still alive… living here?"

"He's still here—in a way."

"Then Kaitlin did kill him after all," Dr. Karanza blurted out with a sly smirk.

"No Doctor… I got rid of Daniel!" Camilla snarled.

"Why would you kill him?"

"Thanks to that awful bastard Daniel, he brought that gypsy witch here with her curse. It's his fault. All of this mess. I couldn't just hide anymore. Stay hidden in the shadows. That night, when this curse finally took William, Liz, and the baby… I had to stop him… stop all of this… once and for all. I knew they would come to investigate. They would find Daniel out there… take him… put him in the hospital like they did with Catherine. It wouldn't be long till they discovered the tunnels, the door, and then me too. We would both become a patient of yours… some twisted play thing for you to torture. I couldn't let him be found, so, I burnt him up, sending him to dwell in hell fire where he belongs."

"But—Charlie said he saw Kaitlin kill him?"

"It was me, Emily. We looked very much alike out there in the dark that night. Don't you see?" Camilla turned her profile, to where Dr. Karanza could see more of her face.

Still questioning and diagnosing, an idea popped into Dr. Karanza's head, and she couldn't help but start sputtering out her racing thoughts—without thinking. "Perhaps you have been exposed to some toxin that has affected your recollection of events. Your symptoms are similar to those exhibited after being bitten by a spider. I vaguely recall treating a patient that developed a form of gangrene after being bitten by a Brown Recluse Spider. The venom caused massive cellular necrosis, an infection that results in thrombosis—an insufficient blood flow, that's right, it caused a slow cell death and a mass of decaying flesh around the bite with a similar appearance, so perhaps you just have a very advanced stage of necrosis from an insect bite, with some delusional aspects brought about by the severity of the infection—of course, that must be it?"

Camilla spun her face back around to glare down at Dr. Karanza. "This is no spider bite Doctor I can assure you of that fact. Perhaps you need more proof—is that it? I should have expected that from you. You don't leave anything to chance, which is exactly why you are here with me now."

"Just how is it that you know so much about *me*?" Dr. Karanza recoiled.

"We all have our secrets. And I, like you, do not leave much to chance. I can't afford to fail this time. This is my last chance. And I have been secretly watching everything and everyone here at this house, since I have nothing better to be doing with my time—obviously," she smirked. "Fortunately, there are tunnels, one going from this room to the main house, and one out to the field. Once inside the house, I can hear almost everything said. And I have learned to be very discreet."

"So then, you've been spying on all of us—this whole time?"

Camilla stepped closer to Dr. Karanza, saying, "I'll give you

the proof you want, to show you that I am not suffering from some delusion, or some spider bite. Then you'll understand how I am able to know so much about you." Her lips stretched into a clownishly big smile. "Would you like that Doctor?" She asked, taking another step closer.

Dr. Karanza nervously agreed.

"Place one of the teeth you have in your pocket on the table there, next to the Grimoire," Camilla instructed.

Dr. Karanza ran her fingers over her pocket feeling the small hard objects tucked inside—before remembering that she had taken several teeth from the fireplaces. *How could she have possibly have known about the teeth?* She thought, as she reached into her pocket and retrieved a single tooth before placing it down on the table in front of her.

Camilla took a small vile of clear liquid sitting on the table next to the tooth. She poured out a small portion of the liquid around the tooth making a small puddle. Taking a match from the box, striking it, she threw the lighted match down igniting the flammable liquid. A flame erupted over the tooth—Camilla looked at Dr. Karanza with a devilishly maniacal smile, and said, "Watch closely Doctor, but don't get too close."

The flame spread across the table, near to the Grimoire. Dr. Karanza jumped up from her seat and reached over the flames to save the book from catching fire. As Dr. Karanza's hands moved over the flames—two human hands of fire leapt out from the flames as if reaching out to grab her. She lifted up her hands just as the fiery hands touched her—the heat almost burning her—before disappearing into thin air. "What the hell!" Dr. Karanza yelled as she threw herself back down into her chair.

"Watch now," Camilla spoke softly. "Hello there Daniel—come on out and play."

Two more human looking arms with fiery hands leapt up out of the fire, grasping wildly at Dr. Karanza. Each fiery finger of his hands strained as they reached out to grab her. Not disappearing

into the air this time, the arms and hands flailed about, grasping in all directions, with fingers clawing, trying to catch hold of something—anything.

"Oh he wants to get out of there—don't you Daniel?" Camilla mocked, "Must hurt being burned over and over again for all eternity—huh Daniel," she taunted him more.

His head and torso emerged in the flame, rising up within the fire. His face becoming clearer within the smoothly flowing red and yellow streaks of flame that were now steadily rising up from off of the surface of the table. His eyes opened wide—glaring out at Dr. Karanza. With raging eyes and gnashing teeth, straining and writhing in agony, Daniel thrashed about as if his living flesh was still being consumed by the fire. She watched in horror as the fire slowly dissipated as the liquid was consumed.

This isn't real—this is some kind of trick she's playing on me—some gypsy magic, Dr. Karanza told herself, as Daniel slowly disappeared with the dying flame. "What in the hell was that?"

"That is no illusion Doctor. That is what is left of Daniel," Camilla explained. "I put his teeth in the fireplaces. And he is not alone. There are others. They speak to me, and I to them. We are all connected somehow thanks to this curse. Whenever my flesh remains in contact with the flame, my mind ignites with images… and I'm able to see whatever they happen to be seeing from within the fire. It is extremely painful of course… but worth it at times. Sometimes it is essential… in order to discover who your true friends are… and those who only wish you harm. Within the fire, we all see with one mind… with one eye. And we have all come to know you now Doctor—just like you will soon come to know all of us. All too well, I'm afraid."

"What are you talking about Camilla," Dr. Karanza responded calmly, falling back into her well-trained Doctor persona, speaking in her reserved, reassuring, professional voice—the one she uses when she's in a therapy session with a paranoid schizophrenic who is delusional, and irrational. "I can help you with whatever is

happening to you. If you know me so well, then you would know that I'm a specialist in treating unique and severe dissociative behavior. I'm certain I can help you deal with this—whatever you are suffering from right now—there are very promising treatments at my facility."

"You should be more worried about treating yourself right about now Doctor," Camilla said with a sinister grin. "Since you now have *it* too."

"Oh, why is that—is it contagious?" Dr. Karanza squirmed, trying to put up a strong front. "I highly doubt that, since I have been exposed to Catherine for years now. Not a sniffle to speak of yet. No signs of infection of any kind. And I've run every imaginable test."

"It's not contagious as you understand it Emily. But this curse is inside of you, whether you choose to believe me or not. It is working on your DNA as we speak, binding it, and tying-off the ends like trillions of tourniquets, stopping you from aging. I like to call it, *the eternal knot*."

"Oh really… so how is it that I got cursed Camilla?"

Camilla smiled wide, and answered in a chilling voice, as if the grim reaper was talking through her. "The red wine you drank up at the house. There wasn't just wine in that bottle. It had a little something extra added in, just for you. A few drops of blood, together with some of the crushed bone of Cain."

"You poisoned me… what did you do to me?" Dr. Karanza murmured, starting to lose her composure—now feeling a little hysterical, while looking down at her hands to see if there were any black spots or sores. Her hands were trembling—but no spots—not yet.

"Oh the irony of it all doctor," Camilla cackled devilishly, "you of all people should appreciate that?"

Doctor Karanza was staring down at her hands, nervously examining them for spots.

"Didn't you read Gitana's papers I left out for you to find doctor—or Forth's journal? Didn't you read any of it?" Camilla asked,

huffing, as if disappointed with a child who didn't complete her homework assignment. "Well, I know you took it to your room with you last night. I presume you read enough of it to have some idea of what is going to happen to you?"

Dr. Karanza looked up at Camilla as if lost, muttering hysterically, "I read some of it… some old folklore… some fantastical imaginary tale about nomads and grave robbers… or something like that—right? None of that is true—an ancient curse couldn't actually exist? I won't accept that. I can't believe that—not without proper testing. Not without some scientific proof—"

"Look at me Doctor," Camilla snapped—snatching Dr. Karanza back to focus on her. She stretched out her hands, with putrid black-death running through her veins, and asked, "Aren't I proof enough?"

"But why Camilla… why did you bring me here… just to do this to me?"

Camilla slinked across the room and slowly sat down in a high-back chair. "Relax, there is plenty of time. I will explain why. I will explain everything. And, I will explain to you, how you can save yourself from this curse—how to save all of us."

Dr. Karanza nodded her head like a humble and scared child, trembling in her seat.

Camilla leaned back calmly, to say in a somber voice, "This curse is very real Emily. Once inside of you, it keeps you alive, as you slowly die inside. Benjamin confided with me on his death bed—telling me how it all happened—how Gitana, and *it*, came to us."

Camilla revealed how Daniel brought Gitana back with him. How she ended up using that book, and her curse, to enslave Daniel, turning him into some kind of zombie like person—all because she wanted to be with Benjamin. They had become secret lovers, and it wasn't long before she became pregnant with Ben's child. Ben said he didn't like what Gitana had done to poor Daniel, but it was the

only way, since he would have tried to kill them both, and the whole town would have turned against him and his business, ruining him and destroying his marriage to Catherine.

So, Ben brought them both here, allowing them live out back in the farmhouse as servants. They sent the newborn baby to live with a country girl named Louise. Daniel was used like a mindless slave, calling him the grounds-keeper. Of course they could never let him step foot off the property. And poor naïve Catherine was none the wiser, and soon she had a son of her own, William, the boy that would later become Kaitlin's father.

Glancing down at her hands, Camilla sadly explained that, "their little lives of seeming bliss was about to change for the worse, so much worse. The black spots soon appeared on Gitana's fingers and toes. And then the burning pain set in, as the curse began to move, slowly eating her flesh like a crawling grass-fire, moving along with the breeze, consuming everything in its path. They tried every remedy known to man before she turned to that book. That burning inside of you—will make you go mad—mad enough to kill. Eventually that's what Gitana resorted to. She lured her son, Nathanial, away from Louise, and she killed him… to use his blood. When he was no older than five, they had Daniel do it—up in the barn. They lied to Louise, telling her Nathanial was killed by acci-dent. But even with that it didn't work—nothing has worked. As the black-death crept up her fingers and toes, the pain grew. Gitana was becoming desperate to find a cure to end the pain. She had to hide herself away from everyone, staying hidden inside the farmhouse all alone. It got so bad that there was no way they could hide it from Catherine much longer. They had to make a decision."

Camilla went on to explain that Gitana wouldn't give up the idea of using the blood of another human to find her cure. She believed she just needed more time—more experimentation—to find out how it worked. It became her only desire—her obsession. All she wanted was to get another sacrifice for more human blood.

On the verge of madness, she even tried to take little William's blood. But Ben caught her and put a stop to it.

Ben would have killed Gitana before he would allow that to happen. He soon realized that Gitana had become a danger to him—to everyone. Camilla glanced around the dark room, saying, "That's when he came up with the idea of building this place that you are in right now Doctor. This underground shelter would become Gitana's home—or final resting place, however you want to look at it," She added with a tepid smirk. "He managed to keep a sharp eye on her for the few months it took to construct this place, but when Gitana finally took up permanent residence here, she just couldn't stand it. All she wanted to do was escape. Daniel was out in the farmhouse, and Ben was with Catherine, while she was left all alone, locked away down here."

Camilla's face soured as she revealed how Gitana quickly grew angry, feeling betrayed, full of jealousy of them all. Forcing that growing hatred and her ever present burning pain into a ball of forged energy—she started digging, day after day, burrowing like a furious badger. Over the passing years she dug tunnels that reached clear up to the main house, the old farmhouse, the cemetery, every-place she go to escape for a few moments of reality—for a little sanity.

At night Gitana would creep inside the house to pretend she was living a normal life, just like the others. It was Gitana's last mistake. Catherine discovered her sneaking around the house late one night. Creeping up to Ben as he slept, she was caressing his hair, with a little kiss. Chasing her away, Catherine accused Ben and Gitana of having an affair—rightfully so, of course. Gitana finally went completely mad and attacked Catherine, trying to kill her. Ben intervened and put a stop to the fight. But Catherine swore that she would contact the authorities and have Gitana locked away—this time forever. Worse yet, she intended to divorce Ben and destroy his reputation. Her last mistake was letting Ben know that she knew—about his affair, his bastard child, and how they had killed him.

Before Catherine could follow through on her threats, Gitana beat her to the punch by creating a potent concoction from out of that book of spells. With her own putrid blood, and some of the bones of Cain, she poisoned Catherine, causing her to slip off into a coma so deep that they believed she was dead. They even dug her grave for her out in the family cemetery. Even put up her headstone. But, on the morning of her funeral, Ben kissed her on the cheek to say his final goodbye. When he did, his glasses fogged over as they caught her warming breath. That kiss saved her from being buried alive. He couldn't bear the thought of living every day, knowing that his wife was buried out behind his home, still alive, clawing at the insides of her casket while cursing his name.

Dr. Karanza remembered Catherine's symptoms, and realized, *that would explain the cellular decay spreading through her capillaries on her fingertips, and toes*.

Benjamin couldn't cope with all of the death he had caused—because of his relationship with Gitana. He hated himself. He hated Gitana. He wanted to do what was right. He, in some way, wanted to pay his debts to everyone he had harmed. So, he came up with a little idea of his own. When Gitana sneaked back into the house that evening, he grabbed her and tied her up tight. Then he dragged her out to the cemetery, where he lowered Gitana down into the grave that had been dug for Catherine. He buried her there with his own hand. Daniel helped of course—getting a little revenge of his own. Catherine was sent off to the hospital. And since there was no traditional treatment for her, she was institutionalized. Upon Ben's death, she was transferred to the State Hospital for one last chance of finding a cure—using *experimental treatments*.

Then, Gitana is still buried alive out there in that graveyard... rotting underground, Dr. Karanza shuttered with the thought, *Ugh!*

"When I arrived here after marrying William," Camilla recalled solemnly, "I had no idea what awaited me. I never would have set a foot in his home if I had known. I'm still not sure about what all William actually knew. And Ben refused to tell us the whole truth...

even after I stumbled across this place. Obviously, he kept Daniel here, and watched after him, out of a sense of guilt, and pity. I never told William what Ben reluctantly chose to tell me. He had suffered enough."

"We were so young… so stupid," Camilla sighed, slumping down with sadness, "And before I knew it, Kaitlin was born. Such a precious, precocious child—she hasn't changed a wit since the day she was brought into this world."

Camilla explained that with a newborn baby, she spent almost every moment of her life at home caring for Kaitlin. William and Ben spent every second of daylight down at the Mill working. Ben was a slave-driver, and he wanted William to develop the same work habits. That left her alone, inside that big house, without much to do except plunder around. That's when she happened upon the small wooden doorway in the basement. Just looking for some old baby things, stuff long stored away by Catherine down there, blankets, a crib, toys, anything she could find in that jumble of clutter piled down there. That's how she happened upon Gitana's tunnel. She followed it, not being able to resist seeing where it would lead—having no idea it would end up right in here. "Curiosity certainly does kill the cat after all," Camilla chuckled sadly.

Dr. Karanza forced a reluctant smile.

Camilla sighed deeply, before saying, "I didn't tell William or Ben about this place—not for a long while. For the next few months I spent most of my alone time in here, with baby Kaitlin sleeping on a blanket right over there, while I was reading, studying, trying to figure out what Gitana had been up to in here. Had no idea who, or what she was, at that time, since Ben hadn't told me the sorted details—not yet. This hidden room became my little secret place to hide away—my tiny escape from boredom. My passion and obsession became reading the Grimoire and trying to make sense out of all the stuff Gitana wrote down, spells, concoctions, potions, all kinds of weird black magic and such. Thought it was all exciting and fun, for a while. I just figured Catherine had become involved in the black arts or witchcraft—silly pretend Satanism and stuff that wealthy bored housewives turn to when their husbands abandon them for other more interesting pursuits."

Dr. Karanza nodded her head.

"Wasn't too long before I stumbled across the most interesting spell of all—it was there calling to me like a siren's song," Camilla sighed again, remembering, "I just had to connect the dots to get the right combination for the spell to work—Oh, how I wanted it to work."

"So what did you do?" Dr. Karanza whispered some encouragement.

"I drank it Doctor." Camilla's forlorn face was cold, and forsaken, as she answered. "I somehow convinced myself that it just might be real—that it just might actually work—that I would somehow, actually, become immortal." Her eyes sank, drooping with her heavy shoulders, wanting to cry, in tearless agony, saying, "the irony is… is that it did work. Now I'm immortal—immortally dying."

A disturbing thought struck Dr. Karanza, and she blurted out, "It was *you* that killed Elizabeth, the baby, and William… to use their blood?"

"No!" Camilla barked back, "never!"

"Then how did they die Camilla… if not you… then who was it?"

Slouching down, Camilla said in a gloomy voice, "after Charles was born, I first noticed the spots on my fingertips and toes. Black spots, that began to spread up through my skin, along with a foul stench, exactly as it had done with Gitana. It was then that I finally told William and Ben about finding this place and what I'd done." With a despondent gaze, she recalled, "I knew what was going to happen to me, and yes, I did consider using their blood to try and cure myself—but I didn't… I couldn't."

Camilla revealed how she visited every doctor and every specialist—without finding a treatment. As the condition worsened, spreading up her arms and legs, she eventually was forced

to quarantine herself inside the house—hiding from the world. It wasn't long after that rumors started to spread around town, with everyone asking about her. William was getting worried. How could he possibly explain her disappearance? She certainly couldn't go out in public—looking and smelling like a corpse. "So, we devised another plan… one to make me disappear for good."

Dr. Karanza listened intently to her, scouring every detail for deceitful discrepancies—still not sure of what she should believe.

Camilla told her how William received an invitation to attend big shin-dig up at the Mayor's house—an annual affair that all the local big-wigs attended to hob-nob, show off, and politic. She got all dressed up, with a long dress dragging the floor, hose, hat, and gloves up to her elbows. The only thing showing was her face. Camilla glanced over at a full-length mirror as she spoke. It was standing against the far wall—turned, it now faced the wall, so she would never have to catch a glimpse of her own reflection.

"It was hard staying away from everyone… far enough so that they wouldn't catch a whiff of my horrid stench," she grimaced.

At the party, they Guzzled booze like sailors on leave, putting on quite the show and making certain that everyone knew that they were obnoxiously inebriated. "By the time we stumbled out the front door, we were as drunk as skunks," she recalled, feigning a half-drunken grin.

About a mile from home, William stopped and let her out of the car. He stomped on the gas and drove straight into a massive oak tree—causing the car to burst into flames on impact. William almost died along with the demolished car. His leg got caught when he went to jump out—twisting it nearly clean off—tearing his muscles and breaking a bone. He never fully recovered, being partially paralyzed on one side, causing him to limp along with the use of his cane. Camilla pretended to be dead, killed in the accident. William told everyone that she had wanted a private funeral—to avoid the fuss. No funeral home, no viewing, just a simple coffin and a quick burial out back with family. And William kept his word, keeping

with the plan he dug her up a few nights later. Taking refuge in the basement room under the barn, she had lived down there ever since—dead to the world above.

"I'm just as dead even without dying… *dead…* even to my own children," Camilla murmured with a forsakenly pitiful frown before falling silent.

"What about Matthew and Elizabeth getting burned alive?" Dr. Karanza spurred her—wanting more answers.

"Just a freak accident Dr.," Camilla said somberly, "In the wrong place at the wrong time. You see, Charles wasn't very good at running the Mill, or any other business for that matter, and he was failing miserably. To make matters worse, he was stealing what little money there was to be had. Knowing that the Mill would eventually fail anyway, he began taking money and hiding it down here in the basement—out there in those steamer trunks. Wasn't long till the I.R.S. got involved, doing an audit. My little Charles couldn't even cook the books well-enough either. After William got word of the audit, he was angry, and he got drunk off his ass. They were upstairs in William's room fighting like I had never heard two people fight before—so loud it frightened even me—since I was hiding out listening in the other room down the hall. Then Charles ran down the stairs with William trying to keep up on his bum leg—thumping along after him."

Camilla paused, looking to the side as if ashamed, and said, "William must not have seen baby Matthew lying there on his blanket down on the floor next to the fireplace where Elizabeth had laid him down to sleep. She had stepped into the kitchen for a moment. William and Charles were still screaming at each other when William threw his whiskey bottle at him. It missed Charles. It shattered on the mantle, spraying alcohol all over the floor—all over Matthew. It caught fire—bursting into a fireball. William turned and hobbled himself back upstairs as Charles and Elizabeth fought to save little Matthew. But they didn't know about the tooth I put in there. Daniel was there in the fire too. I had placed one of his rotten

fallen-out teeth in there. It was a horrible sight with him grabbing them—burning them. Charles managed to pull himself free. But it was too late for Matthew and Elizabeth—Daniel had wrapped his flaming arms around them good and tight—holding them as they burned—till they were gone."

Camilla locked eyes with Dr. Karanza, saying intently, "William was distraught. He went and sat in his chair in front of his fireplace. First, he scorched his own skin with his walking cane, to feel their pain. Then, he took out his gun, and he shot himself." A lost look came over Camilla's face as she said, "I imagine he could see Daniel smiling up at him from inside those flames."

There was a long, silent pause.

Dr. Karanza leaned forward with a furrowed brow—to ask, "But what about us Camilla? Is there a cure to *this… this curse?*"

"That's exactly why you're here Doctor… to find a cure," Camilla answered, with a look of hopeful desperation.

32

LOUISE FELL SILENT as the sun crested the horizon. A soft ray of sunlight crept up the side of her bed, crawling across the quilt—to where it softly illuminated her flour white face. She lay very still on her bed, with her legs and arms straight up-and-down, not moving at all, her head resting atop her fluffed-up pillow, her eyes closed—as a voice coming out of her unmoving mouth spoke to Kaitlin. "Benjamin and I were going to be so happy together. He saved me from that disgusting wretch."

Who's she talking about? Kaitlin wondered. *She must have fallen back to sleep—she's dreaming?*

"That was my baby—my little boy." Her voice groaned louder, as if straining to get the words out, saying, "I was supposed to deliver the Oracle… we were going to be immortal… but that evil bitch tricked me… tricked me… now I'm cursed—cursed forever."

The sunlight drifted up the side of Louise's face—touching the corner of her unmoving slightly opened eye.

Kaitlin reached over to touch her hand, whispering, "What's wrong Louise?" Are you alright… Louise?"

"I am not Louise!" A loud voice snarled as Louise's eyes popped open wide—black eyes with piercing white pupils—swiveling over to stare straight directly at Kaitlin. Louise's corpse like mouth

flopped open limply, with her dentures slipping free, as the woman's growling voice screamed out from deep within her, "I am Gitana!"

Kaitlin jumped to her feet—flinging her chair back thumping up against the wall.

Gitana's pleading voice called out to Kaitlin again—sounding as if the ground beneath her had given way and she was falling into a bottomless pit. With one last chance to be saved—she was calling up to her as she was falling away—falling down-down-down—disappearing into eternal blackness, "Kaitlin… you must free me… free me from this grave… I once was where you now be… prepare with speed to follow me… you must free me from this grave!"

Kaitlin was shaking—staring down at Louise's lifeless looking body. She couldn't hear the loud thumping footsteps stomping into the room—coming up behind her.

"What the hell is going on in here?" Toni bellowed from just inside the doorway. "You again—just what in the hell are you doing? Get away from her… why are back in here?" Toni snarled, as she clamped fingers around Kaitlin's arm like a bull-dog's jaws—pulling her away from the bed like a limp rag-doll.

Kaitlin could only mutter as few words as she was dragged from the room, "We were talking… she told me… I wanted to know… I needed to know… what happened?"

Toni prodded Kaitlin towards the back door, holding up her arms out like she was coaxing a pesky cat to *get out*. "You aint talking to nobody in this room," Toni snarled. "Now go on, get out of here, and let Mrs. Louise rest in peace."

"What, what do you mean *rest in peace*?" Kaitlin blurted out, stunned. Even though her entire body was still trembling, she found the nerve to plant her feet firmly on the kitchen tile, resisting Toni's forceful hands—stopping in a spot where she could still see Louise's prostrate body, her grayish pale face, and her gaping eyes and mouth. *She's dead… but I was just talking with her?*

"Passed away last night about eleven, I figure," Toni mumbled, "but that's no concern of yours." Spreading her legs apart to balance, she planted her hands on her hips like a Sumo Wrestler—readying to body slam Kaitlin if needed—to keep her from going back in the bedroom. "Louise wasn't talking to you or anyone else… that's what I mean—D-E-A-D—dead. Now get out!"

"But I heard her voice… we were talking… just now," Kaitlin stammered.

"Just get the hell out of this house before I throw you out!" Toni demanded throwing her full weight shoving on Kaitlin's back. Toni mumbled angrily as she forced Kaitlin through the door, "Coming in here in the middle of the night… scaring the hell out of me… talking to dead people… everyone said you were crazy all right."

Shoved outside, the door slammed behind Kaitlin.

A swirling cold breeze pulled at her coat and hair as she walked down the sidewalk towards her car. Overhead, swaying trees seemed to be fighting with the same taunting wind. At her feet, swirling brown, orange, and greenish-brown leaves blew in tightly moving circles, making a blurry collage set against the gray concrete walkway—everything was fuzzy, especially the manic thoughts that were swirling inside of her overly tired mind. *Why am I thinking this way… this is not right… how could Louise be dead, but still talking to me… why the hell is Gitana asking me to free her… free her from what? This isn't right… none of this is right… I'm not feeling right…*

Kaitlin didn't notice the young boy standing near the car as she made her way down the sidewalk. Appearing to be about five years old, he was neatly dressed in a short-sleeved Oxford dress shirt, starched and ironed, with a pullover sleeveless sweater, pleated and pressed shorts with a hem above the knee, long socks and wingtip shoes—looking like he was a little rich kid, waiting for a school bus that would whisk him away to a private school.

"Mother!" the young boy called out as Kaitlin reached for the door handle.

Kaitlin spun her head around, glancing in all directions—seeing no one, *it's just the wind playing tricks*, she thought, as a gust of air blew a slew of rustling leaves across the roadway. She lifted the handle. As she turned, her hair was caught by the wind and whipped around her face.

"Mother… she's leaving," the boy called out again, this time tugging with his small hand on Kaitlin's coat to get her attention. "Momma wants you to wait on her," he said, looking up at Kaitlin with a worried plea in his eyes.

Looking down, Kaitlin saw the young boy this time. "What are you doing out here… aren't you cold young man?" She asked softly, trying to seem friendly.

He stood motionless. His perfectly combed, thick brown hair, making a wave over the top of his portly round head, remained perfectly in place as the wind blew past them. Not a single strand of hair on his head seemed to move. Kaitlin pulled her blowing hair out of her face to get a better look at him.

Kaitlin reached out to touch his bare arm.

The squeal of worn brakes being applied stopped her hand. Kaitlin looked up to see a long black hearse pulling up behind her car, and the driver's door already swinging open before it had lurched to a complete stop. An elderly man's head popped out—with long grey sideburns, unshaven face, he was nervously smiling showing his awkwardly crooked and coffee stained teeth. He asked with a jittery—had way-too-much-coffee—voice, "Mornin' ma'am… sorry I'm runnin' late—you Toni?"

"No," Kaitlin answered him, "she's inside."

"Got here as soon as I could get away… busy night… comes in groups of three most times for some reason," he continued babbling before he actually even realized what Kaitlin had answered. "Would've been here last night but we had another service to attend to ma'am… clean on the other side of the county mind you." Dressed in a frumpy black suit that was wrinkled and in need of a cleaning and press, he quickly shuffled over to her on his stodgy short legs. His tie was old and spotted with the same coffee stains visible on his teeth. Sticking his hand out, he announced himself formerly, "names Roger ma'am... here to collect the body."

"I believe you want Toni... she's inside," Kaitlin said curtly, pointing at the house instead of shaking his hand.

"Sorry ma'am," he responded with a nervous pause as if expecting something else to happen, "well... uh... sorry for your loss all the same ma'am," he said with a nod, before scurrying off down the sidewalk.

Kaitlin turned and grabbed the door handle, before remembering the young boy. She looked down. He wasn't there. She glanced down the sidewalk. Roger was knocking on the front door. Looking all around the cars and yard—the boy was nowhere. "Did you see where that boy went?" She called to Roger.

He turned and looked around the front yard, and said, "No ma'am. Didn't notice no boy at all... only saw you there when I pulled up."

Kaitlin looked around nervously, even bending down to look underneath the car.

"Want me to help look for him ma'am?" Roger called to her, just as the front door swung open and Toni stepped out into the sunlight—still dressed in her pajamas and robe.

"Bout time you showed," she growled.

Roger didn't wait for Kaitlin to respond, Toni's angry scowl sent him scampering through the door. Toni swung her glaring eyes at Kaitlin again before slamming the door shut on her—once again.

Cranking the cold engine Kaitlin punched the accelerator and spun the tires on the loose gravel on the side of the road as she sped away. Driving erratically like a drunk heading home after a long night behind a bar, her car meandered around the long bends, crossing the lines on both sides. *I need some sleep... just got to get back home. Home! Ha—listen to me—back home. Back to my cell at the nuthouse more like it,* she chided herself. The road appeared to be slithering like a long black snake in front of her.

Glancing up, into the rear view mirror, she thought she saw the top of a boy's head sitting in the back seat—his wavy brown hair right behind her. *What the*, she thought, before glancing back down at the road just in time to turn the wheels to avoid leaving the roadway with the tires squealing just enough to scare her. With a quick glance back to the mirror, the boy's head was gone. *Keep your damn eyes on the road*, she chastised herself, *don't want to end up lying next to Louise this morning.*

"Thank you for waiting dear," a raspy, yet sticky sweet voice of an old woman said to her from the back seat. "Where are you taking me dear?" the old woman asked.

Kaitlin's eyes jumped back to the rear view mirror to see the face of an old gray haired woman looking back at her. Only half of the old woman's right side was visible. Her short, brittle gray hair, was unkempt, and matted to her head. She was wearing white pajamas decorated with tiny blue dots.

Kaitlin glanced back down at the road—then back up—back down—back up. She was still sitting in the back seat each time. "Louise—is that really you back there?" Kaitlin mumbled.

"Please don't take me back dear," Louise responded. "We have been waiting for so long for this day to come, and now you're finally here. We can finally put an end to all this."

"End… end what Louise?" Kaitlin muttered nervously.

"I see you have met my son Nate." Louise smiled, not responding to the question.

"What are you trying to end Louise?"

"It all started again here with our little Nathanial—isn't that right dear?" Louise responded somberly, stroking Nate's wavy hair. "When Gitana took him from me." Leaning forward to make direct eye contact with Kaitlin in the mirror, she added coldly, "Now it's your turn—to give up your child dear. That's what you have to do, to put an end to all of this, of course."

I don't have a child? Kaitlin pondered, glancing back and forth trying to keep her eyes on the slithering road. "You know I don't have

a child," she groaned, glaring angrily in the mirror just long enough to send the message that she wasn't messing around—and definitely not in the mood for any taunting.

"Don't listen to her Katie," Mary's voice calmly said from the other side of the backseat. Kaitlin shifted her eyes to see Mary's red hair and glaring green eyes staring back at her. Dressed in her school uniform with the all-too-familiar school crest stitched on her chest, she was seated next to Nathanial, glaring back at Kaitlin in the mirror with a fearsome scowl.

Mary abruptly lashed out in her disturbingly grating voice, shrieking, "She's a stinking no good old liar! She's going to trick you Katie just like she did the others."

"Don't listen to her dear—she's the one who plays tricks." Louise softly implored, straining her dry raspy throat.

Oh my God… what is happening to me? Kaitlin's head spun-round. With her blurry eyes she was fighting to keep the car on the roadway. *Just focus on the driving, and get back to the house… back to Dr. Karanza… back to where there's some help.*

"Crazy Katie… did you finally go crazy… did you crazy Katie?" Mary taunted her, with a devilish giggle between each *crazy*.

"Get out of my car! Get out of my mind!" Kaitlin started screaming to drown her out.

Mary just giggled. Leaning up closer, she whispered, "Want to know something I know—but you don't?"

"Don't listen dear, she's trying to trick you," Louise implored.

Mary giggled some more, before saying, "Gregory doesn't love you… he loves someone else. Can you guess who Katie?"

"Don't listen dear," Louise interjected.

Kaitlin focused hard on the road, gripping the wheel tightly with both hands—trying not to listen to either of them.

Mary scrunched up on the seat, leaning in, close up to Kaitlin's ear, to tauntingly say, "He loves Cynthia. But you already knew that huh?"

Kaitlin could feel the muscles twisting in knots as she stiffened

all the way up to the base of her neck—with Mary's disgusting hissing breaths brushing over her.

"But, I bet you didn't know this Katie?" Mary whispered again, "Cynthia's pregnant—with his baby."

Slamming on the brake pedal—the tires squealed and smoked as the car slid to a stop on the blacktop. Kaitlin buried her face into her hands. Shaking her head back and forth… *no… no… no…* her tears flowed.

Mary was gleefully giggling behind her, repeating over and over like a melody, "A baby… a baby… Cynthia's having his baby—"

"Don't listen to her," Louise pleaded. "She'll just trick you… just like Gitana tricked me dear."

"Oh—it's already too late," Mary taunted, "You're already *crazy* Katie. Gregory is going to put you in that hospital right next to Catherine—just like Benjamin did to her, after he knocked up Gitana with this little bastard child." Mary patted Nathanial on his head. "Gregory and Dr. Karanza have it all planned out. Now you're going to be locked up to rot forever—right along with Catherine."

"Is that true Louise?" Kaitlin whimpered. "Is that what Benjamin did to Catherine? Did he lock her up… make her seem crazy… and put her away… just so he could be with Gitana?"

"She's just as crazy as you Katie," Mary interrupted, "I wouldn't listen to a word coming out of her old, crazy, hag, of a mouth. Besides, they just want your baby's blood—how's that for *crazy?*"

"Shut up!" Kaitlin screamed at Mary. "Is she telling me the truth Louise? Has Gregory been cheating on me all this time? Is she going to have Gregory's baby?" Kaitlin's mascara running tear filled eyes strained in the mirror, looking at Louise for an answer.

Louise's face went blank—searching for a good answer, with a stunned, far-off-gaze.

Mary began chanting loudly in her high shrill voice, "She's just crazy… crazy Katie… crazy Katie… crazy Katie… she's just crazy… crazy Katie—!"

Louise finally conceded the truth, nodding—*yes dear.*

Suddenly Mary stopped chanting, and said with a sinister smile, "I know another secret crazy Katie—that's even better. And, I can prove to you that what I am saying is all true. Do you want to see the truth for your own eyes crazy Katie?"

Kaitlin's head bobbed up and down slowly, giving up. Her tearless bloodshot eyes were now numb—expressionless—the look of a trauma patient in shock.

"You can't hear any more of this dear… it's far too much for a mortal sole," Louise pleaded with her, "please just don't listen to her anymore."

But Mary continued, eagerly saying, "Everything that your father told you about your mother was one big fat lie." Sounding as if she were enjoying a delicious meal, savoring every word, chewing her up—ever so slowly—as she added sarcastically, "Shall I continue—*crazy*?" Waiting for Kaitlin's response, she glanced over at Louise, giving her a satisfied look, as if to say, *ha-ha, I win, she's all mine—all mine.*

Kaitlin numbly nodded again with a defeated—*yes.*

Mary smiled wide, before gleefully revealing, "Your mother is still alive Katie. She isn't dead at all. She's only been hiding from you all these years—hiding out in that barn."

"Don't listen to her, you don't want to hear this," Louise tried to interrupt.

"Where is she Mary?" Kaitlin wanted to know she heard her right.

Mary paused, enjoying the moment, before telling her, "She's in the barn, under the ground, down in the basement room—the one place your father never allowed you to go. Now isn't that funny crazy Katie? Turns out, you were right all along!"

Kaitlin slammed her foot onto the accelerator. Spinning the tires with a squeal and leaving behind a cloud of smelly smoking rubber. The car raced down the small country roads, careening off the pavement around every bend or turn, nearly overturning.

Louise leaned forward, feeling desperate and out of control, she had to tell Kaitlin a secret of her own, saying, "Mary is not real Kaitlin. She's just a figment of your imagination dear." The engine roared and the car sped up, swaying hard to the right as they rounded another bend. Louise steadied herself and continued to plead with her, saying, "Kaitlin, you have to believe me. Something very bad happened to you when you were at that school, and Mary died, but she's dead now and you keep bringing her back to punish yourself, but it has to stop. You can't listen to her this time or all will be lost."

The car swung back to the left and accelerated. Kaitlin wasn't listening to anything else—her mind was consumed with her own thoughts swirling in her head. *This is just my imagination. I'm overwhelmed right now… that's all. There are no ghosts in my backseat. Louise's story wasn't true. All of this is just bullshit. This isn't really happening at all. I'm just exhausted, over medicated, overcome with stress from being back here again… dealing with all this mess. It's all just too much for me to handle… probably do need some time away… that's what my body is telling me right now… this is all just too much… just watch the road.*

33

KAITLIN WAS COMPLETELY emotionally numb when she arrived back at the house—exactly the condition Nick wanted her to be in when he got his chance to confront her. He was waiting for her inside. Seated calmly in the front room he was poised like a trap—pulled back and latched with a spring tightly wound up—wanting so badly to be sprung.

He was the last person Kaitlin was prepared to meet as she walked through the front door.

"Hello Kate," Nick announced coldly. She just glanced over at his voice without making eye contact. He recognized her glazed over bloodshot eyes as an opportunity. Not saying another word as he watched her slothfully drift across the foyer into the living room to plop down into the softest chair.

Paul whisked by, walking quickly through the foyer and disappearing into to the kitchen to get a drink of water. Charlie was sitting in a chair opposite Kaitlin with a solemn, pouting, childish expression—as if he had just been scolded for doing something wrong, and was now feeling ashamed.

Nick stood up and shuffled diagonally across the floor as if he were a shifty spider avoiding being detected by his intended prey. Standing directly behind Kaitlin, he said, "You just missed Gregory.

He received an urgent call and had to leave for a little while—medical emergency or something like that."

Kaitlin didn't flinch—or utter a sound.

Nick cleared his throat a little, and said, "You know Katie, we found Daniel." His voice was cool, calm, and exact, sharp and to the point like a scalpel in the hand of a skilled surgeon.

"Oh, and what did he have to say?" Kaitlin responded snidely. She could feel the tension filling the room like a rumbling black storm-cloud developing directly over her head—an unavoidably intense confrontation leading to the inevitable first strike of lightning.

Nick turned up the pressure, by replying; "well now that's very funny Katie. You see ole Dan can't talk to us anymore, not from where he is now. And you know that, now don't you *sweetheart?*"

The clap of thunder in Kaitlin's head was almost deafening as Nick threw out the accusation. She glanced over at Charlie. He was obviously avoiding eye contact with her. Slumping down in his chair and lowering his pouting face, as if hiding himself behind his folded arms. If he were a turtle his head would have disappeared. *What the hell did he tell them… little lying bastard?*

Paul lingered in the foyer, glass of water in hand—listening.

"Just tell me where the hell Daniel is," Kaitlin threw back at him—unwilling to play his cat and mouse games.

Nick pounced on Kaitlin, saying, "We found him just where you left him Katie," while stomping authoritatively around her chair so that he could stare into her eyes. If he had a spotlight, it would be pointing right into her face. "Don't play games with me. I will ask you one more time Katie—where did you last see him?"

Blurring images of her past ran through her mind as she searched for the very last time she saw him; *it was the night he chased after me… out back… out by the barn… just before I was sent away to boarding school… that was the last time. Father moved me up to Atlanta after that—can't remember ever seeing him again?*

Nick didn't give her the chance to respond, letting her know that, "what we could find of him is now in the morgue."

"He's dead?" Kaitlin gushed.

"After you hit him in the head… before burning him alive… well yes, I think it's safe to say he's definitely dead," Nick scoffed, staring down at her like she was insane.

"Go to hell… I didn't kill anybody!"

"Just admit it Kate. You killed Daniel right after you killed the rest of them, including your own father—didn't you?" Nick growled in a loud booming voice that rattled the walls.

How is this happening to me? Kaitlin's mind began racing, trying desperately to come to grips with everything happening to her. *It's not my fault… I was trying to help… everyone… now this… how can this be happening?*

"We have an eye witness Kate," Nick continued his attack, plunging the scalpel in deep, going for her heart—in for the kill. "It will be much better for you in court, better for everyone, if you just confess right now, and just tell me what you did."

Searching the room with her eyes, as if lost, Kaitlin calmly asked him, "A witness—who's the witness?"

Nick instinctively glanced over at Charlie. "Your brother, he's the one that saw everything. Charlie saw you kill them Kate," he said solemnly as if pronouncing her death sentence. "So just go-on and admit what you did, and help us finally put an end to all of this."

Kaitlin looked over at Charlie. His face was buried deeply into his crossed arms. He couldn't look back—not into her frightened, tear-filled, bloodshot eyes.

"Just tell us why you did it," Nick pushed her for answers, "and don't worry we will take good care of you."

Kaitlin looked up, staring deeply into Nick's heartless eyes, to say in a flat emotionless voice, "I did not kill anyone. Now—would you please just leave my house right now?"

Nick paused. He had seen that look many times before during

long interrogations. She had had enough, reaching a breaking point where she would rather die, than answer him. Stewing for a moment, he bit down on his bottom lip—fidgeting, he fought back his urge to launch into another tirade of angry accusations. It was time to retreat, for now, before he pushed her too far. She already had the glassy eyed glare of a prisoner of war that had been mercilessly beaten to the point of exhaustion—to where a person loses a sense of caring about themselves, where nothing matters anymore, and only one thing seems to make sense is not being defeated—where only dying becomes the victory.

Nick relented and drifted towards that front door without saying another word.

Paul stepped in front of him just as he was reaching for the doorknob. He whispered in Nick's ear, "Are you going to arrest her?"

"No," Nick cringed, whispering back, "I can't just yet. I was told by the dumb-ass District Attorney to get whatever evidence I could and bring it back, so he can present it to the Grand Jury. We don't have enough evidence for an arrest yet—because the D.A.'s a damn coward. It's all small town political bullshit."

Opening the front door, Nick paused, to say over his shoulder, "Oh yea, by the way Kate, you're husband Gregory was nice enough to tell me something before he left today. He told me that you were gone in your car, out nearly the entire night on the night of the murders—out long enough to drive all the way from Atlanta to Milledgeville, and then all the way back home again, with time to spare. And as it turns out, I also spoke with a young lady named Cynthia. You might know her Kate. She says she definitely remembers seeing your car driving through town that night. Just a weird coincidence I guess?" With that, he left, pulling the door closed behind him without waiting for her to respond.

Charlie sprung out of his chair and ran up the stairs going back to his room. The walls shimmered as his bedroom door slammed shut.

Kaitlin sat motionless. Closing her eyes, she put her hands to her face.

Paul knelt down in front of her, and asked softly, "Is it true, did you do it Kate?"

Dropping her hands, Kaitlin gushed, "Of course not. Don't you believe me?"

Paul hesitated in deep thought, with that lost look appearing on his face.

His reaction said it all—it was useless. *No one believes me,* she realized while searching Paul's icy unknowing gaze—now the one that left her feeling the most utterly forsaken of all. *My life might as well be over.* She decided as she gave up on him too, and looked away. Wanting to cry, her eyes swelled up—but instead of tears, her eyes felt as dry as desert sand. *No more crying and hiding.* A sudden swell of emotion pushed her up onto her feet. Brushing past Paul she walked resolutely down the hallway, heading for the back door.

"Where are you going Kaitlin?" Paul called to her. He could see in her eyes what Nick had realized before he left. "You look like you need to get some rest Kate," he suggested, trying his best to sound like a sincere friend.

Kaitlin only heard a nurse—someone getting paid to watch after her. "Oh, don't worry about me Paul. I'm just going to end all of this—finally."

Paul sauntered behind and watched the back door slam shut, while pondering; *end it all… what the hell does that mean? Where the hell is Dr. Karanza?*

"Dr. Karanza!" Paul called out. The house was empty and silent. Paul ran out the front door to stop Nick from leaving—but he was already gone. "Dr. Karanza!" Paul called out again, glancing around the front yard.

Charlie heard the back door slam shut as Kaitlin left, and he rushed over to his window. He could see her crossing the back yard, heading for the pathway leading to the barn. *Where the hell is she going now?*

Pacing the floor, he puzzled over what she was up to. It wasn't very long before he had another thought: *Oh shit—the money?* Pacing back and forth like a caged panther with his mind moving faster than his feet—he knew he had to get out of there fast. *How can I get past Paul, to stop her in time, without letting on? If they find the money, I'm done. They'll believe her then—not me.*

Not able to figure out a better plan, Charlie cracked his door to take a peek down the hall. Paul wasn't to be seen. Creeping down the stairs, he shuffled silently to the back door.

Paul entered the front door just as Charlie was walking out the back. Running frantically throughout the house, he started searching for Dr. Karanza, yelling out, "Dr.… where the hell are, you! Dr. Karanza!" Every room was empty. She was now missing—along with Charlie. *This is not good!* Paul fumed as he stormed for the back door. *Oh man… what's going to happen now?*

Kaitlin was moving fast along the dirt path in the direction of the barn. *They think I'm crazy… I'll show them crazy… give them a really good reason to lock me up… not just a bunch of some bullshit lies! I'll burn it all down… everything… starting with that God forsaken barn!*

Mary was hurrying to keep up and staying right behind her—smiling all the way.

Crashing through the thicket of overgrown bushes, the old barn came into view. The air became thick, like molasses, melding around her body, each step becoming harder to take, slowing her down more and more the closer to the door she got. It was her memories coming back to mind that were forcing her to want to stay back. Through her child's eyes, she was reminded of her fear of this place, and she desperately wanted to stay outside. Her feet stopped at the threshold. She couldn't force herself to go through the doorway—not into the darkness. All she could see was her father's anguished face as he lashed the doorway shut with a chain and padlock—while telling her that her mother was dead, that this place was the cause—*a curse*—one that had killed her mother, and that she could never, *ever,* go back inside.

Her thoughts prevented her from stepping inside; *father made me believe that the booze killed her... his moonshine he made in here...that it caused the car accident that killed her. No... he couldn't have lied to me all these years... he wouldn't have... it can't be true... Mary is lying to me again... tricking me... trying to get me inside here to harm me... to make me look crazy. She wants me to behave like I actually believe mother is still alive in here... to tell Nick, Karanza, and Gregory, that she's still alive... plenty enough reason to label me insane and lock me away.*

"Go on Katie," Mary taunted from behind. "See for yourself... if you're not too chicken. Your mother and father are nothing but two no good stinking liars!"

"After I prove you wrong, I'm burning this place to the ground along with Daniel's shack!" Kaitlin yelled back at her. *I'll show everyone that I'm not crazy. Daniel killed them—not me!*

She marched inside. "Oh my God," she gasped, spying the open doorway in the floor.

"See Katie, I told you so," Mary snickered.

Kaitlin's knees buckled to the floor. She planted her hands in the dirt to stop her fall. The sight of the doorway was a sucker punch to the stomach—knocking the breath out of her and spinning her head around till she toppled to the ground like a top that had stopped its twirling. "It can't be true... it just can't be?" She moaned between short breaths.

"Poor little Katie," Mary whispered sarcastically. "Try and keep it together, because it only gets better. Besides, you haven't even seen the best part yet. C'mon, follow me," she motioned with her hand as she disappeared down the stairs—descending into the basement room.

With every ounce of strength Kaitlin had left she lifted herself from off the floor and followed Mary down the stairs. Stumbling on the bottom step, she nearly fell, tripping across the floor she banged up against a steamer trunk. The small room was spinning as she dizzily gazed around. Her eyes tried to stay focused on Mary as she sauntered over to the bookcase mounted on the far wall. Mary turned back to look at her with a devilishly happy grin—with her finger resting lightly on the bookcase that was pulled a few inches away from the wall—dangling on its hinges. With a simple little push she made the bookcase rock back-and-forth, squeaking the hinges.

Kaitlin shuffled across the floor like a drunk. Nearly stumbling before catching herself on the bookcase, she grabbed it and forced it to swing all the way open—revealing the hole in the wall. Steadying herself between the bookcase and the wall, she listened. She could hear a woman's voice talking to someone inside the dark room.

"Go on, take a look," Mary whispered in her ear.

A feeling of nausea wrenched inside her stomach again as Kaitlin lowered her head down to look through the hole. Her heart was throbbing as the sound of the woman's voice grew louder. She took a peek inside, to see a woman dressed in black turning her head slightly—to look directly back at her. *Mother is alive!*

It felt like a bolt of lightning striking suddenly, without mercy.

Although the woman looking back at her was now a grotesque, macabre, corpse of a creature, it was still her mother, and those were still her eyes. Only now, they were black and soulless.

Dr. Karanza didn't notice Kaitlin peeking through the hole.

Camilla intentionally did not react to seeing Kaitlin. She just turned her attention back to Dr. Karanza, as if nobody was there. *It's not time yet. Dr. Karanza isn't ready. She needs more instruction first before she'll know what must be done.*

Mary moved up close to Kaitlin, to whisper in her ear, "She tricked you Katie, not me. It was your own mother. She's the one that betrayed you. The one that made you think you were crazy all this time—it was her."

A feeling of unrestrained hatred swept over Kaitlin. Her mother's lies and betrayal was more than she could withstand. An irrational rage swelled-up inside of her, causing a final and fatal crack to appear in her dammed-up emotions, and she gave way.

A torrent of remorse and guilt gushed out of her—replaced by a murderous rage that filled her back up—pushing her over the edge. *All the years of torment I endured because of her. All the giggling jokes I had to suffer. The whispering lips, accusing eyes, insults, loneliness, isolation—feeling utterly worthless all the time—it was all her fault!*

Kaitlin now realized that it was in fact her mother who had caused her to feel all of those horrible emotions. It was that monster of a mother who had abandoned her with a lie, to make her feel alone, desperate, exposed to years of ridicule and contempt. It was her mother who had caused her to believe she was insane. Her mother caused her to hate her father, to hate everyone, to be forced to go off to that school. All of it was worse than any evil Daniel could have ever conceived of doing to her. *They believe I am a murderer… well now, they will be right!*

Kaitlin surefootedly followed Mary back up the stairs. They now shared the same ominous sinister smile.

Mary sauntered across the dirt floor, over to a small table. She giggled, and daintily pointed down at the brown bottles of moonshine lined up in a row. With her other hand she pointed over at the still and the stack of cut firewood. Lying next to the wood was a box of matches. Mary smiled wide as her maniacal eyes said it all.

Kaitlin picked up a bottle and threw it hard against the wall. Smashing the half-gallon bottle to pieces, the potent grain alcohol sprayed across the wooden walls and piles of cut timber. Mary laughed and skipped around the room as six more bottles flew out of Kaitlin's hands, smashing against each of the four walls. As the last bottle smashed open, the barn filled with a hazy sick-sweet smell of corn mash—smelling just like ethanol enriched gasoline that wafts up from the nozzle while filling the tank.

"Do it," Mary encouraged with wild daring eyes.

Kaitlin lit the long wooden match. Her eyes stared into the tiny flickering flame. *Time to put an end to it all*, she thought, before tossing it onto the floor. Shooting flames burst up in the gas thick air, spreading quickly up the fuel splattered walls.

Camilla and Dr. Karanza listened to the rumbling floorboards overhead and the loud thumps on the walls as the bottles broke. Dirt, dust and bits of plaster rained down. Dr. Karanza jumped to her feet. Glancing skittishly back and forth between Camilla and the ceiling, she asked, "What's going on?"

Camilla remained calm. Staring intently at Dr. Karanza, she responded, "Well Doctor, looks like it's time to make a fateful decision. You have to decide what you are going to do next. You can leave without doing anything further—go back to your life, the hospital, and your patients. Or, you can take the Grimoire and use it to try to find a cure for us. Find a way to make us immortal."

Small plumes of smoke rolled across the ceiling, filtering down into the room through the tiny cracks in the floorboards. Rolling clouds of thick smoke billowed into the adjacent room, flowing across the ceiling and lingering along the stairs like sticky balls of greyish-black cotton candy. A tangy acrid smell filled the basement rooms letting the women know exactly what was coming.

Dr. Karanza stopped moving, with wide eyes she focused on Camilla's fiercely glaring black eyes staring back at her.

Camilla told her, "You can't run away from this curse that now pulses through your veins Doctor. It's in you—eating you—just like in Catherine."

"There's a fire upstairs! We have to leave!" Dr. Karanza yelled out, not wanting to listen to Camilla's suggestion. A haze of smoke lingered in the air—getting thicker by the second. Dr. Karanza choked as she tried to take a deep breath while fighting the urge to run.

"You are the only person who can save us now Doctor," Camilla pleaded, "You are the only person who will have access to her blood. Only you can understand what is in that book. You are the only person left who can save us!"

A thick wall of smoke funneled through the small doorway like a smoke-stack. Dr. Karanza covered her gagging mouth and clenched her stinging eyes as the small room filled up with thick black smoke.

Scurrying over to the doorway, she tried desperately to get through, but the smoke was too thick. As if swimming upstream against a raging current she fought madly into the smoke that was burning in her lungs and in her eyes like acid. Her fingers grasped the edges of the doorway and she guided herself closer to where she almost got her head through the hole before her lungs ached for oxygen and she was forced to open her mouth to suck in—inhaling burning hot smoke. Her eyes cracked open as she fought to see a way through. A churning grey cloud is all she could see through her burning red eyes—before they were forced shut again by the pain. "What do we do!?" she yelled to Camilla as she turned away from the smoke and retreated toward the back wall.

Camilla was gone.

Stumbling over furniture Dr. Karanza fell to the floor. Lost in the smoke she fought for a breath of air as she crawling across the floor like a frightened scurrying rat. Dizzy and blacking out, her subconscious took control and she felt herself moving as if in a dream. Somehow finding the far wall, her fingers scratched along the floorboards searching for a way out. The floor suddenly felt soft and moist as her fingers dug into dirt. She was completely inside the tunnel before she even realized that she was out of the room. With a frantic surge of energy she threw herself forward, landing face first on a dirt floor. Opening her mouth wide she gulped in air like a flopping guppy, desperately gasping for fresh air—until her mind went black—turning as dark as the cavern where she lay.

Charlie moved cautiously along the trail. Like a game-hunter—taking gingerly steps he moved through the thickly overgrown shrubs trying not to make a sound—while keeping his head on a swivel, carefully watching in all directions to make sure Kaitlin or Paul wasn't sneaking up on him, or hiding and waiting, to leap out of a bush to take him by complete surprise. Before he had reached the end of the trail, a wisp of smoke began rising up over the tops of

the trees. Feeling like he had just been bush-wacked, he yelled up at the sky, "Oh hell… oh no… oh you stupid crazy bitch!"

Now furious with the image of burning dollar bills going up in flames, Charlie went off, tearing through the limbs as a charging rhino bearing down on his agitator, with a mindset now impervious to consequence. Breaking out into the clearing surrounding the barn, he stopped, seeing flames leaping out through the open doorway and peeking out through the cracks between the planks of wood. Stomping and huffing, he agonized over the reality of what he had to do. Getting ready to charge in—Paul's hand suddenly landed hard on his shoulder—stopping him cold.

"What's happening Charlie… where's Kaitlin?" Paul asked frantically.

"I don't know. I think she's inside?" Charlie responded with heavy breaths. He could see the passion in Paul's eyes as he prepared himself to run inside—intending to save Kaitlin from the fire. That couldn't happen if he was to save the money first. "Stay here. I'm going in to get her," Charlie said intently. He then darted through the open doorway before Paul could even think.

Paul watched as the smoke rising up into the air above the barn grew thicker, as the flames kept growing larger with each agonizing passing second, eating away at the walls, crawling up and leaping off the roof, getting higher and higher throwing off more and more smoke. "Kaitlin!" he yelled into the flaming barn. "Charlie!" No one answered his calls. Unable to restrain himself another second, knowing that the barn was about to collapse in on itself—Paul covered up his mouth with his arm, squinting his eyelids tight, he threw himself through the open doorway—through the flesh scorching fury. Flying through the air he landed wrong, tripping on something lying on the sandy floor. His body sprawled out on the floor next to the open hatchway in the floor. Gasping for air he flung himself upright and scampered to the basement opening. As he started to scamper down the stairs—he noticed Kaitlin lying unconscious on

the floor. It was her body that he had tripped over, and he realized *Charlie had run right past her… leaving her there to die!*

Scooping her up into his arms Paul carried Kaitlin out of the burning barn where they fell to the ground, coughing and wheezing. Hunched over, Kaitlin coughed up a thick wad of black goo as she gasped for a clean breath of air.

"Where's Charlie?" Paul asked her before she was able to speak.

In between coughs, Kaitlin struggled to answer. Her voice was raspy and weak, "Don't know… he ran past me… disappeared in the smoke… down in the cellar I think?"

Paul pushed himself off the ground and staggered toward the flame enveloped doorway.

"No, Paul, no, don't go in there… it's too late…you'll die," Kaitlin begged.

Paul stopped and looked down at her, and he understood; *she's right—Charlie's not worth it.*

34

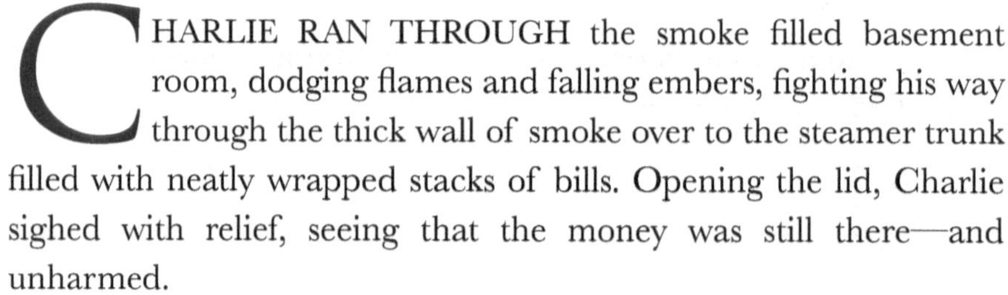

CHARLIE RAN THROUGH the smoke filled basement room, dodging flames and falling embers, fighting his way through the thick wall of smoke over to the steamer trunk filled with neatly wrapped stacks of bills. Opening the lid, Charlie sighed with relief, seeing that the money was still there—and unharmed.

Grabbing the small metal handle on one end of the trunk, closest to the stairs, he pulled as hard as he could, groaning as the trunk began to slide on the slick concrete floor. "Aaaaargh… come on!" He groaned, his face turning a bright red, with pain shooting up his straining arms. His fingers felt like they would pop off at the knuckles he was pulling so hard. Hot smoke gagged and singed his throat when he had to suck in a deep breath. "C'mon, I can do this!" He screamed, as the huge wooden trunk scratched along the concrete floor until his back was up against the stairs. Glancing up the tall stairway behind him, Charlie groaned and gasped for another breath of air before yanking with every fiber in his body until he managed to force the front edge of the trunk up and over the first step.

Every muscle relaxed at once as he sat down on the stairs. Dizzy, with sweat running down his face, he took in another lung scorching hot breath as he paused to recover, preparing for another gut wrenching pull. "I can do this... I got... to... do... this," he groaned, choking and gagging on shallow smoke-filled breaths. Sitting on the stairs, it was all he could do just to stay focused—to stay conscious.

"Look what has become of my little boy," Camilla said, appearing next to him from out of the thick smoke. Standing next to the stairwell, she fixed her black eyes on him like a transfixed snake staring into the eyes of a charmer.

Charlie gasped and choked in a full lung of acrid smoke. "What the hell... what... who... what are you?" He stammered as he began to panic. *I'm hallucinating from a lack of oxygen?* He believed. *I've got to get out of here before I pass out.* Blowing out the little bit of air left inside his lungs, he groaned loudly, throwing himself back hard, pushing his legs down on the floor to pull up on the trunk—with every ounce of strength left inside of him. "Aaaaaagh!" He yelled out as the trunk lifted up another stair, before he gave out, flopping back down limp, with nothing left. "This isn't happening!" Glowing red embers drifted down from the ceiling above, landing on his clothing and head—burning him. It gave him a spark of momentum. He yelled out in desperation as he prepared to lurch himself up for another gut wrenching pull.

"Time to pay your debts Charlie—time to be punished for your sins," Camilla said coldly as she drifted towards him in the blindingly thick smoke. Walking up to the bottom of the stairs she ran her fingers along the bottom edge of the steamer trunk. "Well, looks like you could use a little help," she smirked. Her slender fingers dropped something on the top of the trunk as they slithered across its lid.

Charlie couldn't believe what his eyes were seeing as he stared down at the tooth perched on the trunk.

"Perhaps you got just a little too greedy... hmmmm?" Camilla added with a snarky pout.

Charlie groaned—he could feel the heat from the growing

flames moving in behind him, slowly eating its way down the staircase, burning like a candle's wick, where he was beginning to melt underneath the intense heat. He glanced up at the dim light barely visible through the opening in the floor, with smoke and sweat burning in his watering eyes. *I've got to get out of here!*

"Don't you recognize me son," Camilla chided him with a devilish smile.

Charlie gazed with horror at her decaying face, thinking, *no… this isn't real… I'm seeing delusions… the smoke… I need oxygen… have to get out of here.* Exhausted and lightheaded, he gasped for a breath of air, tensed, and pulled, "aaaaaaah!" But the trunk didn't budge. "No," he whimpered—his strength utterly sapped.

"Last chance Charles," Camilla reminded him, as the fire crept down the stairs.

He looked up to see the wall of flames moving fast, sweeping over the walls, over the ceiling above, falling through the floorboards down to the floor, surrounding him in every direction. Abandoning the trunk he turned to crawl up. Blinking wildly in the blinding smoke, up in front of him, there was only a red and orange glow, as the flames seemed to explode into a thunderstorm of fire. Digging his fingernails into the wood planks Charlie thrust himself ahead, inching up the stairs, straight into the glowing ball of burning flames. Reaching the opening in the floor, his one hand grasped the rim—and he pulled hard. Searing pain swept over his lower body as the flames ignited his clothing, swirling around him the flames tore at him causing his flesh to sizzle. Straining with everything left in him, he couldn't lift his body up through the opening in the floor.

Charlie screamed in agony as the fire took hold—burning his legs first, as if he were being dipped down into boiling oil in a deep-fryer. Looking back down the stairs with agonizing wide eyes—he saw him. Daniel was there—glaring back up at him from within the flames below.

Giddy, looking drunk with pleasure like a ravenous animal

ripping apart a fresh kill, Daniel's torching hands and teeth were busily tearing away at Charlie's flesh.

Before passing out from the overwhelming searing pain—through the blanket of black smoke—Charlie heard his mother saying to him, "Sorry son… you were just a little too late—a little too greedy. Unfortunately, I can't let you do any more damage to my plans. You'll just have to stay right here with me. Please try and understand dear. It's all for the best."

Charlie let out a blood curdling scream as blisters bubbled-up on his skin.

Paul could hear Charlie's anguished screaming coming from inside the barn. He could hear Kaitlin's pleas echoing in his head as he paced around the barn searching for a hole, a crack, someplace where he could peer inside. *If I can see where he is I can probably get to him.* Burning intensely, with flames covering every wall and doorway, the fire quickly spread up the walls to escaping through the roof, allowing the wind to get in—feeding its ferocity even more. Thick black smoke swirled around in the barn like a hurricane making it nearly impossible to see inside. *Shit… there's no way to find him from out here!*

"Help me… please someone… please help me!" Charlie agonizingly pleaded, dangling on the staircase like a rag doll, slowly being consumed with its stuffing smoldering, catching fire, and burning away.

Pulling the double doorway open all the way, to let out as much smoke as possible—Paul was finally able to run inside. "Charlie… where are you Charlie!?" He yelled out just as a rush of scorching air hit him in the face, throwing him back out through the doorway. Flames exploded up into the air filling the entire barn—shooting up through the rood like an erupting volcano—sending fiery bits of wood cascading down all around.

Paul lay stunned on his back. Dazed, almost unconscious, he watched as the barn gave way, crumbling into burning timbers. The rooftop collapsed, and the barn became one enormous bonfire.

"Oh God… Charlie," he moaned. Before blacking out, with his eyes going in-and-out-of-focus, he saw the image of an enormous man leaping up within the flames—flailing about and tearing at the sky like a maniacal madman, who was trying to escape.

Dr. Karanza awoke to find herself in complete darkness. Huffing in air, her throat throbbed with pain—cracked, blistered, and coated with stinging tar. Every breath brought misery. Fighting for consciousness it seemed like an eternity had passed by before she could even remember where she was, let alone, have any idea of just how long she was out.

Lifting up her head to look around, smoke blew into her eyes. Her nose burned with the smell of hot gases. Hunched over on her hands and knees, she had to keep her head down near the ground to breath at all. A thick layer of smoke lingered overhead like a running stream of toxic water.

A small, dim, greyish, glowing point of light was visible through the wall of smoke behind her. She had crawled just far enough away that the heat from the fire couldn't reach her. That was not the way out—turning around would take her back into the basement room where a fiery death awaited. Feeling like a trapped rodent, she realized that she had to keep going down the dirt tunnel in the other direction—to wherever it may lead.

Feeling along the floor for direction, in utter darkness, pebbles and rocks were poking and jabbing into her palms and kneecaps. Occasionally her face would move through a wispy sticky feeling of a spider web that would cling and stick to her skin and hair. She would swat and tear at the invisible strands, hoping that nothing else would be there—to bite her. There were other recognizable objects that had been discarded in the tunnel—empty tin food cans, bottles, paper bags and wrappers, slimy skins of fruits and vegetables, with a vast array of plastic bags and containers—along with the rotten smells that accompany piles of garbage. *Filthy pig!* It made her skin crawl as her hands moved through the mess. With her head low to the ground, her gag reflex kicked-in to overdrive as the pungent, sweetly rotten odors, became as the thick as the smoke above. Straining to breath, convulsing with dry heaves, her throat burned—if a thousand hornets were inside stinging her at once it couldn't have hurt any worse. *I'm going to die if I don't get out of here… now!* She shuffled through the black tunnel as fast as her hands and knees could move.

Without warning she plowed face first into mounded dirt. Jerking her head up out of the dirt, she slammed the top of her head into the top of the tunnel, causing more loose dirt to collapse in on top of her. Now she was gagging on the dust and dirt swirling around her head. It was even thicker than the choking smoke. Coughing and gagging, heaving in a convulsing spasm, the dirt and dust stuck to the walls of her throat as a dry, hard, cracking, crust, blocking off her airway. *I can't breathe in here!* She realized as her fingers dug into the mounded dirt blocking the tunnel. The more she gagged on the dust littered air the less she could take in.

Spinning in place her hands frantically pulled at the loose dirt all around her as her knees shuffled backwards. Her right hand swung out into an empty space where a side tunnel had been dug— recently. Getting dizzy she scurried down the new tunnel faster that she had gone before, knowing that if she didn't get out soon—she was dead.

Within just a few feet her hands could feel the walls expanding outward. Lurching forward she threw herself into the opening. Feeling along the edges, she realized that she was moving around in a small circle. In an instant she had scampered all the way around, until finding the tunnel again—where she had entered. *This is a room. The end of the tunnel… with no other way out!*

Reaching up Dr. Karanza dug at the ceiling like a woman possessed. Her only option now was to go up. Swinging her leg around to brace herself against the wall—her foot kicked an object that bounced off the wall and rolled across the floor, making a distinctive clinking sound as it hit against small rocks; *A bottle?* Frantically running her hands over the floor she found the bottle. *It's a wine bottle,* she realized while running her hands of over its fat bottom up along the slender neck to where the cork was sticking out. Having been opened and re-corked—it was sticking almost halfway out. Her fingers fumbled to yank the cork out with the typical resonating flump sound. Pushing the bottle to her lips, turning it up, she guzzled the liquid down—only taking gasping breaks in-between gulping swallows, to breath in the life-saving air she most desperately needed. "Oh… thank… God," she mumbled between swallows, before sprawling out on the floor, just to breath in fresh air for a while.

While resting, her hand rubbed up against another small object. Fumbling with it—it made a rattling sound like a box of matches. Sliding open the box, her fingers felt inside. *Only one!* Pulling out the only matchstick, she struck it cleanly, sparking to life it lit up the tiny circular dirt room. There at her feet lay a book—the Grimoire. Next to it, there were words that had been hastily scratched into the floor—with a finger:

I once was where you now be,
prepare with speed,
to follow me!

Shadows danced in rhythmic circles around Dr. Karanza as her left hand—holding the matchstick—began to tremble. With her right—she gently fingered three tiny pebble sized bulges inside her front pocket. *I still have his teeth.* Lifting those same fingers to her mouth she slid them across her wet lips. Looking down at the smeared red liquid, she knew then, there was no escaping from what she had become. *Blood… I'm drinking human blood!*

Camilla had left behind everything necessary for her to become just like her—even the tomb. And then, the tiny flame on the matchstick—died.

35

DROPLETS OF A light rain landing on his face woke Paul up again. The sounds of sizzling water and the popping of smoldering embers with the smell of acidic steam greeted him back to consciousness. Only a pile of burnt wood remained of the barn. Small flames jotted up here and there, shooting up out of the white ash as raindrops penetrated the still burning red-hot coals.

Scrambling to his feet, Paul called out in a hoarse voice, "Kaitlin… where are you… Kaitlin!" The only sounds were the popping and hissing of raindrops hitting the smoldering heap of hot ash. Sore pains slowed Paul down when he tried to walk. That's when he first felt the stinging sensations where small blown embers had landed on his clothes. Some of them had burnt through to his skin. Patting himself down, he limped towards the trail.

Kaitlin was climbing into the driver's seat of her Jaguar by the time Paul had raised his head off the ground. She reached underneath her seat and pulled out the purple *Crown Royal* whiskey bag that had a golden sash tied at the top where it was cinched shut. Untying the sash, opening the bag, she pulled out the 38 revolver that was

tucked inside. Gregory had always insisted that she keep the pistol in her vehicle for her own self-protection.

"Don't do it dear," Louise said softly, standing outside her window.

Holding the wooden grip, with her slender finger draped across the cold crescent moon curved trigger, Kaitlin ignored her. Slowly twisting her wrist around—she put the barrel directly to her right temple. Rocking back the hammer until the cylinder turned, clicking, positioning the bullet into place to be fired, Kaitlin placed the cold steel tip of the barrel against her throbbing temple. Her finger quivered as it bore down harder on the trigger. With a fleeting thought of her mother a tear ran down her cheek. "Just do it already," Mary snarled from the passenger seat, "and finally let me get out of your crazy ass head!"

Kaitlin squeezed down hard on the trigger and the hammer fell—*click*—but nothing happened.

"No way—you can't even kill yourself correctly," Mary giggled. "You're so stupid! You didn't even load the gun. You left the bullets in the bag," she taunted her, "How did I ever get stuck with you crazy Katie? Well, it looks like we're stuck together forever now?"

Lowering the gun, Kaitlin grabbed the purple bag and shook it to hear the loose bullets jostling around inside. Mary was right. Popping open the cylinder she slid six shells into firing position and slammed it back shut—this time fully loaded and ready to fire. Louise's soft voice was pleading with her through the window, as she raised the barrel back up to her temple. Her finger slipped firmly around the trigger.

Mary placed her fingers up to her own head, forming the shape of an imaginary gun. Mimicking pulling her own trigger—she blew out her own brains with an enthusiastic smile.

Cocking the hammer back, Kaitlin closed her eyes—squeezing on the trigger.

A car horn blared behind her car, shocking her out of her trance—and the gun fell away from her head. In the rearview

mirror, Gregory's black Mercedes sedan was coming to a stop. Droplets of rain trailing down the rear window obscured the view. It wasn't clear who was inside the car with him.

"Oh no, you don't crazy Katie," Mary snapped at her. "You're not going to get yourself locked away in some nut house—with me right along with you." Mary could see the piercing hatred shooting out of Kaitlin's eyes—burning holes in the rearview mirror like laser beams as she watched Gregory step out of his car. "Don't do it Katie. They'll take you back to that hospital, and we'll never get to leave—never ever," Mary murmured.

"Sounds good to me… it'll be worth it," Kaitlin whispered as she grabbed the slippery-wet door handle. Tucking the pistol behind her right leg, she stepped out of her car, coming face to face with Gregory.

"There you are dear… I've been looking all over for you," Gregory tried to explain. His face was cold and distant—fake—like a talking marble statute, or marionette, with half a smile that was far from convincing. "Detective Thomas finally got a hold of me and told me to get over here right away—is everything OK?"

Kaitlin was stone faced, matching him. He tried to make another smile with his outstretched hands he tried to display some sympathy—but he only revealed his guilt. With a nervous stare and a twitching lip, she could see exactly who he was now—a sneaky little boy who was going to do anything to get what he wanted—if she let him.

Glancing down at her leg where the gun was hidden, he said nervously, "Thomas said there was some trouble… and he's supposed to be on his way here now."

Kaitlin was savoring his nervous agony, *serves him right to suffer just a little, before I put a bullet inside his pompous ass.* "Trouble… there's no trouble here," she said, with a hesitant laugh. "Everything is just wonderful here Gregory. In fact, you arrived just in time. The fun is just about to get started off right this second—with a big bang." The pistol slid out from behind her leg. Tightening her grip on the stock, she fingered the trigger to where it felt firm, steady, and glorious in the palm of her hand—like salvation. She raised it up and pointed it so that Gregory's forehead was perfectly aligned with the site on the end of the barrel.

Nick's car flew up the driveway. Slamming on the brakes he slid to a stop—kicking up muddy gravel in-between Kaitlin and Gregory.

Kaitlin shuttered nervously and let out a gasp as she lowered the gun. Nick leapt out and hustled around the front of his car. A pair of shiny metal hand-cuffs dangled in his plump hairy fingers. Kaitlin shuttered again and took in a sharp breath before raising the gun to Nick's chest—forcing him to stop dead in his tracks.

"It's over Kate. Don't do anything stupid," Nick said in a low voice, hiding his fear the best he could. "Let's talk this out. Everything is going to be fine," he said softly, calling on his training, "but first you need to put the gun down on the ground."

The passenger door of Nick's car popped open. Cynthia stepped out from behind the rain splattered window. "Please don't shoot Gregory. Please Kate… please don't do it," she pleaded hysterically, revealing just how much she felt for him. With her arms stretched out in submission, the sash holding her long coat together came loose. It fell open. A sudden strong breeze blew her coat back. Her thin dress pressed against her body—revealing the recognizable bump of her swollen womb.

All motion and time slowed down as Kaitlin recalled all the things that had been said to her—now all of it being tortuously confirmed—all true—right before her red, sullen, just wanting to die eyes. Mary's whispering and giggling echoing around in her head was pushing her over the edge of sanity—to where passion surpasses anger, defeating self-control. Staring straight at Cynthia's belly, Kaitlin swung the gun around—and fired. "That's supposed to be my baby!" She cried out as the gun discharged.

The bullet passed clean through Cynthia's stomach—passing straight through the tiny hairless head of her gestating baby girl.

Nick caught a whiff of a peppery steel odor filling the air as gunpowder sprayed out of the barrel. He felt its light stinging on his face like a shower of invisible sparks. A concussion thumped the air followed by a thunder clap explosion, chasing him back behind his car for cover.

Paul heard the gun-fire as he rounded the house—in a full-on sprint.

Cynthia slumped down to the ground as Kaitlin swung her gun back around, pointing it directly at Gregory's face. Standing frozen—a deer caught in the headlights of a speeding sports-car—he watched in horror as she squeezed the trigger, ringing out another loud air clapping shot. Whizzing past Gregory's head, the bullet shaved away whisker thin hairs—a mix of natural grey and dyed brown—that puffed into the air as confetti above his ear, before drifting away in the breeze.

Paul slammed into Kaitlin's back like a charging rhino sending them flying off of their feet. Knocked out of Kaitlin's hand, the gun fell at Nick's feet. Paul had crashed down on top of her and his muscular arms roped her into submission with quick instinctive precision—as if she was another one of his out of control mental patients back at the hospital—just as he had done a hundred times before.

Securing the gun in his waistband, Nick straddled Kaitlin and cuffed her, squeezing the metal clasps so tightly that her skin bruised. "Good work Paul," he stated boldly.

Gregory rushed to Cynthia's aid. An artery was severed in her abdomen. Both she and the baby would bleed to death within minutes. There was nothing he could have done to save them. A frantic call to 911 on his car phone was his only option. Only, he was out of range—with no service.

Nick lifted Kaitlin off the ground and dragged her with her feet stumbling to get upright over to his car. "It's all over for you," he snarled as he shoved her into the back seat. Throwing gravel with spinning tires he tore off. Without looking down, he reached down,

taking the radio receiver to contact dispatch, "Civilian down with gunshot wounds… E.M.S. needed at Whitcomb place… pronto," he calmly announced.

"10-4," dispatch squawked back.

Mary tagged along for the ride—sitting calmly next to Kaitlin.

Jostling in the car as they sped down the bumping winding driveway, Kaitlin watched Nick's eyes in the rearview mirror. He looked everywhere except back at her, avoiding any eye contact. Turning onto the main road Nick punched the accelerator. The tires squealed as they spun onto the blacktop.

"That was fun!" Mary said gleefully. "So where are we going now? Huh crazy Katie? Oh yea, I think I know? Off to the crazy hospital where we belong—where we will be locked up forever and forever and ever."

Kaitlin turned her head to the side and stared out the window. Appearing on her lips was a tiny sliver of a smile—one of relief.

36

"GET SOME HELP… go call for an ambulance… go now!" Gregory was yelling at Paul.

As if waking dream from a nightmare, with everything moving slow, his booming voice sounded distant and muted, echoing in Paul's head as if they were far away, and under water. A throbbing ache hit the side of his head, where he smacked the ground—hard. It took a few moments for Paul to focus on the here and now. His mind was racing—heart pounding.

"Paul!" Gregory yelled sharply, finally cutting through his foggy mind. Paul looked him in the eye—slowly focusing. "Please go call for help… do it now," Gregory implored as he cradled Cynthia.

Realizing he was still on the ground—sitting up on his knees—Paul looked over at Cynthia. Her blood was pooling on the ground, making small trails, dark-red streaks moving out in all directions. Gregory was holding a blood-stained hand on her belly, as her blood flowed from the exit wound in her back, trickling from her the corners of her drooping, unconscious mouth. "Right… on it," Paul finally muttered before pushing himself up on his shaky legs.

Staggering into the house Paul picked up the phone. The line was dead. "What the—?" he muttered before slamming the receiver down. "Dr. Karanza!" He yelled up into the house. *Where the hell is*

she? Trotting out the back door he headed across the field to Daniel's house—yelling for her all the way. Stepping onto the creaking porch and peering through the open front door, he called out into the shadowy interior, "Dr. Karanza… Emily… you in here!?"

Sirens blaring down the main roadway pulled his head around. *Thank God*, he thought as he made a quick jog back to the main house. His eyes searched the field and the trees on the way back for any sign of Dr. Karanza. With his heart still racing, breathing hard, his skin turned a shiny red as tiny beads of sweat pushed through his clammy forehead—beating back the cold. *She must have taken off… scared off by the gunshots and commotion? Can't say that I blame her… she's always playing it smart.*

Paul walked through the back door that was left wide open. His breathing slowed and started to relax. By the time he reached the foyer the wailing of the sirens went silent. It was reassuring to hear the calm voices of the medics going to work. Standing in the doorway, he watched them slide Cynthia into the back of the ambulance, with the engine running, they sped away—siren blaring. Gregory followed behind in his car—hugging their bumper.

Kitty-cat-paw footsteps scampered across the floor behind Paul. His neck stiffened before he yanked his head around to look in the direction of the back door—that was gently swaying. "Karanza," he called out softly, "That you?"

Paul walked slowly down the hallway and looked outside. It was quiet. No one was there. *Just the wind,* he thought as he pulled the door closed—locking it. Thumping footsteps on the basement stairs pulled his eyes to the door next to him. A staircase down to the basement was on the other side. Clanging and banging of metal against metal rattled in the basement—sounds of a bucket or tin cans getting knocked over as something brushed by in the dark. And then silence.

Paul grabbed the doorknob and pulled the door open. It was dark—nearly pitch-black at the bottom of the stairs. "Dr. Karanza," Paul called out sheepishly. Waiting a moment, he peered down into

the darkness, trying to see what was there. Nobody answered. *She wouldn't be down there... just a cat or rat... or something?* He thought, while shutting the door.

He had walked half-way down the hall before a thought crossed his mind; *what if Karanza is down there... she could be injured. Kaitlin could have gotten to her... shoved her down the stairs or something?* Turning, Paul stepped back to the door and pulled it open. Without hesitating, he stormed down the dark staircase to the bottom. Light fell over his shoulder from the open doorway at the top of the stairs. It lit up a small circle on the floor like a spotlight over his head. In the dim light, he could make out some of the things around him.

Littering the floor, covered in cobwebs and a thick layer of grey dust, was old stored furniture, toys, nick-knacks, stacks of yellowing books, and the like. Anything and everything usually stuffed into an attic, basement, or storage shed. Musty air lingered, heavy, cold, and dank. Slowly he sifted through the discarded mess, watching shadows for movement. "Dr. Karanza," he called out softly. Gliding stealthily across the dusty floor he could have been a ghost.

At the edge of the light—he stopped. There was an opening situated between two large pieces of furniture covered with tarps, with just enough room between them for someone to scoot through—over to the far wall. It was very dark up against the wall, but he could just make out a small wooden panel, with what appeared to be a handle attached to it. *That almost looks like a door in the wall*, he thought.

The panel suddenly moved—just an inch. "Is someone there?" Paul whispered. Slowly the door opened until Paul could see fingers—then black hair—and then her black eyes peering out at him. "Dr. Karanza... is that you?" he muttered, leaning in to the dark crevice for a better look.

Bursting through the small doorway, Camilla lunged out of the darkness with clawing fingers—going straight for Paul's neck. He stepped back into a slender beam of light just as her hands reached him. Her long, rotten, jagged black fingernails lightly scratched

across his cheeks. He grabbed her wrists—just in time—stopping her from wrapping her boney fingers around his neck. Gnashing her broken and rotting teeth, her desperate black eyes stared into his. She grabbed his shirt with both hands, holding him tight, as her nauseating breath wafted over his face as she pleaded with him, "Please help me… help me get out!"

37

Out of the mind's eye
Present Day
The same observatory room

"TIME'S UP!" THE burly orderly barked as he burst back inside the observation room. Stepping up behind Dr. Edge, he growled, "I said, times up!"

Dr. Edge was non-responsive. With his hand holding the emerald gemstone amulet firmly against Kaitlin's forehead—he was fully entranced.

The orderly's huge hand landed hard on Dr. Edge's shoulder. Grabbing tightly, he yanked him back in his chair—moving his hand away from Kaitlin, grumbling, "You hearing me doc, your hours over—time for you to leave." As Dr. Edge's hand slipped away from Kaitlin's forehead, the gemstone third-eye amulet fell onto the table—tinkling as it bounced about.

Dr. Edge could feel himself pulling away from Camilla's grasp. Her bony fingers tearing away from his throat, as his mind began to separate from Kaitlin. With the sensation of being pulled backwards through a tunnel, Dr. Edge pulled away from Camilla, leaving the basement at the Whitcomb estate as his present senses returned.

Kaitlin reappeared in the present, still seated directly in front of him dressed in a hospital jumpsuit, with her unkempt hair and grayish-white ghostly skin that hadn't seen the sun in ages. Her clutching fingers slipped away from his neck as her hands fell away. The foul stench of rotting flesh hit his nose again forcing him to sit way back, away from her. But he never lost eye contact. Her lips turned up into a soft crescent making a sly smile—the same devilish little smile she had on her face when she was being driven away in the back of Nick's car. It was the smile of blissful relief, knowing that it was all over—over again. It was also a happy smile, knowing that someone else knew what she knew. And this time, that person may actually believe her.

Kaitlin tilted her head a little to the side, as if listening in one ear.

Someone else was now in the room, standing right next to Kaitlin.

Dr. Edge locked eyes with the red-headed preteen girl. Dressed in a school-girl uniform, she was leaning over Kaitlin's shoulder, whispering something into her right ear. *Mary?* Dr. Edge remembered. She glanced up at him as she whispered. Her eyes suddenly widened with the realization that he could see her now. Jolting upright, Mary stepped back before she disappeared—evaporating away into the air like a puff of steam rising off boiling water. Dr. Edge stiffened in shocked amazement—momentarily frozen in place. This was the first time he was able to see an apparition—while outside of a trance.

"You hearing me Edge? Don't make me get physical with you—now let's go," the orderly snarled, taking a handful of Dr. Edge's shirt and pulling him to his feet.

With a swift swipe of his hand, Dr. Edge snatched his amulet from off the table. "Take it easy… I heard you alright," he muttered as he spun to face the enormous brute sent to remove him from the hospital. Whisking past the orderly Dr. Edge made a hasty exit without speaking to anyone else. His mind was focused only on one thing now—getting to the Whitcomb estate.

His *Cobra Mustang*, with a 400 plus horsepower engine, made short work of the twenty country miles between the hospital and the Whitcomb home. Rumbling to a stop outside the large ornate wrought-iron gate, he found a new chain had been wrapped through the bars, along with a very large and shiny new padlock. On the ground, tossed off to the side, he noticed a few rusting links of a chain sticking out from beneath some leaves and dirt. Dangling between the bars was a worn **FOR SALE** sign, hung by a real estate company back in the late eighties. Full of bullet holes, it was covered with rust where the paint had been blistered by the elements. No one would even consider buying the place, let alone spend the night here. The only people coming to visit this place now are the teenagers, those on a dare, or the ones looking to break, vandalize, and steal—all for just the thrill.

Revving the tachometer Dr. Edge sped off, following the roadway along the fence line to find the side entrance. He found the small rutted dirt road leading up to where the barn should be. A small barricade of boards had been erected by the real estate company—to keep the kids out—only to be knocked down and run over by one of the locals, in his makeshift 4X4 monster truck. Inching slowly down the overgrown road as far as his nerves would allow, the Cobra stopped where the gently scratching branches reached out just a little too close for his comfort.

Stepping outside a lingering char smell drifted across his nose. What was left of the barn was just a large pile of splintered lumber sticking up jagged into the air. Underneath was just scorched embers and ash. Circling the pile of debris, Dr. Edge looked for where they had managed to pull Charlie's smoldering corpse from the rubble. The recovery team only dug down into the still simmering coals deep enough to find his unrecognizable body. It was far too risky for them to go any farther. There was a slender path where they had made their way close to the middle of the barn. Gingerly stepping on the charcoaled planks, he cautiously made his way over to where the hatch in the floorboards should have been. Using his shoes to swish away the thick ash, he felt for the opening.

A loud creaking noise gave way to an even louder cracking—as the timbers beneath his feet gave way. He crashed through the floor, twisting around in mid-air before landing hard on his back on what was left of the bottom two steps of the stairs—before flopping over onto the hard concrete basement floor—hitting his head in the process. "Shit that hurt!" He groaned, as the pain set in, "so much for my super spy skills."

Getting to his feet, his eyes scanned the dark room. It was obvious that nothing had been touched since the fire. The steamer trunks were there. The bookcase was intact against the wall. Even the books Dr. Karanza had thrown down onto the floor were still there—exactly where she left them. His pain miraculously disappeared as he excitedly scampered over to the trunks. Inside of them, he found the chemistry lab materials and all of the hidden money. "Hell yes!"

His excitement lasted just as long as it took for him to realize that there was no way for him to get anything out—including himself. The floorboards over his head were weakened from the fire, almost rotted away, and what was left was straining to support the weight of all the debris that had crashed down on top of them. Putting another ounce of weight on them could bring the rest of the floor crashing down. "Damn," he muttered, realizing that the only way for him to get out, was through that metal door in the wall. *Could she still be in there?* He shuttered at the thought. But, he knew, *that's probably the only way out of here.*

Pushing hard against the heavy metal door, it reluctantly swung in—the rusted hinges screeching loudly, letting anyone on the other side know he was coming through. A shock-wave shot up his spine all the way to his teeth as the high pitched squealing screeched out his presence. *Shit!* He squirmed inside. With his cover blown Dr. Edge decided to make a rush for it and plunged his head into the black hole. Seeing nothing at first, he leapt all the way inside the dark room, planting his feet with his hands raised up to block a surprise attack. Glancing around wildly—he could see nothing. The room appeared to be abandoned. "Thank God." He murmured with a sigh of relief.

It still looked just like the room he had seen through Kaitlin's mind. All the furniture was exactly the same—nothing moved. The foul scent of death mixed with musty smoke filled his nose as he relaxed enough to take in a full breath. It was the same rotten smell that had greeted him in the observatory room, but far less pungent. Having permanently permeated the room, only a very lengthy passage of time had managed to soften the odor to a tolerable level. *She must have abandoned this place after the fire*, he surmised.

Finding his way across the room he found the opening to the tunnel. Moving like an anxious hamster in plastic tube he shuffled on hands and knees down the black tunnel—hoping to find his way out at the other end. Zigzagging and backtracking through the tiny black maze for what seemed to be an eternity, Dr. Edge eventually scurried out the other end—crawling out into the basement of the main house. "Thank the Lord above," he muttered as he popped to his feet and scampered up the stairs. Searching through every room of the house, he found it to be empty. Everything inside had been left the same way that it was on the day Kaitlin was apprehended. Only that same distinctive, yet faint, smell of decaying flesh, lingered in every room. Finding nothing of interest, he headed out the back door to search Daniel's old wooden farmhouse.

His excitement grew with each step—all the while running ideas around in his head on how to get the trunk full of cash aboveground. Taking another oblivious step, his foot disappeared into a deep hole—going straight down into the ground—sending him flat-faced into the thick grass. "What the hell," he murmured, as he pulled his leg free of the large hole that had been covered by weeds, vines, and roots. Rolling up onto his knees, he clawed away the natural camouflage to expose the foot-and-a-half in diameter shaft—going straight down about ten feet. The sunlight illuminated the small round cavern room at the bottom. It was only then that he realized what he had stumbled into. *This is where Doctor Karanza was trapped… she did manage to escape!*

Rushing across the rest of the field—while keeping a more watchful eye-out—he entered the farmhouse. Going through every room, he found it the same way—abandoned. Not even finding the slightest of stinky smells this time. Just dust, mold, and rot.

Walking back outside, he surveyed the area, remembering what he had experienced at the hospital with Kaitlin. He couldn't help himself. He just had to take a look at the burn pile and the grave-yard. *Just a quick look around before I head back to the house to get some rope, and whatever else I need to get that trunk out of there.*

The burn pit was unremarkable. Overgrown, it was just a mound of tall weeds and grass now. *I'll head up to the graveyard for just a quick look.* What he really wanted to see, was where Gitana was supposedly buried. It was just too tempting of an idea.

Pushing the waist-high iron-gate open Dr. Edge sauntered inside. He could see the headstones poking up through the tall weeds. There were a couple of discarded beer cans left by some disrespectful teenagers, along with some graffiti sprawled over William's headstone—the tallest one. Walking closer, he noticed the long slender wooden handle of a shovel, sticking straight up from the ground. Someone had jammed the rusting head of the old shovel down deep into the clay next to Catherine's headstone. *Well, that's odd,* he mused. As he walked up to the grave site, he noticed that the ground seemed to have been cleared away in front of the stone. Stepping up to the edge of the grave, he looked down at the reddish clay ground—where he read the words that had been etched with a finger:

I once was where you now be
Prepare with speed to follow me

38

Central State Psychiatric Hospital
Milledgeville, Georgia
Two weeks later, July, 2011

DOCTOR CONRAD WAS tired. Late in the afternoon, he was finishing up his rounds when an orderly stopped him in the hallway, to say, "You got a special delivery Doctor."

Dr. Conrad just nodded, keeping his eyes on the patient file he was reading over.

"It's in your office," the orderly muttered as he sauntered off.

Dr. Conrad didn't give it another thought, not until he saw his last patient for the day, and walked back into his office. Right inside his door was a large steamer trunk. Old and worn, the trunk looked like it had been recovered from the wreck of the Titanic. It stank like an oversized ashtray. "What the hell is this?" he muttered, looking it over with disgust. All he could imagine was the dust and dirt getting spread around the office, and how much of a pain it was going to be to dispose of this *God-awful thing*.

He spied an envelope taped to the lid. *Some kind of joke*, he imagined as he snatched up the paper envelope and tore it open. A small metal key dropped out into the palm of his hand. It was the key needed to unlock the padlock dangling on the front of the old nasty trunk.

Also in the envelope was a short letter. A note of thanks from Dr. Edge, which read:

> Dr. Conrad,
>
> Thanks again for your generous hospitality. This is your share, as promised. It appears that I have stumbled onto something far more valuable than money. Something more valuable than I ever could have imagined. Please take good care of Kaitlin. It just may save your life.
>
> P.S. Don't let her trick you.
>
> Alex

At the same time
In Breckenridge, Colorado

Doctor Edge stepped through the door of a makeshift saloon—a replica of the original—where cowboys and prospectors once frittered away their newly discovered gold, in exchange for glasses of whiskey and the company of saloon girls. Only now it was a family friendly restaurant. It was still an inviting place—preying on tourists, and their loose wallets. A shabby little place with a long wooden bar where skiers would belly-up nightly, to guzzle beer as they try to warm their bones while numbing the sprains and pains inflicted by the spills on the slopes. Keeping with the theme, the room was decorated with an enormous bison head, various antlers of all sizes, and a large stuffed bear—mounted in a standing position to look menacing with snarling teeth and bared claws. Gold mining and panning equipment were hung haphazardly to the walls, along with the ubiquitous WANTED 'dead or alive' posters.

It was four in the afternoon and the bar stools were still empty. A few stragglers from a late lunch were hanging around, not wanting to face the cold again—just yet. Dr. Edge caught the attention of a saloon-girl attired waitress as she passed by with both hands clutching tall pints of frothy beer, saying to her, "Excuse me… I'm looking to find a Paul Pearson, and I understand he works here?"

Without slowing down as she brushed past, she glanced over at the long bar and mumbled an unenergetic response. "He's a bartender… works the dinner shift but he's not here yet… maybe in an hour or so."

Climbing onto one of the tall bar-stools along the bar, Dr. Edge ordered a Red Ale that was brewed in-house. He milked it as long as he could while watching the minute hand achingly-slow circle the antique looking clock on the wall. After forty-long-minutes he was still the only one sitting at the bar. His empty glass sat in front of him for several more long minutes, as the bored day-shift bartender silently willed him into ordering another round.

Half-way down another pint, at five-past-five—Paul finally walked in. A thick furry brown beard covered most of his face, making him look almost like a twin-brother of the stuffed bear looming behind him. Without removing his wool stocking cap or his dark sunglasses that he used for ski-goggles, he quickly scanned the scene. Slow day. He could take his time getting set up behind the bar. Slipping past Dr. Edge he walked into a back room to change into his bartender's outfit—suspenders, bow-tie, and a garter worn on the arm. His plastic name-tag was left inside his locker—by mistake—as usual.

"Another round stranger," Paul mumbled politely.

The other bartender had already stepped out of sight, ready for a desperately needed smoke-break. Dr. Edge looked up from the bottom of his beer. The man he was looking at was younger than he expected—far too young-looking to be over fifty. Dark curly brown hair fell over his smooth forehead. Not one grey hair curled out of his thick beard. His skin was tight and smooth. Not even a crow's feet wrinkle around the eye. Bulging muscles rippled beneath his skin-tight shirt. This guy looked more like some ski-boarding college kid who was putting in some part-time-work over a summer break.

"I'm just waiting for Paul," Dr. Edge replied. He tipped back the pint to suck out the last few drops of beer—thinking the new bartender would leave him alone. Instead, as his glass dropped back down, he was face-to-face with the young bartender. Paul was leaning over the bar, snarling at him with angry eyes and bared grinding teeth—now looking exactly like the menacing stuffed bear.

"Well you found him… now what do you want?" Paul growled in a low voice, so only Dr. Edge could hear. He had sized-up Dr. Edge the second he stepped behind the bar. This guy wasn't in town on a ski trip. The heavy black-leather coat and completely inappropriate dress shoes, oxford button-down-collar shirt and khaki slacks, all screamed cop, reporter, or salesman—no one he wanted to have to deal with right now.

"Paul… Paul Pearson?" Dr. Edge stammered with a gaping mouth.

"Like you don't already know," Paul grumbled, "why the hell won't you people let me be? Like I've told everyone before, I'm not talking about what happened—not anymore."

Having left Georgia, trying to leave his past behind him, he had sought refuge deep in the Colorado Mountains. Supporting himself anyway he could, he became a ski instructor/medical tech, and part of the mountain rescue team, while bartending at night for extra income. All the furious attention had slowly faded away and he hadn't spoken about the incidents at the Whitcomb residence in years—but thought of it every day. Right now, he was worn out from a long day's trek up into the high country to help find some amateur mountain climbers from California. The last thing he wanted to do was have to explain himself to some nosey asshole again.

Paul turned his back to walk away, but Dr. Edge stopped him, saying in a stern voice, "I'm not here to hear what you have to say. I'm here to tell you something… something you have to hear."

Paul spun around with a cold, distrustful glare, to say, "Why should I care what another cop, or some wise ass reporter looking for another story has to say? I've heard it all before. I'm that psycho killer that got away with murder—right?" Stepping back up to the bar, his face turning red, he made his point clear, "I had to leave Atlanta to get away from all those accusations and lies. All those accusing stares and glances… everyone believing I had something to do with those people dying. I won't let you drag all that back out again… not here… not again… so you had better just get the hell out of here before I throw you out!"

"Let me see your hands," Dr. Edge demanded, stopping Paul's angry rant before anyone else noticed. "Your fingers—let me see your fingers."

Stunned, Paul glanced around the room, before slowly lifting up his hands, sticking his fingers up into the air to where Dr. Edge could get a good look. Paul knew exactly what he was looking for. And there they were—as clear as bright stars on a moonless black night sky—tiny black dots on the tip of each finger. Quickly leaning forward, Dr. Edge sniffed the air. His nose wrinkled as it detected the faint stench of death lingering on his fingertips.

Staring down at Paul's finger, the one with the ring on it, he asked, "Interesting ring you got there… what's that carving supposed to be?"

"A Solomon's Knot," Paul huffed, "it signifies immortality and eternal life."

"Don't forget about the other meaning… *hidden knowledge*," Dr. Edge added.

With that being said—they locked eyes with suspicious stares.

"Just who in the hell are you?" Paul groaned, dropping his hands as if giving up. The scorching threats in his eyes went out as his secret was uncovered. Paul realized that this wasn't just another cop or reporter—this guy actually knew something about him, and about the curse.

"My name is Doctor Alex Edge."

"What do you want with me?" Paul asked nervously, wondering if Dr. Karanza had sent him. He snatched up Dr. Edge's empty pint glass and shuffled over to the sink to thrust his hands down in the soapy water. Keeping his hands under the bubbly water he briskly swished the glass clean.

"I've come here to let you know that they've taken her," Dr. Edge replied somberly.

Paul stepped back, still clutching the soapy glass. "Taken who?"

"They've taken your daughter, Fiona."

Paul shuddered. The dripping-wet glass slipped from Paul's limp fingers. His eyes glazed over in distant thought. He muttered over the sounds of the glass shattering on the floor, "She did it… that bitch finally tricked me."

"Who tricked you?"

Looking up—with eyes full of fear of what was to come, Paul answered in a hushed voice, "Malaika, that's who."

"Why would she want your daughter Fiona?"

Paul stepped back up to the bar. Shards of broken glass crunched beneath his shoes. Leaning close, he stared deep into Dr. Edge's eyes. In an emphatic voice, as if he were inside a confessional, ready to relieve himself of all of his burdens, he revealed with a hushed voice, "I am the only son of the Oracle. The only survivor of Siwa… sent out of the desert to hide. It was my reason for living… to protect the bones of Cain."

"Protect them from Malaika?" Dr. Edge joined in.

Bowing his head, Paul replied in a despondent voice, "Malaika will never stop searching for the two things she needs—those bones—and my blood. She escaped her grave in the mountain. By the time I discovered that she was gone—she had already fled up into the Highlands of Scotland with the help of a mindless slave she had captured and poisoned."

"That's where Gitana got ahold of the bones and the Grimoire?"

"That's right, I was preparing a bone fire meant to dispatch Malaika to hell forever… when Gitana showed up. Before I could act, Gitana just up and disappeared with the bones. It took years for me to track her down in Georgia."

Dr. Edge chimed in, "but by then, Gitana was buried and Catherine was already under its curse?"

Paul locked eyes with Dr. Edge, letting him know that he was right on the money—with everything.

Paul continued in a hushed voice. "It was too late for her. And my only chance of locating those bones was if Catherine could speak… to tell us where they were hidden. It wasn't until we took Charlie back to that house that I discovered that Camilla had been hiding beneath that barn… along with the bones."

"Now Dr. Karanza has them, right?"

A look of terrifying foreboding appeared on Paul's face as he spoke, "If that is true… and if this Fiona is truly my daughter… then Malaika may already have what she has always wanted. Fiona is the Oracle reborn. And Malaika will use her immortal blood—to become immortal."

Dr. Edge slipped his fingers inside his coat pocket as Paul was talking. Afraid he was going to hear some nutty unbelievable story—he came prepared. Tickling the silver amulet with the emerald gemstone third eye, he moved his hand up on the bar, to where Paul could see it. In a calculated, calming voice, he asked, "Mind if I try something Paul?"

A slender smile stretched across Paul's lips as he looked down at the gemstone amulet. Locking eyes with Dr. Edge again, he smiled wide, before saying, "Oh, so that's who you are. I've read about you in the papers."

"Then you know what I can do for you," Dr. Edge returned a comforting smile, while moving the amulet into the light. The emerald stone sparkled brightly. "You know what I can see in you."

Paul's eyes thinned. "So, you don't believe me?"

"Let's just say, I trust, but verify." Dr. Edge's hand slowly moved the amulet across the bar—moving it closer to Paul's forehead.

"I wouldn't do that if I were you," Paul whispered.

"Why's that?"

"Because Dr. Edge… you won't survive what you find inside of me."

Dr. Edge's eyes widened a little, as he considered the seemingly veiled threat.

Paul glared deeply into Alex's eyes, saying forcefully, "I'm not one of your usual ghost stories that you're used to chasing around doctor. I'm not some old widow that you can tell fortunes to, while picking her pocket. This is all too real. And if you get any closer to this truth… you're going to get burned alive." As he spoke, he thrust his hand down into his pants pocket to retrieve a vintage cigarette lighter. Flipping the metal lid, his thumb quickly sparked the flint to ignite a fueled wick. A short flame erupted. Just high enough for him to poke his index finger directly into the yellow fire. And he held his finger there an excruciatingly long time—till his fingertip began to glow.

Dr. Edge grinned squeamishly, watching in stunned amazement, as the black dot on the very tip of his finger appeared to melt away—disappearing in the fire.

Paul flipped the lid of the lighter shut, killing the tiny flame. Then he smiled, pleased with the results, showing that there was no pain, before saying, "flesh decays… while the fire cleanses and refines. I have passed through the refiner's fire. I endured the eternal pain. I'm unbound from the eternal knot."

Dr. Edge could see a flickering light erupting in Paul's eyes as he spoke.

Paul leaned across the bar. Opening up his eyes wide, he allowed Dr. Edge to gaze into a raging hellish fire—that is his soul.

Paul then whispered to Dr. Edge, "I once was where you now be… prepare with speed to follow me."